Other books by Henry Denker

Plays by Henry Denker

THE
PHYSICIANS

A NOVEL OF MALPRACTICE

Henry Denker

Simon and Schuster
New York

DESIGNED BY IRVING PERKINS
MANUFACTURED IN THE UNITED STATES OF AMERICA

1 2 3 4 5 6 7 8 9 10

LIBRARY OF CONGRESS CATALOGING IN PUBLICATION DATA
DENKER, HENRY.
THE PHYSICIANS; A NOVEL OF MALPRACTICE.
I. TITLE
PZ3.D4175PH   [PS3507.E5475]   813'.5'4   74-14526
ISBN 0-671-21861-1

To my wife Edith

*"Medicine, of all the arts
the Most Noble...."*
—HIPPOCRATES

ONE

HE WAS never conscious of how intense he appeared as he bent over his microscope to adjust it precisely. Now, as he reached for his scalpel he glanced involuntarily at the wall clock. He ran his fingers through his thick black hair, a sign he felt under pressure. He was urgently aware that he had promised to lecture the mothers of another low-income project this afternoon. Time. There was never enough time.

He applied his scalpel to the sliver of tissue on the slide under his microscope and commenced to count the number of cells in the gray rubbery specimen. His handsome face was grave as he discovered the outrageous degree of damage that might have been avoided if only the mother had understood proper prenatal nutrition. Here was yet another infant who, but for fetal malnutrition, might have been born normal. And who would have survived.

Suddenly the squawk box sounded over his head.

"Dr. Grant! Dr. Christopher Grant! Dr. Grant!"

His instinctive reaction was to ignore it. But he knew he wouldn't. Laying aside the scalpel, he reached for the phone.

"Dr. Sobol wants you, sir."

"Of course," Grant relented at once. Sobol never intruded unless it was urgent. "Ring him!"

In a moment he heard Sobol's voice—old, tired, and a bit apologetic. "Chris, do you mind coming up to ICU? Right away?"

"Be right there."

"Why are all hospital elevators always so slow?" Grant thought as he started racing up the stairs four flights to the neonatal intensive care unit. But with his crowded schedule, he was always impatient. His teaching took a good part of every morning and he always had a full load of tiny patients in the neonate nursery. Add to that his first love, research, and there was little he did not do on the run.

Even as he rounded the last landing, his mind went back to his current paper on brain-damaged infants, those malnourished patients that he had labeled "Reynolds' babies" after one of the major low-income developments in the city.

He was constantly aware of the irony of the fact that his laboratory, his research, the very halls he was striding through, were made possible by the benefactions of the same man who had built the development, John Stewart Reynolds.

Dr. Sobol was waiting in the corridor, just outside the glass wall of the intensive care nursery. With him was a tall man, gray-haired and distinguished-looking. He seemed familiar, but Chris Grant was sure he did not know him. When Sobol spied Chris he started toward him alone, intercepting him halfway down the corridor.

A small man, Dr. Michael Sobol looked even smaller in the stiff white lab coat he wore on his rounds and during his lectures in the medical school. He had a flushed face that seemed perpetually troubled. Behind rimless glasses, his eyes always seemed tearful. His hair was thinning, and mostly gray. He did not seem impressive enough to be chief of the entire pediatric service of a university-affiliated hospital as large and important as Metropolitan General.

"Chris," the little man addressed him softly as they met, "we have a neonate just referred from Parkside Polyclinic. Two to three weeks less than full term, but twenty-six hundred grams so it's not a preemie. Obviously jaundiced though not dangerously. Still, I want you to take this on yourself."

Grant's quizzical expression made Sobol explain. "The infant's name is Simpson. But it might as well be Reynolds." With that, Sobol made a half-turn in the direction of the tall stranger who waited at the door of the intensive care unit. Now Chris Grant made the connection. The distinguished face was indeed familiar. It was the same profile that appeared on the bronze donor's plaque in the foyer of the Research Wing. The man was John Stewart Reynolds.

"So Reynolds' daughter is the mother," said Grant.

"Chris, you know I don't give a damn about power or status. No infant on my service is more important than any other. They all get the best we can give them." Sobol defended himself. "But in this case . . ."

Chris was relieved that Mike didn't take the trouble to explain further. It was painful to him that a man of Sobol's distinguished contributions to science was placed in the demeaning position of being forced to make such explanations. To ease his discomfort, Grant said quickly, "Don't worry, Mike, I'll give it all the time it takes."

"Good . . . good." Sobol was gratified. "And I'll see to it we make up for interrupting your research."

"I know that," Grant said, relieving the old man of all guilt.

"Report to me directly. Every few hours. Even if you have to call me at home," Sobol insisted.

At the door of the intensive care nursery they could not avoid Reynolds. Chris eased the door open, allowing Sobol to enter first. When Reynolds started in after him, Chris shifted his body enough to gently but effectively block the man's access.

"There's nothing you can do in there," Chris explained.

Reynolds' face flushed with resentment. He was not used to being forbidden anything. Chris Grant did not yield.

"That's my grandson. I have a right to know what's wrong with him. What's being done for him," Reynolds said.

"Mr. Reynolds, right now I don't know what you could do except get in the way of people who know their jobs and want to do them for your grandson." Grant slipped into the room, closing the door behind him.

Reynolds, his face stern, made no secret of his resentment. He moved from the door to stare through the huge glass window which permitted him to watch every move Chris Grant made.

At first glance, neonatal intensive care had the look of an efficient private aquarium. Transparent plastic tanks called Isolettes were ranged against all the walls of the room. In each lucite enclosure a sick or premature infant struggled for life. Some were so few hours old that they still assumed the fetal position, crouching so that their tiny protruding ribcages emphasized each spasmodic breath. Many had intravenous tubes strapped to arm splints designed to keep the IVs safely and securely fixed in the tiny patient's arm.

Almost all of them had electrodes taped to their fragile bodies. These were connected in turn to the equipment behind each Isolette which monitored their vital signs. Other sensors helped to regulate the temperature and humidity within the Isolette.

In one such plastic enclosure Baby Simpson, not quite forty-eight hours old, was breathing fairly normally, though its bronzed skin color gave disturbing evidence of its jaundiced condition.

Chris Grant stared at it for a moment. Heir to a great fortune and much power, this infant looked no different from all the others that passed through his hands. Tiny, squirming, its red face wrinkled, its eyes clenched tight, it was a small and pathetic bit of humanity. Unaware of its surroundings, it had only two natural instincts: the need for air and the desire for food. Its tiny body, of bronzed skin and soft bones, did not seem big enough to contain all the complex organs that make up a complete human being. The area where its umbilical cord had been tied off was a bruised reddish blue. It was a newborn child of the human race, facing life with all its uncertainties.

Not the least of which was its present condition.

Chris Grant inserted his hands through the access portholes of the Isolette to lift his patient. He turned it over and back, making a superficial examination, mainly to palpate its liver. With jaundiced babies the root of the trouble could often be found there. Was that organ doing its job of cleansing the bloodstream and rendering the dangerous elements into such form that they could be excreted without harm or damage?

"Liver doesn't seem unusually firm," Sobol commented. With more than a hint of disapproval he urged, "Take a look at the transcript that came over from Parkside."

Chris reached for the record, which the head nurse had ready for him. He began to scan it, till his eye hit the important fact.

"An Rh-negative mother?" he asked suspiciously.

"Read on," Sobol cautioned.

"No previous pregnancy. No previous transfusion. No titer level on her early pregnancy Coombs," Chris read off as he scanned. "Did they test for sepsis?"

"The transcript says they have and found no sign of any infection. But you know Parkside . . ." Sobol cautioned.

That comment reflected the eternal and inevitable war waged between university hospitals and private ones—the research institutions never quite trusting the work done at the private type, the private institutions always accusing the teaching hospitals of being too pedantic, too wedded to theory, research and experimentation to engage effectively in the daily demands of medical practice.

"What was the last reported bilirubin?" Chris asked, reaching for the transcript again.

Sobol anticipated him. "There's only been one. Fourteen milligrams."

"Only one bilirubin? In an infant as obviously jaundiced as this? And with an Rh-negative mother, besides?"

"You think that's something?" Mike Sobol said. "Take a look at the report on the infant's Coombs."

Chris glanced at the record again, then looked up, startled. "Rh incompatibility! How is that possible?"

"At this stage of the game, what does it matter?" Mike asked. "If that result is correct, this baby is going to require very special attention."

"Did they get signed consent for an exchange transfusion?"

"Not according to the transcript," Sobol said.

"Damn, they should have! In case it's necessary," Chris snapped. He had seen enough to know that swift action was necessary. He was about to demand equipment to draw a blood sample, but the head nurse, anticipating him, handed it to him. Passing his hands through the portholes again, he gently and carefully extracted some blood from the heel of the tiny patient. He transferred it to the test tube, sealed it and dispatched the nurse to the lab with it.

"I want a bilirubin. And another Coombs. And have them do a blood smear for sepsis. Stat!" As the nurse left, Chris turned to an intern, briskly, "Dispatch a messenger to Parkside. I want a sample of the mother's blood. Should have been sent over with the transcript! I don't trust any lab results but our own!"

Mike Sobol knew that he could resume his teaching and administrative duties without concern. An angry, determined Chris Grant was Sobol's insurance that the infant would be cared for to the very best of any doctor's ability.

"Chris, you'll check with me every few hours?" Sobol asked. Grant nodded as the older man left for his class in the medical school. On the way he stopped to exchange a few words with John Stewart Reynolds. Reynolds remained an angry conscience, glaring at Grant through the glass wall. He was obviously one of those people who trusted no one. Not even experts in fields about which he himself knew nothing. That alone would have been enough to irritate Grant. The fact that this was also the man responsible for so much Reynolds housing did not temper Grant's resentment.

He turned in such a way that his back blocked Reynolds' view. He examined the infant again. The liver definitely felt normal. "Let's get this little one into a phototherapy unit," he said.

The head nurse moved the tiny patient from the Isolette in which it had rested to another incubator, and refixed the electrode and IV. Then Chris quietly closed the infant's eyes and carefully applied a fabric shield. When he was positive that the mask was so firmly in place that no light could penetrate, he brought down a lid that settled completely over the Isolette. It was more than ordinary stainless, however. Its underside was a battery of twelve short fluorescent tubes, placed so close together that they were almost touching. When Chris threw the switch the lid produced an all-encompassing blue-white light that bore down incessantly on the tiny bronzed patient. Checking once more to be absolutely sure none of the light could penetrate the eye bandage and damage the retina, Chris withdrew his hands through the portholes and watched for a few moments.

When he finally turned away, he noticed that Reynolds still was glaring at him through the window, his doubt and anger more apparent now than before.

"I'll be in my office," Chris said to the nurse. "Call me the second any word comes from the lab."

Before he had fully opened the door, Reynolds confronted him.

"Well, Doctor?"

"I don't like to discuss patients out in the hallway," Grant said. "If you'd come to my office . . ."

"Let's go!" Reynolds snapped impatiently. They hadn't taken more than a few steps when he asked, "What are you going to do? I mean, how are you going to treat that boy?"

"Mr. Reynolds, let's call him what he is. A neonate."

"Which means?" Reynolds demanded.

"A newborn. When we get him safely past that stage he'll be considered an infant. And only then will it become important that he's a boy."

"I don't give a damn about your terminology!" Reynolds protested. "I want to know precisely what he has! And precisely what you're going to do about it!"

"Which is precisely what I don't discuss in hallways," Chris said softly, sensing the wrath that was building up in Reynolds.

There was no further conversation till Chris closed the door of his small cluttered office and pointed out a seat. Reynolds remained standing, preferring, it seemed, to use his height to give him superior position. In the days that were to come, the weeks, and the months, Chris Grant would discover that it was one of Reynolds' favorite tactics, to dominate by the simple expedient of continuing to stand while all others in the room were seated.

Reynolds was tall, spare and in good condition for a man obviously in his sixties. His skin, normally ruddy and somewhat freckled, was not slack but tightly drawn over strong jawbones. His hair was white and short-cropped in military fashion. His voice had a gritty quality which served notice that he could be dangerous if enraged. Many employees and competitors had learned that over the years.

Chris was aware of some of the legends that had grown

up around John Stewart Reynolds. But when it came to medicine, and particularly in his specialty of neonatology, he was not one to yield to most professionals, let alone a layman, no matter how important the man might be.

Once the door was closed, Reynolds reiterated his demand: "I want to know what that child has! And what you intend to do about it!"

"A case of jaundice. And I'm already treating it."

"How?" Reynolds demanded.

"By doing all I *can* do about it. Till those tests come back from the lab, I have to proceed cautiously," Grant explained.

"I didn't see you treat him with anything!" Reynolds protested. "You took some blood and put an intravenous on him. Or is there something special in that intravenous? If there is I demand to know what!"

"Mr. Reynolds, if you want to help you're going to have to do two things."

"If it involves money, or flying in specialists or equipment . . . !" Reynolds seemed ready to pull out his checkbook and start writing.

"First, sit down. Second, shut up," Chris Grant said in a flat, quiet voice.

Reynolds' face grew even tighter, the muscles in his strong jaws swelled in fury. Finally he slipped into the chair opposite Grant.

"Now, Mr. Reynolds, if we can discuss this quietly, I'll tell you everything you want to know."

"What's he got?" Reynolds asked, more temperately.

"We're not sure yet," Chris informed him.

"Does it look serious?"

"Not so far," Chris said. "But we'll know more when we get a confirmation from our own lab on the cause of the jaundice. That's the reason for that blood sample. And those monitoring devices. It's essential in cases of jaundice to keep testing for some hours to see whether his condition grows better or worse."

"But you said you *were* treating it," Reynolds said. "If you don't know what he has, how can you treat it?"

Chris could sense that any architect or engineer who worked on any Reynolds project was put through the same curt cross-examination.

"Jaundice in a newborn can come from any number of causes. In fact, most newborns have it to a slight degree. That is what we call physiologic jaundice."

"If it's so common, why did Coleman get upset?" Reynolds asked suspiciously.

"Coleman?" It was the first time Chris had heard the name.

"The young fellow covering for Dr. Mitchell, my daughter's obstetrician. Mitchell's got the flu and doesn't want to expose any infants," Reynolds explained. "Good man, Mitchell. One of the best. Most meticulous."

"I've heard," Chris agreed.

Reynolds reverted to his original question. "If physiologic jaundice is so common, why did Coleman have the boy transferred here?"

"As a simple precaution." Chris defended Coleman, even though he had never met him. Laymen had a way of blaming doctors, not nature, for illness. "Because the seriousness of jaundice depends on two things. The cause . . ."

"Such as?" Reynolds interrupted sharply.

"Sepsis, an infection of some kind," Chris explained. "Or an ABO incompatibility, where the blood of the mother and child are not compatible. Or an Rh incompatibility which is likely here. Or where an infant is premature. . . ."

Again Reynolds interrupted. "He's not premature! He's only preterm, by two weeks. Three at the most according to Dr. Mitchell. And since he's more than a full twenty-five hundred grams he can't be classified as premature."

Chris was surprised at Reynolds' knowledge. No doubt he

was a man who liked to know everything about any subject he found interesting or important.

"I didn't say your son was premature . . ." Chris began, realizing that he had used the designation son instead of grandson. "But preterms tend more to jaundice than full terms. The reasons have to do with complicated blood chemistry."

"You can explain them to me, I'm no idiot!" Reynolds persisted.

"I don't think it would serve any purpose," said Chris.

"I'll decide that. You just explain it to me," Reynolds insisted, his voice a bit hoarser.

"Mr. Reynolds, I don't intend to give a complete course in blood changes in a neonate to any layman. I haven't got the time. And it wouldn't accomplish anything. Your grandson is getting the best possible care at the moment. We're trying to determine the severity of his condition. We are doing something to diminish the jaundice as rapidly and as safely as possible," Chris said, seeking to bring the interview to an end.

"Look, I'm not one of your ignorant charity parents who can be shut up in this highhanded way!" Reynolds stood up, towering over Chris Grant, who had not moved, had no intention of moving.

He stared up and said calmly, "We don't have this much trouble explaining anything to our 'ignorant charity parents.' They listen. They believe what we tell them. And they go away feeling we're going to do all we can to save their kids."

"You're an insolent young bastard," Reynolds exploded. "I'm going to call Sobol and order him to have you taken off this case!"

"Frankly, I wish you would."

"And don't think he won't do it. Do you know that *I* was the one who insisted on bringing Sobol here from Mount Sinai? When the rest of the board said they were uncertain about bringing in a Jew to head up the department, I said, 'God damn, when it comes to medicine, get the best. And if the best is a Jew, get him!' " Reynolds explained.

"That was very sound," Chris said, refraining from making any more obvious comment. "Sobol *is* the best."

"That isn't the point! Right now the point is that a man who can affect your medical future is asking you for information relating to his grandson, his only grandson. And you can't even be civil enough to give it to him!"

"I've given you all the information we have at this time," Chris said.

"I want to know what the possibilities are. The dangers. And what can be done to overcome them," Reynolds insisted.

Perhaps because the threat Reynolds had leveled was aimed more at Sobol than at himself, Chris Grant decided to make one more effort to assuage Reynolds' anger.

"Mr. Reynolds, it wouldn't do you any good to know all the dangers and possibilities," he tried to explain.

"I have a right!" Reynolds persisted.

Softly, but quite firmly, Chris said, "I should think his mother would 'have a right.' Or his father . . ."

"His mother's recovering from a difficult delivery. And his father is out of town on business. I had to send him to Saint Louis on a deal."

"He works for you?" said Chris.

"Yes, he works for me," Reynolds replied, resentful of Chris's observation.

"And you couldn't have sent anyone else to Saint Louis at a time like this?" Chris asked.

Reynolds didn't answer except to glare at the young doctor. Having made his point, Chris decided that he might as well inform the older man completely.

"Mr. Reynolds, since you arranged things so that you're in charge I will give you all the relevant facts."

The old man's expression softened slightly. He was going to have his way, after all.

"Jaundice is the result of what we call hemolytic disease. Meaning a disease that destroys the infant's blood supply. It can be inconsequential. Or it can be dangerous. Highly dangerous."

"What about my grandson?"

"Listen, and I'll tell you. Jaundice results when, for any one of the several reasons I gave you, the red blood cells begin to break down. That releases a yellow substance into the bloodstream. What we term *bilirubin*. That yellow substance is what gives the jaundiced patient that bronze cast. The seriousness of the problem depends on the percentage of bilirubin in the blood. If the amount is kept low enough and its effects wear off, the bilirubin is excreted and no harm is done."

"But if it isn't kept low enough?" Reynolds pressed.

"If the bilirubin count in an infant gets as high as twenty percent, then it can be dangerous. I like to start worrying at fifteen. Sometimes even less. Depending on the patient," Chris stated.

"You said 'dangerous.' How?" Reynolds demanded.

"If it's concentrated enough, the bilirubin can reach the brain. The amount in which it does can have . . . effects," Chris said.

"Such as?" asked Reynolds, more concerned than ever.

"It can create a condition we term *kernicterus*."

"Which is?"

"It is marked by adverse effects on the main stem of the brain . . . and other areas as well," Chris stated cautiously.

"You mean it can damage that boy's brain?"

"It can do exactly that. Affecting sight. Or speech. Control of limbs. Or general brain ability." Chris didn't shrink from stating the worst aftereffects of a prolonged high bilirubin.

21

"You mean my grandson could be . . ." Reynolds started to ask, then stopped. "Look, I don't give a damn what it costs! Fly in whatever specialists you need. In my plane! I want that child to have the very best of everything!"

"He's getting the best of everything."

"What's he getting, an intravenous to give him nourishment?" Reynolds demanded.

"There's an antibiotic in that intravenous. If there's the slightest chance of infection in his bloodstream I like to medicate instantly, even before the lab reports get back," Chris explained. "That's a part of the immediate treatment."

"Part?" said Reynolds dubiously. "I didn't see that boy get anything else."

"You saw it, you just didn't know what it was," Chris tried to explain.

"I saw what?!" Reynolds exploded.

"Did you see me lower that lid over his Isolette?" The older man nodded cautiously. "That was what we call phototherapy."

"Phototherapy?" Reynolds repeated slowly, making no secret of his distrust and disbelief.

"Phototherapy," Chris reiterated. "It's the process of treating jaundice by the application of intense blue light."

"Those were nothing but ordinary fluorescent lights!" Reynolds protested. "Like they use in supermarkets and offices!"

"That's right."

"You call that therapy?" Reynolds demanded. "What the hell kind of quack medicine do you practice here? Get Sobol on the phone!"

"He's teaching a class right now."

"When my grandson is involved I don't give a damn who's doing what! Get him!!"

"Mr. Reynolds, it wouldn't help your grandson one bit to interrupt Sobol's class. We're doing all we can. We'll know

22

more in a few minutes. Right now, no one, not even Sobol, can tell you any more than I can."

"You get him out of that class . . ." Reynolds suddenly realized he was shouting and his loss of control made him pause. When he continued, it was in a softer voice. "Look, you have to understand. This is my grandson. The only male heir in the Reynolds family. That young man in that little plastic box can be anything he wants! Including President of the United States! He's got to be whole, strong." It was more a plea than an argument.

"Mr. Reynolds, the chances are that he'll make a complete and uneventful recovery without any complications or after-effects. If our reports confirm those in the transcript from Parkside I don't foresee any serious trouble. The percentages are greatly in his favor."

"You didn't seem to think so before," said Reynolds. "Watching you through the glass I could see you were upset. Angry."

"I get angry almost as easily as you do," Chris said, smiling to cover his real concern.

"It was more than that," Reynolds snapped, waiting.

"Yes," Chris admitted. "It was. On the transcript your grandson's bilirubin was higher than ten."

"How much higher?"

"Fourteen," Chris admitted.

"That's bad," Reynolds concluded bitterly.

"Not bad. Just not good."

"Don't play games with me!" Reynolds said.

"Fourteen is worse than ten. But it isn't close to twenty, which *is* quite bad."

"Still, fourteen . . ." Reynolds said, evaluating the situation.

"I said not good. That's why I applied phototherapy at once. That helps to bring down the bilirubin."

"Does it work all the time?"

23

"In nonextreme cases, virtually all the time," Chris said.

Reynolds seemed somewhat relieved. "Just fluorescent lights do it?"

"That's right."

"Doesn't sound possible. How does it work?"

"Well," Chris began cautiously, fearful that at this juncture any explanation was worse than no explanation at all, "the frequency of the light rays in blue fluorescent tubing has the same resonance frequency as the bilirubin. Four fifty-four. If we bombard the infant's body with light rays of the same frequency it breaks up the bilirubin into a form that allows the infant to excrete it in its urine, ridding the body of any dangerous concentration." Reynolds stared back, still unconvinced.

"It's the same principle as a singer shattering a glass by the use of his voice. When voice and glass vibrate on the same frequency the glass will shatter, if it's delicate enough."

Chris could see that John Reynolds was not convinced. "Doesn't make sense," he muttered, "to depend on such a cure for a sick boy."

"Why not?" Chris asked. "It was an old wives' tale for a hundred years. Put the babies with jaundice closest to the window. They recover faster. Till one day a doctor decided to investigate. Was it sunlight that had the strange power to heal? Or any light? It turned out to be just light. And blue light worked best of all. It's become a fairly common treatment in the last few years. And it's certainly the safest step to take while we're waiting for the lab results."

Chris's phone rang. "That's probably the lab right now," he said as he lifted the receiver. But it wasn't the lab. It was someone reminding him about his talk at the project. "I haven't forgotten. I'll be there," he said, then hung up. "Sorry, that wasn't the test results."

The interruption had given Reynolds time to mobilize his anger and his doubts. "My tiny grandson is in there, facing the possibility of brain damage, and all you can do is put on those damned lights."

Chris exhaled sharply. Explain anything to a layman, no matter how intelligent, and he was sure to misinterpret.

"Look, Mr. Reynolds, up to this point nobody has sufficient evidence to conclude that your grandson is in danger of brain damage. You asked me about the possibilities and I told you. Now we have to wait. The lab will tell us if your grandson's condition is growing better or worse. If better, we have nothing to worry about. If worse, then we can decide what steps to take. But till we know, we do not jump to conclusions. We do not take rash or extreme measures. Doctors should not be alarmists. And alarmists should not become doctors!"

Reynolds was never a man to be deterred by the feelings of others. "What if his condition *is* getting worse?" he demanded. "What do we do then?"

If Chris had been less irritated, he might have been amused at Reynolds' use of the word "we."

"If his condition becomes worse, markedly so, *we* will then resort to what *we* call an exchange transfusion."

"Exchange transfusion?" Reynolds asked.

"We slowly exchange the damaged blood of the infant with fresh blood of the right type. Heparinized blood. Until we have given the infant a fresh blood supply twice over. That usually does it."

Reynolds nodded throughout the explanation. He was about to ask more questions when the phone mercifully interrupted. Chris was quick to answer. Once he did, he put his hand over the mouthpiece to say, "The lab."

"Bilirubin, unconjugated? Sixteen. Under the circumstances not too bad. Sepsis? Negative? Good. What about the Coombs?" Chris sat up a bit more erectly. "So it *is* an Rh incompatibility? Are you sure? Run that test again. Why? Because according to the transcript even though the mother is Rh negative there was no prior sensitization.

Run it again!" Chris said. "And I'll want to repeat the bilirubin in two hours."

Chris hung up. Reynolds asked dourly, "Bad, h'm?"

"No. Overall, I'd say it looks favorable."

"What about the Rh incompatibility? You seemed pretty upset about that."

"Not upset. Just surprised," Chris said, wondering how it could have happened. But he had no time to dwell on that. Reynolds was pressing him.

"A bilirubin of sixteen, that's close to the danger zone isn't it?"

"Not too close. But more significant than that is the fact it was fourteen percent eight hours ago and it's only sixteen now. When a bilirubin rises faster than half a milligram an hour we get concerned. No, I'd say if it only went up two mgs in eight hours, that's a damn good sign."

Chris picked up the phone, asked for neonate intensive care and spoke to Head Nurse Carey. "Nan, have Miller draw some blood from the Simpson baby in two hours. Send it down to the lab for stat reports. I'll be back by then. Meantime, might as well get ready. Order a supply of heparinized blood. Laryngoscope and endotrachial tubes and oxygen. Rubber syringe, de-Lee trap and feeding tube. And, of course, some salt-poor albumin. We'll make a decision after the next bilirubin."

Reynolds did not even wait till Chris hung up. "What did you mean, Doctor, you'll 'be back by then'?"

"I'm due down at Rixie Square to deliver a lecture to a group of underprivileged mothers on pre- and postnatal care," Chris said, starting to take off his lab coat and slip into his dark blue blazer.

"Do you mean that while my grandson is in dangerous condition you're going out to deliver a lecture?"

Chris stopped, one arm in his blazer, the other still out. "Mr. Reynolds, there's nothing I can do for your grandson without another bilirubin. That can't be taken for two

hours. Meantime, all we can do is keep him under phototherapy, and wait. I can be more useful lecturing than
simply standing around."

"Look!" Reynolds said abruptly. "I'll pay you any fee you
want! Stay here. Send someone else to give that damned
lecture!"

"If I could accept a fee, which I can't, being a full-time
employee of this hospital, it would be taking money under
false pretenses. There is absolutely nothing I can do for
your grandson right now. We simply have to wait and see,"
Chris said patiently.

"If it's all that simple, how come you ordered all that stuff
to be ready when you come back?" Reynolds challenged.

"If his next bilirubin is markedly higher and I decide to
transfuse I won't want to waste any time," said Chris.
"Which reminds me, if you want to do something for your
grandson, have this consent form signed by his father or
mother." Chris pulled a paper out of the top drawer of his
desk.

"Consent for what?" Reynolds seemed even more dubious
now.

"Consent to do an exchange transfusion if necessary."

"Why do you need a consent form?" Reynolds asked.

"Because exchange transfusions entail a certain risk.
There's a three percent incidence of morbidity," Chris explained.

"Morbidity?"

"Complications," said Chris. "And an almost one percent
incidence of mortality."

"Mortality?" Reynolds said, surprised. "You mean an infant who gets an exchange transfusion has a chance of
dying?"

"Only one chance in a hundred. But that's the reason we
try to check a rising bilirubin with phototherapy and only
resort to transfusion where that doesn't seem to work."

Reynolds nodded, fearful and not so insistently angry as

27

before. Then he reached out for the paper. "Can't I sign that? I don't want to alarm my daughter."

"Hospital regulations say the mother or father," Chris replied, not unsympathetic to Reynolds' concern about his daughter.

"All right," Reynolds finally agreed, "but I'll be right back. Make sure you are, Doctor."

Chris charged the command to Reynolds' long-time habit of giving orders and decided not to let it bother him. He waited for Reynolds to precede him so he could close and lock his door. "See you in about two hours."

Reynolds stopped in the doorway, turned so they were face to face. Chris noticed for the first time how steely blue the old man's eyes were.

"Doctor, you bring that boy through in . . . in good condition . . . and I promise you anything you want. A new lab. A new wing. New equipment. Any appointment you have your heart set on."

"We'll do the best we can," Chris said. "We always do."

The old man did not move. "Think of it as treating a future President of the United States. I want you to give him that much care!" The old man turned and started down the corridor. Chris watched him go, saying to himself, He means it, he really means it.

On his way out, Chris stopped at the intensive care unit to have another look at his patient. There was no noticeable change. But then, there wouldn't have been in so short a time. In two hours Chris would know.

TWO

THE MEETING was held in Public School 146 in the Rixie Square area of the city. The name Rixie Square, in honor of the city's most eminent hero of World War One, was a euphemism for its most devastated slum. Here, amid some of the oldest and worst of the city's tenements, rose some of the newest and tallest of the city's low-income housing units. Several of them were Reynolds-built developments. Public School 146 had been opened three years ago to accommodate the added population that went along with the new housing units.

As Chris Grant sat on the platform of the school auditorium with the principal, a buxom black woman, he watched the mothers straggle in. Some were extremely young, obviously pregnant for the first time, some surprisingly old to be bearing children. Gradually the room filled up. All the seats were occupied and many women stood against the back wall. *The Doctor*, as they called Chris, had a reputation in Rixie Square and these women, mainly black and Hispanic, came to see the handsome young man who talked to them in words they understood. He was solicitous of their questions. He told them everything they wanted to know. He was not as impatient with their halting accents as some doctors in the clinics where they were forced to seek help. He did not ask for anything—neither their votes nor their support for racial causes and actions.

The black principal rose to call the meeting to order. The sounds of voices died out as she introduced Chris.

"*Tu eres una madre antes tener tu bebe,*" he began, using a phrase just learned from one of his interns.

They laughed at his mispronunciations, some of which he committed intentionally to rid himself of the awe in which uneducated people clothed doctors. He wanted them to laugh and relax, to open their minds to what he had to say. Mainly he wanted to tell them in their own language, "You are a mother *before* you have your baby."

Once he had made that point, he launched into the serious discussion in which the words *milk* and *leche* were most prominent. He never used one without meticulously using the other. In addition he stressed the importance of prenatal examinations and the absolute necessity for mother and child to have a good, substantial, balanced diet. He stressed the fact that this country had been made great by its poor. They had raised whole generations of boys and girls who rose from the tenements around them to become successful and respected citizens. But only by force of their brain power. He explained that the secret of brain power lay in proper nutrition in those early months before and after birth. He gave them incentive and desire to accept his words and live by them.

By the time he came to the end of this talk his audience was totally absorbed. Not till he asked for their questions was there a burst of eager voices as the women made sure they understood how to carry out his suggestions. He answered as many questions as he could, glancing from time to time at his wristwatch, without trying to give them the impression that he was in a hurry. When he had only fifteen minutes left to make it back to the hospital within the agreed-on two hours, he excused himself after promising to return and speak again. They rose to give him an ovation as he left the platform. Their cries of "Doctor" and "El Medico" followed him out.

John Stewart Reynolds was still waiting outside the intensive care room, peering through the glass wall at the Isolette in which his tiny grandson lay under the extremely bright blue light of the fluorescent tubes. Doctors might say it had the power to heal. Reynolds would always doubt it. Chris came down the hall. Reynolds turned to confront him. Before he could ask, Chris said, "I just got back. We should have an answer from the lab by now. I'll let you know."

He slipped into the room, went to the Isolette, stared down at the infant. He thought he could detect a change of color, slightly less bronzed than before. But in cases like this a good doctor did not rely on his naked eye. The night nurse in charge came to his side. As he stared down, he asked, "They take that blood sample?"

"More than five minutes ago," she informed him. "The results should come down any minute."

"I'll wait here till they do," Chris said, concerned.

He had actually been very conservative in setting forth the case to old man Reynolds. A bilirubin that would not be disturbing in an infant three or four days old might be very alarming if it showed up in the first twenty-four hours of life.

As long as he had to wait for lab results, he decided to call Coleman, the referring doctor. Fortunately Coleman was making rounds at Parkside Polyclinic so it was easy to get hold of him. Chris wanted to find out what drugs had been administered to Mrs. Simpson during pregnancy. Laymen knew about the much publicized effects of thalidomide. But there were other drugs that had disastrous effects as well. Even aspirin taken in large or continued doses could be damaging.

Luckily Coleman could verify from Mitchell's records

that no such drug had been administered to Reynolds' daughter. He also assured Chris that the membrane did not rupture too early so that the chances of complicating infection were greatly reduced.

But on the main fact Chris wanted to ascertain, Coleman was not very informative. True, the transcript turned over with the infant clearly stated that the two Apgar tests had been made in the delivery room in accordance with standard practice—one, one minute after birth; one, five minutes after. The infant had a normal score on both. But after that the transcript became sketchy. Especially about one important fact. Chris kept pressing Coleman.

"When did you first notice the discoloration in the infant?"

Coleman paused a moment before answering, "Actually, I wasn't the one who noticed it."

"Oh?" Chris responded critically.

"I was called in only seven hours before delivery," Coleman explained impatiently. "Remember, I was covering for Mitchell. But the delivery was in all respects normal. A bit longer than usual. A bit difficult for the mother. But normal. So there was no need for concern."

"Despite the fact that it was a thirty-six-week gestation?" Chris asked.

"Thirty-seven weeks and the infant was full weight," Coleman corrected. "And he checked out perfectly. Both Apgars were normal."

"Yes, I know. But when did you first notice the jaundice?"

"I'm trying to tell you that I didn't notice it. With my own patients to handle, and suddenly having to cover for Mitchell, I wasn't able to get back to any patient as frequently as I usually like. The first I knew was this morning when the nurse called me. . . ."

"This morning . . ." said Chris, making no effort to conceal his surprise.

"I told you I was busy as hell!" Coleman answered

32

sharply. "In fact, I was the one who suggested to the family that we refer the infant to your department."

"Fine, but does anyone know if that infant showed signs of jaundice in the first twenty-four hours or not? I have to know!"

"I'm afraid I couldn't answer that. When I saw the infant, after the nurse called me, it was almost thirty-six hours after birth," Coleman finally admitted.

Chris's further pursuit of that vital fact led him back to the abstract of the infant's chart which indicated that the first time anyone noted a change in the infant's color was some thirty-two hours after birth. Coleman had been called next morning by the nurse in charge. He had ordered an immediate bilirubin and had visited the infant some hours later, only to confirm the nurse's suspicions. Thus no one could accurately tell Chris Grant when the first signs of jaundice had appeared.

The telephone in intensive care did not ring. It flashed. When the nurse started to answer it, Chris took the phone from her. "Ivan? Dr. Grant. What did you come up with on the Simpson baby?"

"Bilirubin, still sixteen."

Secretly, Chris had expected a rise of at least half a percent per hour in the bilirubin. Obviously the phototherapy was holding the situation in check. That was encouraging. Not conclusive, just encouraging.

"Thanks, Ivan. We'll be repeating these again in two hours. Make sure there's someone there to run them through." Chris hung up.

He decided to cancel his date with Alice, and skip his usual subscription performance at the theater. He would wait out the night, or most of it, between his research and intensive care, till some marked trend established itself. Either the bilirubin would resume climbing or else the phototherapy had actually done the job.

He came out of ICU to face John Reynolds. Chris gave

him a complete report, the infant was holding, though not yet improving. In the normal course of things the bilirubin count should now begin to drop. He would stay around to make sure that it did or take countermeasures if it didn't, meaning an exchange transfusion. Had Reynolds secured that written consent from his daughter? The old man handed it over.

"What do we do now?" he asked.

"I'm going to run those tests again in two hours. Till then we just wait."

"It's late. If you haven't had dinner either, would you like to join me?"

"I'd prefer to eat in the cafeteria here. It's easier to reach me."

"Do you anticipate an emergency?" Reynolds asked.

"No. I just want to be around for those lab reports or any contingencies."

"Mind if I join you?" Reynolds asked.

"You'll have to carry your own tray," Chris warned.

"You young bastards are all alike!" Reynolds exploded. "When I started out as a kid, I carried a lunch bucket. I'll bet you don't even know what one of those is! I wasn't born into wealth. I earned it. The hard way. I've eaten food you wouldn't touch. And in places you wouldn't stoop to enter. So don't give me any of that crap about having to carry my own tray!" Then he suddenly asked, "We can't get a drink down there, I guess?"

"No," Chris said.

"If you'd like one, I have a bar out in my car. My chauffeur could bring in a bottle."

"No, thanks. Not when I'm on duty."

"Mind if I have one?" Reynolds asked.

"The day when someone named Grant can tell someone named Reynolds what he can or can't have will be a mighty cold day," Chris responded.

Instead of irritating Reynolds, it made him smile. "You're

a cocky sonofabitch," he said. "But I like that. I was the same at your age. Let's get something to eat."

Though John Reynolds loaded his tray with roast beef, potatoes, salad, dessert and coffee, he ate virtually nothing. Chris came to the conclusion that the old man was hungry only for company. However much Reynolds tried to make conversation about other things, he inevitably came back to the subject of his grandson. Then he veered away from it, deliberately, as if he knew he needed to.

"Must play havoc with your social life, Doctor," Reynolds said, alluding to the late hour when even the hospital cafeteria was almost totally deserted.

"It doesn't do it any good. We were supposed to go to the theater tonight."

"We?"

"A girl I know," Chris said, being intentionally vague about Alice Kennan, the attractive dark-haired instructor of nurses. Chris had met her while enlisting volunteers for his adult education lectures. They had been seeing each other for almost a year now.

"Planning to get married one of these days?" Reynolds prodded.

"Every man plans to get married. One day," said Chris.

Reynolds couldn't refrain from offering. "Look, any night you want to use my box at the theater, just say so."

He didn't have to mention that it was thanks to his huge contribution that they had first-class touring theater in the city. Chris Grant and every subscriber was in Reynolds' debt for that, and had been made well aware of it. There was practically nothing of cultural worth or civic consequence in this city in which John Stewart Reynolds didn't have a substantial hand.

Chris kept eating, silent in the main, but watching the clock on the wall behind Reynolds, waiting for the time to pass so he could go back and draw a blood sample again for that next crucial bilirubin. There was still almost an hour to go and Chris invited Reynolds on a trip around the Babies' Pavilion.

"You've seen it before, but since you paid for most of it you might enjoy an unofficial look at how your money's being utilized," Chris said, smiling.

Reynolds nodded, drained his mug of coffee and they set out. Chris showed him through the operating rooms, the nurseries, the therapy rooms for infants born physically damaged for one reason or another. As they walked through the neurological testing room he saw the older man flinch thinking of his grandson, and Chris continued quickly through to his own laboratory, where he explained his current research, careful not to use the designation "Reynolds' babies," which for the first time he related to a man, not a group of buildings.

The two hours had elapsed. They went back to intensive care. While Reynolds waited outside, staring through the window, Chris examined the infant, thought he detected a favorable change in color, took another blood sample and decided to take it down to the lab himself.

The bilirubin test did not take longer than five minutes. Since there was a lab technician waiting for him, Chris had his result swiftly.

This time when he saw Reynolds waiting down the corridor he was able to approach him with a big smile. Reynolds started toward him.

"Well?" the old man asked hopefully.

"I think we're out of the woods," Chris said, "this bilirubin was fourteen point five."

"Down almost two percent." Reynolds was smiling himself now, relieved for the first time since early afternoon.

"The phototherapy did it," Chris said, kidding the old man by adding: "Those funny fluorescent lights they use in supermarkets."

"I guess it did!" Reynolds exulted.

Chris headed for the door to intensive care, this time saying, "Come on in if you'd like." He held the door open to allow Reynolds to enter first.

They approached the Isolette where Baby Simpson lay under the battery of bright lights. The infant breathed shallowly, but with a distinct semblance of regularity, undisturbed by the IV and the electrodes fastened to its body. Chris Grant reached his hands through the access portholes of the Isolette to turn the infant gently, first one way, then another. When he was satisfied, he looked at Reynolds and whispered, "Yes. I think we're out of the woods."

Reynolds didn't answer. He stared at the infant and his eyes misted up. Suddenly it became strikingly clear to Chris Grant that all that John Stewart Reynolds had ever worked for was wrapped up in this baby.

Chris wondered whether there had ever been a Reynolds' son. Or was Reynolds forced to settle for a daughter.

"Can you tell yet?" the older man asked suddenly.

"I told you, he's definitely improved."

"No, I mean about damage . . . brain damage," Reynolds said, his voice gritty and hard despite its low tone.

"I'll test him as soon as I think it advisable. About a day or two."

"Then we'll know?" said Reynolds, desperately seeking some guarantee.

"It's more complicated than that," Chris began, but Reynolds interrupted.

"Explain it to me! I can understand!" he insisted.

"We'll test him and make a judgment. But that doesn't mean that new evidence can't show up later," Chris explained.

"How much later? A week? A month?"

"Four or five months later. But I'd say we caught it in plenty of time."

"Okay, okay," Reynolds finally whispered. Then he asked suddenly, "Can I . . . can I put my hands through those things and touch him?"

"If you scrub, it couldn't do any harm," Chris agreed.

Reynolds washed his hands as if the life of his grandson depended on it. Chris showed him how to slip his hands gently through the portholes, the openings of which were a flexible plastic fan that retracted easily when Reynolds inserted his hands. Gingerly, the old man let his fingers run lightly over the tiny body. Then he withdrew his hands carefully, allowing the portholes to close again.

Back out in the deserted hallway, Reynolds said, "I want to thank you, Doctor. You certainly know your business. Stay with him for the next forty-eight hours till you're sure and I will be in your debt forever. And if you know anything at all about me you know that I am one man who not only feels gratitude, but knows how to show it."

"Nothing I did was done with that in mind," Chris said.

"Grant, the day will come, I don't know when, but the day will come when John Stewart Reynolds can do something for you. When it does, whatever you want is as near to you as your telephone."

Knowing that one does not put off a man like Reynolds with protests, Chris Grant contented himself with a simple "Thank you."

"First thing we're going to do is make it up to you and your girl friend, about the theater tonight."

"That's perfectly all right," Chris insisted.

"Not at all. What's your next night off?"

"Wednesday."

"Okay. Wednesday," Reynolds said, as if they had just sealed a bargain.

Reassured, Reynolds once more walked with the vigor of a young man as he started down the corridor toward the elevator. Chris Grant watched him turn the corner and disappear, thinking to himself, John Stewart Reynolds must be a great friend to acquire, or a powerful enemy to avoid. He was a man of extreme emotions, capable of great gratitude, and probably relentless vengeance.

THREE

REYNOLDS' OFFER for next Wednesday suddenly reminded Chris. Despite all his intentions, he had forgotten to call Alice. Nor was this the first time. He glanced at his watch. Ten past eleven. She was probably asleep. The question became which was the greater sin, to wake her now or not to call at all. That would lead to hurt questions tomorrow. For a girl as attractive as Alice Kennan, she was quick to be jealous, never quite sure when it was his professional duties or another romantic interest that caused his erratic schedule. It was one of the reasons she kept insisting that she would never marry a doctor. She herself had had too many passes made at her by middle-aged doctors, all of them married, some to nurses whom they had met at Metropolitan General, just as she had met Chris.

No, she had decided, when she married it would not be to a doctor. Certainly not a doctor as handsome or as attractive as Chris Grant. Where other doctors might merely make passes, Chris was likely to succeed.

Each time she and Chris spent the night together she had to caution herself not to become too dependent on him to satisfy her physical needs. Love and sex were for the night, for the moment, for when you hotly desired it. It was for those times of magnificent craving when she enveloped him with her long shapely legs and arms, when they were one in desire and passion to possess each other. Once she was spent, once they could lie in the dark and talk softly and philosophically about love, their love, she could be cool, self-possessed and could insist on her decision not to marry any young handsome doctor.

Still, for all her denials, Alice could not resist being jealous. That amused Chris. If she made less of her independence, she wouldn't have to seem so sheepish when trying to assert her possessiveness.

He had better call. He did. The phone rang six times. At that point he was forced to conclude she was not at home or else deep asleep. To have wakened her and have her get to the phone just as he hung up would be frustrating. To let it ring and confirm for himself that she was not home would have roused jealousies of his own.

At last she answered. Her first response, more a sound than a word.

"Allie . . . honey . . . sorry about tonight."

She had been so deep asleep that she did not instantly remember that they were supposed to have had a date. " 'S'all right," she said too quickly.

"I had an emergency," he explained.

"Uh huh," she breathed, still asleep and going through the dialogue from habit.

"See you tomorrow?" he asked.

"Uh huh," she agreed, again too quickly to give any hint of how angry she must have been earlier in the evening.

"Go back to bed," Chris said, knowing that by morning she would probably not even have any recollection that he had called. At least there had been no scene, no accusations, no need to explain. Without even saying good-bye or good night she hung up.

The mere image of her trudging back to her warm bed aroused him. He would like to be with her now, as he would have been, if they had gone to the theater earlier. He would be embracing her feverishly. She would be pressing his face against her warm, fragrant breasts. She did that sometimes even when she was asleep. Of all the women he had known she was the most satisfying. One day, when she got over her prejudice against doctors as husbands, he would damn well ask her to marry him. For the time being he would accept her on her own terms. His own career made demands that fit that scheme well.

He went across to his apartment in the dorm opposite the hospital. On his way he picked up a copy of the first edition of tomorrow's newspaper. There, dominating the front page, was a glaring headline:

RIOT IN RIXIE SQUARE!

Damn, he said to himself, and began reading the details. Due to some as yet undetermined cause, a riot had erupted in front of Public School 146 shortly after his lecture there. The newspaper account was sketchy as to origins but quite graphic and descriptive as to consequences. Rioters had overflowed the area directly contiguous to the school and invaded the business district, trashing windows, stealing liquor, groceries, television sets and transistor radios.

Finally the police, in cooperation with the firemen, had been able to disperse the rioters. The mayor had promised a full-scale investigation.

Chris kept glancing at the headline as he slipped out of his clothes. If only all that energy could be channeled into constructive uses. Instead, despite his efforts, generations of ill-nourished adults would go on producing generations of poor underequipped infants and children.

He dropped into bed exhausted, pursued by images of those intense young women he had lectured that afternoon.

Perhaps some of them would follow his instructions. His last conscious thought was that he hoped none of those friendly, eager women had been involved in, or hurt in, that damned riot.

Just before her first class in pediatric nursing Alice Kennan called him the next morning. Her students were all assembled, but she had about a minute and a half before the scheduled time and she used that to make one swift call.

"Chris . . ." She was never more demonstrative than that on the telephone, "do we have a date for next Wednesday?"

"You usually keep track of those things. If you say we do, then we do," Chris answered. "I know I'm free."

"*I* didn't say so. But when your flowers arrived this morning, apologizing for last night. . . ."

"Flowers?" he asked, completely surprised.

"Roses, very red. Long stems. And they smell delicious. I like to be wooed with roses," she said.

"Then find out who's doing the wooing," Chris replied.

"There's a card from you apologizing for last night. And it says, we're going to the theater Wednesday night. You said you'll pick me up for dinner at seven."

"*I* said?" Chris asked, confused, but only for an instant. "Oh, I get it. Those roses are from John Stewart Reynolds. When he moves in, he really moves in!"

"If he always sends roses like these, he could move in at my place," Alice said, laughing.

He liked it when Alice laughed, even on the phone. He could see her mischievous dark eyes glistening.

"I guess Reynolds sent those because I didn't have a chance to call and explain."

"Oh, that's all right, provided it's followed by roses each time."

Chris laughed to himself; she hadn't remembered his late

call at all. Well, it wasn't the first time. At least it made Reynolds' roses more effective.

In the few days that followed, Chris Grant found himself inquiring about the lab results on "the Reynolds baby," asking for the chart of "the Reynolds baby," prescribing intermittent discontinuance of phototherapy for "the Reynolds baby," even though the chart and all hospital records clearly designated the infant "Baby Simpson." In Chris's mind, that infant, now recovering so well, was the sole property of John Stewart Reynolds. The term "the Reynolds baby" was quite different in meaning from the term "Reynolds' babies" that Chris had adopted for his research. For a brief time he was tempted to change that designation out of regard for the old man whom he had come to accept, even to like, because of his intense devotion to his grandson but, in the end, the lack of an appropriate alternative made Chris stick with his original term.

Their Wednesday evening at the theater turned out to be more luxurious than Chris had expected. A Reynolds limousine picked them up at Alice's place, took them to the finest restaurant in the city where the maître d' greeted them as if they were familiar and favored guests.

After dinner the car took them off to the theater in time to enter the Reynolds' box just before the lights went down. People in the orchestra section stared up at them, wondering who they were to occupy the Reynolds' box.

Later, as the car drove them back to Alice's, Chris was quite serious when he said, "You could have this kind of luxury all the time if I went into private practice."

But, as she always did when even the hint of marriage came up, Alice avoided it by saying, "You have to make up your own mind about that, Chris. Do what makes you happy." She knew he would never go into private practice. Research and teaching were too important to him.

The car pulled up at her door. She said loudly enough for the chauffeur to hear, "Call me in the morning."

"I can at least see you to your door," he said, surprised.

"I'll make it," she said and was gone, her sudden flight irritating him sufficiently to make him call as soon as he arrived home.

"What the hell was that all about? What did I do to upset you?"

"It wasn't you," she said.

"Then *what?*" he demanded. "I thought we'd finish off a very delightful evening in an even more delightful way."

"Oh, it was a fantastic evening. But did it ever occur to you how John Stewart Reynolds knew about me or my address?"

"I never even thought about it," he said.

"Well, I did," she replied testily.

"I give you my word, I didn't mention your name."

"Could it have been Sobol?" she asked.

"Of course not!" Chris said. "Mike's too respectful of other people's privacy."

"Then in some way your Reynolds, the omnipotent, found out who I am, where I live. And if I'd let him, he'd have found out all about my sex life, too. Well, I didn't choose to let him!"

"Good God!" Chris exploded. "Only a woman would think of something like that!"

His annoyance and frustration were short-lived. Alice said softly, "If you still want to, why not get into a cab and come over now?"

He did.

On the way, he thought about how suddenly and completely John Reynolds could invade and take over someone's life, if one let him. The man was dangerously likable and highly ingratiating when he chose to be. One had to be on guard.

The Simpson-Reynolds infant had recovered nicely. Its bilirubin count went down sharply in the seventy-two hours after its exposure to phototherapy. Insofar as it was possible for a neonatologist to check out so young an infant, Chris Grant had assured himself that there were no after-effects. To make doubly sure, he asked the pediatric neurologist to examine the tiny patient. He confirmed Chris's findings. From all tests and reactions possible at this early stage the infant's development seemed fine. At the end of eight days, Chris released the infant to his mother.

On the day that Baby Simpson was discharged from the neonate intensive care unit at Metropolitan General, a new Continental Mark IV bearing MD plates was waiting in the hospital parking lot. The keys and the registration were in an envelope left with the attendant for Dr. Christopher Grant. There was a simple note on the engraved personal stationery of John Stewart Reynolds; it said merely, "Dear Chris, thanks." And it was signed "John."

That night, in a note expressing his appreciation but rejecting the overly generous gift, Chris returned the keys. Two days later the car was driven out of the parking lot. John Stewart Reynolds was forced to limit his gratitude to an extremely complimentary letter he wrote to the board of trustees profusely praising Dr. Grant not only for his highly efficient and effective treatment of the tiny patient but for his consideration of close relatives and the trouble he took to make sure those relatives completely understood the patient's situation.

The Simpson-Reynolds case appeared to be closed. The treatment successful. The patient recovered. The result as good as could be expected.

Mike Sobol was particularly grateful to Chris, since he

had plans for a new laboratory specifically for neurological research on neonates, a specialty still too deprived to achieve maximum effectiveness. It would take costly new equipment, some of which had never been built before. The tightening of federal monies meant that Sobol would have to go hat in hand to a few wealthy men, prime of whom was John Stewart Reynolds. Mike Sobol was a fine doctor and a brilliant researcher, but a poor beggar. Chris had made his unhappy task much, much easier now.

Or so it seemed, for a time.

FOUR

FOUR MONTHS had gone by. Dr. Christopher Grant was delivering his research paper, with the appropriate slides projected on the huge screen beside him. His audience were the members of the Neonatological Society of the Eastern United States. It was not his first lecture on his Reynolds' babies, but it was the first time he had been invited to address so large and distinguished an assemblage. There were several specialists in his audience who were legendary names when Chris was just a medical student.

He opened by giving credit to the men who had researched the problem before him and said that he had been able to take his research one step further by studying the surviving siblings of the dead Reynolds' babies. These children lived, yes, but their failure to develop mentally or physically at any rate approaching normal strongly corroborated the earlier findings.

The grave and silent manner in which Chris's audience listened encouraged him as he drew to his conclusion. He was about to present his personal comments when he noticed a man enter anxiously through the side door of the auditorium. The intruder whispered something to one of the doctors who then pointed at Chris. The intruder seemed distressed, but nevertheless was, if not content to wait, at least resigned.

Chris forced his attention back to his address.

"The special importance of these infants whom I have chosen to designate as 'Reynolds' babies' is not medical alone. These children are the product of a so-called enlightened society. Their families were moved out of the slums into new housing projects surrounded by areas of green grass. They are presumed to exist above the poverty level. Yet under my microscope I find clear evidence that all these steps did very little to improve the brain cell count of these unfortunate children."

Chris noticed that the man with the note sitting near the door was becoming restless again, handling a slip of paper as if it were a weapon. But Chris continued, for this was the substance of his talk.

"Billions of dollars are used in an effort to help these children *after* the damage has been done. With far less money they could have been born normal, productive human beings if their mothers were simply taught the importance of proper prenatal nutrition. A generation ago the stereotyped Negro in our most popular forms of entertainment was a lazy, shiftless, sleeping-in-the-sun, apathetic, lethargic black man. People laughed at him and some in their indulgent and self-righteous moments felt sorry for him. All the while, never taking the time to consider that the two most notable characteristics produced by severe malnutrition in children are *apathy* and *lethargy!* What some of us have been taking to be a racial characteristic or a genetic inferiority is really something that by deprivation *we* have bred into a substantial portion of our black population.

"I say a reordering of priorities is demanded. But it has to start with us, the neonatologists who have the evidence in our hands. We must use our medical knowledge to make sure that our nation's social and economic programs are the right programs. Not based on theory and speculation, but on hard medical fact. If we don't, one deprived generation will breed another, and another and another. And we will waste our time, our efforts and our substance on programs that are too late. And we as doctors will spend our lives trying to treat patients who are untreatable from deficiencies that were completely preventable in the earliest days of pre- and post-birth. I will ask, before this convention is adjourned, that we pass a resolution urging the government to consider and act on these findings."

He would have gone on but for the white slip that fluttered in that persistent hand near the door. The applause that greeted his conclusion was strong except for the area immediately in front of him where the older and more conservative doctors sat by virtue of right or because they had trouble hearing.

Chris was neither surprised nor disappointed. At the moment he was most anxious to discover the identity of the man who was pushing his way through the crowd. Reaching over the heads of the doctors he waved the note, saying, "Dr. Grant! This is urgent! Urgent!"

Chris reached for the slip and glanced at the brief message. "Call your hospital at once!"

"Excuse me . . . excuse me . . ." he said abruptly to the doctors who were trying to talk to him and followed the little man out of the auditorium to a phone.

As he accompanied the man a number of disturbing thoughts flashed through Chris Grant's mind. The main one was that Mike Sobol might have had a second heart attack. Between teaching duties, research, administrative chores and his desperate effort to secure enough money to launch the new neurological lab, Mike had been overworking. Twice Chris had suggested slowing down. But Sobol

49

seemed not to hear, or else not to take well to the suggestion.

When Chris contacted the hospital switchboard, the operator put through his call without even asking whom he wanted to speak to. When Chris heard Sobol's voice he was greatly relieved.

"Mike!"

"Yes, Chris." The old man sounded tired and almost breathless. "I hated to interrupt you, but this couldn't wait. This morning John Stewart Reynolds called me. Chris, he said that the Simpson baby shows evidences of being retarded."

"What did you say?" Chris demanded, unbelieving.

"The Simpson baby appears to be subnormal."

"Brain-damaged?" asked Chris.

"Those are the indications," Sobol said gravely.

"I won't believe that till I examine that infant myself!"

"That may not be easy."

"Why not?" asked Chris.

"Because Reynolds is blaming you for the whole thing." Before Chris could recover sufficiently to answer, Sobol went on, "Chris, get on a plane! Come right home! Get on the very first plane!"

Chris went straight to his room to start packing. But even before he had put his few shirts into the bag there was a knock on the door. Two men were there. Jeremy Bingham of Children's Hospital in Boston and Carl Ehrenz, head of pediatrics at UCLA.

Bingham was smiling as he said, "We're not here as a committee but as competitors. We caught each other in the same elevator, each in the act of sub rosa headhunting."

Ehrenz, though he had no need to, introduced himself, "Carl Ehrenz, UCLA."

"I know, sir. I've read all your papers," Chris said.

"What it comes to, Grant," interrupted Bingham, "is that

we both want you. And at optimum terms. The choice is up to you. Do you want to practice in a civilized community like Boston? Or would you prefer to do covered wagon pediatrics out in frontier country?"

Both men laughed but Chris, thinking of Reynolds' implacable anger, was tempted for a moment to accept any offer that would take him away from Metropolitan General and a confrontation with the Reynolds empire. If it hadn't been for Mike Sobol's troubled voice, still fresh in his memory, Chris might have discussed the proposals. Instead he said simply, "Doctors, I thank you both. But I've just been called back for an emergency. Please don't think I'm rude. But I do have to pack and get down to the airport."

Bingham dropped his casual smiling façade to say very soberly, "Grant, if you change your mind let me know. Immediately!"

"Of course, sir."

On the flight back Chris considered all the possibilities. Could the Simpson infant have been turned over to him too late? In preterm babies an early onset of jaundice damage could be swift. Still, the infant's bilirubin never reached dangerous levels. The phototherapy had worked. As it worked in almost every case. Yet here it was four months later and there were signs of brain damage. Impossible, Chris decided.

Most likely the child was not retarded at all. An overanxious, overambitious grandparent like John Stewart Reynolds probably just expected too much of the infant. And, perhaps, he had goaded his daughter and her husband into expecting too much. Come to think of it, hadn't he mentioned to Reynolds that signs of brain damage were most likely to appear at four to five months? Well, the old buzzard must have been waiting and now was diagnosing

any sign that displeased or disappointed him as brain damage.

Chris refused to be alarmed.

"I don't know what to tell you," said Mike Sobol. "The
man is unreasonable, I know. But because he is, we have
to be careful. Extremely careful."

"Who examined the infant?" Chris asked.

"Mitchell."

"Anyone else?"

"Mitchell is a good doctor. True, he likes money, but
I still respect him as a practitioner. If he says that child
shows evidence of kernicterus, I have to believe him."

"What if I wanted to examine the child?" Chris asked.

"We'd have no right, no legal right, that is. It would
have to be arranged. As a courtesy."

"And Reynolds is in no mood for courtesies?"

"Not the way he sounded on the phone," Sobol said, then
added, "I could call him, I could ask."

"Not yet." Chris was too stunned to trust his own im-
pulses. "I'm sorry about what this might do to your plans
for a neurologic lab, Mike."

"We live at the mercy of royal largesse, no matter what
laymen think. But I'll work it out," Sobol tried to reassure
him. "I'll work it out somehow."

Yet Chris could tell by the way the old man's wispy hair
was matted to his damp scalp that this was a severe blow
to his plans. Sobol had counted heavily on Reynolds, not
only for his personal contribution, but for aid in securing
funds from the rest of the community.

"Before I believe there are any neurologic sequelae I
want to examine that baby!" Chris said suddenly. "You
know parents. Most times their complaints are only a reflection of their own insecurity."

Sobol nodded, still dubious that an examination would

52

reveal anything to alter or improve the situation. He was about to reach for the phone when Chris continued, "I'd like to examine the mother. And question the father."

"I can't promise anything, Chris, I can only ask. After all, we have no right to demand."

"But a complete history is important in making any diagnosis," Chris persisted.

"I'll try and explain that," Sobol said, sounding a bit apologetic for his inherent reluctance to engage in power struggles. It had always gone against his nature that doctors had to be, on certain occasions, persuaders and politicians.

He pushed aside some papers on his desk and found the phone. His hand rested on the instrument a moment before he lifted it and said, "Get Mr. John Reynolds, please." They were both silent during the moments it took to put through the call.

"John, this is Mike. Mike Sobol," the old man began softly.

"Yes?"

"Grant is back from that convention. He is naturally distressed, greatly distressed. And he thinks that perhaps there's been a misdiagnosis."

Reynolds cut in, "Mitchell is our doctor. And I trust him!"

"With all due respect to Mitchell, no doctor in this world is infallible. It can't hurt to have another opinion . . ." Sobol suggested.

"It may not hurt, but I don't see how it can help!" Reynolds said curtly.

"John, please. We are as much concerned about that child as you are. Do you think we'd do anything to hurt him? We're only trying to help," Sobol pleaded.

"I don't know . . ."

"John, perhaps Mitchell is too close to the case. Perhaps he's too tense because he knows how you feel about that child. It can color a doctor's judgment."

There was a long pause before Reynolds said, "Where

would it take place? The examination?"

"Here at the hospital," Sobol said quickly, since he could sense Reynolds relenting.

"No!" Reynolds said sharply. "But if you could do it at home, at my home, and if Mitchell would be in attendance, then I think it might be arranged."

"Good, good," Sobol said, gratified.

Chris suggested, "Ask about the mother, it's important."

Sobol tried to make it sound like a casual afterthought when he added, "And, John, there might be some questions that only your daughter could answer. Could she be there?"

"I think that's an enormous imposition, considering the situation that Grant has inflicted on her!"

"John . . . we're not sure yet what the situation is. Or who is responsible. So let's not make accusations." Sobol's face was beginning to grow red as much from anger as from tension. He did not like his young men assailed in this way.

"He may examine the child in Mitchell's presence, if he wishes. But my daughter will not be there!" Reynolds said so loudly that Sobol didn't have to repeat the statement for Chris. Chris hesitated, then deciding that any examination was better than none, nodded his acceptance.

"All right, John. Would this afternoon be too soon?" Sobol asked.

"This afternoon. Four o'clock," Reynolds said with crisp impatience and hung up.

FIVE

THE REYNOLDS home rose up from the highest point in the exclusive Walnut Hill section of the city. From the time Chris Grant and Mike Sobol first entered the grounds of the estate it took some minutes to arrive at the house. There was already another car with MD plates parked in the circular driveway. Mitchell had obviously arrived before them.

They were admitted to the house by a butler and led across a huge marble-floored foyer, over an ornate crimson and gold Oriental rug, toward the broad staircase. Chris noticed on the wall several Monets and a Van Gogh. John Reynold's wealth, always in good taste, never suffered from overstatement.

They were shown into the room where the baby rested. Chris was surprised to find that it was a completely equipped nursery. More the sort of room that well-to-do parents would equip rather than grandparents. It reinforced his initial feeling that John Stewart Reynolds regarded the infant as his son rather than his grandson.

Reynolds greeted them with grim reserve. He introduced them to Mitchell, whom Sobol knew fairly well but whom Chris Grant had never met before. Mrs. Reynolds, a birdlike woman, tiny and fragile as a fine translucent china cup, waited near the crib. She attempted to smile at them but did not quite succeed. Evidently she was under great tension, as if in some way she too were on trial. When she extended her hand, Chris found it as cold as some patients he'd seen who eventually lapsed into psychotic breakdowns.

He stared down at the child. It was a fine-looking infant. Blond, red-cheeked, with a small delicate nose. It was the kind of infant that all proud parents secretly believe looks even more beautiful than those healthy beaming ones used in ads for baby food and diapers. But Chris Grant knew that sometimes the most terrible of mental illnesses afflict the most beautiful infants, as if by some perverse and merciless rule of nature.

As he looked at the child, waiting to see what its reaction to him would be, he asked Mitchell, "He eat well?"

"Moderately," Mitchell said.

"Sleep?"

"Not too badly," Mitchell admitted.

So far so good, Chris thought.

"Weight gain?" Chris asked.

"Below normal," Mitchell replied, his manner making a comment as well.

Chris reached into the crib to run his fingers lightly over the infant's head. There were no signs of pronounced cranial deformity. That was to the good. Though when he used his tape, he confirmed for himself his first serious suspicion. The infant's head was slightly less than normal size. He reached into his pocket for his flashlight and passed the lighted end before the infant's eyes. It evoked no tracking reaction. He tried again. And yet another time. The eyes remained aimless and unfixed, not at all stimulated by the light.

He reached down and picked up the tiny patient. It was almost completely limp in his hands, "dish-raggy" in the vernacular of his specialty. Chris felt the first strong pang of fear. Aware that John Reynolds was glaring at him, Chris carried the infant to the bassinette and placed it face down, hoping that it would respond by raising or at least trying to raise its head. It lay there, inert. He gently lifted the head. But he could tell that the tonic quality of the neck muscles which should have evidenced itself by three months at the latest was lacking. His hands ran the length of the tiny warm body only confirming that it was limp, underdeveloped.

He brought the infant to a sitting position, but it could not maintain itself and slumped out of control. He placed it on its back. As he turned to find a diaper, he could see Mrs. Reynolds in the background, trembling with the tension that had accumulated in the room since Chris began his examination. Mike Sobol was perspiring so profusely that he was wiping his cheek with his bare hand. Mitchell remained silent, vindictive.

Chris took the diaper and placed it lightly over the child's face. An infant four months old should, by instinct, make some effort to move it away. The infant under Chris's professional scrutiny did not move.

Chris recalled bitterly words he had used in his paper on Reynolds' babies: "Apathy and lethargy are clear evidence of neurologic abnormalities." The syndrome was staring up at him, in the person of an infant who, though it had not been nutritionally deprived before birth or after, was clearly mentally defective. Mike Sobol glanced at Chris who finally dared to meet his eyes. Their worst fears had been confirmed.

"We should do an electroencephalogram," Chris said softly.

"After all you've seen, Doctor?" Mitchell prodded. "Atonic body. Failure to track. Failure to lift its head from a prone position. No reaction to a diaper test. Do you really think an EEG is necessary?"

Chris knew the evidence was overwhelming. Mitchell

was right. An EEG or a brain scan was a desperate measure that could accomplish no more than confirm findings that were already too apparent.

Reynolds broke the silence by asking in a tone of suppressed hostility, "Well, Doctor, what now?"

Chris turned to him. "I would have to concur in Dr. Mitchell's diagnosis." Then he added suddenly, "I want to talk to the mother!"

"Young man, you will talk to *me!*" Reynolds answered sharply. "Come along!"

Chris looked to Mike who stared back, helpless.

Knowing her husband's temper, Mrs. Reynolds impulsively tried to intervene. "John . . . please . . . what good . . ."

Reynolds silenced her with a look. He opened the door, waited till Grant and Sobol preceded him, and pointed the way down the broad stairs to a paneled library.

On a huge antique walnut desk there was a battery of phones that connected John Stewart Reynolds to his various nationwide enterprises. On one corner of the desk was an electronic computer screen on which Reynolds could summon up the price of any stock or commodity on any exchange with the touch of a button. It seemed to Chris that the man might run the whole world from this spacious room surrounded by antiques, costly paintings and whole walls of old books which gave the appearance of having been collected but never read.

Reynolds took his place behind the desk but did not sit down.

"Well?" He accused and convicted Chris with a single word.

"John," said Sobol, "there are two questions to be concerned with here. . . ."

"There's only one!" Reynolds interrupted fiercely. "My grandson is mentally damaged! There is no dispute about that, not even by your brilliant young Dr. Grant. That leaves only one question. Whose fault was it?"

"Before we go using words like fault . . ." Sobol began.

Reynolds would not be deterred. He turned to Chris. "Doctor, you knew how much this infant meant to me. What plans and ambitions I had. I told you. I am a man who does not play with words. That child *could* have been President of the United States! As far as any evidence we have, he was perfectly normal at birth! What did you do to him?"

"Mr. Reynolds, I still say I want to talk to your daughter!" Chris replied.

"You'll talk to me! Truthfully. Something you did not do before, young man!"

"That's not so!" Chris defended himself.

"Isn't it?" Reynolds challenged. "Why didn't you tell me everything?"

"Everything?" Chris asked, puzzled, looking to Mike Sobol for some explanation. But Sobol was equally confused.

"Yes, everything!" Reynolds accused viciously. He moved from behind his desk. "You damn doctors, you think you have a monopoly on understanding. When I asked for detailed information on what you were doing to my grandson you brushed me aside as if I were some fool charity patient. Well, I am not. Once the symptoms began to appear, and *I* was the first to spot them, I went to the medical library myself!

"Yes, I looked it all up. All the signs and symptoms of neurologic deficiencies in infants from birth to age four months. Those tests you did up there, *I* did them myself. *I* was the one who called it to the attention of my daughter. To Dr. Mitchell's attention. Where my grandson is concerned, I no longer trust anybody!"

"John, nobody can feel this as strongly as you can," said Sobol. "I know how you dreamed about this child. But some things are out of the hands of doctors."

"This wasn't!" Reynolds accused.

"There was clear evidence of jaundice. Your own doctor

said that. That's why the infant was turned over to us."

"There was jaundice. And that child needed treatment."

"That's what Grant did. He treated the child, as quickly, as efficiently as possible," Sobol explained. Actually it sounded more as if Mike were pleading and it hurt Chris to have put the old man in that position.

"Mr. Reynolds," said Chris, "you were there. You watched every step of the treatment for the first twenty-four hours. You saw the jaundice diminish within twelve hours. You stood over his Isolette, I gave you permission to put your hands through the portholes to touch him. Don't you remember?"

"Oh, yes, I remember that!" Reynolds began to shout. "But what I didn't know at the time, and what you deliberately concealed from me, were the aftereffects!"

"What aftereffects?" Chris demanded.

"I found out a number of interesting things in that medical library, young man! All about your precious 'photo-therapy'! Why didn't you tell me the whole truth? Why did you deliberately mislead me?"

"I didn't mislead you!"

"When my grandson's future was in the balance you lied to me. 'It's a magical treatment. You just shine some light on the child and it works like a miracle.'"

"I never used those words!"

"Not the words. But that was the impression you gave. You put a jaundiced infant under those lights and behold, like magic, because of the light frequency or some other damn nonsense, the bilirubin goes down. The jaundice disappears! The infant is cured! Why didn't you tell me about the risks? The aftereffects? Why?" Reynolds demanded, his anger now tinged by self-pity.

"You should have told me. I would have understood. I would have called in other doctors, tried other treatments. You should have told me . . ." His voice trailed off.

"What, John?" Sobol asked softly. "What 'aftereffects'?"

"Of that damned phototherapy," Reynolds answered. "It upsets their tiny stomachs. It gives those poor little things rashes. It can cause eye damage."

"The first two effects are transitory," Chris said. "And I guarded against eye damage. You saw that yourself. Any doctor will tell you that child is not suffering from retinal damage."

"What about his head size?" said Reynolds, his voice rising again. "What about that? There's a paper written on that subject, young man! I've read it! One doctor who reported that in some infants phototherapy results in inhibiting head growth!"

"There's been opinion both ways, on that," said Chris. "And recent papers dispute it altogether. Including one by that same doctor."

"What good does it do me to hear that when upstairs my grandson is lying there, his head smaller than normal and destined to remain that way forever! What good does it do me to hear there are doctors who dispute that! You never should have done it! Never!"

"John, it's a recognized form of treatment . . ." Sobol said.

"Mike, I don't trust any doctors anymore! Not even you!"

Sobol's face flushed, but he said nothing. Reynolds continued, as if talking to himself.

"A lifetime, a whole lifetime he'll live that way. That little boy will spend the rest of his life . . . and *my* life . . . being a benign little idiot. Forty years I've waited for a male heir. If not my son, then my grandson. And when he finally did come along, he was destroyed, destroyed! By men who are supposed to know. By men who are supposed to be the souls of honor. But who lie. Who conceal. Who tell you everything is going to be fine. When it isn't. Who tell you all about the benefits of treatment without telling you about the risks!"

He turned on Chris Grant. "Well, young man, don't think you're going to get away with it! Before I'm through with you, you'll regret the day you ever decided to go into medicine! Damn you, I'll destroy you before I'm through!"

"John . . . ?" was all Mike Sobol dared to whisper, trying to discover what Reynolds had in mind.

"Young man," said Reynolds, ignoring the interruption, "I am going to sue you for malpractice. Five million dollars! I don't give a damn if I don't collect a dime as long as I destroy you! Then try to get an appointment at any other hospital. Try to retain your license when I'm through with you! You are finished as far as medicine is concerned in this country."

"John, if you have no regard for anything else, think of what you'll be doing to our hospital, a hospital you helped to build and maintain," Mike pleaded.

"And the one time in my life when I needed it, really needed it, what happened?" Reynolds demanded hoarsely. "I don't give a damn about that hospital from now on."

"You can't mean that," Sobol said softly.

"When John Stewart Reynolds makes a promise, or a threat, he means it."

The degree to which he had planned his vengeance became apparent when he added, "It won't just be Reynolds' money you'll be missing from now on. It'll be state money and federal money. I have power I haven't begun to use!"

He turned on Chris Grant again. "You bastard, I'll break you for this if it's the last thing I do."

JOHN REYNOLDS SIMPSON an Infant, by his father, LAWRENCE SIMPSON, and LAWRENCE SIMPSON
                                                    Plaintiffs

- against -
METROPOLITAN GENERAL HOSPITAL, CHRISTOPHER GRANT, M.D., and MICHAEL EDWARD SOBOL, M.D.
                                                    Defendants

Plaintiffs, above named, complaining of the Defendants by their attorneys, PARKINS, SEARS and WADLEIGH, respectfully allege:

Chris Grant stared at the heading on the legal document, the first that had ever been served on him during his lifetime. Then he read through the rest, trying to get to the heart of the matter. He was charged with having been guilty of malpractice in the treatment of the infant, John Reynolds Simpson, resulting in serious and permanent injury. The amount of damages sought was five million dollars. Ridiculous, he knew. But he could still remember Reynolds' threat, though Reynolds' name did not appear anywhere in the papers.

Mike Sobol was also served with a copy, as was the administrator of the hospital. Since Parkins, Sears and Wadleigh were counsel to Metropolitan General as well, they asked to be relieved of that duty because of the obvious conflict of interest.

The real defense, therefore, fell to any law firm to be selected by Medical Underwriters, the insurance company covering the hospital for all malpractice suits. Since under the terms of the policy Chris Grant and Mike Sobol were both employees of the hospital, the company was obligated to defend them as well.

As soon as the suit was filed it received extensive coverage in the press, both because the name Reynolds was involved and because of the huge amount of damages at stake. During the next ten days Chris Grant received two letters within a day of each other. One was from Boston, from Jeremy Bingham, informing him that "Due to the urgent need to fill the position, we have had to settle on another physician as assistant professor."

The second letter came from Carl Ehrenz at UCLA. The language was different, though equally diplomatic and courteous. The effect was the same. The offer Ehrenz had made so insistently at the neonatologists' convention was being withdrawn.

The medical mark of Cain was on Christopher Grant, practically at the outset of his career.

63

SIX

CHRIS STARED through the transparent lucite wall of the Isolette at the full-term but pitifully undersized infant whose brown body struggled to catch breath. Its high-pitched crying was interrupted only when its tortured body convulsed in a spasm and a greenish vomit erupted from its twisted mouth. The intensive care nurse at Chris's side stared down angrily.

"Damn it, they should have forced an abortion in a case like this!" she said.

"Where's the mother?" Chris asked.

"Ward C, Maternity."

"Anyone ask her?"

"She says she didn't have a fix for three days before delivery."

Staring down at the struggling infant, Chris whispered angrily, "That's a lie! She say how much of a habit she has?"

"Two bags a day."

"I'll talk to her," said Chris, and added, "Get me a kit and some chlorpromazine."

She turned away to fetch the injection kit and the bottle of medication. Chris assembled the hypodermic, extracted

64

a small dose from the bottle. Reaching through the portholes of the Isolette, he sterilized an area of the infant's thin buttocks. He swiftly inserted the needle and delivered the drug. The infant struggled slightly, then seemed to surrender to the procedure. Chris handed back the needle and asked for some gauze pads. He reached in and tenderly wiped away the greenish matter which the tortured infant had spewed out. He waited till the drug began to take effect.

"He'll sleep now. When he wakes feed him. Every time he wakes, feed him. Get as much food into him as he'll take. He won't retain it all. But whatever he does retain is to the good. Now I'll go see the mother."

As he started away from the Isolette, a young nurse in training was holding the phone out to him.

Chris took the receiver. "Grant. Yes?"

It was Sobol. "Chris, aren't you supposed to be in my office?" It was a command only phrased in the form of a question. That wasn't Mike Sobol's way.

"I've got a neonate addict at a highly dangerous stage. I've got to talk to the mother right away," said Chris.

"The investigator is here from the insurance company."

"He'll have to wait!" Chris said brusquely. He resented the threat involved, to himself and to his patients whose welfare from now on might be subordinated to the demands of a lawsuit.

Sobol persisted, in his low, temperate voice, "How long?"

"As long as it takes me to get the whole story out of her!" Chris snapped back. He was immediately sorry that he was letting Sobol bear the thrust of his anger. More gently, he added, "Mike, I've got to get as much of a history from that woman as possible. I doubt this one's going to make it, but I have to try. Time is vital."

"Okay, Chris. I'll hold him off. Call me the minute you can."

"Of course," Chris promised.

Off Ward C was a small private room for use of those occasional ward patients who required extreme quiet or might disturb the other patients. The addicted mother had been consigned to that room for fear that during her withdrawal she would cry and moan loudly enough to upset the whole ward.

As Chris approached her door, the nurse was coming out, carrying a covered porcelain basin. He had no need to be told. He could smell the sour contents. The mother, not unlike her tortured infant son, had been retching.

"How is she?" Chris asked.

"Bad," the nurse replied. "I think she's got to have a shot."

"She'll talk for it," Chris said bitterly.

The mother was hardly more than a girl herself, not over sixteen. She was dark in color with features that attested to a mixture of bloods in some previous generation. Thin and ravaged by her self-inflicted disease, the skin of her face was drawn tight over basically good bone structure. Her lips twitched though she tried to control them. She stared at Chris with eyes that were pleading and angry at the same time.

"You a doctor?" she asked. Chris nodded, studying her face. "You got to give me a shot! It's allowed! A doctor can do it!" Her voice was rising desperately. Suddenly she leaned over the side of the bed away from Chris. He could hear the sound of her retching, could see her body convulsing in spasms. She recovered. She turned back, foul-smelling spittle still on her lips.

"Wipe your mouth," Chris ordered. She did. "Now, there are some things I want to know."

"I need a fix!" she countered desperately.

"I need some answers," Chris said flatly. "Your baby is in bad shape. And we're doing what we can. But there are some things we have to know in order to treat him properly."

66

"Can you save him?" she asked softly.

"The statistics are not very good."

"How good?" she asked, tears coming to her eyes.

"At the best, one chance out of three."

"Jesus," she said softly, tears spilling over. For the moment she seemed to have forgotten her own misery.

"Now, you have to be absolutely honest with me." She nodded, but turned to hide her face from him. "How many bags a day?"

She hesitated, then admitted, "Ten."

Chris was surprised. "When did you have your last shot?"

"This morning." When Chris seemed shocked, she explained, "A friend. A good friend."

"I meant, when did you have your last shot *before* delivering?"

"Before delivering . . ." She paused to think of an answer that would satisfy Chris. "The night before. . . ."

"The night before?"

"I need a shot," she demanded.

"You're sure it was the night before?" Chris persisted.

"I need a shot! I need it now or I'll . . ." She rolled over on her side and retched again.

Chris moved closer to the bed. "Look, you're not my patient. Your baby is. I don't give a damn what happens to you. I want the correct information. Did you have a shot just before you started for the hospital?" When she didn't answer he seized her by the shoulders and turned her about. He held her convulsing body in a painful angry grip. "Did you?"

The girl struggled to break free. Chris held her tighter. "Did you have a shot before you started for the hospital? It's important for me to know when you had your last shot before delivering. It might help save your child!"

The girl continued to struggle until Chris promised, "Tell me and I'll give you a shot."

She looked up, doubting, and he nodded.

"In the cab . . . on the way here . . ." she finally admitted in a whisper. "Now, please . . . please . . ." She started to weep.

"In the cab . . . on the way . . ." Chris repeated, evaluating his tiny patient's prognosis. "I'll see that you get help," he said.

As he opened the door he heard her desperate voice again, "Please . . . Please . . ."

He stopped at the floor desk. "Find her doctor. Get an order. She needs something. Stat!"

He had returned to the neonate ward where he stood over the Isolette in which the infant was somewhat calmer, its mouth making slight sucking movements. When it woke it would feed. That was good. If it retained, that would be even better. Edith Riley, the nurse in charge, came to his side.

"Edie, see that it has another shot of chlorpromazine within five hours from now."

"Yes, Doctor," she said, then added, "They're still waiting."

"Who?" Chris asked.

"Dr. Sobol and the investigator, they're waiting."

His visit with the baby's mother had driven the lawsuit out of his mind. The light on the phone flashed as he lifted it.

"Chris?" It was Sobol again.

"Be there in a moment," he promised. He turned to the nurse. "Watch this one closely. If it evidences tremors, or shows uncontrolled vomiting after being fed, get me no matter where I am."

"Even in Dr. Sobol's office?"

"No matter where I am."

Chris strode down the corridor wondering if all the care spent on the infant would be worth it. Even if he could save its life, though chances were against it, to what purpose? No one had studied the later life of such children to know the

68

eventual effects of having an addicted mother. Perhaps this infant had been born with a predisposition to addiction that would haunt it all its life and would, in the end, destroy it anyhow.

There were days when all pediatrics seemed futile. This was one of them.

He reached Sobol's office. The outer door was open. Sobol's secretary was waiting for him. "Hi, Marcie."

"Go right in," she said without any of her usual warmth. Her manner was only a hint of what awaited him inside Sobol's office. He knew it the moment he saw Mike's red, tense face.

"Chris, I want you to meet Mr. Colwell. He's the investigator from the insurance company."

Charles Colwell was a middle-aged man, tall and stout. Chris estimated him to be at least twenty-five pounds overweight and dangerously flabby. Colwell held out his hand allowing Chris to shake it. It, too, was soft and limp and the man's florid complexion bespoke many lunchtime martinis. When he spoke, his voice was soft and ingratiating. He had an annoying tendency to smile at the end of each sentence, even when discussing the most ominous possibilities in their case. He accompanied his smile with a slight sound, "H'mmm?" which Chris took to mean, "Do you understand me, do you realize the danger of your position?"

Before even a few minutes had passed, Chris Grant formed a distinct dislike of Charles Colwell. But he continued to listen and to answer all questions as fully as he could.

"We've had some preliminary conversations with Reynolds' counsel," Colwell said. "After all, none of us has anything to gain from long, protracted litigation, do we? We'd like to avoid a trial, if possible. For all our sakes. Especially yours, Dr. Grant."

Chris glanced sharply at Sobol, who said, "Listen to the man, Chris. It's important to all of us."

"I'll do what I can to cooperate," Chris said, more for Mike Sobol's sake than for any other reason.

"Cooperation, that's the key to success in lawsuits," Colwell said, smiling. "We'll all be better off in the long run if we're frank and honest with each other."

"Mr. Colwell," said Sobol, his temper showing for the first time since he had learned of the suit, "what gives you the feeling that Dr. Grant is going to be less than completely honest and frank?"

"I didn't say that. I merely like to state the ground rules so everybody understands. We have a right to complete access to the hospital records, to the doctor's private records, even to the doctor's thoughts at the time of this alleged malpractice. What a doctor thought at the time is possibly as important as what he did in these cases."

Colwell put aside his yellow legal pad and got up from his chair. Standing, he was taller than Chris had suspected.

"For example, sometimes a doctor puts a note into the patient's chart that, on reconsideration, he regrets. It might be important to know what he was thinking when he made that note. In fact, sometimes it's possible that the doctor might want to change his notes, to make the record a clearer, a more honest presentation of what actually happened. . . ." Colwell let his statement hang in midair as if he had opened the subject to discussion.

"Are you suggesting that a hospital chart should be subject to alteration?" asked Sobol.

"To correction," Colwell suggested, smiling again. "After all, notes in a hospital chart are not the Ten Commandments. They're not engraved in stone."

"They're not intended to be tampered with either," said Sobol.

"Who said anything about tampering?" Colwell defended himself. "Corrected to reflect a more accurate picture of what happened at the time."

"There's nothing in that record that I would want to amend," Chris stated flatly.

Colwell was not put off that easily. "Doctor, perhaps if you realized what you're up against you wouldn't be so damned noble. It's a dirty business, malpractice. Plaintiffs will resort to almost anything. Especially a man like John Reynolds. His name isn't on those papers that were served, but it's his hand throughout. He'll be telling his lawyers what to do and how to do it. And you're the one he's after, Doctor."

Colwell drew a cigar out of his breast pocket, removed the cellophane wrap, bit off the end and toyed with that shredded remnant.

"I'm only saying, if you're going to make any changes in that record, this is the time to do it. Before he gets his hands on them. Because he will. He will," Colwell warned.

"And if he does?" Chris demanded. "There's nothing in there I'm ashamed of, professionally or personally."

"Doctor, I think that's for other people to say. Like the insurance company's lawyers." Again Colwell was warning him with that faint smile that was becoming more and more irritating.

"You should examine that record, Grant. Before anyone else does. Just in case there's something in there that might be 'misinterpreted.' "

"I know that record and the chart. There is nothing I want to change. And even if there were I wouldn't alter it."

Colwell nodded sadly. "I wish I could be that cavalier about my career." He glanced down at his pad as if to pick up the trend of his questioning.

While still glancing down, he sucked at the end of his cigar before observing, as if to no one in particular, "Oh, there's going to be a letter from the insurance company in a few days . . . unless you've already got it . . ."

"Letter?" Sobol asked, alert to a new danger. "To whom?"

"The hospital. You. And Dr. Grant. You see, where the amount of the suit exceeds the amount of the insurance coverage then the individual doctors and the hospital can be liable. So you have a right to call in your own counsel," Colwell said, looking up for the first time, to see if his point had struck home.

Sobol leaned forward in his chair. "I thought the insurance company supplied all the legal defense. That's what the policy calls for."

"It does," Colwell was quick to answer. "Except that if we get hung with a verdict exceeding the three-million-dollar coverage in your policy, the excess will fall on the hospital, and on you and Dr. Grant personally. So you all have a right to consult lawyers on your own even though they can have no official standing in the case."

Chris made a mental note to check on Colwell's statement. It might be a threat, or it might be true.

"Doctor, I don't think you fully appreciate the significance of what I just said," Colwell continued. "It's proof that this is a personal vendetta. Reynolds doesn't need the money. He knows, and his lawyers know, that five million is an outrageous sum. But it's the only way he can keep you from hiding behind the hospital's insurance company. He wants your head. So I'd think seriously about what's *in* that record. And then about what you'd *like* to have in it. It's your last chance for the benefit of hindsight."

"That record stands!" Chris said firmly.

"Okay." Colwell seemed to resign himself to the worst consequences. "Well, now, let's get down to cases. There are some questions I have to ask."

"About the record?" Chris asked sharply.

"Yes and no," Colwell said. He lit his cigar. "This phototherapy is fairly new, isn't it?"

"It's been used very effectively for more than ten years," Mike Sobol declared, protectively.

"Used?" Colwell said.

72

"In some of the finest hospitals in this country," Chris added, taking over his own defense.

"How firmly established is it, really? I mean, do you know of any reputable hospitals where it *isn't* in use?"

"There are some. What about it?" Chris asked angrily.

Colwell smiled. "Grant, as an old hand at this law game, let me give you some good advice. When you answer questions in a legal case, don't give vent to your feelings. Give straightforward answers without emotion. No one, especially a judge, is interested in how you *feel*. He wants factual answers. Just as I do."

"Straightforward answers, like let's take the true entries out of the record and substitute phony ones," Chris said bitterly.

"Chris," said Sobol, hoping to pacify his angry young disciple.

Colwell continued his questioning. "Now then, according to our company doctors, there are certain very fine hospitals that don't employ phototherapy as standard practice."

"True," Chris conceded. "And there are many fine hospitals that do. There are also hundreds of papers written on that therapy by excellent men in the field of neonatology."

"Perhaps we can get some of them to come and testify on your behalf," Colwell said, almost as an aside. "But we'll get to our defenses later. First, you never presented this therapy to your Human Experimentation Committee, did you?"

"There was no need to," Sobol said quickly.

Colwell turned to the older doctor. "Direct answers to direct questions. Either you did or didn't put this form of therapy to your Human Experimentation Committee."

"We didn't," Sobol said, bristling at the investigator's arrogance. "And there's a reason."

Colwell finally yielded. "All right, what's the reason?"

"The best of all reasons," Sobol explained. "By the time we adopted the therapy it was no longer in the experimental stage."

73

Colwell nodded, not agreeing, just absorbing the statement and evaluating it.

"In fact," said Sobol, "that was one of the reasons I tried so hard to get Grant to join our staff."

"What was?" Colwell shot back quickly.

"Phototherapy. He had had experience with it in his previous post and I wanted such a unit set up here. At the same time, he wanted to be sure that we would adopt phototherapy if he did come here. Our interests being the same, we were able to arrive at a mutual agreement. I must say I have never regretted it."

Colwell nodded soberly. Then the small unsettling smile flicked across his face. "You just proved my point better than I ever could," he said, enjoying Sobol's puzzlement and discomfort.

"Proved what?"

"I merely asked whether you put this procedure to your Human Experimentation Committee. And you gave me a lot of information I never asked for. Information that would invalidate your testifying with any effectiveness on behalf of Dr. Grant. You admit he's your protégé. You brought him here to practice phototherapy. You're prejudiced in his favor. You'd make one hell of a lousy witness on his behalf."

Colwell bit off the wet end of his cigar. "Remember, both of you. Only answer what you've been asked. Don't explain. Don't apologize. Don't argue. Just answer."

"Look," Sobol fought back, "we're doctors, not professional witnesses. Oh, I know doctors who are. And I myself have testified three times, no, four, in my career. But I don't devote my time to it. Nor do I want to. I'll do what I have to in this case because I believe in Grant and what he did. But don't circumscribe me with rules and regulations, and a manner of conduct that is foreign to my nature. I am not an actor who learns a part and then repeats it as he's been directed!"

Colwell kept smiling his unnerving smile. "I'm your

friend. I'm on your side. Wait till you meet the opposition. You'll wish you *were* an actor."

"Is there anything else you want to know?" Sobol asked, impatient to end the confrontation.

The phone rang just then. Sobol answered.

"I told you not to disturb us, Marcie!" he said to his secretary who rarely heard him sound annoyed. "Oh . . . yes, yes." He handed the phone to Chris.

"Yes?" Chris spoke crisply into the phone.

It was Edith Riley in neonate intensive care. "Doctor, the Grove infant, it's vomiting again."

"Badly?"

"Very. And it's developed respiratory trouble. Also very bad."

"I'll be right there!" Chris said, hanging up.

"One minute, Doctor!" Colwell said.

"I have a terribly sick infant up there. Terminal, I think." Chris started for the door.

"Dr. Grant, I have to warn you." Chris turned to face the tall fat man. "Malpractice cases are messy. Time-consuming. This one is going to be even worse. We're worried down at the company."

"Your company gets paid to worry!" said Chris.

"In most cases we have the professional witnesses on *our* side." Colwell spoke swiftly now. "It's the plaintiff who normally has to scrounge for doctors to testify to the malpractice of another doctor. But Reynolds has muscle. There'll be a long line of very good doctors who'll testify against you!"

"I'm sorry about that. Now, I have a patient . . ."

"One thing more. You may not like me. But believe it or not, I'm trying to help you," said Colwell.

Once the door closed behind Chris, Mike Sobol asked, "You weren't just saying those things to scare him into cooperating, were you?"

"We are worried. We think they can go for the whole

bundle, and get it!" Colwell said. "So you'd better warn that young man, he's in bigger trouble than he suspects."

"It could ruin his career."

"That's why I wanted to get a firsthand look at the young man."

"What difference does that make?"

"Well . . ." Colwell equivocated, as if debating whether to reveal the information. Finally he said, "There's been talk down at the company of settling. For a very fancy figure. But malpractice isn't like other kinds of liability. Any other case, auto accident, fire, theft, if we decide to settle we make our offer, haggle a bit and then settle."

"Why not malpractice?" Sobol asked.

"Because it's the one kind of liability in which you have to get the insured's permission."

"Yes, I can see that," said Sobol. "After all, the hospital's reputation, the doctor's reputation are involved. And a settlement is an admission of guilt."

"*Some* doctors think so. Others are just glad to have the whole mess finished and forgotten," Colwell said.

"Forgotten? Things like that are never quite forgotten. Not in our profession."

"He's not likely to agree?" Colwell asked gingerly.

"Not likely," Sobol said. "And I'll tell you something, Mr. Colwell, I'm not likely to agree either."

Colwell glared at the older man.

"That's right," Sobol said quietly. "Your company is haggling over money. A lot of money, true, but still only money. I am dealing with the future of a young man, a brilliant young man. Hotheaded, yes. Resentful, yes. But devoted. That infant upstairs is probably going to die, but it's still more valuable to him than you and your whole damn company."

"We'll see, we'll see . . ." Colwell said, shoving his papers into his briefcase. "We're only at the beginning of things, Doctor."

Sobol suddenly realized that he had been nervously fingering the lapel of his starched lab coat until it was limp. He ceased instantly. He did not want to evidence any further uncertainty in the presence of this offensive man who was supposed to represent them but had done little more than issue veiled threats during the entire distasteful interview.

The Grove baby died in a convulsion at twelve minutes past ten o'clock that night. Chris felt no sorrow as he watched its struggle end. It had been a losing battle from the start, with a bad prognosis in the event of survival.

He went down to the ward to inform the mother. He discovered that earlier she had slipped out of the hospital unobserved. Obviously the needs for her habit had driven her back on the street again. It was no surprise to him that when the hospital checked they discovered the name Grove was fictitious. Nor was she known at the address she had given upon admission. It was quite usual in such cases.

Before he left the hospital, Chris stopped at Mike Sobol's office, but the head of pediatrics had left several hours earlier. Chris would have to wait until morning to confer with Mike about their sessions with Charles Colwell.

chapter SEVEN

THE BOARD of trustees of Metropolitan General was composed, as most hospital boards are, of lawyers, successful businessmen, and, recently, two women who, because they were wives of wealthy men, had the time and the personal drive to offer themselves to public service. Every member of the board was proud of the reputation of Metropolitan General, which was outstanding not only in the city but in the nation. Doctors who trained there went on to become chiefs of service at important hospitals throughout the country. Research papers by men on staff were numerous and well received. The many grants from public as well as private sources testified to the excellent research being done at the hospital.

Thomas Brady, chairman of the board, and a respected banker, had had the unpleasant duty of calling the meeting to discuss *Simpson vs. Metropolitan General, Christopher Grant, M.D., and Michael Edward Sobol, M.D.* Avery Waller, senior partner of the law firm which had been called in to represent the hospital, thought the meeting grave enough to appear in person rather than delegating one of his junior partners. It was the first time in the long history of the board of trustees that every single member was in attendance.

The large board room was paneled in rich dark oak. A lush Oriental rug covered the hand-pegged floor. The long table was of a single slab of South American mahogany that had been rubbed until it glistened. Matching chairs waited to accommodate the sixteen members. To open the meeting Thomas Brady, a tall man, white-haired and tanned, summoned all the trustees to the table by simply saying, "Shall we?"

Once they were all settled Brady began: "I'm sure all of us are equally distressed by the reason for this special meeting. It's sad enough when a hospital like ours is on the wrong end of such a lawsuit. But it is especially distressing when the plaintiffs have been so generous with this institution.

"But we can't let our past association with John Reynolds enter these deliberations. We must think first about this hospital, both its reputation and its obligation to the community."

Several of the other trustees nodded as Brady added: "To begin I think we must get an assessment of our position from our counsel, Mr. Waller."

Waller, short, plump, rosy-cheeked, one of those few who had always resisted the fashion that disposed of men's vests, was toying with the Phi Beta Kappa key on his gold chain. Now he leaned back in his huge armchair and cleared his throat.

"I've had our men go into this thoroughly. We've answered the summons and complaint and admitted only one fact—Doctors Sobol and Grant are our employees. As for all the other allegations, we deny them. We were not guilty of any negligence. Nor, for the record, was either doctor guilty of malpractice. We have also served a Demand for a Bill of Particulars. Their bill will be served shortly. Then we will know the specific detailed acts of negligence and malpractice the plaintiff alleges.

"Now I must warn you at the outset that since Dr. Grant

79

is a full-time doctor on staff he is our employee in the legal sense of that word. We are therefore responsible for his actions under the theory of *respondeat superior*. So there is no legal basis on which we can escape liability if his malpractice is proven."

The gloved hand of Mrs. Elliot Forster went up sharply. Without waiting to be recognized she said, "We *are* covered, aren't we? I mean it's really the insurance company that will have to make good?"

"I'll get to that in a moment, Mrs. Forster," Waller said gently, though he resented the interruption.

"I say 'we' can't escape liability because in this case the amount sued for is in excess of the coverage of our policy. If a judgment is found for the plaintiff over and above the amount of that coverage, then this hospital as well as Doctors Grant and Sobol will be financially responsible. And I needn't tell you who will actually have to pay."

Mrs. Forster was openly distressed by that announcement.

Waller continued: "Now, my office has examined the hospital records, including the patient's chart, the order book, the nurses' notes and all lab findings. It is our considered recommendation that this board should try and reach a settlement. We've discussed this with the insurance company and they agree. Especially since their investigator reports that our Dr. Grant does not promise to be the best of witnesses. His tendency to be combative would make him very vulnerable on the stand."

The distressed faces of the board members made it clear they understood all the implications involved.

Then Waller added what seemed only an aside, "Of course, it doesn't enhance our case that behind the plaintiff stands the figure of John Reynolds. Any jury will know that he is not motivated by money but a desire for justice. Which presents us with another ugly aspect of this case—public reaction."

Mrs. Forster was quick to volunteer, "I can imagine! People will be saying, if that's the kind of treatment Reynolds' grandchild got, imagine what our own children can expect from Metropolitan."

Cyrus Rosenstiel, the department store owner, sitting alongside Mrs. Forster, added, "And I wouldn't blame them. I say, let's get it over with. The longer this drags on, the worse it will look!"

"Exactly!" agreed Ellis Jackson, the chairman of Tool and Die Industries.

Rosenstiel addressed Waller: "Do we have any indication from the insurance company as to the disposition of the Reynoldses to settle?"

Chairman Brady leaned forward. "That's really what this meeting is about. We'd like to settle. The company would like to settle. But up to this moment there has been absolutely no indication from the Reynoldses that they are willing to settle. In fact . . ." Brady turned to Waller who said grimly:

"One of our lawyers plays golf with two partners of Reynolds' law firm. He tried to feel them out on the issue of settlement and ran up against a stone wall."

Brady resumed, "What we'd like to decide tonight is this. Whoever here is on the best terms with John Reynolds should go visit John and discuss the matter with him. Tell him what we feel, how sorry we are, how we are willing to assume the blame. But also what damage can be done to this hospital if he persists in taking this matter into court.

"We might also," Brady lowered his voice somewhat, "promise him that Dr. Grant will be dropped from our staff as soon as possible."

Mrs. Forster was the first to speak. "I certainly would volunteer to serve!"

Several of the men smiled, but it was Cy Rosenstiel who said, "I'm afraid, Mrs. Forster, that John Reynolds is not so enlightened that he would be moved by a woman's arguments. I would suggest, if I may, Tom Brady, Ellis Jackson and Ed Clarke."

Brady waited to see if there were any other suggestions, then said, "If Ed and Ellis are willing, I would undertake to head such a committee."

Brady was about to adjourn the meeting when there was a sharp knock on the door. When Rosenstiel opened it Mike Sobol came in wearing a dark suit instead of his accustomed white lab coat. "So, it's still going on," he said. "Good!"

"Actually, the meeting has just been adjourned . . ." began Brady, but Sobol interrupted more sharply than anyone expected.

"As long as the entire board is here it will save time."

Brady looked about the table. Most of the trustees would have preferred to leave the issue closed, but they were reluctant to offend one of their most revered staff chiefs. Brady finally said, "Unless there is someone who has to rush off . . ."

The members resumed their seats and Brady gave the floor to Sobol with a brisk gesture. The doctor took his place at the head of the table and spoke with an unaccustomed determination.

"All of you know that I am not one for meetings and boards. But tonight, because of what's at stake, I felt I had to come before you. I can guess what went on here before I arrived. And I don't fault you. Of course, save the hospital! Save our reputation! Silence all the bad publicity! I can understand that. But I must warn you that sometimes the easiest way out results in the most difficult consequences. And I have too much respect for human life to see one of my staff offered as a sacrifice."

From the trustees' reaction, Sobol had no need to be told. "Yes, I can imagine you've already made your decision. John Reynolds has suffered an enormous blow. He must be appeased. And since John Reynolds already has a surfeit of material things, payment must be made in blood. Specifically that of a young doctor, who in good faith pursued a proper course of treatment in this case. Something went wrong, but precisely what no one knows. What we must decide is whether to face the future objectively or follow some primitive rule of vengeance. That's the issue before this board. How will it help Reynolds or his grandson to destroy the career of Christopher Grant?"

There was a considerable amount of throat-clearing before anyone chose to answer. Waller, counsel for the hospital, spoke first.

"Dr. Sobol, I wish the issue were as simple as you choose to make it. Your interest in this matter and ours are not precisely identical. You approach it from the point of view of a chief of service trying to help one of your staff. Believe me, I understand. You feel responsible for that young man. And why not?"

Swiftly and angrily Sobol turned to face the lawyer. "If you're suggesting that I'm protecting him because I was responsible for bringing him here in the first place then you are wrong! If anything, I judge him *more* severely. If I thought he was guilty of malpractice I would be the first to call for his resignation."

Sobol had hit precisely on the point Waller intended to make. Still the lawyer tried to evade. "I simply wanted to say, you are concerned with running a single department in the hospital. We are charged with its overall well-being. We have to ask: "What's best for Metropolitan?"

"Exactly." Chairman Brady assumed the burden of the argument. "Mike, with government monies becoming harder and harder to come by, we can't be too zealous in protecting the reputation of this hospital. When we apply for funds for some worthwhile project—one of your own projects, for example—we can't have this unsavory lawsuit hanging over us. It is our considered judgment that our duty is to protect the hospital, not any single individual."

"So you're determined to settle," Sobol said sadly.

"*If* we can," said Waller. "I'm not sure Reynolds'll let us."

"Oh, I think he will," Sobol remarked caustically, "if you bring him Grant's head on a silver platter like John the Baptist!"

"Now wait a minute," Waller said, half in surprise, half in indignation. He had not expected such an attack from the usually mild-mannered physician.

"What else would you call it? What name would *you* have for this dirty business? You want to trade away the future of a brilliant young doctor to soothe the angry vanity of a man because he has great power?"

"He's done a great deal for you, Mike," Brady pointed out.

"Of course! No one knows it better than I," Sobol admitted. "But that doesn't mean that I have to stand by while he deliberately destroys a man. No one has proven Dr. Grant guilty of malpractice and I doubt anyone will."

"Reynolds' lawyers think they will," Brady interrupted. "They're so sure that we can't say now they'll even entertain talk of settlement."

Sobol raised his voice. "I repeat, nobody has proved that yet! And I don't think they will. Not to my satisfaction."

"Unfortunately, Mike, they only have to prove it to a jury's satisfaction," said Waller.

"Till they do, I maintain Chris Grant is innocent. But it isn't even his innocence that is paramount in my mind. What I am thinking about is what happens to this hospital, this medical school if we don't stand up for Grant. How do we attract the best men if we get a reputation for ruthlessly abandoning young doctors at the first sign of trouble? These days if you want good young men you have to search them out, and offer them the best conditions. Why, in the two years since Grant's been here he's had a dozen different offers from other hospitals.

"I say, if you try and settle this case it will be a mark against our institution. Every young man we want from now on will ask himself, 'If I go to Metropolitan General and get into any kind of trouble, will they crucify me?' And most of them will not come. They simply will not come."

"What do you want us to do?" Mrs. Forster asked, honestly perplexed. "There is the unfortunate child. And there is the damned lawsuit. We can't ignore either. Why my own husband said, 'There's only one way to straighten this out. Heads have to roll. We do it in business all the time.' "

"So that's what your husband said," Sobol remarked bitterly. "Well, may I have the temerity to point out that your husband may know how to run an advertising agency but he doesn't know a damn thing about running a hospital!"

"Mike, please—" Brady tried to interrupt.

Sobol would not be stopped. "There is a difference between business executives and doctors. Executives can go from failure to a better job. For doctors it's not so easy. They bear the scars for the rest of their lives. And, unfortunately, we don't have so many good young men that we can afford the spectacle of seeing 'heads roll.' We have to take considered action. Even if it means a long, tough, hard fight."

"Exactly what would you have us do?" Waller demanded.

"First, you must not settle this case!" Sobol declared. "That's the same as admitting that Grant is guilty of malpractice. Second, we have to give him the best defense we can."

"Do you realize, Mike," Waller said, "if we do that and lose he'll surely be ruined because of the massive publicity?"

"I can't say we'll win. I only say we have to fight," Sobol said doggedly.

"And there's the expense," Cy Rosenstiel argued. "If we fight and lose, the hospital can be liable for any judgment over and above the policy."

"Unfortunately," said Sobol, "fighting always carries with it the possibility of losing."

"That's no answer, Mike!" Rosenstiel declared angrily, as if these two men had never shared a *seder* on Passover.

"What kind of answer do you want, Cy? You want me to go to the bank and sign a note in blood that I will personally pay the amount of any judgment? Okay, I'll sign it!"

"Now, that's ridiculous, Mike! Nobody expects it or asks it," Chairman Brady said, hoping to put an end to the discussion.

Sobol persisted. "I want that young man defended!"

Brady decided it was time to close the discussion. "Mike, we understand your position. But we are still the trustees responsible for this institution. We have decided on a course of action we think is temperate, wise and expedient in very difficult circumstances. As a member of the faculty you have to abide by our decision."

Sobol nodded slightly, not in agreement, but in recognition of the fact that no matter how high he had risen in his field, he was in the end a hired hand. What the board decided, he must accept. Well, he still had a trump card.

"Gentlemen, you seem to have overlooked one point. Where malpractice is involved an insurance company can't settle without the consent of all the insured. And I can tell you right now that Grant won't give his consent. Nor will I!"

Waller waited till the trustees absorbed Sobol's statement. Then he said, "You're right. Up to a point."

"And that point is?" Sobol asked.

"If this was Grant's policy, or yours, you could prevent a settlement. But this is the hospital's policy and nothing you or Grant can do can prevent us from settling."

Mike hesitated, reaching into his mind for some final argument to reverse the board's decision. Finally he spoke. Very softly, this time.

"Then I'm afraid I have to tender my resignation."

"Mike, don't do anything foolish!" Cy Rosenstiel rushed to say.

"Foolish? What's foolish about taking a stand beside a

young man in whose abilities and ethics I have the highest confidence?"

Sobol turned and walked out of the room. Rosenstiel rose from the table. "I'll go after him. I'll talk to him."

But Brady said, "No, Cy, no. Wait."

Brady thought for a few moments before speaking. "Twenty-one years. The man made that statement after twenty-one years in this hospital. I don't think anyone would do that out of loyalty to one young doctor. Even if he looks upon him as a son. No, I am inclined now to accept what he says. That he sees this as a blow to the medical school and our hospital. Mike Sobol is a man who has suffered considerable frustration here. He has done his share of waiting, pleading and begging to improve our facilities. Such a man does not indulge in whims. The question no longer is, do we let one young doctor stand in our way? It is, do we sacrifice a man like Mike Sobol or do we fight? On that issue, I think we have to reconsider our stand. If someone will make a motion to reopen this meeting. . . ."

Waller tried to intervene. "Before we get carried away with sentiment over Mike Sobol . . ."

"Damn it, Avery!" Brady exploded. "This isn't a matter of sentiment! The man has said he would rather resign than watch us damage Metropolitan. When a man lays his career on the line that's not sentiment. Do I hear a motion to reopen?"

The motion was made by Mrs. Forster and seconded by Cy Rosenstiel.

In the more than two hours of debate the board of trustees of Metropolitan General decided that at this time they would not give permission to the insurance company to settle *Simpson vs. Metropolitan General, Christopher Grant, M.D., and Michael Edward Sobol, M.D.*

CHAPTER EIGHT

"TWENTY THOUSAND dollars?" Chris Grant repeated, stunned.

"That's right, Chris," Mike Sobol said glumly. "That's what he said."

Chris shook his head.

"He's a good man," Mike said. "One of the best litigation lawyers in the city. He said he had to consider the time-consuming paperwork, the examinations before trial, and of course the trial itself. Altogether on an hourly rate, which is how lawyers figure their fees these days, it would come to twenty thousand dollars."

"That's almost as much as I make in a year," Chris said.

"It might even run higher," Mike warned.

"Do we have to have attorneys of our own?" Chris asked finally.

Mike Sobol had never told Chris about his meeting with the trustees, but the older man knew that even though he had prevailed that evening, he might not be so fortunate the next time, which is why he had begun to investigate the possibility of personal legal counsel. The fees unhappily seemed out of the question.

A man like Mike Sobol who had devoted his life to academic medicine did not accumulate large savings. Instead of huge fees which he could invest in stocks, real estate and other business ventures, Mike had a little money put aside. Twenty thousand dollars would represent a sizable part of his savings, if he yielded to his temptation to foot the legal bill himself.

"You think it's absolutely necessary that we have counsel of our own?" Chris asked, hoping to avoid the problem.

Mike nodded. "After that meeting with Colwell, yes. If they're suggesting now that you falsify records, who knows what they'll come up with next? And when you refuse, as you no doubt will, we don't know how well our interests will be protected. We need someone we can trust, someone who is working for us, and only for us."

"But Colwell said our own lawyer wouldn't have any official status in the case. Would merely be advisory."

"The lawyer I consulted agrees," said Mike. "But he feels it's essential we know how well we're being protected by the insurance company."

"Still, twenty thousand dollars," said Chris.

Mike reached for the dry pipe which he merely sucked on since his heart attack. He fondled it, then placed it between his teeth and, after a moment broached his real purpose.

"Chris, suppose there were someone young. Not in the same league as a lawyer with a twenty-thousand-dollar-a-case retainer but good, thorough, counsel with an excellent law school record who has been working with a solid firm for several years and whose fee would be nominal."

"What do you mean, nominal?" Chris asked, still overwhelmed by the twenty-thousand-dollar figure.

"Say anything *we* set," Mike said.

"Why would one lawyer ask twenty thousand, and another be willing to do the same job for whatever we can afford?" Chris asked.

"Because she happens to owe me a favor," Mike said softly.

"*She?*" Chris asked, surprised.

"Yes, *she,*" Mike Sobol repeated. "She happens to owe me a favor and she's been waiting for the chance to pay me back. This is it."

"A favor?"

"Her life," Mike said gently. "She was born a preemie. It was highly doubtful she'd make it."

"You pulled her through," Chris concluded.

Mike nodded. "The family was so grateful that Rose and I were asked to be her godparents. We've known her all her life. She calls us Aunt Rose and Uncle Mike." Then Mike added sadly, "Or used to when Rose was alive."

"A girl," Chris observed again.

"A bright girl. A thoroughly good and nice person. I don't think she'd ask you to falsify records or commit perjury," Mike said. "But she'd give us the best advice she could. Advice we could follow."

"At least the price is right," Chris said, permitting himself his first smile during this discouraging discussion.

"I don't want you to say yes merely because the price is right. Or because I think she can do it. Before you agree, I want you to talk to her. I think it's essential that we only retain someone in whom we both have confidence."

"Sure. Okay," said Chris.

Mike had his secretary put through the call to Miss Laura Winters.

"Laura? Uncle Mike," Sobol began. "I'm sitting here with my associate. Or do I say my co-defendant? I think it might be a good idea if you two met first and discussed the matter. Wait, I'll ask." He turned to Chris. "What would be a good time?"

"I'll be done in the lab at about eight this evening. If there are no emergencies, how about eight-thirty?"

Mike relayed the information, then turned to Chris. "Where?"

"Anyplace," Chris said. "Her office. Whatever is most convenient for her."

Mike spoke into the phone again. "It can't be here, because I don't want anyone in the hospital to see you two together. Not yet. It can't be Chris's place because he lives in the hospital complex and I don't want any inferences drawn. But there is an excellent Italian restaurant called La Scala, where I am well known. I'll arrange a table and you two will be my guests for dinner. Just mention my name to Guido, the owner. He'll put it on my bill, which he never lets me pay. So, La Scala, at eight-thirty? Right, that's the place. I'm glad you remember. Where Rose and I took you when you graduated from high school."

Mike hung up. "Eight-thirty. La Scala. I'll give you the directions."

Chris tried to concentrate on his research but hadn't been able to. When he had first learned of the malpractice suit his reaction had been combative and defiant. He was sure he had chosen the correct treatment and that he would be vindicated. But ever since his confrontation with Colwell he had begun to appreciate the grim, tiring process of the law. It was not all like those flashy courtroom scenes one saw on TV, and now, when he should be working on his new paper, he found his mind grappling with legal problems instead. Why had Mike been so assiduous about seeking counsel from other lawyers? Did Mike have reason to suspect they might not get all the personal protection they were entitled to from the hospital?

And a woman lawyer. From the way Mike talked, not even a woman, a mere girl. He left his work with considerable reservation and started downtown to La Scala.

Guido, owner and maître d' of La Scala, seemed to recognize Chris as soon as he entered.

"You are, no doubt, the doctor who is a friend of Mike Sobol?"

"Yes."

"Good. The lady is already here and waiting." With a menu as a pointer, Guido indicated a table in the far corner. Chris glanced in that direction. Good God, he thought. She barely looked twenty and from this distance she seemed tiny as well. If lawyers went by the pound this was one lawyer he could afford. As he followed Guido among the tables, he kept staring at her. She was blonde. Her hair was neat and obviously feminine in its arrangement. She was dressed in a dark silk outfit with a touch of red at the throat. Close up she was a bit more mature than he had first thought and not so small.

When they shook hands he looked down at her from his six-one and found her to be an extremely attractive young woman. For some reason, that also made him doubt her qualifications as a lawyer. If she suspected that, she didn't give any hint. She simply said, "Sit down, Doctor," putting their relationship on a straight professional basis with her first words.

She kept it that way throughout dinner, doing all the ordering herself, including the wine. While they waited she talked about Mike, their early relationship, the close ties they had, possibly because Rose and Mike had had no children. A great pity, Laura Winters observed, because Mike and Rose would have made great parents.

Only once she had set Chris at ease did she begin to discuss the case. Even then only by indirection. She asked Chris about his research, his teaching, his hospital practice. Gradually she had him talking about himself. Something he did not like to do. He even told her about the addicted Grove baby and how he had been forced to stay in Mike's office talking to Colwell while the infant was embattled in its vain struggle.

Then he said, "In a way I'm glad it died. It would have been an orphan before it was a year old. That mother's going to OD before very long. And where would that leave him, with no one to adopt him because of his prenatal addiction? What a hell of a way to begin life."

Laura didn't answer, just stared across the table, studying Chris's face. When he glanced at her, he noticed that she had very blue, extremely warm eyes. They made him self-conscious and he started picking at his food again.

When they finished dinner they still had a great deal of talking to do and she suggested they go to her apartment. The invitation was couched in such terms that there was no doubt it was a purely business meeting and would remain so.

Her apartment was a reflection of herself. Small, neatly arranged, warm and yet efficient. She put some coffee on to brew, then settled down in a large comfortable chair, drawing her legs up under her. Chris sat opposite her on the couch.

"Do you have any idea," she asked suddenly, "how long a lawsuit like this takes? And if one side or the other wants to stall, it can drag on for years. In fact, Doctor, it could take as long to resolve this case as it did for you to go through medical school."

"Four years?" Chris asked, astounded.

"Or longer, Doctor." She lit a cigarette. Her eleventh, Chris noted with disapproval. She continued:

"There'll be constant interruptions of your work. They'll make your life hell. They'll schedule an examination before trial, you'll arrange your time to accommodate it and at the last moment they'll find some reason for a postponement.

"The insurance company lawyers will be after you to tell your story over and over to experts they intend to hire to testify for you during the trial. They'll come up with bright ideas from their dirty tricks department—and don't think

Colwell's suggestion was the exception. That's the rule. The law can be a dirty business. Just as medicine can, I suppose."

Chris didn't comment.

"Of course, if a lawyer made such a suggestion to you directly he would be subject to disbarment. That's why they sent Colwell. He's only an investigator. But you can be damn sure that idea was born in the mind of some lawyer. The significant thing is that the suggestion was made."

She reached for a fresh cigarette. This time he reacted with open disapproval. She noticed and said crisply, "Let's get two things straight, Doctor. First, I don't intend to listen to any lectures from you about my smoking. I smoke too much. I know it and it won't help if you keep reminding me of that fact."

Chris smiled. "And second?"

"Second, this can only work out if it remains a purely professional relationship," she asserted, and in so doing confirmed his own thought that they might find each other extremely interesting as man and woman.

He didn't answer, merely nodded his head slightly.

"Now, as I was saying, what's significant is that they felt impelled to suggest that you falsify your records. That means they feel vulnerable. That your case isn't too strong. That they have doubts about the judgment you exercised in treating the infant. Always remember one thing about insurance companies. They'll throw anyone to the wolves to avoid a big settlement. That's why Mike had to battle so hard at the trustees meeting. . . ."

The look of surprise on his face stopped her.

"I guess you weren't supposed to know about that," Laura said apologetically.

"I don't want Mike taking risks for me," Chris protested.

"He did. And he will," Laura said simply. "You know Uncle Mike."

Chris nodded.

94

"I'm not sorry I told you," she said. "I don't believe in concealing anything from a client. We have to be honest with each other, that's why I'm taking the time tonight to explain things. When I'm done, you may not want me for your lawyer. And I may not want you for a client."

They had finished the first pot of coffee and were working on the second. Laura Winters had led Chris Grant through the entire procedure that he had followed in treating Reynolds' grandchild. When she mentioned the possibility of many experts testifying for the prosecution, he protested.

"Nobody, certainly no honest doctor, can testify that what I did was malpractice!"

"Dr. Grant, a firm like Parkins, Sears and Wadleigh doesn't go serving a summons and complaint without having the word of some respected doctors that they *will* so testify!" Laura explained.

"If John Reynolds commanded it, his law firm would bring bastardy proceedings against St. Joseph for siring Jesus Christ!"

"Now, just a minute, Doctor!" said Laura sharply. "Just as doctors realize certain things from experience, lawyers do too. And I know this. Sure Parkins will try to please Reynolds in any way they can. But that's not why they're his lawyers. They are his lawyers because they know their business. And because he respects them. If they thought he had no suit they would have told him so. Because if they didn't, then sooner or later he'd discover they'd given him bad advice and they wouldn't be his law firm any longer. So I say if the Parkins firm is handling this there's substance to it. And if the insurance company is worried enough to ask you to commit forgery . . ."

Chris reacted.

"Yes, legally that's what it is. If they're passing the word along to you, then they are damned well worried. And if *they* are, *you* ought to be, too. And if you're not, then *I* am!"

"You mean you don't want to take on the case?" Chris asked.

"I mean," she said softly, "that an idealistic shnook like you needs a lawyer more than most men."

She lapsed into thought, but only for a moment. "One other thing I know. Parkins, Sears and Wadleigh is not the type of firm that usually handles malpractice suits. Before very long we're going to see some eminent counsel pop up to take over at the trial."

"What does that mean?" Chris asked.

"You have specialties in medicine. Well, we do in the law. Men who do one thing to practically the exclusion of all others and do it so expertly that they are virtually invincible. If I had to make a guess, John Reynolds must have said, 'Get me the best and the most expensive negligence trial lawyer in this state!' And that means only one man."

"Who?"

"Harry Franklyn," Laura said. "We'll know how far they're willing to go if we hear that name because I can tell you now, Harry Franklyn doesn't take any case he even suspects he might lose. And in a courtroom, he's the most disarming and effective lawyer I've ever seen."

"Harry Franklyn," Chris repeated, a name he'd never heard before but which suddenly embodied the enemy.

Laura Winters was silent for a time, then she announced, "Yes, I'm going to be your lawyer. Even merely as a consultant it'll be fun to watch little Harry Franklyn at work."

From her description, Chris had expected an idealized Perry Mason. Laura smiled. "Yes, little. Franklyn's no taller than I am. And never speaks above a whisper if he can help it. But then a cobra doesn't make much noise either."

She reached for another cigarette. He glanced at her reprovingly, and at the ashtray which was laden with burnt-out stubs.

She noticed and snapped impatiently, "I need a cigarette. I know it's a sign of weakness and I know all the reasons why I shouldn't. But I know as many doctors who smoke as women."

She lit up, took a few puffs. "Look, let's keep one thing straight. Let's not try to run each other's lives. Okay?"

"Okay," he agreed.

"Goodnight, Doctor," she said, ending the evening.

He left. On his way home he had to admit that he had been greatly impressed by her professional attitude and probing questions. Yet he couldn't help regretting that he hadn't met her on a more personal level, with no professional relationship involved. She was an attractive young woman. A girl, really. Younger than he was. But in her own way she seemed to be at least as capable.

NINE

HE WAS in bed with Alice Kennan when he became aware
of the change in himself. Actually she had noticed it first.
In the habit of lovers, they had indulged in the small provocative tactics that each had come to know the other
desired. And their desire had built to the point where it
was inevitable that they would become one. For himself, he
felt as strong, as hungry, as vigorous as he always had. His
need for her was, if anything, greater than ever. He felt
her responding under him. Her arms and her long, strong,
graceful legs seemed to envelop him with even greater
ferocity than usual. Their bodies reached the peak of intensity at the same instant. As he relaxed, spent, he could
feel the pulsating throbbing that told him she too was
satisfied.

They were silent in the dark. His face was pressed against
her soft warm shoulder, inhaling her perfume. She was a
completely satisfied and satisfying woman. In moments
such as these he had twice mentioned the subject of their
getting married. Always she had responded in the same
way.

"Chris, darling, if I ever marry a doctor, it'll be you."

She would laugh, not because she was making light of his proposal, but because she was uneasy with her own response. Whatever her inner fears and feelings about marriage, Chris suspected it did not truly relate to doctors. For if it did, why did she continue to work at a medical center?

Once, subtly as he could, he suggested she go see a psychiatrist. But she only laughed and said, "What if he told me to give you up?"

Though the self-deception in Alice's life was clear to Chris, he could never make it clear to her. So he accepted their relationship for what it was. An affair between two people of fortunately matching desires who had careers they pursued with avidness and a sense of satisfaction. It suited Alice and as long as she understood the demands of his career, it suited Chris as well.

Yet tonight something was missing. He thought of it as they lay in the dark, their bodies curved to fit each other, and even as he was thinking about it, she voiced it.

"There *is* something different," she said in her middle-of-the-night whisper. "You're worried about that examination before trial tomorrow."

"It's nothing to be worried about," said Chris. "Any doctor who's had to stand up before an audience of other doctors shouldn't be scared of a few lawyers sitting in a conference room asking questions."

"Worried or not, it was different tonight," Alice said, in a voice he had never heard before.

"Don't be silly." He drew her warm body even closer. Letting her know that his desire for her had started to grow again.

"Alice? Honey?" he whispered.

She shook her head. Her long black hair rustled against the pillow. He tried to turn her to him so he could kiss her on the lips, but she did not respond. That had never happened before.

"Allie?" he asked, his hand reaching to envelop her breast.

"If it ever changes between us," she said, "I want you to tell me. I don't want pretenses. I don't want lies. I want to know."

"Don't be silly," he protested.

"I want to know," she insisted, before turning to accept his kiss. Soon they were ready for each other, but this time because of either what she said, or what he had only suspected before, this time it was different. He was thinking when he should only be feeling. He was reserving some corner of himself when he should have been giving all of himself. Was he really tense about tomorrow?

Or was he simply concerned over the infant who had come into intensive care just before he left the hospital to meet Alice? A neonate whose heart could not pump an adequate supply of blood to its frail body. In the morning they would have to decide whether or not to operate. The choice was not a promising one. Left on its own the infant would be an invalid for its short life. Operated on, it might die under the scalpel. He and Frank Walp, the pediatric surgeon, would decide in the morning.

Having convinced himself that it was this decision that had been troubling him, he rested against Alice's fragrant body and allowed himself to fall asleep. Alice was not so easily or surely persuaded. She remained awake, holding his strong, capable hand tight against her.

The infant breathed spasmodically. Its ribcage, a tortured structure, seemed fragile as eggshells. Chris Grant examined the infant swiftly so it could be returned to the safety, warmth and oxygen of its plastic enclosure as soon as possible. Walp, the surgeon, stood beside Chris, ready to carry out his own examination. It didn't take long to confirm Chris's findings. The stethoscope clearly revealed the existence of a defective heart valve which rendered the infant incapable of forcing enough blood through its system to carry vital oxygen to all parts of its body.

"Keep it on a respirator," said the surgeon. "So I have time to prepare. See you in the operating room. Say an hour and a half."

The surgeon left. Chris lifted the little patient which felt like a naked frightened chicken. Its frantic heart fought so to compensate for its defect that he could feel it thrusting against the flexible ribs. The urge to live was as strong, as desperate in a day-old infant as in older, stronger patients Chris used to see on the wards during his days as an intern.

Chris scrubbed before entering the OR to observe. Alongside him, Walp, in his green surgical gown, went over his hands, fingers and nails with special vigor. When he was done, the nurse who stood by to assist pulled the gloves down over his raised hands. They snapped into place with a brisk sound and she tied on his mask. Similarly gloved and masked, Chris followed him into the operating room.

If the patient seemed tiny in its Isolette, it appeared almost insignificant in the midst of the shiny equipment. The anesthesia was completed and Walp painted the field of the operation with an antiseptic solution. Checking his assistant who was standing by with miniature retractors, Walp proceeded to make his first incision.

Chris watched, fascinated by the facility of Walp's skillful hands. In his early days in medicine Chris had considered quite seriously becoming a surgeon. Open-heart surgery was reaching prominence when he became a medical student, and it fascinated many doctors who were deciding on a specialty.

Consciously, Chris had finally opted for neonatology out of concern for those children who confronted danger in their earliest hours of life, and unconsciously, his choice had its roots in events that took place when he himself was only four years old.

His mother had been a decent, conscientious woman. She had worked hard to make up for Chris's father. Phil Grant was one of those men always destined to be a marginal worker. During World War II he was deferred from the draft because he was married and had a child. He worked in a shipyard and earned the best wages of his life. When the war ended and Liberty ships were phased out, Phil Grant was one of the first to be let go.

He found work as a bus driver. It did not require special ability, so he kept that job for some time. But since it did not require much skill, neither did it pay well. It was enough for a family of three to live on. When his mother became pregnant again it was even enough for them to welcome the baby. Chris's mother was happy during her pregnancy. She continued with the laundering which she took in until her last weeks of pregnancy. Chris would play under her ironing board while she talked to him about the baby that was coming. He could not remember now having been greatly affected except to ask if it would be a brother or a sister.

His mother used to smile and say only, "We'll see. We'll see."

The trouble came in the last days. She was so big with child that Chris had secretly wondered if she would ever be the same size as he remembered her. Then one afternoon the phone rang, and from her first few words Chris knew, even as a four-year-old, that something terrible had happened. Terrible enough to frighten him. Terrible enough so that he never would forget the feeling of sudden terror.

He remembered she had hung up, reached swiftly for her coat, saying, "You'll have to stay with Bernard and Mrs. Molloy. But I'll be back as soon as I can. . . ."

She didn't finish that sentence. Or her next one. Which was more a sound of pain than a word. Then she made her way to the door and cried out, "Edna! Mrs. Molloy!!"

Fortunately, Edna Molloy was home and quick to answer.

She had barely reached the Grant door when his mother said, "Oh, my God."

He noticed that his mother was becoming dark and wet around that forbidden area of her body. When Mrs. Molloy opened the door, his mother called out, "My water. It broke!" Mrs. Molloy, an older woman, and used to trouble, went to the phone at once and called for an ambulance. She guided his mother to the bedroom and forced her to lie down, despite her protests that she would soil the bed. But Mrs. Molloy insisted. Even as she lay down he could remember his mother saying, "He needs me . . . he needs me . . ." It wasn't until later that young Chris realized that his mother was not talking about the baby as yet unborn, but about his father.

Mrs. Molloy kept assuring his mother that everything would be fine, right up to the moment when they heard the heartening sound of the ambulance as it rounded the corner and pulled up before the tenement in which they lived. Once that sound released her, Mrs. Molloy gave vent to her fears as she called desperately to the doctor, "Up here! She's up here!" She was definitely relieved when an intern, young as he was, took over.

They wrapped Chris's mother in a blanket and put her on a stretcher despite her protests, "He needs me . . . he needs me . . ." They carried her out of the apartment, loaded her into the ambulance and slammed the doors. It pulled away sounding its siren.

They had watched it from the front door, little Chris, Mrs. Molloy and young Bernard. Chris was crying. Soon Bernard was too. To Bernard, Mrs. Molloy said, "Shut up or I'll give you one." But to young Chris Mrs. Molloy said, "Come upstairs and I'll give you some milk and cookies. You're not to worry about your mama. She'll be all right."

"She won't die?" young Chris pleaded.

"What do you know about dying?" Mrs. Molloy had asked. "A young child like you?"

He didn't know. He didn't even know why he had mentioned it. Except that, somehow, he knew that dying was the worst thing that could happen to anyone. Certainly the worst thing that could happen to mothers of little boys.

His father came home later that afternoon. His hand was bandaged. From the way he carried it, Chris knew that it hurt very badly. As soon as Phil Grant discovered what had happened he rushed to the hospital. He came back late, so late that Chris slept with Bernard Molloy.

In the days that followed, especially after his mother came home from the hospital without the long-promised baby, Chris discovered from the little that was said that his father had had an accident with the bus. Someone had been killed. And, though after a while his father was not in trouble with the law, neither did he get his job back again.

From that time on his mother did all the work, going out to do laundry in other people's homes. She came back in time to make supper for him and his father. During the rest of the day his father took care of Chris, making his breakfast and lunch, eventually taking him off to kindergarten. His father occasionally found odd jobs but nothing steady, nothing that lasted. Eventually he became a thin, quiet man who spent most of his time alone. He did not smoke. He did not drink. He was simply alone, reading the newspaper so carefully that he seemed to be rationing it to last the day.

Puzzled as he was, Chris Grant did not ask many questions. His father never had answers and his mother had too much grief answering them.

But one question could not be ignored. What had happened to his new brother or sister? Mama had gone away looking so big and come back so empty. Nights when he was supposed to be asleep in his small bed he could hear his mother in the big bed sighing, and sometimes weeping. His father slept, or pretended to. Then she would get up quietly and slip out of the room to go sit in the kitchen.

Even when it was freezing and they had no heat, she would sit in the kitchen in her thin cotton nightgown.

Sometimes Chris would slip out of his bed and listen. Once he dared to open the door and slip silently to the kitchen. He stood in the doorway, watching her. She did not seem to notice him, yet she said, very softly, "Come, darling. Come."

He went to her and she reached out to draw him close. Cold as he was she felt colder. Her thin body could give him no comfort except closeness. Her breasts seemed small now. Her face was damp. Her eyes red and staring, even in the dark. He pressed against her.

He dared to ask, "Mama, are you crying for the baby?"

She didn't answer.

"Did it . . . die?"

Again she didn't answer, only held him tighter.

"Why, Mama? Why did it die?" In a while he asked, "Will I die, too?"

"Oh, no, no!" she said, lifting him into her lap. "It died . . . it died because it couldn't breathe."

"Couldn't breathe?" Chris asked, puzzled. Everybody breathed.

"Babies before their time, their lungs are too small, or their hearts, and they just can't breathe. So they die. . . ."

"Where do they go when they die?" he asked.

"To heaven. Little babies are always clean and innocent. They all go to heaven."

"Will I go to heaven when I die?" Chris had asked.

She pressed him closer. "You won't die," she protested, rocking him till he fell asleep, but not before his face was wet with her tears. When he woke the next morning he was in his own bed.

He never asked her about the baby again. But she never stopped weeping for it. For the rest of her life, at times when he had forgotten all about it, Chris would be aware of his mother leaving the big bed and going out into the kitchen to cry. She never blamed his father, never said that it was his accident that caused her premature delivery. But his father apologized to her for it for the rest of their dismal lives. Neither of them ever recovered from the loss.

Chris recovered, but it left a mark. The events that began that terrible day could well have motivated him to elect the field of pediatrics, and the subspecialty of neonatology, so that tiny infants, born defective, or stricken in their early hours, would have a chance. So that mothers would not have to sit alone in the dark and weep for what could not be properly mourned or retrieved.

As he stared down at the small field of the operation now under the surgeon's hand, Chris Grant found himself wondering, as he usually did during neonate surgery, what the defect was that robbed him of his little brother.

Today the operation was going well. Walp was through the soft bones of the ribcage and into the chest cavity. With skillful fingers he found and corrected the defective valve. Fortunately it was of the type that needed correction, not substitution. In a short time the repair was made. Walp began the process of withdrawal. He did not turn over the final suturing to any assistant but insisted on doing it himself.

As Walp turned from the table, leaving the infant in the care of a pediatric nurse, he said to Chris, "I'll be up on the ward about three o'clock right before my rounds. See you then."

"I won't be there," Chris was forced to say.

The surgeon's look demanded an explanation.

"Lawyers. There's an examination today."

"Oh," was all Walp said. Chris did not know if that was meant to express solicitude or disapproval. Walp never mentioned the subject again.

The infant was safely back in its Isolette with an IV in its arm and an oxygen tube taped to its nose. Chris slipped out of his operating room greens and into his own clothes.

Ten minutes later he left the hospital to go down to the financial district where most of the large law firms had their offices. He started out well in advance of the appointed time because Laura Winters had insisted they meet and go over strategy before his first confrontation with Parkins, Sears and Wadleigh.

Laura was employed by a firm of lawyers who, though they did not have the prestige of the Parkins firm, were substantial and well regarded. Chris found her office to be a comfortably efficient room, with a window overlooking Courthouse Square. When he caught sight of her at her desk, blonde hair in slight disarray, giving instructions to a secretary about some papers she had just finished dictating, he was even more impressed. This small but very nicely proportioned young woman had a surgeon's approach to her profession. That she was attractive besides in some way amused him. Attractive women had no right to be so efficient and businesslike.

She dispatched the secretary, turned to Chris and said crisply, "Oh, yes," as if he were just another order of business on her crowded calendar. Then she relaxed a bit and said, "Sorry, Chris, but it's been one of those days. Do sit down."

When he was in the leather desk chair she rose and stared out the window, her back to him. She said nothing. For what seemed to Chris like a long time she simply stared out the window.

"It's going to be very difficult to explain this to a layman," she said suddenly. He was unused to having himself referred to as a layman, but on reflection, insofar as the law was concerned, that was what he was.

"Each lawsuit has its own demands, its own complications." She paused. "And its own emotional cost."

The gravity of her manner gave Chris the identical sinking feeling that he had experienced as he left the hospital less than an hour ago.

"Medical malpractice," Laura continued, "means the questioning of a man in that area of his life that is most precious to him—his profession." Her blue eyes were carefully focused on him. "If the jury decides that you are guilty, your whole view of your life and your profession will be affected. A man facing such an accusation can become highly emotional. That's why this talk before we go across the square to the Parkins office."

Laura paused, then said, "You cannot, you must not, under any provocation, give vent to anger during this preliminary examination. No matter what charges are made, what questions asked, what snide inferences are suggested, you must steel yourself to answer the questions as directly as you can. Do not volunteer. Do not argue. You are only a witness. Don't step out of that role. Do I make myself clear?"

In that instant Laura was lawyer, mentor, and mother all in one, warning her little boy that he must behave. He could not resist smiling and saying, "Yes, Mother, it's perfectly clear."

Angered, Laura said, "And that's another thing! This case cannot be treated as a source of amusement. Even when we are alone. It is one relaxation that I will not abide. It endangers you. It belittles me. I will not have that!"

It seemed to Chris that in that brief moment she had become a bit emotional and involved herself. She felt it too. For she regained her composure and said, "Now we're ready to go across the square. Just remember what I said."

She took her gray businesslike jacket from its hanger on the back of the door and slipped into it. When Chris helped her he caught the fresh clean smell of her perfume. It was totally feminine. If the perfume hadn't told him that, the curve of her breasts as they disappeared into that sober jacket made it eminently clear.

But now there was serious, possibly dangerous, business to attend to.

TEN

THE OFFICES of Parkins, Sears and Wadleigh were impressive. On the high walnut-paneled double doors that led to the large waiting room were gold leafed the names of fourteen senior partners. Below the dividing line and in smaller gilt lettering was a list of junior names too numerous to count. Parkins, Sears and Wadleigh did not enter any battle undermanned.

Paul Crabtree, who had been retained to represent the insurance company, and James Spalding, from Waller's law firm, representing the hospital, were waiting for Chris and Laura when they arrived. Crabtree, a tall, rangy man, with an easy smile and a warm, deep voice, pretended to be delighted to meet them. Actually he was as concerned as Laura about what impression their key witness would make. He knew from long experience that the fate of an entire case was sometimes determined in a few sharp, probing examinations before trial. Somehow in the informal atmosphere of an office witnesses were inclined to be more careless than they might be in a courtroom. He had seen doctors make admissions in examinations before trial that doomed their entire testimony in court. It became almost like a laydown hand in bridge. Or a chess match resigned after the first three moves.

So, though Crabtree greeted Chris quite warmly, the lawyer's real purpose was to evaluate his worth to the defense. Later he would report back to the insurance company his objective opinion of their chances.

James Spalding, who was here to protect the interests of the hospital, seemed reserved and pleasant. He was one of those men who, when it came time to shake hands, was somehow always occupied with his pipe and tobacco pouch. He was doing that as he greeted Chris. His attitude was reflected in his one word, "Doctor," polite, reserved, noncommittal. It gave Chris a strange feeling. This lawyer, whose interests should be identical with his own, was too detached. But then, Chris reminded himself, Spalding, like Laura, played only an observer's role in this proceeding. Crabtree was the only lawyer legally empowered to act for him. The other two could only advise.

The four of them were shown into Conference Room B. When the page opened the door for them, Chris was amazed to find a long table that could easily accommodate forty people. If this was Conference Room B, Chris thought, then Conference Room A must be as large as The Reynolds Center for the Performing Arts.

The four of them were dwarfed in the huge room. In a moment two more lawyers entered. Arthur Cross, a tall, gray-haired man with a measured but unrevealing smile. He shook hands all around, pausing only to comment when he shook Chris's hand, "Ah, yes, Dr. Grant." Cross introduced William Heinfelden, who would obviously conduct the examination since he carried the file and a yellow pad filled with questions. Heinfelden was of medium height, with broad shoulders testifying to his days as a star football player at a Midwestern university. They waited only an instant for the stenotypist to appear. While she was setting up her machine, Cross remarked, pleasantly, "These days it's even harder to get a doctor to make an office call than a house call."

He intended it as a joke about Chris's being a bit late, but Chris was not amused.

"I was in surgery until forty-five minutes ago!" he answered crisply.

Laura wished he hadn't answered, because she could tell that Heinfelden now realized how edgy the doctor was. Chris himself knew he had already done the one thing Laura had warned him against. He assured himself that once they got onto the questions that mattered he would be in complete control.

They lined up at the table like two teams in combat. Laura, Chris, Crabtree and Spalding on the one side; Cross and Heinfelden directly opposite. The stenotypist sat at the end of the table, as if she, at least, were neutral. Cross gestured to the stenotypist who administered the oath. That done, Cross leaned back and let Heinfelden take over. Cross himself would act only as an observer. He, like Crabtree, had come to evaluate the strengths and weaknesses of the case.

Laura sat alongside Chris, praying that he would keep his temper in check.

Heinfelden's first questions were routine, harmless— Chris's full name, residence, his schools and medical training. In the course of eliciting the information the lawyer also discovered that Chris had worked his way through high school doing a series of odd jobs, from hawking hot dogs at a baseball park to making deliveries for a florist. His college education was financed by similar work, though the jobs were somewhat more interesting and better paying. He had earned enough to cover his books and tuition, and even enough to bury his father when he died.

Medical school was easier. He had been awarded scholarships to two universities and chose the one closest to his home because he knew that his mother would not long outlive his father. Chris had always believed she stayed alive only to take care of his father and himself. Once his father died and Chris had proved self-sufficient, Mary Grant had no obligation to go on. She died, clinically from coronary failure, but in fact from loss of will to survive.

Throughout the early part of the examination, Heinfelden might well have been Chris's own attorney so solicitously did he elicit the details of his background. Neither Laura nor Spalding found anything to object to, and after a while Heinfelden's questions seemed almost aimless. So much so that Laura found herself growing more and more uneasy. Heinfelden was neither inexperienced nor inept. He must have some reason for his leisurely approach.

Finally he got to the subject of Chris's research and his various published papers. Did Chris have an unusual interest in the field of brain-damaged children? All brain-damaged children? Or only special groups?

"Tell me, Dr. Grant, what was it that first interested you in the arrested brain development of malnourished children?"

"I don't know, truthfully."

"Could it have been your own past? I mean, coming from a poor background did you have a special affinity for those children?"

"I don't know. Perhaps."

At that point Laura leaned forward and glanced sharply at Paul Crabtree. Crabtree cleared his throat and said in a quiet but firm way, "Off the record. . . ."

Heinfelden looked across the table at him innocently. "Something wrong?"

"A good deal of this testimony seems irrelevant. Time-consuming. Without purpose. I don't see what bearing any of Dr. Grant's papers have on this litigation. And we object to his answering any further questions of this nature."

"Even those that might prove to be relevant?" asked Heinfelden.

"If you have relevant questions, get to them!" Crabtree said impatiently.

Heinfelden smiled, turned back to Chris and asked, "Doctor, the treatment involved in this lawsuit, would you say it was a matter of doctor's discretion?"

"Every treatment is a matter of the doctor's discretion. A doctor's function is to evaluate the patient's condition and to apply the therapy that in his judgment seems best indicated," Chris replied. From Laura's movement at his side he knew he had answered more fully than he had need to.

He began to regret it at once for Heinfelden asked, "A doctor's judgment is an extremely subjective thing isn't it? I mean, two doctors facing the same set of symptoms might differ on the treatment to be applied."

"Yes," Chris responded, determined not to use any extraneous words.

"Why, Doctor?"

"Why?"

"Yes, why would two doctors in identical circumstances prescribe different forms of therapy?"

"There could be many reasons."

"Such as?" Heinfelden insisted.

"Different experience. One doctor has success with a certain form of therapy or a certain drug and has confidence in it. Another doctor's experience might be slightly different and he might favor another drug, or another therapy."

"So it depends on a doctor's personal experience."

"Yes, you could say that."

"It's not what I could say, the question is would *you* say that?" Heinfelden continued.

"Yes," Chris admitted.

"In referring to the doctor's past experience, do you mean only his medical experiences?"

"Yes," Chris said firmly. "What other experiences would influence a doctor?"

"An interesting question," Heinfelden said, leaning a bit closer to the table. "What other experiences *would* influence a doctor's judgment?"

Laura glanced at Crabtree who said, "Is this an examination before trial or a discussion of medical motivation? If you've got a point, get to it. If not, let's finish up for today. Though I warn you now we won't produce the doctor every time you gentlemen snap your fingers. In fact, considering all the questions asked, I think any judge would be reluctant to grant you further examinations."

"We're not done for today," Heinfelden responded, turning back to Chris. "Dr. Grant, was there any other course of treatment open to you at the time you decided to give the Simpson infant phototherapy?"

"Yes."

"Such as?" Heinfelden asked, as if he were not already primed on the subject.

"It would have been possible to do an exchange transfusion."

"But you didn't choose to do that?"

"No."

"Why?" Heinfelden pursued.

"In my judgment the condition didn't warrant the attendant risks," said Chris.

"What risks?"

"The risk of infection for one."

"Any others?"

"It is a time-consuming procedure. In my judgment the infant could benefit more from exposure to phototherapy. Certainly until the tests came back from the lab."

"Oh, there were tests going on at the same time?" Heinfelden asked, with an excellent pretense at being surprised.

"When an infant comes into intensive care with distinctly noticeable jaundice the first thing we have to do is determine the cause. I sent a blood sample down to the lab to find out if jaundice was due to sepsis. Or to ABO incompatibility. In this case it was due to an Rh difficulty," Chris explained.

"And while that was going on you merely put the infant

into a plastic box and let the fluorescent light shine down on it?" Heinfelden asked, attempting to denigrate the treatment and its potentials. Laura visualized now how such a question could affect a jury of laymen.

"No," said Chris, growing resentful. "I started an IV, intravenous that is, to nourish the infant and to administer an antibiotic. If there was sepsis, I wanted to treat it at once."

"I see." Heinfelden seemed impressed. "And at the same time you put it under those fluorescent lights?"

"Yes," Chris said.

"But you did not give the infant an exchange transfusion?"

"No."

"Why?"

"I explained that," Chris said, becoming impatient. "In my opinion, phototherapy was the best and safest form of treatment."

"In view of the ultimate result, you would still say that?" Heinfelden asked.

"Yes."

"Even though the other doctors might have handled the case differently?" he pressed.

"I was the doctor in charge at the time. The infant was my patient. I decided that phototherapy was the indicated treatment. And I was right."

"Oh?" Heinfelden asked.

"The bilirubin began to go down. Not dramatically, but it did go down. The phototherapy reversed the trend."

"And that justified your decision?" Heinfelden asked.

"High bilirubin is the problem. If you bring it down to nondangerous levels then the treatment has succeeded," said Chris.

"But if it is not brought down in time to avoid complications . . . say, brain damage . . . then would you say the treatment had succeeded?"

"We object to that question," Crabtree said quickly.

Heinfelden nodded, not conceding defeat, but temporarily accepting Crabtree's protest. Backtracking, apparently to stall for time, he asked, "You were saying that the decision of a doctor as to the most desirable form of therapy is a personal matter."

"I didn't say personal. That's your word," Chris pointed out.

"Well, then, it's at least a professional decision arrived at on the basis of personal experience?"

"Professional experience," Chris corrected.

"But still personal to the doctor, insofar as different doctors might employ different techniques in the same given circumstances. H'mm?"

Chris nodded.

"We'll need an answer, Doctor."

"Yes," Chris said.

"So whether we put the word 'personal' on it or the word 'professional' it becomes each doctor's own decision. And what motivates him to make such a decision . . ."

"Object!" said Crabtree loudly.

"We consider that highly material and relevant to this case. And we mean to get a ruling on it from the judge before we go any further!" Heinfelden dropped all pretense at pleasantness.

Crabtree pulled back from the table and rose to his feet. "We are not concerned with personal feelings. The only question is whether the defendant used an accepted form of treatment, in a competent professional way. Everything else is irrelevant!"

"We can let that one go for the time being," Heinfelden finally conceded. "May we go on to another subject?"

"Something more relevant, I trust?" Crabtree shot back.

"I think so," Heinfelden said casually, yet it had the sound of a threat. "Doctor, this phototherapy, it's not without risk, is it?"

116

Chris glanced at Laura who indicated that he answer.

"In the sense that no therapy is absolutely without risk, no. But the risk is so minimal that for all practical purposes it does not exist."

"Is it possible that the use of phototherapy can inhibit the proper development of an infant's head growth?" Heinfelden asked suddenly.

"That was reported in earlier papers, but has since been disproved," Chris said flatly.

"But there were such reported cases?" Heinfelden persisted.

"There were," Chris conceded. "But that finding has been disproved."

"Is that why you never told John Reynolds about it?" Heinfelden asked.

"I did tell him about it!" Chris protested.

"Are you sure?"

"Yes, I'm sure! We went to my office and I gave him a full explanation of the therapy."

"And of the risks?" Heinfelden interrupted.

"I didn't mention that finding about head size since it has proved to be invalid," Chris was forced to admit.

"But you told him everything else?"

"Everything that was pertinent. I wanted to set his mind at ease," Chris explained. "He was quite concerned, and naturally so. After all, this infant was his only male heir."

"He made a point of that, did he?"

"He made a point of almost nothing else!" Chris retorted.

"So you made a full disclosure of the facts in the infant's case. . . ."

"Insofar as I knew the facts at the time," Chris said.

"Doctor, when you just said, 'Insofar as I knew the facts at that time,' what did you mean?"

"I'd sent the blood specimen down to the lab for tests. At that point I didn't know if there was sepsis involved. Or precisely what the infant's bilirubin was. Or even if that

Coombs finding was correct. I didn't trust the report from Polyclinic. I wanted our own lab to check everything."

"So it was while you were waiting for the reports to come back that you had your conversation with John Reynolds?"

"Yes," Chris responded. "Once I'd taken the immediately indicated steps—the antibiotic, the IV feeding, the photo-therapy—then there was time to have a lengthy conversation with Mr. Reynolds."

"Ah, exactly," Heinfelden exclaimed.

Chris, Laura, Crabtree and Spalding all tensed.

"Tell me, Doctor," Heinfelden continued, "did you explain any of this to John Reynolds *before* you took those steps?"

"There was no time," Chris tried to explain.

"No time?" Heinfelden probed.

"The infant was obviously jaundiced. Treatment had to be started immediately," Chris said, his impatience no longer in check.

Laura touched his arm to calm him down. The gesture did not escape Heinfelden's notice, though he seemed to be looking through his notes.

"Dr. Grant," he said, "earlier in this examination you told us that it was possible for two doctors, equally well trained and of course equally well motivated, to differ on what course of treatment to follow in any given case."

"Yes," Chris agreed gingerly.

"In this case the choice was between, as I understand it, phototherapy and an exchange transfusion. Is that right?"

"Yes," Chris conceded.

"With such a choice to make, did it ever occur to you to call in another doctor and ask for his opinion in this case?" Heinfelden asked suddenly.

Chris hesitated, then answered, "No, no it did not."

"Doctor, was there any chance at all that another doctor, as well qualified, or perhaps even better qualified than you, might have decided that perhaps a transfusion rather than phototherapy was the answer?"

"As I said before, there's always a chance that two doctors might disagree in any given case," Chris conceded.

"Is it possible, say, that Dr. Sobol might have decided on an exchange transfusion?"

"I would doubt it," Chris said, becoming impatient again.

"You doubt that he would have decided on a transfusion? Or that it was *possible* he might have decided on a transfusion," Heinfelden pursued.

"I doubt he would have prescribed a transfusion in this case," said Chris.

"Meaning, that under no stretch of the imagination would he have prescribed a transfusion?"

"I would say so," Chris was growing more and more resentful at Heinfelden's semantic game.

"Doctor, have you ever seen Dr. Sobol prescribe an exchange transfusion?" Heinfelden asked blandly.

"Of course I have," said Chris. "All pediatricians on occasion prescribe transfusions when conditions call for it!"

"So that when you said you doubted that Dr. Sobol would have prescribed a transfusion you were only guessing. Since he had resorted to that procedure on other occasions by your own admission."

"Look, I'm trying to answer your questions. But you're playing guessing games!" Chris exploded.

"I just want to be as clear about this as you do, Doctor. You have seen Dr. Sobol prescribe transfusions in a number of cases, but it was your assumption that he would not have prescribed one in this particular case. Am I correct?" Heinfelden asked with meticulous care.

Chris hesitated, trying to evaluate whether he was being trapped. Finally he said, "Yes, that's correct."

"On what basis did you arrive at that conclusion?" Heinfelden asked.

"The condition of the infant, the results of the tests, the total picture," Chris said, openly irritated.

Laura would have liked to intervene, but Crabtree did not respond to her signal, or else did not notice it. Heinfelden continued.

"In other words, Doctor, you decided that Dr. Sobol agreed that phototherapy was the sole and proper treatment in this instance?"

"It wasn't up to Dr. Sobol to decide. The patient had been turned over to me. It was my responsibility. I acted according to my own evaluation of the situation," Chris said.

"Ah, I see. So that you were determined to make your own evaluation, your own diagnosis, carry out your own method of treatment regardless of any other doctor's opinion?"

"I didn't say that!" Chris shot back, angrily.

"Oh, I'm sorry if I misunderstood. Could you tell me how I misquoted you?"

"You tried to indicate that I was being stubborn and willful about this treatment and I was not!" Chris exploded. "I did what I thought best in the circumstances and I didn't think there was a need to seek a second opinion."

"Oh, I see," Heinfelden pretended to sudden enlightenment. "So you didn't think it necessary or desirable to seek a second opinion."

"Not in the circumstances."

"You didn't want to be overruled, is that it?"

"There was no reason to expect that I would be overruled!" Chris shouted.

"If that is really so, Doctor, wouldn't it have been more professionally correct to pick up the phone and check with Dr. Sobol, before making such a momentous decision on your own?" Heinfelden asked pointedly. When Chris did not answer at once, the lawyer said, "Or would that have been asking too much of a vain young man who is so sure he is always right that he wouldn't deign to ask for a more experienced opinion?"

"Object!" said Crabtree.

"Object, hell!" Chris shouted, standing up. "I want to answer that question!" Before anyone could stop him, he said, "Vanity had nothing to do with it! But if you've had experience and know your business you don't go checking your opinion every time you are faced with a choice. If you do, you're a poor excuse for a doctor!"

Laura blanched. Crabtree exhaled in impatient defeat. "Doctor," Heinfelden asked gently, "don't you know that failure to consult with other doctors can be deemed malpractice in certain circumstances?"

With that Heinfelden and Cross glanced at each other and Cross said, "This examination is over for now. We may decide to recall the doctor later."

When they reached the street, Crabtree and Spalding seemed in a hurry to leave. Laura delayed them by saying, "Gentlemen, I think we ought to discuss this *together*." She had let them know that she suspected what was in their minds and that she did not intend to accept it. Crabtree was about to plead another engagement, but Spalding said, "Yes, I think we should meet. Come across to my office."

The Waller firm, of which Spalding was a partner, had its offices in another of those tall steel-and-glass office buildings that have become standard in the American business community. It seemed to Chris that lawyers were encapsulated in glass Isolettes like infants in intensive care.

Before anyone could speak, Chris Grant indicted himself. "I did it. Despite all the advice I lost my temper, gave away information." He dropped into a soft leather chair, sighed in fatigue and despair.

After a long minute Crabtree said, "Doctor, let's just say you didn't help your cause. Or ours either."

"Sorry," Chris said.

"Fortunately," Spalding tried to find a bright side, "they didn't dig too deep or in the right places. From now on we can shield Dr. Grant by pleading that he's busy, that he has already submitted himself to examination. If they didn't make the most of their opportunity, that's their fault, not ours. We can't go taking the doctor away from his medical duties to satisfy their whims. At least it'll keep him out of their hands till the trial."

Laura had been silent and thoughtful. The other two lawyers appeared about to leave until she said gravely, "Gentlemen! I think our problem may be even greater than you think."

"How so?" Crabtree demanded.

"You said it yourself," Laura pointed out. "They didn't make the most of their chance. Why? Because they're inexperienced? Inept? Sloppy? I doubt it. Not that firm. I think from their point of view the examination was eminently successful. They found out what kind of witness Grant is."

Chris felt a surge of resentment, but Laura was still speaking.

"Grant is excitable. When he is challenged in areas of his own professional judgment he tends to fly off the handle. He is a pushover as a witness in that he volunteers too much information."

"I've never done this kind of thing before," Chris said angrily. "I can learn."

Laura turned on him sharply. "Doctor, one thing people never learn. How to control their emotions. They either can or they can't." Having disposed of Chris, she turned back to Crabtree. "I think they got one thing more they were fishing for."

"Oh, you do?" Crabtree said, feeling now that his own professional expertise was under attack.

Laura smiled. "Doctors, it seems, aren't the only sensitive professionals." Crabtree's face reddened. "I think before long we're going to be presented with a new and additional cause of action."

"Such as?" Spalding asked.

"Failure to obtain informed consent."

"In a treatment like phototherapy? Ridiculous!" Crabtree scoffed.

A bit morosely, Chris admitted, "You know there are hospitals, not many, but some, in which it's standard practice to obtain consent before using phototherapy."

"Why the hell didn't you tell us that before?" Crabtree glared at Chris.

"It's so unusual," Chris tried to explain.

Crabtree turned to attack Laura, "What do you and your client talk about in your meetings? How did a thing like that slip by you?"

Rather than being cowed by Crabtree, Laura asked, "How did a thing like their strategy escape you today?"

"What does that mean?"

"That maybe they didn't probe too deeply because they didn't want to expose their line of future cross-examination. Maybe they're saving that for their trial counsel so that Dr. Grant won't know what to expect. Maybe whoever is making the moves behind the scenes wanted today's examination conducted in just this way."

"Whoever is making what moves?" said Spalding, surprised.

"Take one guess," Laura invited.

Crabtree and Spalding spoke at the same time: "Harry Franklyn."

"My money's on that," Laura said.

Abruptly she summoned Chris with a gesture of her hand. She was ready to go, and she wanted her client to leave with her.

By the end of the week, Laura Winters' first prediction came true. Parkins, Sears and Wadleigh applied for leave to amend their complaint to include a new cause of action, failure to secure informed consent. Judge Bannon, into whose hands the case had passed, granted their motion.

The question now remained, would her second prediction turn out to be correct? Would Harry Franklyn appear in the case as trial counsel for the plaintiffs?

ELEVEN

CHRIS GRANT moved down the hall of the ward past ambulatory patients, most of whom were mothers who had delivered within the past day or two. The patient whom Chris was on his way to see was still confined to bed. Having given birth prematurely, with great pain and effort, she was still forced to take nourishment intravenously. Chris was coming to see her now because her infant was struggling for its life in an Isolette up in neonate intensive care. He wanted as much of the woman's history as he could get that might relate to the infant's difficulties.

The woman was confined to one of the small private rooms for the seriously ill. The door was ajar so that the nurses could check her as they passed. Chris glanced in to see if she were dozing. She seemed to be until she sensed his presence. Frightened, she opened her eyes and stared at the unfamiliar face.

"Mrs. Melendez?" Chris asked softly.

The woman tensed. Finally she nodded and Chris picked up the chart that hung at the foot of the bed. A glance revealed that she was running a fever of a hundred and one and a half. But her other vital signs were close enough to normal to cause no great concern.

"I feel good," she volunteered, hoping to be alone again.

"Fine," Chris said, moving to her side. "Mrs. Melendez, I'm your baby's doctor."

She turned back slowly. "He's sick?"

"He's very sick," Chris admitted. "But we're doing all we can for him."

She nodded, vaguely.

"Mrs. Melendez, there are a few questions. If you remember, tell me. If not, don't worry about it."

She tensed again, cautious, on guard.

"Mrs. Melendez, did you have any trouble with your other deliveries?" She didn't seem to understand. "The record indicates that this baby is your fifth. Did you have trouble with any of the first four?"

She hesitated and he tried to focus her thoughts by adding, "The first one, did you have trouble delivering the first?"

"No," she said finally.

"It was full term, the whole nine months?" She nodded. "And the delivery was normal? The doctor had no trouble?" She shook her head.

"And the second?" She shook her head again. The same for the third and fourth.

"But this time, there *was* trouble. And the baby came sooner than the nine months," Chris stated softly.

She barely nodded, as if it caused her great pain.

"Mrs. Melendez, during the pregnancy, especially in the first months, did you do anything different from the other pregnancies?"

"No. I work all the time. Then come home. Do my cleaning, cooking. And the kids. You know, you got to keep them clean. And school. You got to make them go to school." When she talked in longer sentences her accent became stronger.

"Mrs. Melendez, after a woman has had several *bebes,* two, three, four, she shouldn't have the kind of trouble you had. And the baby shouldn't be born early. Can you think of anything that happened differently this time?"

She turned away to avoid his eyes.

"Whatever it is, if you tell me it might help your little one," Chris prodded gently.

She shook her head.

"Did you take any pills of any kind?"

"No."

"Even if a doctor gave you the pills, did you take anything? You can tell me." She would not answer. "I know from your chart you're not on drugs. So if it was anything, it had to be some kind of medicine. Some pills. What kind?"

She buried her face in the pillow, withdrawing as far from Chris as she could.

"Mrs. Melendez, in the first three months, did you try to get rid of the baby?" Chris asked softly.

She did not answer. She did not even draw breath.

"Did you?"

Without facing him she began to talk in a flat, expressionless tone. Her words were without emphasis or inflection.

"There is Cesar. He is already twelve. And he go to school. I tell him to be careful. '*Pórtese bien*,' I say, '*cuidado!*' I mean not to go with bad boys. Not go with bad girls. A boy twelve already is old enough to get in trouble with girls. I tell him not to steal. Not to do anything except go to school and play ball."

She stopped, as if she had come to the end of her story. Chris waited.

"Cesar, he don't listen. One day I see he is not the same. Not noisy. Not asking for more to eat. He always asks for more to eat. But not now. And he is out of the house a lot, especially at night. I start to watch him. One night . . . one night just after I am pregnant again, I stay up, I wait. He don't come in. I go downstairs, in bare feet not to make noise. I find him with two other boys under the stairs. I see it. The little match burning. I see Cesar's face. One of the boys is holding a spoon over the match. Then there is the needle and I know. I know."

Chris could hear her weeping softly. "I start to cry. I beg with him. It do no good. He only hollers at me. It is my fault. I make him live in this rotten place. Make him go to a rotten school. My fault."

She turned slowly, daring to face Chris.

"Is it my fault? I work hard. I do all I can. I have three others. How much can I do? To work and take care of four *niñitos*."

"Your husband, Mrs. Melendez?" Chris asked. "Doesn't he help?"

"He is gone. When I tell him there is one more child he say no. He blame me. I should do something. He say he can't take it anymore and he go away. Maybe that's why Cesar . . ."

"Mrs. Melendez, when your husband said that to you, *did* you do anything?"

"A woman at work. She had some pills. She said if I take the pills, no more baby."

"And you took them?" said Chris. "Did they make you sick?"

She nodded.

"Make you retch, vomit?"

Again she nodded.

"But they didn't abort the baby. The baby was still there."

She did not deny it.

"Did you do anything else?" he asked.

She hesitated, then nodded.

"What?" She refused to answer. "Did you try to put something into yourself? Some sharp instrument?"

She finally gave a single nod of the head. He did not pursue it. There would be no purpose served in dragging the loathsome details out of the tortured woman. He already knew enough to appraise the unfortunate problem that awaited him back in intensive care.

"The baby is bad?"

"Very bad," he said gently.

"Very bad . . ." she echoed painfully.

Because she was so obviously miserable, he patted her gently on the shoulder. Without turning to face him, she seized his hand and gripped it tightly.

"Doctor, the baby, they tell me is a boy."

"Yes."

"Do something for me . . . let him die."

Involuntarily, Chris started to draw back his hand but she held it tighter.

"Please, Doctor?"

Chris said gently, "You know I can't do that."

"He is sick, very sick. You say that yourself. Then just . . . just let him . . . that's all." She said flatly, "I don't want him to be like Cesar . . . I can't anymore . . . I can't . . ."

"Don't worry about it now," Chris said, without much conviction. "We'll see what we can do later."

He retreated from the room, fleeing the sound of Mrs. Melendez's soft weeping, and made his way back to the neonate ward. The Baby Melendez was struggling to breathe, despite the oxygen tube taped into its tiny nose and the respirator which tried to assist in the vital process. The nurse handed Chris the latest lab findings.

He could continue the treatment, assist the infant's labored breathing, possibly even attempt surgery. The infant was not really fit for an operation, but in desperate situations a doctor could not rule out any alternative.

Chris was considering all the possibilities when he felt someone come up alongside him. It was Sobol.

Mike, who had been briefed on the case, reached for the chart. He glanced at the figures written there, the notes as to medication and therapy, and let the chart slide gently back into place.

"Can I see you, Chris, for a few minutes?"

"Of course, Mike."

He turned away from the Isolette, spoke to the nurse, "I'll be in Dr. Sobol's office. If anything changes let me know. And if it happens too fast for that, then do me a favor. Go over to Maternity, room two twenty-seven. Go over and tell Mrs. Melendez." Suddenly he changed his mind, "No, call me. I'll go tell her."

They were seated in Sobol's office. Mike reached for his unlit straight-grain briar which he still held in times of stress. He was silent for a few moments. Chris assumed that Mike was having trouble broaching a subject that had been bothering Chris himself for weeks and he decided to take the initiative.

"I can say it, Mike. Maybe even better than you can."

"You can?" Sobol asked, mildly surprised.

"I've been aware of it longer than anyone else."

"Have you?" Sobol asked, curious now.

"In your place I'd feel the same way. These past weeks, I haven't been up to it."

Sobol started to remove the pipe to answer but Chris went right on, "My research hasn't been progressing. And my classes, well, if they *seem* to be doing well, that's only because I've been going over ground I've been through with other classes in the past."

Chris hesitated a moment. This time Mike Sobol did not make any effort to intrude. He sat back, listened, sucking on his old pipe.

"But when it comes to patients, Mike, that's what upsets you. And it should. When it comes to making a diagnosis, or prescribing a therapy, I'm no longer sure of myself. Every decision becomes a debate. Not about is it the *right* way? But is it the *safe* way? Will I be able to *justify* it?"

Chris rose from his chair and started to pace as he continued.

"Look, Mike, if you really feel I should resign I will. But I don't want to. I want to fight no matter what it costs me in effort and self-recrimination." He stared down at Mike and said softly, "Please, Mike, give me that chance."

"So that's what's been going through your mind all this time? I'm glad you got it out finally," Sobol said.

"I'll do whatever you decide, Mike, you know that. If it'll make it any easier for you, I will offer my resignation."

Sobol leaned back in his swivel chair. "Chris, my decision, which you have just agreed to abide by, is this. You stick in there. It won't be easy. You'll have your doubts. And your recriminations. But you stick with it. Make your decisions, tough as they are. Think about yourself, natural as that is. But even with these extra demands on your time you are as good a doctor as I want on my staff."

Chris stared at him.

Sobol continued, "Of course you can't put this whole legal thing out of your mind. But what you *can* do is say, despite it, 'I'm a physician, I have a job to do and I'm going to do it.'

"In any case, Chris, I wouldn't let you quit, even if you wanted to. Not for your sake, but for the sake of the hospital. For the sake of all the other men who'll have to resist similar pressures in the future. What Reynolds was trying to force that board of trustees to do I am not going to let you do for him. If he wants you out, he's going to have to fight me to do it. And if he has to fight *you* as well, it's going to make my job a little easier. So don't give in."

"Is it fair to my patients?" asked Chris.

"That's my job to decide. I say it is and if the time ever comes when I don't think so, I'll let you know."

Chris Grant nodded, for he knew that though Sobol was a kind man, he was also a realist. He would never allow his professional judgment to be corrupted by personal feeling.

"Okay," Chris agreed. "But if it wasn't my resignation you wanted to discuss with me, what was it?"

Sobol had to stop and try to remember. Then he remembered. "Oh, yes. The insurance company lawyer called me today."

"Crabtree?"

"Yes. They want me to appear for an examination before trial tomorrow."

"Oh, I'm sorry about that."

"There you go. I didn't blame you. But you blame yourself. I only wanted to say two things. First, would you take over my afternoon class?"

"Of course."

"Second, I want to apologize in advance if I say the wrong thing. They tried to coach me on what to say, but you know me. I'm no actor. I'll just have to answer as best I can. Damn it," he added, "I wish this were all unnecessary!"

The phone rang. Sobol answered, his voice mild again. He handed the instrument to Chris.

"Doctor?" Chris recognized the nurse's voice. "The Melendez infant just went out."

"I'll be right down." He hung up. "The Melendez baby."

"Are you going to blame yourself for that, too?" Sobol asked.

"No," Chris said, "but I'm going to verify it. And then go see the mother."

"Those are the tough ones," Sobol commiserated.

"Not in this case," Chris said, and he left.

Mike Sobol, accompanied by Laura Winters, presented himself at the office of Parkins, Sears and Wadleigh at two o'clock as he had been instructed. They met Paul Crabtree and Jim Spalding and were immediately shown into the conference room. Heinfelden was alone this time with the stenotypist.

The early part of the examination went swiftly. He covered Mike's background and then asked Mike his opinion on phototherapy, on Chris's work, on the reason why Mike had entrusted the Simpson baby to Chris's care. Mike explained that he favored phototherapy, that he had brought Chris to Metropolitan General because of his familiarity with the treatment, and that he had turned the Simpson baby over to him because of the enormous confidence he had in him.

Did Mike notice any unusually alarming symptoms in the Simpson baby on his first examination? No, he did not. Were there any neurologic symptoms? No, but then there most likely would not be at such an early age unless they were gross and obvious abnormalities.

For some reason Heinfelden seemed to dwell on the fact that Chris was in the research lab when Mike summoned him. The lawyer pressed Mike to reconstruct the conversation, which he did. He could not recall the exact words, but he did recall apologizing for interrupting the younger doctor's research.

Heinfelden's manner was so casual that neither Mike nor Laura could guess what he was probing for. He seemed not to uncover anything of great significance. He simply plowed on with his list of prearranged questions.

After a while, Sobol relaxed. Perhaps the advice he had been given was true: if you answered all questions directly and limited yourself to the specific information requested, being a witness was not so difficult.

It was only at the very end that Heinfelden asked Sobol's feelings about many young doctors' devotion to social causes. Mike allowed that young doctors did seem more sociologically oriented today but he saw no harm in it. In fact, he added, these young men might just be more constructive doctors than were his own contemporaries.

Seeing Laura stiffen in her chair, Mike Sobol suddenly had the feeling that he had volunteered some information that might arise to plague him later.

He was even more uneasy when Heinfelden added, "Would you say, too, that those young physicians might sometimes consider their sociological theories more important than the treatment of individual patients?"

"I would not!"

Heinfelden smiled and retreated with an apologetic, "Sorry, Doctor, no offense." He consulted his pad, discovered no further questions and called the examination to an end.

As Mike and Laura walked away from the office building he said, "I didn't do too well there at the end. I should have kept my mouth shut about young men and their ideals." He paused uncomfortably.

"Frankly, Mike, I wasn't even thinking about that," Laura said, evidently troubled.

"What then?" he asked.

"It's too easy. Like the proverbial calm before the storm. They're not digging, not asking compromising questions."

"Only trying to find out how an old fool responds under pressure so they'll know how to attack him in the courtroom, h'm?" Mike asked.

"Please, Uncle Mike, don't disparage yourself. You did better than you should have. That's what worries me," Laura reassured him.

"Is that all that worries you?" he asked pointedly.

She hesitated, then said, "No. It was just that disturbing little thought that he introduced about young doctors. It's an iceberg, only the tip is showing. But I'm afraid we won't learn to rest until Harry Franklyn makes his appearance."

"What is this Franklyn, a monster, that lawyers quake at the sound of his name?" Mike asked impatiently.

"He's not called the Napoleon of the courtroom for nothing."

Mike sensed that there was more to her concern. He asked, "Laurie, darling, tell me something. And if you don't want to tell me, that'll be answer enough."

"What, Mike?"

"Laurie, is there anything between you and Chris?"

"Of course not," she answered, a bit too quickly. "What makes you ask?"

Mike smiled. "Because Rose always used to say if I didn't become a doctor I would have made a very good *shadchen.*"

She looked at him, puzzled.

"Jewish for matchmaker," he explained. "When I see two young people, both attractive, both dedicated, I have this irresistible urge to bring them together. In fact, seeing the two of you together during the past few weeks, I've asked myself a number of times, did I have some ulterior motive in mind when I brought you into this case?"

"Well, there's nothing to it. Nothing at all," said Laura. "We've never had a date. And I wouldn't encourage it if he asked. A lawyer who represents himself has a fool for a client. A lawyer who represents someone with whom she has an emotional involvement is even more foolish."

They walked along in silence. Mike couldn't resist stealing a glance at her. She was lovely, even when her face was as serious as it appeared now.

"Do you always worry this much about a client?"

She glanced at him quite sharply. "When a client's fortune is involved that's one thing. When his life is involved that's quite something else."

"His life?" asked Mike.

"Well, I have a hunch," said Laura. "Almost a premonition. Between them, Reynolds and Heinfelden have already worked out a strategy not just to prove Chris wrong, to disgrace him in the medical community. It's deeper than that, more malignant."

"What could be worse than that?" Mike asked.

"We'll see. We'll see," was all that Laura would say for the moment.

CHAPTER
TWELVE

THE ANNUAL Conference of Pediatricians had been scheduled at Metropolitan General long before *Simpson vs. Metropolitan General, Grant and Sobol* ever became a fact. To cancel or transfer the meeting to another university hospital would have entailed enormous disruption of travel and hotel reservations. It would also be construed to be a prejudgment of the case.

So the conference proceeded with its scheduled meetings, discussions, and lectures on new discoveries and techniques, but it placed an additional burden on Mike and Chris who were forced to endure countless, though well-meant, references to the trial.

Chris was surprised when Laura had expressed a desire to attend the conference. But she explained she only wanted to attend those sessions during which Chris spoke or lectured on phototherapy. She wanted to get the professional feel of the subject matter as well as seek out some potential witnesses for the defense.

She was quite impressed by Chris's presentation, not only the thorough way in which his research had been done but the earnestness of his social attitudes. Some of the older men around her expressed their disapproval by overtly fidgeting. One got up and walked out. But most of the younger doctors were intent listeners.

Laura decided that Chris could make an impressive witness if handled properly in the courtroom. She also made a note to mention to Crabtree that he should try to get as many women on the jury as possible. Women would not only be receptive to Chris's ideas on prenatal care but also be extremely receptive to Chris as a man. She did not consciously include herself. After her talk with Mike, she had deliberately banished all such thoughts for the duration of the trial.

Because Laura had attended some of the lectures, Chris felt obliged to invite her to the final banquet. Watching many of the wives compete in attesting to their husbands' success through their jewels and gowns, Laura was glad she was not married to a physician, though a number of the older women assumed that she was and wanted to know all about her husband.

They were just leaving the ballroom, hastily making their way among the tables, when Chris was intercepted by Harvey Bellamy, a classmate at medical school.

Harvey was a well-established pediatrician and with his blond hair, tanned face and easy smile, Laura could imagine how safe new mothers must feel in entrusting their infants to a man who exuded much magnetic confidence. His wife, Claire, was not only beautiful but beautifully dressed.

"Chris, it's been so long," said Bellamy, "and we haven't had a minute alone this week. Let's have a drink?"

"I'd love to, Harv, but it's late. Laura has to be in the office first thing in the morning . . ." Chris started to say.

Bellamy interrupted, amiably enough. "Chris, that's part of what I want to talk to you about."

"What?" he asked, puzzled.

"I talk better sitting down than standing up. Let's all have a drink."

They found a booth in a dark corner of the cocktail lounge. Until they were served Harvey Bellamy made small talk about medical practice in Southern California, stressing the ease of living for families with young children.

But once the waiter had brought their drinks, Bellamy became quite direct. "If we didn't know each other so well, I'd have to do a lot of fencing around."

Chris didn't respond.

"You're a goddamned fool! When you first made the decision to go into academic medicine, I said to myself, 'He'll get over it. After a while he'll realize that scrounging for grants and money to carry on research is a demeaning way to practice a profession as much entitled to respect as any other.'

"Remember the week we finished internship, I begged you to come into practice with me. Well, now I'm making that offer again. Leave this mess. Even if you lose this case, what will happen? No jury will ever vote a five-million-dollar judgment. You won't be touched."

"*Financially!*" The single word encompassed all the many comments Chris might have made.

Bellamy was not deterred. "I say it again. Financially you won't be touched. The insurance company will take the whole loss."

"The insurance company is willing to settle," Laura volunteered.

"Let 'em! *Make* 'em!" Bellamy urged. "Chris, for your own good, get it over with."

"It's not that simple," Chris argued.

"Why?" Bellamy challenged. "Only because *you* won't let it be! Right?"

"If a man doesn't protect his own reputation, who will?" said Laura.

"If by reputation you mean that Chris won't get another university appointment at a salary one tenth of what he's worth, I agree with you. Loss of reputation will only mean that he'll be forced to do what he should have done in the first place. Go out in the real world and practice medicine!"

Chris didn't respond, he only fingered his glass.

"Chris, did you hear me?"

"You just don't understand, Harv."

"Don't I? Chris, I'm not one of your medical hacks. Don't forget that in medical school we ranked one, two. And sometimes two, one."

Chris nodded.

"I could have taken your route, but I didn't. Was I wrong? You tell me. I don't have to depend on grants. I don't have to depend on a boss or a board of trustees. I have a twelve-room house. And from my living room I can see the California desert on the one side and snow-capped mountains on the other. My children go to the best private school in the whole area. My wife has two live-in servants. Her own Mercedes three-fifty SL. And a climate you won't believe. Everlastingly lovely. But those are only superficial indicia. More important, I have my own medical group. I own the land and the building. And have a half-interest in the pharmacy on the premises. There are eight doctors in my group. We have the latest and best equipment. As to my income, I don't want to be vulgar. You can assume anything you want and don't overlook the advantages of a professional corporation under the new tax law. You'll be fixed for life in only five years!"

Bellamy paused to drain his glass.

"It isn't only money, Chris. It's the way of life. When was the last time you were out on the golf course? No, I forgot, you don't play golf. But tennis. You used to love tennis. When was the last time you played?"

Chris shrugged, he couldn't remember.

"When did you last have time off? I mean really off, away from telephones. Away from calls from your chief. Well, I have every Wednesday and Sunday off. And half a day on Saturday. My golf handicap is four. At the Racquet Club

139

I'm always in the top seed. And I have time for my family. For my wife."

He glanced at Laura to enlist her help and she suddenly realized that Bellamy was presuming a relationship that did not exist. When she didn't answer Bellamy continued, "There is no rule that says a doctor has to give up his right to be a realist. We're living in a world where economics has taken the place of religion. There's no place for zeal any longer. There's certainly no place for misguided zeal. Chris, we need a well-trained pediatrician. You can't just sit back and let them ruin your career. Come into practice with us and your gifts and training won't be wasted."

"Look, Harv, don't," Chris began.

But Bellamy overrode him. "Don't say no yet. I'm not talking about a job. I'm talking about a full share partnership, Chris. In the first year alone you could be drawing better than a hundred thousand. We would make one hell of a team. And you could have an ideal life."

"Harv, don't think I'm being ungrateful . . ."

"What else can I think, if you won't even consider my offer?" Bellamy challenged.

"I have to see this through first."

"I tell you, out where I practice nobody gives a damn about a legal suit," Bellamy assured him.

"Well, right here where I live, people *do* give a damn. *I* give a damn!" Chris said sharply.

"Chris, you're trying to win a war that is not worth winning. Even if you say no to my offer, don't let this case go to court."

"Harv, I can't back out now. If for no other reason, I couldn't leave Mike Sobol holding the bag."

"Mike Sobol . . ." Bellamy picked up the name at once. "Do me a favor, Chris, go to Mike Sobol. Discuss this with him. He'd be the first to tell you to settle."

"I don't think so . . ." Chris said.

"Look at him. All those years in academic medicine and

now he has to fight for his job, because some madman wants vengeance. Is that what you want, Chris? For the rest of your professional life?"

"Sorry, Harv," Chris said, not wanting to enlarge the field of battle.

Bellamy would not be put off. "You know your trouble. You're still trying to pay off some imaginary debt to your past. Just because you grew up in a slum doesn't mean you owe the poor anything."

Chris put down his glass; Bellamy knew the conversation was over. He said only, "I want you to think about it. I'll hold it open as long as I can. And remember, I want you, because you're the best pediatrician I know."

The last was spoken with complete sincerity. For the first time Chris recognized the old Harvey Bellamy of medical school days.

"I give you my word, I'll think about it," Chris finally said.

"Talk to him," Bellamy urged Laura. "He owes it to you if not himself. He owes you a good life. That's what you both want, isn't it? A good life together, kids, everything that makes life worth living."

Laura smiled and said simply, "If we had any kids together it would be embarrassing to say the least. Chris is my client, not my fiancé."

"Well, I'll be damned. Watching you two, I could have sworn . . ." Bellamy returned to his attack. "Promise me you'll think about it!"

"Okay, I'll think about it," Chris said, to bring the conversation to an end.

On the way back home, Chris drove Laura's car. They talked little. Finally the silence goaded him into making an explanation.

"Harv is a first-rate physician. I wouldn't hesitate to entrust any child of mine to him. The rest of it, the money, his life-style, his business setup, don't let that fool you. He wouldn't be that successful if he weren't good."

"I don't know why you feel you have to defend him to me. I haven't said a word," Laura reminded him.

"It's just two different ways of approaching medicine. Harv decided his interests lay in private practice. I don't fault him. But I don't have to choose the same way. Do I?" Laura didn't answer. He repeated, "Do I?"

When she didn't respond, he asked frustratedly, "Don't you have any opinion?"

"As a woman? Or as a lawyer?"

"Both," Chris said.

"As a woman I say to myself, it does sound like a great way to live. Did you see her sable coat and that dress? An original St. Laurent. It was in *Harper's* two months ago."

"Do you read *Harper's?*" Chris asked, surprised.

"Both," she answered a bit testily. "Plain old *Harper's* as a lawyer. And *Harper's Bazaar* as a woman. I wasn't born wearing a gray flannel suit."

He realized she was joking, yet underneath there was a solid protest against his having obliterated her femininity so completely.

"Look, that was your idea for this relationship from the start. Remember?"

She didn't answer and neither of them said anything more until they reached her apartment where he insisted on seeing her to the door. Hoping to end the evening on a lighter note, he said, "Come to think of it, Harv isn't as good a diagnostician as I used to think."

"Because he misinterpreted our relationship?" she said defensively, then added, "Well, he isn't the only one."

Chris stared down into her mischievous blue eyes. "What does that mean?"

"The other day, Mike asked me the same question."

"Mike?"

She didn't answer, putting her key in the lock.

"Mike," Chris repeated, this time as a statement. He

reached out and turned her about to face him. "You mean everyone can see it except us?"

He was about to kiss her when she made one last protest, "It'll be wrong . . ."

He kissed her anyhow and could feel her small body press urgently against him.

Feelings they had both so scrupulously suppressed erupted. She made no pretense at sending him away. With the swiftness that only mutual desire can mobilize, they were lovers. Urgent and eager in her bed he found her body more voluptuous than he had imagined. Her passion, too, was more than he had expected. He wondered if her severe pose as a lawyer was necessary for the very reason that she was, underneath, an unusually passionate woman. Her intensity was so great as to be painful to her. But when he released her she whimpered like a child.

His cheek rested against her left breast and he could feel the beating of her heart. His fingers traced a pattern across her soft, rounded belly. She tensed and seized his hand. Then she raised it to her lips and kissed it. His fingers traced the outline of her profile in the dark, until he felt the dampness of her cheeks.

He whispered, "Good God, it's not something to cry about."

She just shook her head and soon he was caressing her body, holding it fiercely against his own. She did not resist him. With unexpected strength she was giving him all of herself and expecting the same in return.

It was dark in the room and very quiet. He could hear the soft sound of her breathing. Neither of them had spoken but Chris was thinking of Alice Kennan's last words to him. Now he knew his feelings toward her had changed because of his unconscious desire for Laura. He felt guilty about Alice, but it was over now.

He stared up at the ceiling, and said gently, "Tell me now, was it something to cry about?"

More gravely than he expected, she said, "It was, it was . . ."

He raised up on his elbow, stared down at her. Her eyes were closed but she could not stop the flow of tears.

"Laura, honey?" he asked.

She shook her head, refusing to answer.

"What's wrong?" he demanded. "That silly notion that lawyers and clients have to keep each other at arm's length?"

"It's more than that," she said.

"What?" he asked, afraid that she was going to try to end their relationship.

"I told you. The toll malpractice trials can take is enormous. Many times the patient dies of the treatment, not the disease."

"I know, you warned me." He tried to draw her close but she would not be stilled, not by his caresses, not by his kisses.

"No," she protested, "I have to say this. So we both know what can happen. Men who have been through lawsuits, libel, malpractice, where their character was in question, where they've been forced to justify past lives or professional conduct, even though they are vindicated in the end, suffer quite terrible consequences."

"Even if they win?" Chris asked, disbelieving.

"Even if they win," she reiterated gravely. "Somehow their marriages dissolve. Wives who have stuck with them loyally through the entire fight leave them when that fight is over. And their careers are never the same either."

"Why?" Chris asked.

"Maybe it's because people never can forget the charges that were made against them. They can forget the man's defenses. They can even forget the fact that the man won. But somehow the charges endure and maybe wives begin to believe some of the lies too. But whatever the reason, the relationships are never the same."

"It won't happen to us!" he protested fervently, but she was not reassured.

"This isn't even an ordinary malpractice suit. Reynolds isn't out to win. He's out to destroy you. And your only way out is to settle."

"That means publicly accepting the blame for that damaged child?" Chris concluded grimly.

"Yes," she said.

"I can't do that," Chris said.

"I know you can't," Laura said. "That's one of the things I love about you."

They were both aware that she had used the word. It had a comforting and fine sound, but she did not let it rest.

"Because I love you, it makes the danger greater. He'll destroy us both. It would have been better if we hadn't fallen in love."

"That's something to cry about," Chris said softly. He reached out and drew her close to him, holding her head against his chest.

"As long as we know the danger we can fight it," he tried to assure her.

She did not respond and in a while he said, "Of course, there's Harv's offer. If we did decide to settle."

"Yes," Laura agreed. "The house. The view. The expensive clothes. The servants."

"Look, I don't want an inventory," Chris interrupted. "I want an answer."

"The inventory *is* the answer. The golf club, the Racquet Club. God, a woman could go to lunch three times a day. And sign the check every time. Did you ever notice how the rich disdain any contact with money? Never touch the stuff. Just sign, sign, sign."

"Laurie," he interrupted impatiently, forcing her to give him an answer.

"I was only adding up the pluses."

"Well, get to the minuses!" he exploded.

"That's it," she said.

"What?" he demanded.

"What just happened," she replied very gently. "If you can't even talk about it without getting angry, then the answer is obvious."

"What did I say?"

"Chris, darling, what makes it all a perfectly nice, delightful way for Claire Bellamy to live is that her *husband* thinks it's a perfectly nice, delightful way to live. But give those same things to a woman whose husband hates them and in a very short time every convenience, every luxury, even the everlasting lovely climate would become a rebuke. You couldn't live with it. So neither could I. I'm afraid we have no choice but to see the case through."

"Despite what it might do to us?"

"Nobody ever said there was a good answer to every question," she said sadly. "At least for the time being, we have each other."

She kissed him. Not to arouse any passions in him but to seal a compact. They had each other. For whatever that might bring.

THIRTEEN

CHRIS GRANT was in the neonate nursery, staring through the Plexiglas dome of an Isolette at a bronze-skinned infant which was gasping for breath. Without looking up, Chris observed to Phil Carey, his resident, "We'd better put an oxygen hood on this little one." The nurse who stood by to assist did not wait for the order. She hurried to the supply room to secure it.

Chris inserted his sterilized hands through the portholes to palpate the infant's liver. He didn't like what he felt.

"Get me a transfusion setup," he ordered.

"Right," Carey said.

Chris lifted the chart that hung from the Isolette. *Lopez, Baby. Premature. Thirty-four weeks gestation. General appearance conjunctive, yellow. Skin, generalized icterus. Eyes, yellow-orange.* Notes made three hours ago.

Chris could see now that those signs had become even more ominous. The nurse returned with the oxygen hood, a square transparent plastic box with a small curved opening to accommodate a baby's neck when the box was placed over its head. As the nurse began to lift the cover, Chris said, "Hold that. We're going to do an exchange."

"On this one?" the nurse asked softly.

Irritated that his judgment was being questioned, Chris ordered in a brusque whisper, "Damn it, search that chart and let me know if there's consent for a transfusion! I have to prepare."

"Yes, Doctor," the nurse said quietly, though it was obvious her feelings were hurt.

As Chris scrubbed, the nurse flipped through the pages of the chart. Before she was done, Carey had returned with the proper supply of heparinized blood, the catheter, needles and dosage of protamine.

Chris checked the infant's heartbeat, observed its respiration, then began to exchange. Slowly he inserted the needle of one catheter into the infant's umbilical vein. Using an empty hypodermic he withdrew 20 cc of the infant's damaged blood. Then, as cautiously, he injected 20 cc of the anticoagulating heparinized blood into the artery. He stopped to check the infant's heartbeat.

There seemed to be no bad effects and he resumed the slow, painstaking process, withdrawing another 20 cc and injecting a fresh 20 cc of heparinized blood. Each time he checked the infant's heartbeat and the respiratory responses.

For this unfortunate baby only an exchange transfusion would be effective, but its chance of surviving the procedure without complication was small. As is frequent, the patient demanding the most difficult treatment was also least able to cope with it. It would take Chris at least twelve or thirteen repetitions of the slow withdrawal and infusion of blood to complete the process. Only then would he have any indication as to whether it would succeed. For the sixth time he infused 20 cc of fresh blood.

The light on the telephone began blinking with monotonous persistence. The nurse answered. Holding her hand over the mouthpiece, she informed, "Dr. Sobol. He says it's important."

148

Chris completed infusing an additional 20 cc of fresh blood before answering. "Tell him I'm doing an exchange. But I'll be there as soon as I can."

The nurse hesitated. Then with Chris staring at her, she relayed the message. Chris continued with his work. Though she said nothing, they all knew that any competent resident could do an exchange. Why had Chris refused to turn the patient over to Carey? Perhaps it was that as the demands of the case encroached more and more on his work he had become increasingly resistant to any interruption. It was as if he were tied to that case by some invisible legal umbilical cord.

Determinedly, Chris completed the transfusion and left Carey to administer the protamine. "Keep close watch on this one. Frankly, I think the prognosis is bad. If there's any radical change, call me in Sobol's office. And if Marcie says I can't come to the phone, insist!"

"For God's sake," Mike shouted the minute he saw Chris, "you didn't do it? Did you?"

"Do what?" Chris asked, honestly puzzled.

"You didn't give that TV man any information, did you?"

"Mike, what are you talking about?"

"What the whole board is talking about! The news story last night about the hospital."

"News story?" Chris said, puzzled. "What did it say?"

"We'll know soon enough." Mike began to explain with no little anguish, "At three o'clock this afternoon there will be a meeting in the board room. They are going to play the tape and then ask us to explain how it got on television. Most of the board will be there as well as a few 'friendly' doctors."

"Oh." Chris was dismayed, knowing that Mike was referring to the private practitioners connected with Metropolitan General. Unconsciously, Chris glanced down at his watch. It was almost five minutes to three. "Did you call Laura?"

Mike Sobol shook his head. "The board does not want any outsiders."

"She's no outsider. She's our lawyer."

"To them she's an outsider," Mike said.

Chris noted that the old man was paler, thinner, the lines in his face deeper. Perhaps the only decent thing for Chris to do was go along with a settlement. A man with a massive coronary behind him was not a good subject for this kind of stress. Before Chris could say anything, though, Mike started off for the board room.

Through the influence of one of the trustees, the local TV station had been convinced to surrender the segment of last night's news dealing with Metropolitan General. By the time Mike and Chris arrived the members of the board and the insurance company attorney were all in attendance. In addition, there was a committee of three doctors that included Dr. Arthur Spencer, one of the most successful practitioners in the city.

The TV film, which took only two minutes and seven seconds to run, was narrated by a slight young man whom the screen identified as "KTNT Community Relations Reporter Juan Melez." Melez stood before a number of different and changing backgrounds as he spoke. The original main building of Metropolitan General, the new Pediatrics Wing known as Reynolds Babies' Pavilion, the courthouse where the trial would take place, the huge estate of John Reynolds, and finally Public School 146, where Chris had delivered his lecture.

Melez praised Chris Grant, calling him "the kind of dedicated young doctor this community needs," and lauded him for his lectures to the mothers in the housing projects. Then, standing before the Reynolds estate on Walnut Hill,

Melez said, "Secluded behind this high, ornate ironwork fence lives the man who is attempting to destroy Metropolitan General. The charges he has leveled against this vital institution are shameful and destructive. If he is allowed to prevail, not only will a number of medical careers be ruined, but more important, Metropolitan General itself will be hurt, and the monies it uses to help the needy sick will dwindle."

At that point the camera zoomed in slowly on Melez's intense young face. "Whatever wrongs John Stewart Reynolds imagines have been done to his grandson, can they be so great as to demand this kind of destruction? Must Reynolds' anger be assuaged at such cost to this city? We will continue to cover this case as it proceeds."

Before there was any discussion, Chairman Brady insisted on running the tape again. Afterward he addressed Chris. "Dr. Grant, did you have anything to do with this?"

"Of course not," said Chris.

"He didn't even know about it till I called him less than half an hour ago," Mike Sobol said.

This time Brady let Dr. Arthur Spencer answer. His handsome face tanned from a recent Florida vacation, Spencer spoke as a man used to wielding influence among the powerful.

"It's worse than distressing. It's disgraceful! Damn it, I have spent most of my life helping to build Metropolitan General's reputation. And now comes this lawsuit which is damaging enough. Add to it this kind of television publicity and our hospital can lose its fine reputation. How do you suppose it makes the private patients feel, when they see such a story on the evening news?"

He was not through, and Brady did not seem inclined to interrupt him. "You fellows had better understand one thing. What revenue this hospital derives it derives from doctors like myself. At this moment I have twenty-seven beds in the private pavilion occupied by paying patients. If

Caldwell and Gross," Spencer referred to his two colleagues at the meeting, "joined me in leaving Metropolitan along with a couple of other doctors on your staff, you would lose up to five million dollars of revenue each year. And believe me we have all considered resigning our clinical professorships!"

If it was not an ultimatum, it was surely a serious threat. Mike Sobol paused before attempting to answer.

"Dr. Spencer," he began formally, though both men had been on a first-name basis for years, "I agree that you and your colleagues are indispensable parts of this hospital. But without our full-time teaching staff you practitioners would probably be out on the street as well!"

Before Mike could go on, Brady interrupted, "Gentlemen, please. I'm sure we all have one interest in common—to protect this institution. And now that Dr. Grant has informed us he had nothing to do with that unwelcome TV publicity, I accept his word. I just hope such incidents can be avoided in the future."

Spencer was about to speak, but Waller leaned forward in his chair and said quickly, "Not all aspects of this development are as negative as we have feared."

Chris and Mike exchanged glances.

Waller continued: "Whether it was the pressure of that newscast, or not, doesn't matter, but Crabtree has what we feel is good news."

Crabtree steepled his fingers and drummed them nervously.

"This morning," the lawyer said softly, "we were officially notified that Harry Franklyn has been retained to handle the case if it proceeds to trial."

Chris remembered all of Laura's forebodings.

Crabtree smiled, "Well, Harry and I are old antagonists. So this morning I called to welcome him aboard. During any lawsuit one may need a favor so it doesn't hurt to be on friendly terms with the adversary. In the course of our conversation he let me know that he's been masterminding this case from the beginning."

"Is that supposed to make us feel good?" Chris demanded.

Crabtree turned on the young doctor with an impatient stare. "I know that Harry Franklyn is too shrewd a man to be that informative without having some motive. I'm certain he was hinting, 'You know me, Paul, I'm a practical, reasonable man. If you've got an offer that makes sense, I have Reynolds' ear.' "

Mike Sobol interrupted, "I thought this board voted *against* settling this case!"

"Mike," said Rosenstiel with unnatural gentleness, "no one has said anything about the board changing its mind."

Mike and Chris glanced at each other, Mike's look saying, I think this is all prearranged.

"Cy," exploded Mike, "were we brought here to discuss that television newscast? Or to go into the matter of settlement again?"

"Mike, please, nobody said anything like that." Rosenstiel again acted as spokesman.

"Then why are we discussing it?"

"Mike, please!" Rosenstiel begged. "After all, you should be the first to admit that if it wasn't for the ability of this board of trustees to reconsider its position you wouldn't have half the modern equipment you have in your department. How many times have you been turned down? And then come back a few months later and persuaded us to change our position and vote you the funds."

Mike Sobol acquiesced, with a single impatient nod of the head.

"All we're asking is that you adopt the same open-minded attitude. At least listen to what Mr. Crabtree has to say."

"I guess the least we can do is listen," Mike said finally, but he could not bring himself to glance at Chris.

Crabtree tried to maintain a reassuring tone. "Like you I only want to protect Dr. Grant. But one has to define that word 'protect.' Frankly, Doctor"—Crabtree turned to Chris with exaggerated concern—"you did not make a very good witness on your examination before trial. I can imagine how you will react when Franklyn introduces a succession of distinguished witnesses to criticize your treatment."

Crabtree did not take his eyes off Chris. "I say we have to carefully evaluate what is the best means of protecting you, Dr. Grant."

Chris wished that Laura were present. She'd know if Crabtree was misstating the situation for some purpose of his own. He studied Crabtree, who continued, "I thought as long as I had Franklyn in such a cooperative mood I'd make a stab at settling. He fended it off, but not too strongly, so when he hung up I immediately called the insurance company. They surprised me with the biggest offer of settlement I've ever heard them make. Half a million dollars. I relayed it to Franklyn, who called me early this morning."

Crabtree paused and glanced at Brady and Spencer. "Franklyn's answer was that the *figure* would be acceptable."

Crabtree's strange emphasis on the word "figure" set Chris on edge.

"Speaking on behalf of his clients, Franklyn said they were not primarily interested in financial compensation. Their chief concern was to protect other families using Metropolitan."

Chris felt an angry rush of blood to his face, but Crabtree did not pause. "Franklyn said that they wanted a complete admission from the defendants that the treatment was undertaken in error and that there was a willful failure to disclose its inherent risks at the time the therapy was applied."

Brady tried to appear cool and dispassionate as he observed, "Well, that's certainly something to consider."

Before Chris could reply, the phone rang. Brady answered it with great impatience. "Damn it, we were not to be interrupted by any calls!" Then he moderated his tone, "Dr. Grant? Yes, yes, I suppose so." He held out the instrument to Chris, who listened a minute, then said, "Oh? I see. Well, complete your notes. I'll add mine when I get back." Chris hung up, turned to Mike. "The Lopez baby didn't make it."

"I expected that," Sobol said, then turned to the others to observe, "Exchange transfusions aren't necessarily the right answer every time either."

Chris remained standing. "Gentlemen, my own counsel has told me you can settle this matter over my head. But when it comes to my own culpability, then I do have rights. What John Reynolds wants—is my professional death warrant signed by my own hand. If Reynolds were a less important man, any psychiatrist would tell you that this is highly suspicious conduct. Enough to reflect on his mental state. But one doesn't dare have such suspicions about John Stewart Reynolds. Does one?

"Well, I am not about to give in to his outrageous demand. You gentlemen can negotiate with the enemy, I do not wish to be part of it. Mike?"

Sobol rose to join Chris, but Cy Rosenstiel intervened.

"Mike, at a time like this, an older man can be of great value in helping his young associate see the light."

"You know, Cy," Mike said softly, "you remind me of the joke about two Jewish prisoners standing before a firing squad. Their hands were bound behind their backs. The squad had raised their rifles. Then the officer in command asked, 'Do you wish blindfolds?' Meyer accepted. But Abe said, 'To hell with your blindfold! Shoot!' And his timid friend Meyer cautioned, 'Abe, don't make trouble.' You can be Meyer. I'll be Abe, if you don't mind. Gentlemen, to hell with your blindfold!"

Mike turned and preceded Chris out of the room.

FOURTEEN

LAURA WINTERS was standing across the street from Parkside Polyclinic. She was some minutes early for her appointment so she waited, admiring the building's strong clean lines. Not nearly so large as Metropolitan General, it had been designed by a famous architect in white sandstone and comprised a main building and two smaller wings, one of which contained the two free wards needed to give the hospital its tax-free status. Some of the most expensive and reputable doctors in the city were its chief stockholders, and no doctor was invited to join the staff without the proper social as well as professional recommendation.

Laura glanced again at her watch. It was time. For days she had been discreetly trying to establish contact with someone inside Parkside, preferably in the records office. Finally, it turned out that one of her clients, Judson Dahn, for whom Laura had handled several delicate private matters, not only knew someone but was most happy to help.

Dahn, a tall, impressive man, was vice president of a large advertising agency, surviving on his charm as well as his ability to entertain clients. When he was in the city he had a little black book from which he provided freely for the pleasure of his out-of-town clients. When Dahn traveled he expected the same in return and was rarely disappointed. The first few times he and Laura had met at her office he made undisguised attempts to develop a sexual relationship. When he finally accepted the fact that Laura would not acquiesce, their relationship settled down to the conventional one of client and lawyer.

It was Dahn's son and his sports car that had finally made Judson a friend. Young Dahn had run his sports car off the parkway and into a road light, collapsing the stanchion and wrecking the car. He had also forced another car off the road, injuring its two occupants. For reasons Dahn did not disclose at once, he had chosen to assume the resulting legal difficulties personally instead of through his insurance company. Laura had finally discovered that young Dahn had been extremely high at the time of the accident.

It took some months, but Laura was able to settle the civil suits brought by the two victims and get young Dahn off with no publicity. From that time on Jud Dahn never made any inappropriate advances and he was always quick to remind her that he was anxious to help anytime she needed a favor.

Now, thanks to Jud Dahn's contacts, Laura Winters had made the necessary contact at Parkside Polyclinic. She went directly to the information desk, asked for the woman whom Dahn had recommended. She was directed to an office on the basement level floor where Ethel Grayson was waiting. At first glance, Laura could guess the relationship between the two. Miss Grayson was tall and amply built. Her dark eyes were warm, frank, penetrating, and she radiated sexuality.

Obviously the woman had been well prepared for Laura's visit. She greeted Laura with a smile and locked the door to her office as inconspicuously as she could.

"Jud told me what you want," she said in the hushed tones of a conspirator. "The reason you had to wait a few days is that I had to pull the file. I didn't want to do it on the same day you came, in case someone made the connection."

"I understand," Laura said. "And I want to thank you."

"I'm doing this for Jud," Ethel Grayson said, cutting her off. "I don't know what good this will do you—I'm not a doctor—but that's up to you."

"May I see . . ."

Again the Grayson woman interrupted, "I'm going to go up to the admitting office on the main floor. I'll leave you here alone. For about fifteen minutes. The file is in the bottom drawer of the green metal file cabinet. Whatever notes you can make in fifteen minutes is okay with me. Just remember, I never showed you anything."

"Yes, of course."

Ethel Grayson started out, then turned to take a long, appraising look at Laura. "Just what is it between you and Jud?"

"I'm his lawyer. Didn't he tell you?"

"Oh, he told me," she said, "but when I saw you I wondered." Evidently Ethel Grayson wanted possession, or at least the illusion of possession.

As soon as the door was closed, Laura pulled out the bottom drawer of the file. There lay a solitary, thin file, labeled SIMPSON, BABY. In parentheses appeared (c/o JOHN STEWART REYNOLDS).

Laura scanned the hospital chart which had been kept during the forty-odd hours that the infant had been a patient at Parkside. Dr. Coleman's report indicated the infant was the result of a somewhat difficult but not abnormal delivery, weighed over the required 2500 grams, and was thus not labeled premature. From all other indications the child appeared normal. Both Apgars, the first over-all examinations at the time of birth, presented no evidence of any defect. Although Laura did not understand the lab report which Chris would have to evaluate, the file seemed only to reinforce the claims made by Parkins, Sears and Wadleigh. An infant with a somewhat higher than average though not dangerous bilirubin had been referred to Metropolitan General for treatment.

Since Laura suspected this was the only chance she would have to examine the file she drew a Minox camera out of her purse, laid out the papers under the desk lamp and trusted that her flashless film would pick up clean, legible copies.

She was just returning the file to the drawer when there was a knock at the door. Laura turned the lock as silently as she could and opened it.

Instead of Ethel Grayson, a young man who, but for the stethoscope in his pocket, seemed too young to be a doctor, stood before her. "Miss Grayson not in?" he asked.

"She'll be back any minute."

"Then I'll wait, if you don't mind."

"Of course not," Laura said, anxious to leave before he had a chance to remember her. Fortunately, Ethel Grayson returned. She had already been alerted by the fact that her office door was open and she addressed Laura at once.

"Miss Scott, I'm afraid that the records you want can only be gotten through the accounting office. Ever since Medicare all our business records are in a mess. If you have any trouble, do call again."

"Thank you very much," Laura said, pleased to make good her escape.

Once the door closed, Ethel Grayson turned to her visitor. "What can I do for you, Dr. Coleman?"

"The file and the chart on the Simpson baby, could I see those again?" he asked.

Knowing what it might mean to admit that the file was in her office at that moment, Ethel Grayson said quickly, "We keep that file in a special place. For obvious reasons. But if you give me an hour I'm sure I can make it available."

"Good," Coleman said. "I'll want to take it home so I can look it over tonight at my leisure."

"I'm sure that can be arranged," Ethel Grayson said, as pleasantly as she could. When Coleman left her office, she locked the door and picked up the phone. Jud Dahn answered on his private line. Ethel Grayson said, "She was here and she saw the file. But you almost put me in a hell of a fix."

"Did she get what she wanted?" Dahn asked.

"I let her look at everything we have."

"Good."

"Jud, sweetie, don't ever do that to me again. You hear?"

"I had to. I owe that girl a lot," said Dahn.

"Don't owe her too much," Ethel warned.

"What does that mean?"

"You said your lawyer was coming, and not to be surprised that she was a woman, but you never said she was beautiful. If I ever find out there's anything between you two . . ." She left it hanging as an open threat.

"Ethel, honey, I take an oath, there's nothing between us."

"Okay," she relented. She was about to mention the fact that Dr. Coleman had just inquired about the same file but decided it was more important to end the conversation on a personal note.

Laura took her film to the photo shop in her office building. Within the day the prints were ready and she called Chris at the hospital and invited him to her apartment for dinner. From the sound of her voice he knew it was to be strictly a business meeting.

She had prepared a simple meal. Before she cleared the table, she said, "You look at this while I do the dishes."

Chris settled down in the easy chair and took the copies of the file from their envelope. "Laurie, where did you ever get these?" he asked, shocked.

"Never mind," she called, as she loaded the dishes into

the washer, "just read them."

He was done. She asked anxiously, "Well?"

"Very interesting."

"Never mind interesting! Does it answer any questions?"

"How did you ever get hold of this?" he asked again.

"Answer me, *does it help?*"

"If you expected there would be any information that you could dramatically hold up in a courtroom and cry out, 'Your Honor, we have the whole solution to the case right here in this file,' the answer is no."

When she responded with a look of disappointment, he asked, "Now, tell me. How did you get hold of these?"

She told him. When she finished, he got up from his chair and took her in his arms. "Was there anything illegal about what you did?"

"Illegal? No," she said. Then admitted, "There was a breach of hospital confidentiality as far as Miss Grayson was concerned. That was illegal. Yes."

"Look," he said, holding her tightly, "I don't want you to take any risks because of me. You're doing enough already." He kissed her. "No risks. Promise?"

"Okay. Promise," she said. "But as long as we have them, look at them again?" He examined the records carefully.

"Do they contain any information that might be at all helpful? That might reveal any other cause of that infant's damage?"

"Frankly," Chris said, "they don't even contain enough vital information to make them particularly useful to a doctor. Very sloppy record-keeping. It was hardly worth the effort."

"We'll keep them anyhow," Laura said, gathering them up.

"They won't be of any use," Chris warned.

"They just might," Laura said in a way that provoked him.

"In what way?" he asked.

"Chris, darling," she said, leading him over to the sofa, "the law is a rough business. Or do I have to tell you that after the Watergate hearings? Remember what that insurance investigator suggested you do?"

"Alter my notes?"

"Yes. Well, suppose during the trial Coleman is called upon to introduce his records and they don't quite match the set that we have . . ." She didn't complete her sentence.

"You mean that Coleman might change *his* records?"

"I mean that doctors have been known to do just that. It's possible that if there's something in the file that Harry Franklyn objects to, he might ask Coleman to remove it."

"I doubt it."

"I don't," Laura said quickly.

"There's nothing in there to embarrass Coleman. Why should he make any changes?" Chris asked.

"When we get to court, we'll see," was all Laura would say.

He embraced her, more passionately this time, then suddenly remembered the meeting in the board room that morning. She sensed his change of mood and whispered, "Chris?" He told her. About the newscast, the offer of settlement, the statement Reynolds wanted him to sign and Mike's response.

"Of course," she said sadly. "Mike and you, the same, innocents, believing that if you practice medicine honestly, ethically, you are entitled to vindication."

She pulled away from him to look for her cigarettes. He was about to say something, but he had learned that his warnings only made her more stubborn. She lit up. The flaring match illuminated her face which seemed very tired. "Chris, if you were treating that infant again would you do anything differently?"

He was surprised at the directness of her question.

"Would you?" she persisted.

"I think about it," he admitted. "I go over every step,

the transcript from Parkside, the appearance of the infant, our own lab reports. . . ."

"Would you have done anything differently?" she repeated.

"Sometimes," he confessed, "sometimes I think to myself, if I'd done a conventional exchange transfusion maybe this whole mess could have been avoided."

"*Would* it have done any good?" she insisted.

"You never know. Medicine is full of ifs. But you have only one chance in a case like this."

"I want your honest opinion. Do you think it would have made a difference?"

"I don't know. Nobody will ever know," he admitted.

She ground out her cigarette, trying to avoid his glance. "Chris, on cross-examination, you must never admit to any second thoughts."

He looked at her, surprised and disapproving.

"Just consider what you've admitted this evening," she said defensively. "Parkside's records are correct. An exchange transfusion is a more conventional treatment. You do have some second thoughts about not doing one. Worse, there was no room for ifs. Your decision *could* have doomed that baby."

Chris shrugged hopelessly.

"Imagine what Harry Franklyn could do with such statements. That's why you can't admit to any second thoughts. Ever."

"But if it's the truth," he argued.

"They'll turn it into damaging evidence."

"But how can I deny . . ."

"You have to!" Laura insisted. Then she sighed. "No, you're right. How could you say anything but what you believe to be true." She turned to him, kissed him. He did not respond. Softly she said, "I was wrong. Treating you like just another client."

"Is that what you advise your other clients?" he asked.

She reached for another cigarette before she could answer. He caught her hand, took the cigarette, asked again, "Is it?"

"That's what it's like. You learn the rules only to figure out ways to circumvent them. You discover the truth only to keep it from being told. Most times the more unscrupulous the means you use, the greater hero you emerge. But everyone does it."

He turned her about, stared into her eyes until she admitted, "That's only a rationalization. It's the new American morality. The new standard of values and virtue. Nothing we do is wrong as long as we can compare it with something equally wrong that someone else is doing." She asked in a whisper, "Hold me?"

He embraced her and they were silent, each seeking strength from the other. Finally she said, "Chris, the trial will start soon. In the days we have left we can't think about us. We have to think about you. I want you to keep asking yourself if there was any possible way that infant could have been damaged that was unrelated to your treatment."

"Could have?" Chris echoed impatiently. "Anything *could* have happened."

"Chris," she cautioned, "in a case where we don't have any idea what did happen, we have to line up as many *could have happeneds* as we can. Where the facts aren't clear, we have to put up a smokescreen."

"That's only another way of distorting the truth!" he protested.

"You don't know the danger you're in!"

Now he couldn't stop her from lighting her cigarette. It seemed to calm her. Her voice was less urgent when she said, "The difference between doctors and lawyers is that doctors try to bolster their patients' morale by telling them the best aspects of their cases. Lawyers try to scare their clients into cooperating by giving them the worst." She smiled. "Just this once I'd like to have a well-prepared dishonest witness."

He took her in his arms and began to kiss her, no longer attempting to refrain from his passion. The last thing she whispered was, "Chris . . . darling . . . we can't . . . all our arguments . . . all our discussions can't end up in bed." He kissed her again. And that was the end of any more talk.

Later, much later, she lay beside him in the dark, her fingers delicately tracing designs across his chest.

"I worry about Mike. If we lose, what options are open to a man his age?"

"I don't know. Retirement, I guess," Chris admitted.

"To give him more time to spend in that empty apartment. Where Rose used to be and isn't anymore. It'll kill him."

"I know," Chris said grimly. "That's the only reason I'd ever contemplate settling. And that's the only reason why he wouldn't."

"Chris," she said, drawing his hand close. "Just don't stop thinking about what might have damaged that infant aside from the phototherapy."

"Damn it, why do you keep thinking it was the phototherapy?"

"Because you can't tell me that it wasn't," she answered coolly. "And eventually we'll have to have an answer, if we expect to have any chance of winning."

He nodded, though he was not hopeful that he could supply the answer.

Suddenly she asked, "What was it you said about Reynolds at the board meeting?"

"That if he wasn't such an important man . . ."

"That's right," she said. "How did you phrase it?"

He tried to recall exactly. "I think I said, 'Any psychiatrist would tell you his conduct is suspicious. Highly suspicious.' That?"

"Yes, that," she said, giving Chris's words special significance. "I'd feel better if Reynolds were less compulsive. Or less powerful."

She embraced him with an intensity that bespoke her fear. She held him close not to arouse him but to protect him. "I wish we didn't have to go through this trial. I wish . . ." She never did say what she wished. She just clung to him, protectively, yet needing his protection at the same time.

FIFTEEN

CHRISTOPHER GRANT, M.D., stood at the foot of the wide steps and stared up. He had seen photographs of the old courthouse many times, usually as a background for a demonstration or for a politician making some pronouncement having to do with a case being tried within the building. But Chris Grant had never before had reason to ascend those broad, worn stone steps.

Now he stared up at the sooty-gray Greek columns with apprehension. He was a man on trial for his life.

Before he could start up with Laura at his side, they were intercepted by a reporter carrying a microphone. Just behind him trailed a cameraman who was focusing a hand-held movie camera.

"Doctor?" the newsman called. Chris turned, resenting the intrusion. "You are Dr. Grant, aren't you?"

Chris was about to continue up the steps when he recognized the young man. He had seen that thin dark face before. It was the TV commentator whose newscast had so upset the board of trustees only a few weeks earlier.

Melez persisted. "Doctor, how does it feel standing up against the power of John Stewart Reynolds?"

Before Chris could answer, Laura said, "Dr. Grant is forbidden to make any statements to the press."

"By Mr. Reynolds?" Melez asked, smiling.

"By his attorney!" Laura responded curtly, seeking to end the conversation.

But Melez moved swiftly, securing a position two steps above them and blocking their passage. "Look, I'm on your side. I've done a whole series on your problem."

"Yes, we know," Laura replied. "But the thing you don't understand is that no publicity would be even better for us than favorable publicity."

"Lady, before this is through you're going to need all the help you can get," Melez persisted. "Now, let the Doctor make any statement he chooses and I'll see that it gets on the air."

"We intend to try this case in the courtroom," Laura said firmly.

"Okay," said Melez, "but you're going to need friends. You've got enough enemies."

"Thank you, we know that," Laura said, gripping Chris's arm, a signal to him to start moving.

Melez did not give in at once. "Look, when you do need help, remember me. I'll do what I can. I just hope it won't be too late."

"Thank you," Laura said.

They climbed the steps, their feet slipping naturally into grooves that had been worn into that stone for half a century by thousands of lawyers, combatants and witnesses, each of whom had come here ostensibly in a righteous cause. Much law and some justice had been dispensed in this old building in decades gone by.

Behind them were Paul Crabtree and Avery Waller, who represented the corporate interests of the hospital. Though Waller had no more official standing in the case than Laura Winters, he and Crabtree functioned like partners. They had held many meetings from which Laura was excluded and they had agreed on their strategy.

"Like to place a bet before the game starts?" Crabtree asked.

"No," Waller responded gingerly. "Oh, did they tell you? We took another crack at Sobol last night. Couldn't budge him."

"If he'd only realize," said Crabtree, "the last thing that belongs in a courtroom is principle."

"God save me from the client who demands justice," Waller agreed as they reached the top step.

The corridor of the courthouse reeked with the accumulated smoke of millions of cigars and cigarettes consumed over the years by nervous witnesses. No small amount came from the millions of cigars handed out to courthouse clerks and attendants as gratuities for small favors. A cheap cigar could bring forth a much sought after file in a short time. A more expensive cigar might elicit some bit of information about a judge's disposition or his attitude on a particular motion.

"Smells like a cancer factory," observed Chris as he and Laura walked down the hall.

"It is," she replied, "in more ways than one."

Still she couldn't help smiling. He never missed a chance to let her know how he felt about her only weakness.

They found Courtroom 405. Outside the leather-covered doors a neat plaque announced the fact that Justice Timothy Bannon was presiding. When they entered, Chris and Laura found two uniformed court attendants lolling in the jury box.

When Crabtree arrived he called both clerks by their first names. They knew what the impending case was about and looked forward to seeing it unfold.

There were few spectators in the courtroom when the

opposing parties took their places at the respective tables. Chris and Laura sat at the far end of their counsel's table. The chair provided for Mike Sobol was empty. When summoned to testify he would appear. Until then he would continue his hospital duties uninterrupted.

At the plaintiff's table sat William Heinfelden and a junior from Parkins, Sears and Wadleigh. Though Heinfelden busied himself laying out papers and memoranda, it was obvious that he was awaiting trial counsel to assume the plaintiff's case. Only minutes after the court attendant had led in the first thirty potential jurors a sound of excitement was heard outside the courtroom. Chris and Laura turned to look. When the doors were thrust open John Stewart Reynolds entered, calling behind him, "Gentlemen, it is far too early for me to make any statement. But when the proper time comes, you may be sure I will not remain silent!"

Having disposed of the press, Reynolds started briskly down the aisle followed by a smallish man dressed in a plain dark blue suit, white shirt and solid maroon tie. The man wore rimless glasses which added to his undistinguished look. He shook hands with Heinfelden, and with equal pleasantness approached the defense table and shook hands with Crabtree and Waller.

"Dr. Grant, Miss Winters," said Crabtree, "this is Harry Franklyn."

Chris shook the little man's hand. It was soft, limp, almost effeminate. Surely it was not the grip or the hand he expected after all the warnings he'd heard about Harry Franklyn.

But this was exactly the effect Harry Franklyn intended to produce. He had spent years cultivating his courtroom appearance so that it was inoffensive, disarming, almost nondescript. In his wardrobe were nine suits which he alternated for work. Each was navy blue British worsted.

Each was tailored in London. Each was single breasted. His courtroom shirts were all plain white Egyptian cotton broadcloth, soft as silk, but otherwise indistinguishable from the average white shirt. His courtroom ties were all the same proper shade of maroon. He never wanted any juror to feel that Harry Franklyn was superior to him in any material respect. He liked jurors to become his friends, to feel sorry for him if possible, to sympathize with his client certainly. Above all, he did not wish to give any juror the feeling that he was such an inordinately successful trial lawyer that for each of the past seventeen years his fees never totaled less than a million dollars a year.

Franklyn retired to his own table. John Reynolds was already ensconced in his armchair, gazing about the courtroom. When his eyes swept over Chris Grant there was not the faintest glimmer of recognition, not even any hint of resentment. It was as if Chris Grant did not exist. In John Stewart Reynolds' mind he had already been wiped out.

Suddenly the clerk called for silence. At the command "All rise!" the door from the judges' robing room opened. The Honorable Justice Timothy Bannon entered. He was a tall man, thin, and, though handsome, his worn face seemed to exude character.

Bannon took his place in his high-backed chair, smiled his greeting to those lawyers whom he knew personally and ordered the clerk to commence the jury selection. The clerk spun the drum and began to draw names out of it. As he announced the name each prospective juror took his place in the box. When fourteen men and women had been named and seated, the clerk arranged the cards on the jury board and handed it to Harry Franklyn.

The lawyer leaned across the rail of the jury box and spoke in a voice so low and confidential that most of his words escaped Chris. Franklyn outlined the case so that the potential jurors could answer some questions that might

171

qualify or disqualify them from hearing it. In the course of his explanation Franklyn introduced each of the persons sitting at both counsel tables.

When Franklyn had assured himself and the court that no potential juror personally knew any of the parties or counsel involved, he began to question each by name. One by one he dismissed those jurors who, for one reason or another, seemed prejudiced or unwilling to serve. Franklyn seemed particularly interested in eliminating anyone who had been involved in a medical case or who had relatives or close friends who were in the medical profession.

As some jurors were excused others took their places. The procedure droned on till Chris began to lose interest. If this was the law in all its exciting majesty it was a damned bore. He slid lower and lower into his chair, though Laura remained tense and attentive throughout. By the time the lunch recess was declared, Chris was relieved to rise and stretch. For some reason Laura did not seem in a hurry to leave. She lingered till all the others had gone and they were alone in the empty courtroom.

"Franklyn must get paid by the day," Chris observed.

"Don't be snowed," Laura said in a curt whisper. "Didn't you notice what he was doing?"

"Aside from boring everyone to death?"

"He was slowly but surely stripping that jury of black people. Oh, sure, he excused a few whites. But one thing is clear. He doesn't want any blacks on that jury if he can help it."

"Why?" Chris asked.

"That's what I'd like to know. Not a single doctor involved is black," Laura said.

"Then what possible reason could he have?" Chris asked.

"Some lawyers believe that white jurors having a higher standard of living tend to vote bigger verdicts. But money isn't the game here. It won't make any difference to Reynolds if he wins five dollars or five million."

"Would it make a difference to Franklyn?" Chris asked.

"Usually he'd get a percentage. But in a case like this I'll bet he's been paid a huge retainer and about two thousand dollars a day for each court appearance, so he can't be thinking about the size of the verdict," Laura said. "But we'll see. We'll see. Let's go get some lunch."

The afternoon seemed equally dull. Franklyn questioned jurors in his soft voice, Bannon sat on the bench scanning papers from other cases, except when Crabtree made some objection. Then Bannon would rule, most times in favor of Franklyn, and the juror would be excused.

When Laura tried to point out to Crabtree the fact that the prosecution was eliminating all the prospective blacks he shrugged it off with a kind of amused boredom.

Then Crabtree's turn came. As an insurance company lawyer, he tried to eliminate all jurors who had ever been involved in litigation or who were closely connected to a lawyer. He also tried to eliminate as many unemployed as he could. Then as many employees as he could. He favored those who were self-employed, on the theory that they had a greater respect for money, and thus would favor a smaller verdict. For his own purposes, Crabtree seemed to be playing along with Franklyn, since most of his challenges tended to eliminate blacks, too.

By the following morning Justice Bannon began to evidence signs of restlessness. "Any twelve honest citizens make up a good jury. Let's not be too finicky, gentlemen," he kept urging.

By the end of the day Franklyn and Crabtree had arrived at twelve jurors and two alternates whom they both deemed acceptable. Of the fourteen persons who remained in the jury box thirteen were white, one was black. Of the thirteen whites, nine were women, four were men. The sole black, a woman, was one of the alternate jurors. Whatever Harry Franklyn's strategy, he had succeeded in securing his twelve white jurors.

Justice Bannon swore in all the fourteen persons selected and ordered Franklyn to be ready to begin the plaintiff's case as soon as court convened the next day.

Promptly at ten o'clock, Harry Franklyn in blue suit, white shirt and maroon tie was ready to make his opening statement. He approached the jury box, rested his arm on the rail and spoke in a tone so intimate that even Bannon had to lean forward and cup his ear to catch the words.

"Ladies and gentlemen, some of you may have sat on juries in the past. But I am sure none of you has ever before contemplated a case of this magnitude. I don't know about you, but, to me, if you deprive a man of his arm or his leg, that is horrible enough. But what do you do for an infant who in the very first hours of its life has been doomed by a doctor's negligence to the existence of a brain-damaged vegetable?"

He paused as though the gravity of the case he must present had already overtaxed him.

"That is the case we are involved in. We know that a normal child was born to Mr. Lawrence Simpson and his wife. The delivery was a bit premature and a bit difficult but the infant was perfectly healthy. You will hear the obstetrician testify to that. After birth a condition developed in that child that called for further treatment. Two eminent doctors will testify to the child's condition and to what sort of treatment was needed. And, because it was deemed advisable, for the reassurance of the parents, and the safety of the child, the child was turned over to Metropolitan General Hospital, specifically to Dr. Michael Sobol, who in turn referred that helpless infant to Dr. Christopher Grant, one of the defendants in this case."

Franklyn turned slightly to direct the jury's gaze toward Chris, who instinctively withdrew.

Franklyn continued: "The child was then subjected to a

treatment too complicated for me to explore here, but a treatment that resulted in brain damage. We will introduce physicians, the best in their specialty, to give testimony to that effect. As we will introduce physicians who will, unfortunately, testify to the present sad condition of that infant.

"While we take the position that no amount of money can repay either the child or its family for the damage that has been done to it, a large verdict may teach other hospitals and doctors to exercise more care in the future."

Franklyn hesitated a moment, as if to seal a bargain with the jurors. Then he turned and started back to the table.

"Mr. Crabtree?" Judge Bannon invited the defense to make its opening statement.

Crabtree rose to his full height and moved to the jury box. Where Franklyn had been small, almost timid, Crabtree was large and made no attempt to restrain his booming voice. Whether he strove for contrast with Franklyn or not, he achieved it. The jurors sat up and listened intently.

Crabtree began by expressing great regret over the unfortunate child, but he assured the jury that neither the hospital nor the doctors were responsible. He cautioned the jury that the mere fact of brain damage did not mean that anyone was at fault. Sometimes such tragedies were unfortunate accidents of nature. He would prove, through the testimony of eminent and respected doctors, that the steps taken in relation to the unfortunate child were good and accepted practice, carefully carried out. Thus neither the hospital nor the doctors were either legally or morally culpable.

Crabtree went no farther. Since the burden of proof was on the plaintiff he did not wish to commit himself to proving more than he had to. Even Laura felt that it was a perfectly effective opening.

Once Crabtree sat down, Franklyn took up the task of establishing his prima facie case for the plaintiff. In careful, methodical manner he began with Hugh Mitchell, the doctor who had the first contact with Mrs. Simpson from the moment when she suspected she might be pregnant. Silver-haired and distinguished, Mitchell answered every question in a benign and helpful way.

Franklyn led Dr. Mitchell through his long career, starting with medical school, his excellent record there, internship, residency, hospital affiliations, the extensive list of offices he held in local and national groups including the American Medical Association and the National Obstetrical Society, of which he had been vice president twice and president for one term. Slowly, precisely, Franklyn created the portrait of a doctor with excellent training and an impeccable reputation. Finally he brought Mitchell to his long-time affiliation with Parkside Polyclinic Hospital.

Having assured himself that he had sufficiently impressed the jury with the veracity and professional eminence of his witness, Harry Franklyn launched into the testimony he sought to elicit.

"Tell the jury, if you will, Doctor, about your first contact with Mrs. Simpson."

Mitchell turned slightly to address the jury. "On August tenth two years ago I received a call from Mrs. Simpson's father asking me to see his daughter. As a long-time friend of Mr. Reynolds' I immediately arranged to see Arlene Simpson."

"That day?"

"The next morning."

"And, Doctor?"

"I did a complete examination. There was no doubt that she was pregnant."

"And then, Doctor?"

"I drew some blood to make all the indicated tests, I congratulated her and her husband and sent them home to await the outcome of the lab reports."

"The tests you referred to, Doctor, what were the results?"

"Normal in all respects. Except for one thing. Mrs. Simpson's blood was Rh negative."

"Is that bad, Doctor?"

"Not in this instance," said Mitchell.

"Could you explain that?" Franklyn asked, pretending ignorance of the medical facts.

"Well, the fact that a potential mother is Rh negative in blood type is not important in the bearing of her first child, though it can have dire consequences for succeeding children. Or at least I should say, it *used* to have dire consequences. Now with the advent of a substance we call Rh-O-Gam we are able to prevent damage to second children by treating the mother after the birth of the first child."

"So that since the infant was Mrs. Simpson's first child, there was no danger at all of its having an Rh problem?"

Mitchell turned to Franklyn as if to disagree. "Well, not exactly."

"Why is that?"

"Well," Mitchell equivocated, as he'd been instructed. "The explanation is quite complicated."

"I'm sure the men and women on this jury are highly intelligent and will understand." Having flattered the jury, as well as prepared them for a complicated medical discussion, Franklyn gave Mitchell free rein, saying, "Please, Doctor?"

"First, the term Rh-negative blood sounds worse than it is. Everyone in this world is either Rh negative or Rh positive and there is no difference in the quality of the blood. All negative means is that a certain protein substance is not found in the red blood cells. The only time it becomes important is when a woman becomes pregnant and it only presents a problem when the baby is Rh positive."

Mitchell extended the same fatherly concern to the jury

177

that he adopted with his young pregnant patients. "During the birth of a first baby there is a chance that some of the baby's Rh-positive blood will cross over into the mother's bloodstream. The mother's body will treat that Rh-positive blood as a foreign substance, and will begin to manufacture antibodies against it. This does not affect the child that is already out of the mother's body, but if that woman has any future babies that are Rh positive, then her blood, which now has antibodies, will fight the unborn baby's blood cells, slowly destroying it, either while it is in utero or after it is born."

"Even after it is born?" Franklyn questioned.

"Right, Mr. Franklyn. If it is born alive, that second Rh-positive baby can suffer from what we call Rh hemolytic disease of the newborn."

"So that you are always extremely careful to test any pregnant woman for her positive or negative type?" Franklyn brought Mitchell back to his earlier statement.

"Of course."

"Even though it is a first child and that child is immune from any Rh problem?" Franklyn prodded.

"There is the possibility of another problem connected with an Rh-negative mother. Even with a first child," Mitchell said.

Pretending that he had been surprised by that bit of medical fact, Franklyn stated, "But you said before that first children were immune."

Mitchell smiled indulgently. "I warned you this could become complicated. There is another way the Rh-negative antibodies in the mother can be triggered even before a first baby."

"Oh?" Franklyn had a highly developed knack of being able to respond with as much interest and curiosity as any juror. He seemed to reflect their moods while actually playing on them to extremely good effect.

Mitchell was continuing his explanation. "If the mother

had at any time been given a blood transfusion of Rh-positive blood, she would then be sensitized and her body would manufacture antibodies that could affect even a first child."

"And did you check Mrs. Simpson?" Franklyn asked.

"Yes. I asked her if she'd ever had a transfusion. And though she said she had not, I checked with her internist who made it quite clear that she had never had reason for a transfusion."

"Anything else, Doctor?"

"I had the lab run a test on her blood to determine the titer level of her blood."

"Titer level?" Franklyn repeated, pretending to be confused.

"That tells us the level of the antibodies in her blood, if in fact there are any," Mitchell explained.

"And in Mrs. Simpson's case?"

"The report came back from the lab. The Coombs on Mrs. Simpson relieved us of all concern."

"Coombs?" Franklyn asked.

"One of the tests we use to determine the titer level in a woman's blood," Mitchell explained.

"And the Coombs test done on Mrs. Simpson's blood clearly showed that she had no antibody problem in her blood that would affect the birth of her first child?" Franklyn nailed down the point he had really been aiming to make all along.

"That is correct."

"So that Mrs. Simpson had, in all respects, a normal full-term pregnancy?" Franklyn asked.

"Not quite full term. I would judge that it was closer to thirty-seven or thirty-eight weeks. But not premature," Mitchell responded.

"Now, at the time of delivery," Franklyn began, "is there a test done on every baby right in the delivery room?"

"Yes. It's called an Apgar score, after Dr. Apgar, the

woman who devised it," Mitchell volunteered.

"And precisely what is that test and what does it establish?"

"It's a test designed to assess circulatory, respiratory and neurological status. It's done one minute after birth and then repeated five minutes after birth," Mitchell responded.

"What does the test consist of, Doctor?"

"We score the infant for heart rate, respiration, color, reflexes and muscle tone. The infant is graded on each from two to zero. If the score totals from seven to ten, we know we're dealing with a normal infant," Mitchell said.

"And were the Apgar tests made on the Simpson baby?"

"I wasn't there, Mr. Franklyn," Mitchell responded simply, as he had been instructed to do.

"You weren't there?" Franklyn echoed.

"When it came time for Mrs. Simpson to give birth I was ill with the flu. I'm afraid you'll have to ask Dr. Coleman about the actual details of the delivery."

"I see," Franklyn said. "So that your last contact with the Simpson family was just before the delivery?"

"Oh, no," Mitchell corrected. "About a day and a half after the delivery I received a call from Dr. Coleman. The infant was beginning to evidence not only a bilirubin count that was disturbing, but a Coombs that showed an Rh problem. Coleman wanted to refer it to Metropolitan General where it could benefit from more intensive care, but he wished my approval."

"And did you concur?" Franklyn asked.

"Unfortunately, yes," Mitchell replied.

Crabtree rose at once to object to the word "unfortunately." Bannon ordered it struck.

"Doctor, when you agreed with Dr. Coleman that the infant should be turned over to Metropolitan, did you have any idea what sort of treatment was going to be administered?"

"I had expected that it would be given an exchange . . ."

Crabtree rose before Mitchell had finished. His objection was strenuous and Bannon ruled in his favor.

Franklyn had to content himself with, "That will be all for the moment, Doctor." He did not intend to press his luck. He had too many experts ready to testify as to the desirability of a transfusion over phototherapy. He turned the witness over for cross-examination.

Crabtree began gingerly. He wanted to be quite sure that he did not ask any question that would allow for the doctor to express an opinion on the method of treatment followed by Chris Grant. "Dr. Mitchell, you testified that to make sure that there were no antibodies in Mrs. Simpson's blood you had a Coombs test done."

"Which revealed that her antibody titer was nonexistent," Mitchell volunteered.

"Doctor, is a Coombs the kind of test you would consider one hundred percent reliable?" Crabtree asked.

Mitchell smiled. "No medical test is infallible, Mr. Crabtree. But a Coombs is a perfectly acceptable test and reliable for our purposes."

"Isn't it true that there are other tests for the same purpose? Such as saline agglutinins, plasma albumins, tryepsinized cell tests?"

"And even more," Mitchell agreed. "Including bovine measurements for one. But I rely on the Coombs and so do most doctors I respect."

"Yet you yourself have just admitted that it is not infallible."

As if addressing a student rather than a lawyer almost as old as himself, Mitchell said, "My dear man, a doctor doesn't rely on the test alone. But taken together, a negative Coombs, a woman having her first child, with no history of a transfusion, no serious illness, one doesn't have to pursue the matter further."

"Not even so far as taking a second Coombs?"

"In a case like this to what end? To prove what's already

been proven?" Mitchell said impatiently.

Judge Bannon intervened. "Dr. Mitchell, the attorneys ask the questions here."

"Would you care to rephrase your answer, Doctor?" Crabtree asked.

"Taking all the factors into account, I didn't think there was any need to pursue the question further."

"Despite the fact that you admit a Coombs isn't always a hundred percent correct?" Crabtree was trying to salvage something from his cross-examination.

"Yes," Mitchell persisted.

Since pressing Mitchell further would elicit his opinion on Grant's treatment, Crabtree indicated that he was through with the witness.

Franklyn had one last question, which he asked in a soft voice, from his place at the counsel table. "Doctor, what percentage of obstetricians would you estimate use the Coombs as opposed to the other tests which Mr. Crabtree mentioned?"

"About eighty percent," Mitchell said confidently.

"Thank you, Doctor. But please remain available for recall to the stand after the next witness."

SIXTEEN

DR. ROBERT Coleman was the next witness.

Franklyn led the handsome young doctor through his early training to his present affiliation with Parkside Polyclinic. He established his experience and expertise and brought him finally to the day when Dr. Mitchell had called, asking him to cover his practice until he was over the flu. It was not the first time Coleman had covered for Mitchell and he had no hesitation in undertaking the responsibility despite his own heavy schedule. Mitchell had briefed him carefully on all his patients, and most especially on Mrs. Simpson, the daughter of Mitchell's long-time friend, John Stewart Reynolds.

As soon as she evidenced the first signs of labor, Coleman had ordered her into the hospital. There, she remained for some eighteen hours, a long, but not necessarily overlong labor for a woman having her first child. Her delivery was not easy, but involved no real medical complications. Franklyn dwelled on that point at some length, finally asking, "Doctor, did you find it necessary to use forceps in this delivery?"

"I did not."

"So there were no marks on the infant, and no chance of any injury to the head as sometimes results from use of forceps?" Franklyn persisted.

"No chance whatsoever," said Coleman. "The birth was not complicated. The infant was not injured in any way."

"Doctor, were you present when the Apgar tests were done?" Franklyn asked.

"Of course," Coleman replied. "In fact, even though it is customary for the delivery room nurse to do both Apgars, I did the first one myself. I wanted to be absolutely sure, in view of Dr. Mitchell's close relationship with the grandfather of the child."

"And what did you find?" Franklyn pursued.

"What my report indicates. . . ." Coleman replied.

Franklyn turned to Heinfelden who held out the hospital record. After Coleman testified that it was indeed his report, Franklyn offered it for identification. Judge Bannon examined it and passed it to Crabtree, who found nothing to object to. He was about to hand it back, when Laura intervened.

"I'd like to see that!" She seized the document from Crabtree's hand. Both she and Chris went over it carefully.

Finally, Chris had to admit in a discouraged whisper, "Exactly the same as the one you photographed. He didn't change a thing."

Laura allowed the report to be marked and received in evidence. It was handed back to Coleman.

"Doctor, according to your report what was the result of the Apgar you did on the Simpson baby?"

"The one-minute Apgar was seven. Certainly in the normal range," Coleman said.

"And the five-minute Apgar?" Franklyn asked.

"Done by the nurse. With a score of nine," Coleman said, using the record to back up his statement.

"Was that the extent of your examination, Doctor?"

"No. I did a complete physical. The infant was in excellent condition, a healthy, active, newborn baby," Coleman reported.

"And did you so note?" Franklyn asked.

"As you can see," Coleman said, brandishing the report.

"Dr. Coleman, what did you do after examining the baby?"

"I instructed the head nurse to keep close watch for any changes and to notify me at once if there were any. Otherwise I would be back on my usual rounds. I also wrote the infant's prescribed diet in the order book. Then I left."

"To resume the other duties involved in your practice?" Franklyn suggested.

"Yes."

"And in your opinion, that was sufficient and proper in such a situation?" Franklyn inquired.

"Considering the uncomplicated delivery, the fact that this was a first child and without apparent Rh involvement, yes."

"Tell me, Doctor, did you notice at that time any indication at all of a jaundiced condition?"

"None whatsoever!"

"Did you get back to see that infant during your afternoon rounds?"

"Actually, no. An emergency arose, an ectopic pregnancy that required immediate surgery. Naturally I had to deal with that first. But I did maintain contact with the nursery staff, frequent contact."

"And what did you learn?"

"That the Reynolds baby . . . I mean the Simpson baby . . . was doing quite well. Eating and retaining food. Sleeping normally. There was no apparent need for concern."

"Did that condition continue, Doctor?" asked Franklyn.

"Unfortunately, no. The next morning the nursery informed me that the infant was exhibiting slight jaundiced coloring."

"And what did you do?"

"I immediately ordered a bilirubin and a Coombs test and left instructions to be called the minute those reports came back from the lab," Coleman stated righteously. "Even if I was in surgery. I was scheduled to do two hysterectomies that afternoon."

"And were your instructions followed?" Franklyn asked.

"They were. When the results came back I was paged in the OR, operating room, that is."

"And then?"

"When I came down from the OR, I examined the lab reports."

"And what did you find?" Franklyn asked.

"The infant had a bilirubin of fourteen."

"Doctor, would that in your opinion be cause for alarm?" Franklyn asked.

"Cause for concern, not alarm. Until a bilirubin approaches twenty there is no real danger. But at fourteen I like to watch them very closely, especially since the Coombs test revealed that the infant was suffering from an Rh incompatibility."

"And when you discovered that, what did you do?" Franklyn prodded.

"I ordered an immediate follow-up bilirubin, and waited right there for the result. I didn't want to waste time."

"And what was the result of that second test, Dr. Coleman?" Franklyn asked routinely as if he expected a direct answer.

"Before the results came down from the lab I called Dr. Mitchell at his home and told him what I'd found. He suggested that I refer the Simpson baby to Metropolitan General at once."

"Did that strike you as unusual advice, Doctor?"

"It did not. It's done all the time," Coleman replied.

Franklyn allowed that to settle before going on. "Doctor, can you explain to the jury why you, a thoroughly

186

trained, experienced doctor, would refer an infant to Metropolitan General?"

"Of course. Metropolitan General is a teaching hospital with interns, residents and a much larger nursing staff than Parkside Polyclinic, which is a private institution. The Simpson baby needed constant observation. Frankly, I would have preferred to do it myself, but with my own practice, plus Dr. Mitchell's, I felt it in the infant's best interest to refer it."

"Having decided that, what did you do?"

"I called Mr. Reynolds and he said . . ."

Crabtree interrupted. "Mr. Reynolds can testify to what he said. Otherwise, this is hearsay evidence and we object to it."

Judge Bannon nodded in agreement.

Franklyn continued, "Doctor, did you call Metropolitan General yourself?"

"I did not."

"Why not?" Franklyn asked blandly.

"Because . . ." and here Coleman looked to Judge Bannon, "I can't answer that if I can't refer to my conversation with Mr. Reynolds."

Bannon contemplated that for an instant, and then ruled, "Just tell us what *you* did and said."

"I called Mr. Reynolds. Then I spoke with Dr. Sobol at Metropolitan General. An ambulance was coming to pick up the Simpson baby. He asked me to have a transcript of the infant's hospital record ready, which I did."

"Tell me, Dr. Coleman, when you made your last examination of the Reynolds baby . . . I mean the Simpson baby, did you notice any signs at all of any neurologic difficulty?"

"None, as my report indicates."

"So that the only problem that existed was the somewhat jaundiced color, the positive Coombs and the lab report of a bilirubin of fourteen?"

"Correct," Coleman stated very firmly.

"Have you had occasion to examine the Simpson infant since that time?"

"No, sir. By the time the baby was released from Metropolitan Hospital, Dr. Mitchell had recovered from the flu."

"So that you can say quite definitely that at all times when you examined that infant it was not suffering from neurologic damage of any kind whatsoever?" Franklyn asked, allowing his voice to rise only slightly.

"Quite definitely!" Coleman said with great conviction.

Franklyn turned away from the witness indicating that he had completed his direct examination. Crabtree rose to undertake the cross-examination, but without much enthusiasm. Coleman had been a good solid witness. There was little to attack him on.

"Tell me, Doctor, why did you decide on Metropolitan General as the proper place to refer your patient?"

"I already testified to that," Coleman retorted. "They had the personnel and the facilities for intensive care. I couldn't devote all the time I would have liked."

"Can we assume from your choice that you think Metropolitan General is a fine hospital?"

"Yes," Coleman declared.

"With first-rate, capable personnel?"

"Yes," Coleman assented, a bit less forthrightly than before.

"You wouldn't have chosen Metropolitan unless you had utmost faith in its staff, would you?"

"Of course not," Coleman said, hesitating slightly. He had no way of knowing where Crabtree was attempting to lead him.

"If you had had any doubts about Metropolitan General and its staff, it would have been malpractice on your part to have referred a patient to them, wouldn't it?"

"I made a professional decision based on my own knowledge of the hospital and its excellent reputation," Coleman declared.

"And from your knowledge and based on its reputation Metropolitan General and its pediatrics department are among the best in the country?" Crabtree persisted.

"I would say so, yes."

"The reputation of Dr. Michael Sobol was known to you?"

"It was. His reputation is excellent."

"Have you ever read any of his research papers?" Crabtree asked.

"I have. They are professionally very sound."

"Dr. Coleman, were you also aware of the reputation of Dr. Christopher Grant?"

"I was not," Coleman said crisply. "And if I had known that the Simpson baby would end up in his hands I would never have consented to refer it."

Chris started to rise but Laura's delicate but firm hand restrained him. Instead of settling back, Chris whispered fiercely, "I want to question him!"

"You can't, you're not a lawyer," Laura said. "Even I can't. I have no official standing here."

"Then I want to talk to Crabtree!" Chris insisted.

By this time even Judge Bannon had to take cognizance of the flurry.

"Will counsel see to it that his client does not interrupt the progress of this case?" he instructed Crabtree.

In a whispered conference Crabtree reprimanded Chris sharply. "This kind of conduct isn't going to help, Doctor!"

"We can't let him get away with it."

"You'd better get used to hearing things like that about yourself, Grant. Because this is only the beginning. Don't forget you wanted this!"

"Ask him about the phone call!" said Chris.

"What phone call?"

"I called him to get more information than was on the

abstract. He couldn't even tell me exactly when the first signs of jaundice appeared," Chris declared.

"Is that important?"

"You're damn right! An infant who exhibits jaundice in the first twenty-four hours is at greater risk."

"Anything else?" Crabtree asked, genuinely interested for the first time.

"Yes, what happened to that second bilirubin test? It never showed up."

"And?"

"Let's see what he says first," said Chris.

Crabtree turned back to the witness. "Dr. Coleman, did you at any time have any conversation with Dr. Grant about the Simpson infant?"

"Yes, I did. On the telephone."

"Did you call him or did he call you?" Crabtree pressed.

"He called me. He wanted some information that was not on the transcript that was sent over with the infant."

"What additional information?" Crabtree asked.

"I didn't make notes, but to the best of my recollection he wanted to know who first noticed the jaundice. I told him, as I just told you, the nurse noticed it first."

"Doctor, why wasn't the time when those signs first appeared on that hospital transcript?"

"I couldn't answer that," Coleman said.

"Do you think it would have been desirable for the other doctor to have that information?"

"Yes, I think so."

"Doctor, isn't it a fact that it is *crucial* for a doctor to know the exact time, since a child who evidences signs of jaundice in the first twenty-four hours is at greater risk than one who evidences jaundice two or three days later?" Crabtree demanded.

"Yes, that's true. And I told him that it was the nurse who first observed the signs and that she did not notice them till the end of the first twenty-four hours," Coleman said.

Chris signaled to Crabtree, but the lawyer shrugged him off. He knew what Chris wanted and he was getting to it. He referred to his notes and while still looking down, asked suddenly, "Dr. Coleman, you said you ordered a second bilirubin test. But we never did hear what it disclosed. Can you tell us?"

"I'm afraid I can't," said Coleman. "Once the infant had been referred that report became academic since I knew that they would do their own tests at Metropolitan."

"You were never curious about what that second test showed?"

"Mr. Crabtree, in the press of daily practice a doctor doesn't have time to indulge his curiosity. He does what he can for those patients he has to treat. That was especially true since I was covering for Dr. Mitchell."

"Did you ever follow up by calling Dr. Grant to inquire about the progress of the Simpson baby?"

"Since I assumed the infant was in good hands I also assumed it would receive proper care," Coleman said. "Frankly, I have had enormous regrets since that time. If I had had any idea of the kind of therapy Dr. Grant was using . . ."

Crabtree interrupted, "Object!"

But Coleman overrode him to conclude, "I would have gone down there myself and taken that infant back!"

Bannon banged his gavel to cut off Coleman's answer, but it was futile. As was his order to the jury to ignore Coleman's last words. Crabtree decided not to pursue his cross-examination any further. He felt that he had at least raised some cloud over Coleman's testimony, though silently he cursed himself for letting the examination get out of hand in that last moment. He felt no better when Harry Franklyn passed up the opportunity to continue with Coleman on re-direct examination. With a slight gesture of his hand, the short attorney indicated he was finished with the witness. If Franklyn didn't pursue the matter, Crabtree knew that his adversary was delighted to have had the question of phototherapy raised in such a provocative way. The jury's appetite had been whetted. Franklyn was willing to let them ponder the matter for a while.

Crabtree retired to the table where Chris exploded in a burst of angry whispers. "Damn it, why did you let him get away with it? How could any doctor *not* care about the results of that second bilirubin?"

Crabtree turned on him. "Look here, Doctor, you stick to medicine! Let me take care of the law. There's a basic rule in cross-examination: never ask any question to which you don't know the answer. How do we know what that second test showed? Or that it could have helped us? You saw what happened at the end. We're in deeper now than we were before I asked your damned questions."

SEVENTEEN

In line with his original strategy, Harry Franklyn now re-called Dr. Mitchell to the stand.

"Doctor, when you and Dr. Coleman agreed that the Simpson baby should be transferred to Metropolitan General, what did you have in mind?"

Crabtree cut in sharply, "Object!"

"Let's hear the answer first, Counselor," Bannon ruled. "Doctor?"

"Well, I thought that they could give the infant more intensive care, due to their large staff."

Franklyn assisted him. "For the reasons Dr. Coleman mentioned before?"

"Yes. At Parkside we have a concentration of excellent practitioners, but Metropolitan has a larger staff with more facilities. For example, they could do the exchange blood transfusion that was clearly indicated . . ."

Before Mitchell could finish, Crabtree rose and objected. Bannon reluctantly sustained him. Franklyn smiled, then continued.

"You had no reservations about referring the infant?"

"Not at that time," Mitchell said.

"But you did have reservations later?"

"It was impossible not to have reservations later, in view of what happened."

"What did happen?" Franklyn asked, a simple question but intended to open up the basic situation upon which the lawsuit rested.

"You mean the day I got that terrible call from Mr. Reynolds . . ."

Judge Bannon leaned across his bench. "Dr. Mitchell, allow Mr. Franklyn to conduct the examination. He is quite able, as you will discover."

Mitchell smiled sheepishly. "I'm sorry, Your Honor."

Without raising his voice, Franklyn resumed, but this time he moved to the far end of the jury box, forcing Mitchell to turn and face the jury as well. The move was not lost on Laura who nudged Chris gently. It was clear that Franklyn was depending heavily on Mitchell's forthcoming testimony. Both Laura and Chris edged closer, ready to make notes.

"Dr. Mitchell," Harry Franklyn asked, "you referred a moment ago to a call you received from Mr. John Reynolds. May I take you back before that time, so that the jury will have an orderly and continuous history of what happened to that point. After the Simpson infant was released from Metropolitan General what was your relationship to it?"

"By that time I was over the flu and able to examine the infant thoroughly. It was apparently in good health, but I studied the transcript and all the lab reports from Metropolitan General anyway."

"Were you favorably impressed by what you found, sir?"

"Yes. And no."

"I'm afraid we will have to insist on a more precise answer than that."

"I was favorably impressed by the *apparent* result. I mean the lab report showed a steadily decreasing bilirubin. The charts indicated the infant's vital signs were all good. I felt we were very lucky," Mitchell said.

"Lucky?"

"It's what I meant before when I said yes and no. I was not that pleased by the method chosen to treat the infant at Metropolitan Hospital."

Franklyn glanced at the jury to determine the degree of their involvement before he asked, "Dr. Mitchell, exactly what kind of treatment are you referring to?"

"This . . . this phototherapy that was used."

"Doctor, could you explain for the jury precisely what phototherapy is?" Franklyn asked.

"Well," Mitchell began, his tone indicating disapproval of the entire procedure, "it is a treatment for jaundice which consists of placing the sick infant under a battery of fluorescent lights for from a few hours to a few days."

"Doctor," said Franklyn, incredulous, as if he had just learned this piece of information, "are you saying that putting an infant under ordinary fluorescent light is an accepted form of treatment?"

"There are doctors who believe in it, sir."

"When did you first learn that such treatment had been used on the Simpson baby?"

"When I read it in the transcript that accompanied the infant on its return to my care."

"Were you disturbed . . ."

Crabtree half rose. "Counsel is leading his witness!"

"Sorry," Franklyn said with a deferential turn to Crabtree. "Dr. Mitchell, what was your professional reaction when you read the record?"

"Frankly, I was greatly disturbed," Mitchell said, using the word Franklyn had suggested to him.

"Would you tell us why?"

"To my mind, phototherapy is too uncertain a treatment, still too undefined in terms of its eventual aftereffects, and not nearly so satisfactory in this kind of case as an exchange transfusion."

195

"Despite the fact that, as I understand it, it is used in some very fine medical institutions?" Franklyn asked, pretending to impeach his own witness.

"That's the trouble with institutions which practice academic medicine! Mind you, young men *do* have to have places to learn, to train, but the tendency in such places is to lean too far in the direction of experimentation."

"Object," Crabtree sang out.

But both judge and jury were too interested in this aspect of Mitchell's testimony, and Bannon barely breathed "Denied," before continuing to listen to Mitchell.

The doctor went on: "There is a vast difference between men who practice medicine as a profession and those who approach it as a field for the testing of new ideas." Mitchell hesitated as if not wanting to expose to laymen the internecine warfare that was waged among professionals.

But Franklyn was eager to get the statement into the record before Crabtree objected. "What difference, Doctor?"

"Well, academicians tend to forsake the tried and true for the new and experimental, just to see the results," Mitchell declared.

"Using the patient as a guinea pig, so to speak?" Franklyn suggested.

Crabtree was up out of his chair and this time Bannon did sustain his objection. Franklyn apologized for his remark, then continued:

"Tell me, Doctor, why would any doctor do that?"

"Why?" Mitchell echoed rhetorically. "How else are these young men going to make names for themselves? They carry on their experiments, they write their papers, they have them published in all sorts of medical journals. Their next promotion depends on what they've had published in the last year or two."

Mitchell would have gone on if Crabtree hadn't objected.

But Bannon found the testimony to be relevant and enlightening and permitted Mitchell to continue. Franklyn urged him on.

"Tell the jury, Doctor, if you will, more about this phase of medicine, which I am sure is as interesting to them as it is to me."

"It is natural, I suppose, for there to be friction between those men who practice the profession and those who teach it. The demands are different. We practitioners must deal with the day-to-day problems. When it comes to applying a cure to a patient our standards are not the same. We are more exacting, more cautious. We pay more attention to experience. We are more likely to be conservative. To put it simply, we'd rather be safe than sorry."

"Exactly how does that apply in this case, Doctor?" Franklyn prodded.

"I am sure if a reliable method such as an exchange transfusion had been used on this unfortunate child we would not be in this courtroom today. That child would be perfectly healthy and normal," Mitchell declared.

"Doctor, when was the first time you had occasion to discover that the infant was damaged?" Franklyn asked.

"The day I referred to before, when Mr. Reynolds called and asked if I could come to his home and examine the child."

Franklyn then, slowly and methodically led Mitchell through the details of his neurologic findings.

"And what did you conclude from all this?"

"There was no question about it. The child had suffered brain damage."

"Has the condition changed since that time?" Franklyn asked.

"It has become more marked."

Franklyn moved closer to Mitchell. "Doctor, in your expert opinion, what caused the condition in this child?"

"Based on a study of the laboratory tests involved, the doctors' records, the hospital records, the treatments prescribed, the only possible cause could have been the phototherapy applied by Dr. Grant," Mitchell stated with great regret, as if he were reluctant to place blame.

"How can you pinpoint the cause so exactly?"

"Because at no time was there a bilirubin recorded that exceeded sixteen milligrams per one hundred milliliters. An infant born only two weeks preterm, at twenty-six hundred grams, is not likely to suffer brain damage from a bilirubin that does not climb up to twenty."

"Doctor," Franklyn pursued, "why do you put so much stress on the infant's weight and the fact that it was only two weeks preterm?"

"Because in a really premature baby, meaning one born before full term and weighing less than twenty-five hundred grams, a bilirubin much less than twenty has, in some cases, caused brain damage. But that was not so in the instance of the Simpson baby."

"Dr. Mitchell, if your advice had been sought at the time the Simpson baby was being treated by Dr. Christopher Grant, would you have agreed with the decision that was made to use phototherapy?"

"I would not!" Mitchell declared dogmatically.

"Would you have advised the use of a complete exchange transfusion of the infant's blood?"

"I would!"

"In your opinion, then, Dr. Mitchell, did the use of phototherapy constitute a departure from good medical practice?" Franklyn asked, a bit more loudly.

Chris felt Laura stiffen. She had warned him during their strategy sessions that the key factor in any malpractice case was whether the defendant had departed from good medical practice. Once that question was introduced and answered in the affirmative, Chris's chances with the jury were not favorable. He waited for Mitchell's answer.

"In my opinion, in this case, the use of phototherapy was

definitely a departure from good medical practice," Mitchell stated firmly.

"One more question, Doctor. With phototherapy in its present state of development, would you consider it necessary for a doctor to receive informed consent from the parents or the guardian of the infant about to be so treated?"

"The relative responsible for any patient should be informed of all the dangers of any therapy before consenting to have it used," Mitchell declared. "I understand it was not done in this case."

"Move to strike that last!" said Crabtree.

"Strike it!" Bannon ruled, though he appeared almost annoyed at the objection.

"That is all, Doctor," Franklyn said quietly, but as he moved to the counsel table there was no disguising the fact that he was satisfied he had laid a solid foundation for his case on two grounds: malpractice and failure to secure informed consent.

Crabtree accepted that fact as well. Instead of rising to cross-examine Mitchell at once, he asked for a brief recess to confer with his client. Crabtree's strategy was manifold. He did want to confer with Chris, but he also wanted to give Mitchell a chance to cool off. Some witnesses build up an emotional involvement in testifying. Given a chance to relax, their momentum slowed, they are easier to handle on cross-examination.

Crabtree, Waller, Chris and Laura huddled at the far end of the corridor outside the courtroom.

"Is Mitchell vulnerable on any medical ground?" Crabtree asked.

"He is," Chris replied. "Look at all those papers I gave you on phototherapy, the hospitals where it's used, the statistics in thousands of successful cases."

"I've got all that," Crabtree said. "I want to know did he

make any misstatements of medical fact? Is his suggested treatment subject to attack?"

"The material we gave you on exchange blood transfusions," Laura said. "There's enough there to attack him on."

Recalling no error in Mitchell's facts, Chris began to point out the differences in the two schools of medical thought.

Crabtree cut him off. "I know all that. It's not enough. Two schools of thought that disagree, naturally every doctor takes one side or the other. But that doesn't impeach Mitchell personally and professionally. I need some specific thing he said on which I can trap him, because he is hurting us badly."

"I wish we had a transcript," Laura said thoughtfully. "But I could swear that Coleman said Mitchell suggested referring the baby. Whereas Mitchell testified Coleman called him to suggest it."

"That's right," said Chris.

"I'd better check that before I try it," Crabtree said. "Mitchell is so strong now that I wouldn't want to wind up looking like a fool."

The clerk was summoning all parties back to the courtroom. Before they reached the door young Juan Melez fell in alongside Chris and Laura.

"Dr. Grant," Melez began.

Laura intervened. "No comment."

Melez smiled. "I can understand how that would apply to the doctor. But not to me."

"Look, we're wanted inside," Laura said.

"Lady, I'm here because the young mothers in my part of the city are asking for *El Medico*. They all want him to treat their babies. They found out he's on trial instead of being in the hospital and they're upset. I'm here to try to reassure them, but it's going heavy on you, Doctor. Real heavy. If I can help in any way . . ." He renewed his earlier offer.

"We have to go back," Laura insisted.

"Okay, just remember what I said," Melez said.

Mitchell resumed the stand. Crabtree, a sheaf of notes in his hand, rose to confront him. He had to wait a few minutes until it was quiet, for since midmorning more and more spectators had abandoned other cases to fill the courtroom.

Silence within the courtroom was finally ensured by a wry comment from Judge Bannon: "All right, folks, this isn't a TV show you're watching. You're not allowed to talk while it's going on. Nor can you get up and get a beer. And we do not allow potato chips. They make too much noise. So let's all settle down. Else I'll clear this court as quickly as you can change channels."

Crabtree decided to attack at once. If he could shake Mitchell at the outset, he might have his way with him for the rest of the cross-examination. Referring to his notes, none of which bore the information he was about to use, Crabtree began.

"Dr. Mitchell, in your various discussions with Dr. Coleman about this case, did the two of you always agree?"

"We did, indeed. We were both shocked at the method of treatment Dr. Grant used and appalled at the outcome," Mitchell asserted.

"At no time did you two disagree?" Crabtree persisted.

"At no time. Not when it was decided to refer the infant. Not when we discovered that phototherapy was used. And I might add, not in any conversation we have had since."

Though Mitchell's answers were exceeding the questions, Crabtree did not protest. The firmer Mitchell was now, the more unsettled he might become later.

"Doctor, have you known Dr. Michael Sobol for a long time?"

"Many years," Mitchell said, adding, "An outstanding man in the field. I found it hard to believe that he would sponsor a man like Dr. Grant."

"Doctor, if you had known Dr. Grant was on Sobol's staff, would you have been so quick to suggest that the Simpson infant be referred to Metropolitan General?"

"Would I . . . I didn't suggest referring the infant. Dr. Coleman did. Of course I agreed," Mitchell stated in such a way as to correct Crabtree's error.

"That's strange," Crabtree said, turning to the stenographer. "Mr. Blau, would you be good enough to read the question and answer I had you mark in Dr. Coleman's testimony?"

The court stenographer looked up at Judge Bannon who nodded gravely. Blau read: "Question by Mr. Franklyn, 'What did you do?' Answer by Dr. Coleman, 'I called Dr. Mitchell at his home and told him what I'd found. He suggested that I refer the Simpson baby to Metropolitan General at once.' "

"Thank you," Crabtree said. Mitchell's face had changed from pink to red. "It is Dr. Coleman's testimony that *you* suggested referring the infant. Is it still your testimony that the suggestion came from Dr. Coleman?"

"As I . . ." Mitchell began. "To the best of my recollection it was definitely Coleman's suggestion. Though . . ." Mitchell stopped.

"Though?" Crabtree pressed, for his gambit had achieved the effect he sought. When Mitchell did not answer, he repeated, "Though, Doctor?"

"Though I don't see what difference it makes, as long as we both agreed it was the proper thing to do," Mitchell said.

"I was merely trying to qualify your previous statement that you and Dr. Coleman agreed on everything involved in this case. Can we say that, on this point at least, there is some area of disagreement?"

"If you get any comfort out of saying that," Mitchell conceded, dismissing the entire matter as inconsequential. But Crabtree could tell the old man had been shaken.

"Dr. Mitchell, are you thoroughly familiar with the literature on phototherapy?"

"I make it a point to keep abreast of all new developments," he declared, bristling.

"If you had to make a random guess as to how many hospitals use phototherapy, what would you say?"

Mitchell stared upward a moment and then declared, "Several hundred."

Crabtree pursued, "Can we be more precise, two hundred, three, four, five? What is several hundred?"

"Several hundred," Mitchell repeated. "But if I had to be more specific I'd say three or four hundred."

"Would it surprise you if I said there are as many as a thousand hospitals using phototherapy?"

"It wouldn't surprise me. Nor would it impress me. A mistake does not gain medical credence by the number of times it is repeated. I can cite hundreds of instances where a treatment or medication gained worldwide acceptance and was later discovered to be dangerous, even fatal," said Mitchell.

"Do you always tend to be conservative in your adoption of new methods, new drugs?"

Mitchell smiled for his first time on cross-examination. "Among experienced practitioners we have a rule. Use any new medication on strangers first. Then on patients. And finally on your own family if the other two groups survive."

Even the jury enjoyed that, laughing aloud. Bannon made no effort to silence them, though he did glare at the spectators. Rather than go against the tide of feeling, Crabtree permitted himself a broad grin. "Doctor, if you had to make another rule, would you say that young doctors tend to adopt new techniques and new medications sooner than more mature doctors?"

"Older men with more experience tend to be more discerning, more skeptical. Younger men, seeking to build careers, are more willing to accept the new. Especially in these times," Mitchell said.

That last phrase intrigued Crabtree and he decided to pursue it. "In these times, Doctor?"

"With so much activism in the world, young doctors have become politicized. Try to get some of them to show up in a hospital with their hair a proper length. Or without beards."

"Do you object to beards on doctors, Doctor?" Crabtree asked.

"It happens that I do! A doctor's appearance is a part of his total professional demeanor. It affects the patient's confidence."

"Doctor, haven't there been some great doctors with beards? Sigmund Freud for one?"

"I would not want to have one of *my* patients treated by Sigmund Freud. His record of cures was very poor."

Crabtree smiled. "Doctor, do you disapprove of young doctors because of the way they look or because of their ready acceptance of new methods of therapy?"

"You are certainly correct as to the latter."

"And you feel that way about phototherapy, the treatment used in this case?"

"Most decidedly!" Mitchell said.

Suddenly Crabtree changed course. "Doctor, do you know that an exchange blood transfusion can produce serious complications?"

"Of course," Mitchell said.

"Can you explain some of them to the jury?"

"If you wish," Mitchell said grudgingly. "In some cases an exchange can lead to infection or shock, but the mortality rate is very very low."

"So the exchange transfusion, which you would have prescribed in this case, can have serious complications?" Crabtree tried to pin Mitchell down.

"Any treatment can. But the exchange transfusion is the most effective treatment and presents only infinitesimal risks."

"Doctor," Crabtree began, "do you of your own knowledge, know any young doctor who used phototherapy and induced an infection in an infant?"

"Infection? I don't see the relevance . . ." Mitchell protested.

Franklyn rose from his chair. "Your honor, there is a sound legal point in the doctor's observation. The question is irrelevant."

Bannon nodded and turned to reprimand Crabtree. But the defense attorney was swifter in his argument, "Your Honor, the essence of this case is a form of medical treatment applied to an infant. I think it of the utmost relevance to discover what other forms of therapy were available to the defendants in making their professional decision."

Bannon hesitated, then murmured, "I will allow it."

"Doctor, in case you've forgotten the question, do you know of any doctor who has induced an infection in an infant by using phototherapy?"

"I would say no. No, I do not."

"Do you know of any case where phototherapy has induced convulsions in an infant?"

"No," Mitchell conceded.

"Or an irregular heartbeat?"

"No."

"Yet those are complications that can result from an exchange transfusion, are they not?"

"Not if it's done correctly!" said Mitchell, his pride damaged by the admissions Crabtree had elicited from him. "A proper exchange transfusion is done very very slowly. If the infant begins to react, if its vital signs show any marked deviation, the transfusion is stopped at once."

Crabtree had allowed Mitchell to go on at length for it served to prove the point he was about to make next. "Then, Doctor, is it correct to say that the alternative treatment available to Dr. Grant was not without risk? In fact, it might have turned out to be far more risky than the photo-therapy which was used. Might it not?"

"Not at all!" Mitchell declared surprisingly.

"Despite what you've testified in the last few minutes, Doctor?"

"Yes!" Mitchell was quite firm. "At least with an exchange transfusion the results are immediate and can be dealt with. But with phototherapy you never know. The effects can show up weeks later or, as in this case, months later!"

"Object," said Crabtree. "There is still no proof that phototherapy had anything to do with the condition of this infant!"

Bannon leaned forward, stared down at Crabtree. "Mr. Crabtree, the court has granted you great latitude in your cross-examination. I think you have to be bound by the results. The doctor's answer will be allowed to stand."

Chris tried to remain impassive, mainly because Laura had a firm grip on his forearm under the table. The more damaging Mitchell's testimony had been, the more necessary it was for Chris not to explode into a confrontation that would only bring a rebuke from Judge Bannon and reinforce the episode in the jury's mind.

Crabtree sought to retreat gracefully from the trap he had set himself. "I'm sure when my client takes the stand he will answer that, Dr. Mitchell."

"I'll be interested to hear what he has to say," Mitchell challenged, completing the cross-examination.

Saving his most powerful ammunition for subsequent battles, Harry Franklyn excused the witness.

Since it was too late in the day to put a new witness

on the stand, Bannon excused the jury with a warning not to discuss the case among themselves or with anyone else.

They stood on the top step of the courthouse. Paul Crabtree, Avery Waller, Chris Grant and Laura Winters. They were grim and serious. Crabtree tried to put a better face on things by saying, "The plaintiff always has it his own way on the first day."

"We should have attacked Mitchell more strongly!" Chris exploded.

"I wouldn't worry about that if I were you," Crabtree warned. "I'd worry why Franklyn didn't exploit him more. What's he holding back?"

"That old bastard Mitchell is prejudiced and behind the times!" Chris shot back. "The jury should have had that pointed out!"

Crabtree answered more directly. "Look here, Doctor, any time you want to take over this defense just get my company off the hook."

"Paul, let's not fight among ourselves." Waller tried to assuage Crabtree. "It was a bad first day, but maybe things'll improve tomorrow."

"You know Harry Franklyn, he doesn't shoot his wad the first day." Angrily turning his back on Chris, Crabtree started down the courthouse steps. Waller hurried after him.

"You're too edgy, Paul. It wasn't that bad."

"Wasn't it?" said Crabtree. "My instinct tells me otherwise. It's more than two very impressive-looking doctors telling a story that is basically beyond attack. That little maneuver about who first suggested sending the baby to Metropolitan didn't fool anybody. Both doctors agreed on all the major points of testimony. I couldn't shake them."

"You didn't have a chance. But it'll come, it'll come."

"With Harry Franklyn?" Crabtree smiled bitterly. "Did

I ever tell you that they offered Franklyn a lifetime retainer to work for the insurance company?"

"They did?"

"Not that they wanted him to work *for* them. They just didn't want him to work *against* them. And it was worth a half million dollar a year fee to make sure of that. He turned them down flat."

"With his practice and his reputation, I don't blame him."

"I'll hold my own in a courtroom against anyone, even Franklyn. But I need something to work with. We haven't got it," Crabtree said vehemently.

EIGHTEEN

THE SECOND day of the trial opened quietly. Harry Franklyn introduced the first medical expert for the prosecution. Dr. Walter Lawler. Tall, big-framed, with a healthy complexion and sharp brown eyes, Lawler was an impressive-looking man. The medical credentials and affiliations that Franklyn elicited quickly qualified him as an expert in pediatric neurology. The court accepted him without protest and Franklyn launched into the body of his testimony.

"Dr. Lawler, have you ever examined an infant named John Reynolds Simpson?"

"I have."

"And what did you find?"

"The infant was definitely brain-damaged. It did not respond in a normal way to the tests I made. For a child of almost one year it is decidedly and grossly retarded," Lawler said soberly.

"Were those the usual tests that you perform on an infant to make such a determination?" Franklyn continued.

"The usual tests that I, and all other pediatric neurologists, make on such infants," Lawler explained.

"Doctor, based on your own experience and expertise, do

you believe that the damage is reversible?"

"It is not," Lawler stated categorically.

"Not even if some new discovery were to be made?" Franklyn asked softly.

"No. Brain tissue is not self-regenerating. Once damage is done, it is done. Irreversible means just that, never subject to change or improvement."

"Doctor, based on the tests you've made, would you give us your estimate of the degree of functioning power that the child has now, or will have?"

"In my opinion John Reynolds Simpson will, at the optimum, achieve a mental age of about six."

"And will never exceed that level?" asked Franklyn.

"Not in my opinion," Lawler said more firmly than before.

Franklyn paused to let the jury absorb those shocking facts. After consulting his notes, he continued:

"Doctor, could you tell us the various causes of brain damage in infants?"

"Well, brain damage can be hereditary."

"Was it in this case?" Franklyn asked.

"No, sir. Or the child would not have had a normal Apgar at birth."

"Any other causes?" Franklyn asked.

"Brain damage can result from other traumas such as a disease suffered by the mother during pregnancy, usually in the first three months."

"Did that happen in this case?"

"No!" Lawler declared flatly, then went on to explain, "Such damage, in the majority of cases, is revealed in the initial Apgar."

"Any other causes of brain damage, Doctor?"

"Certain medications given to the mother can have severe effects on the infant," Lawler replied, volunteering, "the most recent well-known cause being thalidomide."

"Did you consider that possibility in this case?"

"Of course. But the records show that no questionable medication was administered to the mother."

"What did that lead you to conclude, Doctor?"

"That the cause of brain damage in this case was kernicterus."

"For the benefit of the jury, Doctor, exactly what is *kernicterus?*"

Lawler faced the jury. "It is a condition that results from an excess of bilirubin in the blood. As a general rule, when it achieves a concentration of twenty milligrams per one hundred milliliters or more it will destroy the brain-stem and cells."

"Doctor, as far as you know, was the bilirubin count in infant John Reynolds Simpson ever as high as twenty before he was transferred to Metropolitan General Hospital?"

"No."

"Then when the infant was referred it was jaundiced due to an Rh incompatibility, but not near the danger level insofar as the bilirubin count was concerned?"

"That is exactly right," Lawler said.

"So that any damage that occurred must have occurred *after* the infant was referred?"

"There is no doubt about it," Lawler's certainty was growing with each positive answer that Franklyn encouraged him to give.

"Doctor, is it significant to you that there is no laboratory report on record which shows that infant to have a bilirubin of over twenty?"

"Not particularly."

"Why not?"

"Because we've had evidence of brain damage in cases where the bilirubin never quite reached twenty. I become apprehensive when a bilirubin exceeds fifteen."

"And when it reaches fifteen or sixteen, Doctor?"

"I am inclined to urge an exchange transfusion at once," Lawler stated flatly.

Chris sat staring at Walter Lawler. A respected man, with a distinguished history as a pediatric neurologist, Lawler's was the most damaging testimony yet. He was beginning to make the direct connection between Chris Grant's treatment and the damage done to the child. Harry Franklyn certainly knew how to build and present a malpractice case.

Even the jury sensed the importance of Lawler's testimony. They were perfectly still, leaning forward in their chairs. John Stewart Reynolds leaned forward too, his face cupped in his hands, his elbows resting on the counsel table.

Not wishing to disturb the air of quiet expectancy he had so carefully built up, Franklyn spoke even more softly than before. "Doctor, are you familiar with the medical treatment known as phototherapy?"

"I am."

"Have you ever used it?"

"I have," Lawler said.

"Do you find it effective?" Franklyn asked.

"Under certain limited conditions," Lawler conceded, "it is helpful."

"What conditions?" Franklyn led him further.

"If there is no urgency, if the jaundice is not too severe. Then it might be helpful as a safeguard."

"Based on what you know of this particular case, would you have prescribed phototherapy?"

"I most decidedly would not!"

"Why?"

"The need here was to get the situation under control as soon as possible. Though the bilirubin was only sixteen there was an Rh problem and a blood exchange was clearly indicated."

"And that's the procedure you would have followed?" Franklyn asked.

"The effects of a blood exchange are immediate. Phototherapy takes longer. When a child's mental condition is

212

hanging in the balance one does not take halfway measures."

"So that even though phototherapy might be beneficial in other cases, it is your opinion that it was the wrong procedure to follow in this case."

"It was."

"And you say that based on your study of the child's medical record."

"On that, and one other thing."

"Which is?"

"The present condition of the infant. That's the ultimate proof that phototherapy was the wrong procedure to follow," Lawler stated with a firmness that indicated his opinion was not subject to correction or change.

Chris Grant slumped back in his chair, his shirt damp against his body, his pulse rate so swift and hard he was aware of every beat.

The fact that Lawler had been so effective made Crabtree's cross-examination vitally important, for this was not one of the two doctors involved in treating the child, but an eminent and independent expert.

Crabtree rose quickly. "Doctor, did I understand you to say that, confronted with the facts that appeared in the record, you would have resorted to an exchange transfusion?"

"Yes," Lawler replied.

"Then may I ask you if your answer would be the same if you had examined the record as it was initially presented to Dr. Grant?"

"Of course," Lawler said.

"Without even knowing what facts were presented to Dr. Grant?" Crabtree asked sharply.

"Well, I assume they were the same. Laboratory results. Vital signs."

"Doctor, do you know whether the facts contained in that file were actually the same as those presented to Dr. Grant?"

"Now that you ask, no," Lawler conceded.

"So that it is incorrect, or at least unfounded, for you to express an opinion on what you *might* have done in a given circumstance without knowing precisely what that circumstance was, isn't it?"

"I was going on the basis of what I had seen and read in the medical reports."

"Did any test in the files show a bilirubin of higher than twenty?"

"Sixteen was the highest reported bilirubin."

"Would you term an infant with a bilirubin that peaked at sixteen as severely endangered?"

"I don't acknowledge your terminology, sir," Lawler retorted.

"Was there any record in that file that indicated that the infant was in imminent danger?"

"That's a subjective judgment to be made by the doctor," said Lawler.

"Doctor, the fact that there was no lab finding indicating a dangerous bilirubin count—wouldn't that have played some part in determining the therapy you would have suggested?" Crabtree insisted.

"It would have," Lawler admitted. Crabtree afforded himself a moment of reassurance until Lawler volunteered, "Except for one thing."

Crabtree's first instinct was to have that part of the answer struck, but he knew the jury would remember it. And worse, Franklyn was sure to exploit it in his redirect examination. Crabtree had no choice but to ask.

"What one thing, Doctor?"

"The fact that the infant was being referred from another hospital, by a doctor with good credentials. That alone would have alerted me. I would have had to assume that an imminent danger did exist, or was suspected, regardless of the lab findings," Lawler explained. "Certainly I would have felt obligated to apply the most immediate effective steps available."

Whatever Crabtree had achieved by his first questions was swept away by that explanation. It was necessary for him to attack again as quickly as possible. "Doctor, did you testify that an exchange transfusion has an immediate effect, whereas phototherapy takes much longer?"

"Yes," Lawler declared.

"Dr. Lawler, have you never heard of cases in which phototherapy has had an effect within a few hours?"

"Well, there have been cases reported . . ." Lawler evaded.

"A few cases? Many cases?"

"I wouldn't know how to answer that," said Lawler.

"Would it help if I offered you some papers substantiating the facts that have been published in recognized pediatric journals?"

"I would accept the statement that there have been a number of cases in which phototherapy has worked quickly," Lawler said, "but not so swiftly as an exchange transfusion."

Crabtree didn't mind Lawler's postscript. At least he had forced the imperturbable doctor to back away from one of his most significant statements. He was no longer the unassailable witness he had appeared at first. Crabtree decided to exploit his advantage.

"Dr. Lawler, what is the obligation of a doctor in any given situation, as it relates to the patient?"

"To do his best to diagnose and treat the condition involved, as expeditiously as possible."

"Is it your opinion that Dr. Grant did not follow that course of action?"

"Based on the results, I would have to say he did not select the best course of treatment."

"That's not what I asked, Doctor. My question was if,

by your own definition, Dr. Grant did his best to diagnose and treat the condition he found, as expeditiously as possible!" Crabtree argued.

"The results tell us otherwise."

"Do they?" Crabtree countered. "Or does hindsight tell us that you, knowing what you know *now*, would not have followed the same course? There is a difference, Doctor, isn't there?"

Lawler hesitated and Crabtree enlarged on his question: "Or are you telling us, Doctor, that anyone who disagreed with your opinion or used a different therapy from you had to be wrong?"

"I didn't say that."

"Well, perhaps we can clarify things if I restate my question. Is it a doctor's professional obligation to achieve a cure in each case? Or is it his duty to exercise his best judgment, in a conscientious professional way and in accord with accepted medical practice?"

Lawler contemplated the consequences of his answer, then replied, "I would accept that, sir."

"Then I ask you, without having examined the patient at that time, relying solely on a file, are you in a position to state that Dr. Grant did *not* do his best, in a conscientious professional way and in accordance with accepted medical practice?"

"I think you're toying with words, Mr. Crabtree."

"Doctor, do you make it a practice to give medical advice over the phone?" Crabtree asked suddenly.

"Sometimes," said Lawler.

"Do you mean, Doctor, if I called you in the middle of the night and described a child's condition to you, would you unhesitatingly give advice on the phone?"

"Only if I knew the child."

"But you never saw the Simpson child until some days ago, did you, Doctor?"

"No, I did not," Lawler admitted.

"So that for you to express an opinion now as to what you would have done a year ago, when you had not examined the infant, is, to say the least, presumptuous!" Crabtree attacked.

"Object!" Harry Franklyn called out, indicating that he had a powerful voice when forced to use it.

"Sustained," Judge Bannon ruled, coming to Lawler's defense. "Counsel will confine himself to questions, not observations."

For the first time Chris Grant felt that Crabtree was not only determined to protect him, but was a competent lawyer. He glanced at Laura who seemed to share his new optimism.

Crabtree, meantime, rephrased his attack. "Dr. Lawler, would you say that a doctor who has examined a patient is in a better position to make a decision as to treatment than a doctor who has never examined that patient?"

"As a general rule, yes," Lawler conceded. "But not in this case."

"Why not?" Crabtree challenged.

"Because in this case we know the result," Lawler said vindictively. "And the result was disastrous."

"Dr. Lawler, in the course of your long practice have you ever made a mistake? An honest mistake?

"Come now," said Crabtree when Lawler remained silent, "you can admit to being human. Surely you're not about to tell us that doctors are perfect?" Crabtree had deliberately softened his approach to give Lawler a graceful way to agree with him.

"No one pretends doctors are always perfect," said Lawler.

"Isn't that why doctors are judged by a more intelligent standard: Did he do his job conscientiously and in accord with good medical practice?"

"Yes," Lawler agreed.

"Doesn't it also follow that only another doctor who was

present, who actually examined the patient, could really pass judgment on whether the doctor followed good medical practice?" Crabtree asked, confident he had maneuvered Lawler into a defenseless position.

Lawler's answer caught him by surprise. "Not in this case."

"Why not?"

"With a choice of therapies, he chose the wrong one, the slow one, the unsure one. You simply do not gamble with the life of an infant under such circumstances!" Lawler declared, dogmatic once again.

Everything Crabtree had structured so carefully was swept away with that single reply. Yet he had to continue.

"Doctor, isn't it true that a doctor may make a mistake without being guilty of malpractice?"

Before Lawler could answer, Chris Grant stood up, thrusting aside Laura's restraining hand. "No matter what this lawyer says, I do not admit to having made a mistake! He's not my lawyer. He was hired by an insurance company and I don't want him making any admission for me!"

Judge Bannon banged his gavel and glared down from the bench. "Young man, you will sit down and refrain from any further outbursts. As it is, we will now have to consider the effect of your interruption on this trial. Counsel will approach the bench!"

Crabtree, Waller, Franklyn and Heinfelden came forward and an intense whispered side bar discussion followed. Mere disclosure that an insurance company was involved could be grounds for a mistrial since juries were known to react with great antipathy toward large companies, both in determining liability and in the size of the verdicts they voted. On the other hand, Crabtree had to speculate on whether he would be better or worse off with a new trial. He decided there was nothing to be gained by starting over. For his part, he would waive any claim to a mistrial.

Displaying some false reluctance, Franklyn agreed to go

along. For he had reconfirmed something that would be of enormous value to his case. Chris Grant had revealed himself to be young, emotional, dedicated and hence, as a witness, extremely vulnerable. Whatever else happened, Franklyn knew that he could win his case during his cross-examination of Chris Grant. No, Harry Franklyn wanted no mistrial.

Crabtree resumed his cross-examination. To lighten the moment he said, "Dr. Lawler, where was I, when I was so rudely interrupted?" The witness smiled, some of the jurors laughed. Chris Grant burned with resentment but Laura kept him quiet if not calm.

"Oh, yes," Crabtree recovered, "I was asking if a doctor's mistake is always to be considered malpractice."

"No, not always," Lawler agreed.

"So that if a young man exercised his best professional judgment, and did so in conformity with accepted medical practice, he might be wrong, but not culpable?" Crabtree tried to arrive at some favorable conclusion to his examination.

But Lawler would only say, "As a general rule, yes. In this particular case, no."

"Despite all the literature on the subject, all the proof that has been amassed, all the hospitals that use phototherapy as part of their daily practice?" Crabtree tried to wring a concession from Lawler.

"The fact that a therapy is approved and used does not mean that it is proper or indicated in a given circumstance," Lawler declared. "In my judgment, in this case, it was a mistake. A sad and costly mistake."

Crabtree realized that he had lost his momentum. The witness had slipped from his fingers like the fish an angler loses while trying to unhook it. Inwardly he cursed Chris's interruption.

The session was over. At the plaintiff's table there was an air of satisfied confidence. Chris noticed John Reynolds exchange some words with Harry Franklyn. They were a strange pair. Reynolds, tall, solid, physically strong. Franklyn, short, slight, a ferret of a man, with sharp dark eyes. Even when he smiled it was a frugal display of emotion. Chris knew that before the trial was over he would have to face that small man. And he had already come to fear him.

At the defense table, Crabtree and Waller said nothing. But the desultory way they gathered up their papers clearly revealed how badly the day had gone. Crabtree pleaded a need to go to the law library before the morning session, Waller had other obligations that took him off. Chris and Laura were left standing alone at the foot of the courthouse steps.

"I'd better get back to the hospital," he said. "There are two cases I've got to look at."

She nodded, she understood.

"If you care to wait, we could have a late dinner," he offered. "Or you could come to the hospital with me."

"No, I've got some research to do, too," she said.

"Okay."

He leaned over to kiss her good-bye. She seized him suddenly, held him tight, but avoided his lips.

"Laurie?" he asked, apprehensive.

"I don't know why I did that," she admitted. She kissed him on the lips, with her usual intensity. He watched her as she ran down the stairs briskly and got into a cab. Something had changed, but whether it was in her or in him he wasn't sure.

NINETEEN

PAUL CRABTREE made the phone call the moment he reached his office. He spoke to Tom Brady, Chairman of the Board of Trustees of Metropolitan General.

Three hours later, Crabtree, Brady, and a majority of the trustees were assembled in the paneled board room. Crabtree recited the unhappy events of the day and then made an urgent recommendation that they reopen contact with Reynolds' law firm to try to reach a settlement.

"Regardless of the consequences to Dr. Sobol and Dr. Grant?" Brady asked.

"Regardless of any other factor but the future and the reputation of Metropolitan General," Crabtree asserted. Avery Waller agreed. He could foresee only disaster if the trial was allowed to continue.

Brady was inclined to discuss the matter with Mike Sobol, as were a few of the others, but Crabtree was opposed.

"He misled us once before."

Mrs. Forster came to Sobol's defense. "I resent that. I think Dr. Sobol is one of the most honorable men I've ever known. He helped take care of my own Emily during a pregnancy that most other doctors advised be terminated. He and the obstetrician brought her through beautifully. Nights when I put my grandson to bed I think that he might never have been born except for Mike Sobol."

Crabtree leaned back from the table, a gesture of disapproval which Mrs. Forster was quick to resent. She glared across at him. "It's not merely a matter of sentiment! He's a fine man and he made quite a strong argument when he said that we must consider the effect on future applicants if we didn't defend our own when they were under attack."

Crabtree turned to the chairman. "Mr. Brady, may I have your permission to speak frankly? Very frankly."

"God, man, that's why we're here," Brady declared. "This is no time for small courtesies."

"Well," Crabtree began, "when a lawyer is in a courtroom, marshaling his facts, watching the other side present its case, he sometimes gets the first clear view of his entire case.

"I must admit I was moved by Dr. Sobol's plea at our last meeting. But sitting in the courtroom this morning, hearing those doctors testify, knowing it was only the beginning of a tidal wave of testimony, the whole picture was suddenly clarified. Dr. Grant is going to sustain a number of attacks which he will not be able to survive. And while today the emphasis was on Dr. Grant, soon there will be insinuations that it wasn't just Grant who was responsible, but Metropolitan General. Else why would we be there defending him?

"How do I know? Because we started this trial with an empty courtroom, but today spectators were lined up outside the door, including a number of newspapermen. Soon the general public will be saying that it's this hospital that's guilty of practicing therapies that are questionable while shielding and defending doctors who are unsound and not sufficiently concerned with the safety of their patients."

"What's that to do with Dr. Sobol?" said Mrs. Forster.

"That nice, able, gentle man, without meaning to, has misled us. If you reconsider in light of what happened today what he said, you will see that his is the precise reason why we have to end this lawsuit as fast as possible. Sobol convinced us that promising doctors wouldn't want to come here if we didn't defend Grant. Well, let me ask you, how eager will they be if the reputation of this hospital is destroyed?"

Brady was perplexed. Moved by the soundness of the argument, yet concerned about the effects. "Shouldn't we discuss this with Mike Sobol before we do anything?"

Waller interceded. "I advise against it. You people are charged with the responsibility of running a hospital. You cannot be guided by a man who, at best, is only an employee. This board has to make its own decision and the sooner the better." Waller looked around the table. "If it will make your determination any easier we'll withdraw and wait outside. On the other hand, if there is any information we can offer . . ."

Mrs. Forster's hand went up. "What do we do if Mike Sobol says he will resign?"

"That is an unfortunate consequence. But men pass on. Hospitals endure, *if* they are properly run," Waller said.

At Brady's invitation the two attorneys left the room.

It was just past midnight when the board voted to empower Paul Crabtree and Avery Waller to engage in discussions which might lead to an early settlement of the case. Word of that vote, unanimous except for Mrs. Forster who abstained, would not reach Mike Sobol or Chris Grant for several days.

Before court opened the next morning, Paul Crabtree met in chambers with Judge Bannon and informed him that, under the proper auspices and without prejudice to either side, it might be possible to discuss settlement. Bannon received the advice with a simple nod of the head. He would bring his good offices to bear.

By the time Harry Franklyn was introducing his first witness of the morning, a folded note from Judge Bannon's secretary was placed on Crabtree's table. It invited Crabtree and Waller to a luncheon meeting at the Downtown Athletic Club. The impending meeting might have caused Franklyn to proceed at a leisurely pace now. Whatever the reason, the quiet little man seemed to be taking his time this morning.

The expert was Dr. Elliott Baker, from a renowned medical center in Baltimore. An expert in pediatrics, head of neonatology, and a man whose published papers it took Franklyn more than half an hour to introduce, Baker was younger than one might have expected. But there was no doubt in anyone's mind that he was an eminently qualified expert.

Baker's testimony differed little from Lawler's the day before. He, too, had examined little John Reynolds Simpson, had found him to be brain-damaged, and was quite sure from the records he had seen, especially the early Apgars, that the child had been normal at birth. In his opinion, mistreatment in the subsequent few days had been responsible for the difficulty.

Baker had a more tolerant attitude toward phototherapy. It was used at his hospital. He had himself used it on numerous occasions. But he did not rely on it solely.

Throughout Baker's testimony, Chris and Laura listened attentively. Soon Chris found himself agreeing with much that Baker was saying. In fact, rather than being an expert for the plaintiff, Baker seemed to be completely impartial. Nor did Franklyn seem particularly intent on leading Baker in either direction.

Then, just when it seemed that Franklyn was content to

have Baker merely reinforce Lawler's testimony, he suddenly asked, "Dr. Baker, does the phrase 'masking symptoms' have a particular meaning in medicine?"

"Definitely," Baker agreed.

"Can you give us a layman's explanation?"

"Well, it means prescribing treatment or medication that serves to cover or diminish symptoms so that the illness is either completely masked or difficult to diagnose."

"Can you give us an example?"

"The most common form is the administering of painkillers. Pain is sometimes necessary to diagnose an illness. Suppressing pain may only serve to mislead the patient and the doctor into believing the situation is less serious than it actually is." Baker enlarged on his original statement.

"Do I understand that phototherapy may accomplish the same result, Doctor?"

"Indeed," said Baker. "There is no doubt that in almost all cases phototherapy will decrease the amount of bilirubin in the blood. But by doing so one may also mask the true condition."

"In your expert opinion, Doctor, is it possible that is what happened in this case?"

"More than possible. Likely." Then Baker volunteered, "Especially with a younger man who hasn't had the length of experience . . ."

Crabtree rose to object. Judge Bannon sustained him. Franklyn returned to the attack.

"Finally, Dr. Baker, given the facts established in the record, the bilirubin of sixteen, an Rh-negative incompatibility, in your expert opinion what would have been the course of treatment demanded by sound medical practice?"

"Only one thing—an immediate exchange transfusion."

Crabtree rose to begin his cross-examination, but Judge Bannon intervened. Aware of the luncheon conference, the judge asked, "Mr. Crabtree, don't you think that we can forego the cross-examination of Dr. Baker till after the noon recess?"

"Yes, Your Honor," Crabtree readily agreed. Chris leaned across Waller to whisper angrily.

"Get at him now while what he said is still fresh in the jury's mind!"

Crabtree snapped in a low voice, "I'll handle this my way, Doctor!" Then he addressed the bench: "Your Honor, we are agreeable to an early lunch recess. But we ask that Dr. Baker remain available for this afternoon's session."

Once the doctor had agreed, court was recessed till one-thirty.

Though they left the courtroom as seeming adversaries, Franklyn, Reynolds, Crabtree and Waller were all soon gathered around Reynolds' special table in the corner of the old oak bar of the Downtown Athletic Club. Over drinks they talked of everything but the case. They made jokes about their golf scores, their wives, the national administration.

The captain of the dining room approached their table and whispered to Reynolds. He nodded and escorted his guests to a private dining room, where the table was laid for four. Reynolds considerately suggested the club's best dishes, giving detailed instructions to the captain as to how each dish was to be prepared. He did not order anything for himself. Coffee would be enough. The reason for that became apparent once the meal was served. While Franklyn, Crabtree and Waller ate, Reynolds spoke.

"Gentlemen, before you go into the legal aspects of this situation, I want my say. In the final analysis any settlement will depend on my son-in-law. He is the plaintiff on behalf of himself and my grandson."

Crabtree and Waller glanced at each other, mystified as to Reynolds' purpose.

"I have no doubt," he continued, "that my son-in-law will be guided by my advice."

Nor did anyone else in that room. Crabtree looked across the table at Franklyn, hoping to detect some clue. But the little man continued to concentrate on his food which he seemed to enjoy enormously.

"Now, we can save a lot of haggling," Reynolds said, "if we acknowledge one thing. We will not accept any settlement of this case insofar as defendant Grant is concerned. Is that clear?"

Both Waller and Crabtree ceased eating. Crabtree glanced at Franklyn who still seemed unconcerned. That in itself told Crabtree that Reynolds had already discussed settlement with his lawyer. Franklyn knew exactly what Reynolds wanted and agreed with him. So there was little room for actual negotiation. Still, as counsel for the insurance company, Crabtree had to respond now.

"Mr. Reynolds, you understand our position. According to the policy that covers the hospital, my client is obligated to defend that institution and all its employees."

Reynolds nodded, but only to allow Crabtree to finish his explanation.

"Naturally, if we can't settle on behalf of Grant as well as the hospital and Sobol we haven't improved our position at all. The company is still obligated to provide Grant with a defense. And to bear the cost of any verdict, if there is one. Under these conditions I don't see the advantage of settling. Nor could I advise the hospital to do so."

Reynolds glanced at Harry Franklyn, who wiped his lips with the large napkin and cleared his throat slightly. Now, when he talked, he used his full voice and not the soft courtroom tones that evoked such rapt attention from the jurors.

"I think I can explain what Mr. Reynolds has in mind. He bears no grudges against Dr. Sobol or Metropolitan General. But he does feel, for the protection of the general public, of course, that a doctor like Grant should be called to account for flagrant negligence and malpractice."

"But how do we separate these defendants?" Crabtree asked.

Franklyn toyed with his fork as he continued: "Well, as we see it, if the insurance company chooses to settle, then the hospital can be *forced* into a settlement . . ."

"That may not be necessary," Waller interrupted, anxious to further a settlement for the hospital if he could. "I will say frankly that we are quite amenable to settling."

"Fine," Franklyn said. "Then we have several parties who are willing. The plaintiffs, the insurance company and the hospital."

"That leaves Sobol and Grant," Crabtree warned. "We'd still be on the hook."

"Unless . . ." Franklyn began, then paused to take a sip of coffee.

"Unless?" Crabtree coaxed.

"Crabtree, I've studied that policy very carefully. Under its terms if the insurance company wants to settle, it needs the hospital's agreement."

"But the hospital is willing to talk settlement," Waller insisted.

"Please," Franklyn said, as if reprimanding a junior in his office. "The point I make is that Grant is *not* a party to that insurance contract. He is not bound by its terms. Meaning he has no obligation to settle. And at the same time he is not a beneficiary of your protection under that contract once he separates himself from the hospital's stand. In a word, if the hospital agrees to settle and Grant does not, you gentlemen are completely off the hook."

Waller answered first. "Yes, but what if Grant chooses to settle rather than go it alone?"

Franklyn turned to Reynolds. "Gentlemen," he said, "everyone thinks that I've made my fortune by being a keen student of business. Nonsense! I've done it all by knowing human nature. Grant won't settle! Not that arrogant young bastard! I'm willing to stake the outcome of this case on it."

Crabtree attempted to clarify his options. "Since I'll have to report back to my client on this, I would like to confirm this. You are willing to settle whether or not Dr. Grant chooses to carry on this defense alone. Any settlement we reach is final. I mean, we don't want our settlement upset if Grant decides to quit, after all."

Reynolds smiled grimly. "I'm willing to take that gamble. I want that young man alone in court."

"What about Sobol?" Waller asked.

"I'm sorry about Sobol," Reynolds said, "but he can make his own decision."

Waller finally said, "Well, at least we have a definite proposal to take back to our clients."

Crabtree began to hedge. "Of course we haven't talked arithmetic yet."

"Don't worry about that!" Reynolds said briskly. Money seemed the farthest thing from his mind. "I'd like this done quickly."

As far as John Stewart Reynolds was concerned, lunch was over.

It took two days to arrive at the exact terms of the settlement. During that time the trial continued, but at a low level of excitement. Franklyn introduced medical experts, all of whose testimony served to support Lawler and Baker. Crabtree only went through the motions of cross-examining them. Despite Laura's insistence that he press the witnesses harder, the jurors sensed the absence of any real conflict.

During a midmorning break on the third day Grant led

Laura to a corner of the corridor outside the courtroom.

"What the hell's going on? Nobody is actually doing anything!"

"I know," Laura said, not daring to vent her own fears which were even stronger than Chris's. Whatever the strategy was, Crabtree was not nearly aggressive enough on behalf of his chief client, the insurance company. Since he had been retained by them many times before and would hope to be retained many times in future, his conduct was suspicious, unnerving.

It was the end of the day. Judge Bannon had recessed the case till morning and as Crabtree gathered up his papers he observed to Laura, "I think we'd better have a little meeting."

"I think so, too," she agreed swiftly.

"I mean all of us. You, Grant, Waller and myself."

"Anything that'll unify this defense," she said pointedly.

Crabtree stared at her, undecided whether to argue or simply smile. He did neither. "Look, I suggest we go across to my office."

As soon as they were all comfortably seated, Crabtree began summing up the trial, interspersing his interpretations, including the degree of impact on the jury as he perceived it. But it was merely a prologue to his final statement.

"So we, all of us, came to the conclusion that the only intelligent course is to settle. We put out some feelers and got some responses. We're at the point now where we've just agreed on the figure."

"Without telling us?" Laura demanded angrily.

"Since you have no official standing in this case, we felt we were within our rights to proceed on our own. However, now that we have reached a decision, we'd like you to know."

Chris broke in. "Did the hospital agree to this?"

"Yes," Waller said firmly.

"And Mike Sobol?"

"Dr. Sobol is in the same position you are. It would be nice if he would agree, but legally not essential," Crabtree said.

Chris looked at Laura who nodded, giving credence to Crabtree's statement.

"Now, I would think that you'd use this as your chance to bury this whole sad affair," Crabtree advised, but Chris interrupted by rising from his chair with a violence that led Crabtree and Waller to exchange concerned glances.

"Grant?" Waller said.

"I'll let you know." He burst from the room, slamming the door behind him.

Laura paused only long enough to say, "You bastards!" Then she raced after Chris, catching him just as he stepped into the elevator.

In the office, Crabtree and Waller sat back, undisturbed by Laura's outburst.

"You think Grant will?" Waller asked.

"Frankly, I don't give a damn," Crabtree said. "This wasn't the strongest case I've ever had."

"I hope he doesn't do anything foolish, that's all," Waller said.

"He will," Crabtree said. "He will. I think Reynolds was right about him. Headstrong. And with a knack for putting his neck in a noose."

Mike Sobol received the news during a small meeting in the hospital board room. He was still in his white lab coat, having been summoned from the clinic to meet with a committee consisting of Tom Brady, Avery Waller, and Cy Rosenstiel.

Mike listened, scarcely reacting. Either he was too pre-

231

occupied to understand, or too tired to react as strongly as the situation demanded. When they were done, Sobol asked only, "And where is Grant?"

"We don't know. He hasn't come back to the hospital yet."

"This doesn't mean he's terminated, does it?"

"Of course not," Brady reassured him. "We're settling for the express purpose of getting this over with so we can all get on with the business of this hospital—Grant included."

But it was an assurance given too blandly and too easily to impress Sobol.

"The thing is, Mike," Rosenstiel interjected, "we thought it would help Grant make a wise decision if you set the example. We're looking to you, Mike. Depending on you."

Sobol nodded, only admitting that it was something to think about.

"We know it isn't easy, Sobol," said Waller. "I have the same situation at my office. Young men come along and I look on them as sons. You advise them. You steer them. But in the end they have to make their own decisions, determine their own future."

To himself, Mike Sobol said, "Why are you feeding me platitudes when I have to make such a decision?"

Aloud, he said, "I'll . . . I'll have to think about it."

Brady pressed. "Mike, we know it isn't easy. But you have to consider *all* your loyalties."

"What does that mean?" he demanded.

"You owe this hospital something, too," Brady reminded him.

"Have I ever given you gentlemen cause to doubt that?"

"Mike, please," said Cy Rosenstiel.

"Gentlemen, I'm fully aware of *all* my loyalties and responsibilities. I will ponder them and come to some conclusion."

"Soon, we hope," said Waller.

"Soon, soon," Sobol promised.

"It would be very helpful if we could have a decision by morning," Brady said.

"All right, by morning," Sobol agreed testily.

Brady and Waller excused themselves. Rosenstiel lingered. As soon as they were alone Rosenstiel said softly, "Mike, settle the damn thing. And if you can't get Chris to settle, then he's on his own. You've done all you can. You can't jeopardize your position here for an outsider like Grant."

"Outsider?"

"A gentile with his record, his looks, can go somewhere else and eventually do well. He can go into private practice. He's got nothing to worry about."

"Any doctor, gentile or not, with this on his record will be destroyed where it counts. No hospital with good research facilities will have him," Sobol said.

Then he paused, and began wearily, "Cy, do me a favor? Never talk to me again. Please?"

"Mike?"

"Yes, I mean it. To me the worst anomaly on the face of this earth is a Jew with prejudice. There are only two kinds of doctors. Not Jews and gentiles. But good and bad." Sobol turned wearily away.

"You'll have my answer by morning."

TWENTY

THEY WERE coming to dinner, Chris Grant and Laura. Mike Sobol had spent almost two hours shopping for what he thought was needed for the kind of dinner that Rose used to prepare. He would watch her in the old days. On holidays like Passover or Rosh Hashanah, he would invite all his Jewish students, interns and residents whose homes were in other cities. Sometimes Rose had the burden of feeding as many as twenty-five people. All of them young, all of them hungry as well as longing for a taste of home.

On those days Mike Sobol used to come home from the hospital a bit ahead of time to help. And Rose would let him, though, if she had wanted to tell the truth, most of the time he was underfoot. She used to say to herself, how can a man so adept in a research laboratory be so clumsy in a kitchen?

Now, tonight, four days into the trial of *Simpson vs. Metropolitan General, Christoper Grant and Michael Sobol,* Mike Sobol was having company for the third time since Rose had died. So it was an occasion and Mike had determined that he would serve a real homemade meal.

First he would serve mushroom and barley soup. This he

couldn't make so he bought it at the one "kosher-type" restaurant in the area. He had also brought in fresh vegetables for a healthy green salad. And nut cake from the Viennese bakery near the hospital. But the main dish, veal chops with fried potatoes, he would cook himself from scratch.

It went off extremely well. Mike had set a presentable looking table, using the best of Rose's linens and her holiday silver.

In the middle of the main course Mike suddenly said, "Oh, my God!"

Laura asked anxiously, "What's wrong, Mike? Don't you feel well?"

"The green vegetable! I forgot to defrost the broccoli!" Mike apologized.

"We'll live without it," she said. "We have that terrific salad."

"Rose's own dressing. Don't ask me how she arrived at it. All I do is follow her recipe. Being a chemistry major, she wrote down everything as if it were an experiment," Mike explained.

Chris said little during dinner. It was only during coffee when Laura lit her after-dinner cigarette that he spoke up.

"Laurie, please!"

Without hesitation, Laura inhaled deeply. Chris looked to Mike for help. "Tell her, Mike."

But Mike only said, "You're old enough to know that the last basis on which to appeal to a woman is reason." He smiled at Laura and she smiled back. After that, though, there were no more smiles. They had to either talk about the case or not talk at all.

Laura finally said, "Look, while you men are talking, I'll clear and do the dishes."

"No guest in my home does dishes," said Mike. "That is, not without some help. Come, we'll do it together."

When they finished and were seated again in the living

room, he told them about his meeting with Brady, Waller and Rosenstiel.

"Well?" Chris asked.

"Well," Mike said, stretching the word into three syllables, "I decided to call my brother in Chicago. He's a lawyer, a damned good one, and he said they were not lying to us. They *can* settle without our consent. All we can do is decide whether to go on and defend the suit or back out. Unless . . ."

"Unless what?" Laura asked, a lawyer challenging what another lawyer had said.

"Unless Reynolds could be convinced to drop their suit against us."

"You know he won't do that," Chris said bitterly.

"All right," Mike admitted sadly. "John Reynolds is not going to drop any lawsuit against you. He's like a man possessed. All the years I've known him, I've found him to be practical. Stubborn at times, yes, but in the end practical. It's hard for me to understand his attitude now. I admit that this situation cuts him deeply. He wanted a son, Chris, more than anything. You've met his daughter, haven't you?"

"No."

"Well, if you had you'd know what I mean. She walks around with an eternally apologetic air, as if she doesn't rightly own her small space on this earth, as if she's an impostor. A nice girl, but so self-effacing that it isn't natural. Which is a reflection of how much John Reynolds wanted a son. Why there never was one I don't know, but eventually John had to look forward to a grandson. Why not? A natural feeling."

All the while that Mike talked, Chris kept asking himself, doesn't Mike realize that in a way he's talking about himself? Where is his son? His grandson? But he didn't interrupt.

"The tragedy that happened, happened," Mike continued. "I can understand a man being griefstricken. But this vindictiveness, it's not like him."

"That day at the hospital," Chris said, "he told me the ambitions he had for that boy—President of the United States. And it was no idle grandfather's dream, he meant it."

"In these times, when only rich men can run for office, there is enough Reynolds money to make a President," Mike said soberly. "In any case, whatever his reason, Reynolds wants to witness your destruction. The question is, do you fight him? Or do you give him his wish by simply saying, 'I surrender, I admit my guilt'?"

Chris didn't answer.

"I've done a good deal of thinking since yesterday," Mike said. "There's the principle involved, but there's the practical side as well. What do we do for a defense? Without the insurance company footing the bills, do you mortgage your whole future to defend yourself against a madman with unlimited money?"

Laura spoke up very firmly, "I'm qualified to carry on this case alone."

"One girl against Reynolds' whole law firm? And that Harry Franklyn, he's a shrewd little bastard. And when he has to be, completely unscrupulous."

Mike turned to Laura, looked into her lovely, open, determined face. "You'd go up against all that by yourself?"

She smiled. "Only one lawyer at a time can examine any witness, so it doesn't matter to me how many men they have. Frankly, I could do ten times the job on this case that Crabtree's been doing. And that's not female chauvinism, either!"

Mike smiled. "Exactly the kind of thing Rose would have said. But, Laurie, my dear, can you stand back and make an objective judgment about one thing?"

"I can try."

"Can you appraise this case honestly? After all, we are

dealing with a man's judgment. That's what it comes down to. Did Chris make the right decision or didn't he? Now, could you ever believe that he *didn't* follow good practice? Could you admit to yourself, as a lawyer, mind you, that this is a bad case?"

"It isn't the best I've ever seen."

"Well, at least we have our feet on the ground. Now, let me ask you, realizing that, do you think the case is defensible?"

She hesitated, took a long moment, then said, "Yes."

"Now the final question. What do you think the odds are?" Mike asked pointedly.

"Less than good," she admitted.

Mike turned to Chris. "There, that's the basis on which we have to make our decision."

Chris slid his hand free of Laura's grasp. He rose to his full six feet one and looked down at Mike. "There's one other factor to consider."

"Reputation?" Mike Sobol anticipated. "I've been thinking about that, too, Chris. Settle and the issue is always left somewhat in doubt. Fight and lose and the blemish is there forever. That *is* something for a young man to consider."

"That isn't what I was referring to, Mike," Chris said in a tone that made the older man look up guardedly.

"What, then?"

"I'm determined to go on with this case," Chris Grant said. "But I want you to settle."

"Why?" Mike demanded.

"I've been doing *my* share of thinking, Mike. You were here long before I came. You built the department. You can hold it together no matter what happens to me. You're an institution, Mike."

"So I'm an institution, am I?" said Mike. "Like one of the old buildings. *I* belong. *You* don't. You very nice idiot! I'm yesterday. You're tomorrow. You count. We both settle or neither of us does."

"Mike, you have to be practical!"

"Oh, I'm practical, don't worry about that. I have thought it all out very clearly. At sixty-four I don't have much time left. No university wants a man this old to head up anything as rapidly changing as pediatrics. And no drug or chemical firm needs a man that old to head up research. I know," Mike finally confessed. "I've been making inquiries. . . ."

Laura and Chris turned to each other to stare silently.

"Yes, the past few weeks I've been putting out feelers to old friends who always used to say, 'Anytime you're ready to make a change, Mike, just let us know.' Well, Mike was ready to make a change. So he let them know. You should see the stack of beautifully phrased letters that all say no. Someday, someone is going to publish a collection of letters that all say 'no' without ever using that simple one-syllable word."

"All the more reason why *you* have to settle," Chris insisted.

"Reasons! All our lives when we have a tough decision to make we set down all the reasons *for*, all the reasons *against*. Then we decide. On the basis of all the reasons? Nonsense! We make our decisions with our emotions. Just as I make mine now."

"Mike?" Chris asked.

"Before you came, when I was in the kitchen cooking, I kept thinking of Rose. I know what she would be saying now: 'Mike, that young man needs all the help he can get. If you're there alongside him, that'll count. And if there are consequences, so what? We were going to retire to Florida one day anyhow. And maybe you'll meet a nice rich widow there. . . .'"

Mike tried to make a joke of it at the end but he couldn't

quite bring it off. One thing he knew, he was doing what he had to do.

"Mike," Laura said, "tell me honestly, you don't mind putting your fate in the hands of a woman?"

He smiled. "Never tell an old Jew about what a woman, even a small woman, can accomplish. After all, where do you think the legend of the Jewish mother started?" He suddenly became brighter, his eyes which had been sad, lit up and sparkled. "Let's have a toast." He went to a closet in the kitchen and came out with a bottle of wine.

"The last bottle Rose and I bought for Passover."

He poured three glasses, held up his own. "To all the foolish people of this world, who can't reason themselves into doing the wrong thing."

TWENTY-ONE

"JOHN STEWART Reynolds!" the court clerk summoned the next witness to the stand.

A muffled tremor of excited anticipation erupted in the crowded courtroom. No one felt the shock more than Laura Winters, unless it was Chris Grant who sat beside her at the defense table. They had no preparation, no hint that Harry Franklyn intended to allow John Reynolds to take the stand in this trial.

Franklyn had, in fact, gone out of his way to appear gracious and understanding when Laura took over the sole defense of Chris and Mike Sobol. He had readily agreed to the three-day recess she had requested to prepare herself. Then, this morning, when trial did resume, Franklyn agreed that Judge Bannon instruct the jury not to speculate on the reason for the substitution of defense counsel. Through it all Franklyn had seemed almost fatherly in his concern for her.

Laura had expected to settle down to several more days of Franklyn's expert witnesses, qualified doctor after qualified doctor who supported his case. Laura had long sheafs of yellow legal paper with many questions prepared to dispute, cross-examine, and force those experts into retreating from their strongly held positions and opinions. She had spent hours with Chris and Mike the past three nights to frame those questions. She was not at all prepared for the witness who now stood in the witness box, hand raised, taking the oath.

Laura whispered to Chris, "Get on the phone! I want Mike here right away!"

By the time Chris returned, Harry Franklyn was already leading John Reynolds through his early background. Still apprehensive and puzzled, Laura did not object but awaited Reynolds' testimony, wondering at its pertinence and value to Franklyn's case. Wondering, too, if Franklyn had been saving Reynolds till just this time, when she had the sole burden of the defense.

As Franklyn elicited the story in his soft voice, Reynolds revealed that he had come from a large family, a poor family. It seemed important to Franklyn to fix that fact for the jury. Reynolds had risen from a hod-carrying construction worker to a contractor with one truck. When the Great Depression struck and most large contractors were being eaten up by huge overhead, his small business started to expand. By the time the Depression began to recede, he was expanding in geometric strides.

During the Second World War, as a patriotic duty, of course, he was ready to go into huge-scale shipbuilding and airplane parts production. Before the war was over, his plants were turning out propellers for B-17's, bombsights, torpedo fuses, and more than three hundred other products for various phases of the war effort. By the time the war was over the foundations of the huge Reynolds fortune had been securely laid, and in the wave of prosperity that followed, Reynolds's fortune multiplied into the hundreds of millions.

Slowly, surely, Harry Franklyn was establishing John Reynolds not only as an eminently successful businessman but as a patriot, a man of principle. Franklyn also pointed out that Reynolds' grandson had been treated in a building made possible by a huge contribution from the Reynolds Foundation, and he made sure to nod sadly at the irony involved in that fact.

Though the courtroom was filled to capacity with press and curious spectators, there was not a sound from the audience throughout Reynolds' testimony. The jurors leaned forward attentively. For all fourteen of them it was their first close look at a legend about whom they had been reading for a generation. Far from being the stern, forbidding giant they had believed, Reynolds was warm and compassionate. He had come from the same modest background they had. He was a human being rather than a tycoon, a grandfather rather than a nationally known industrialist.

Whatever impulse Laura might have had to attack or object, she knew she had to allow Franklyn to have his way or run the risk of antagonizing both jury and press.

Mike Sobol joined them just as Franklyn was ready to begin his real examination. The doctor slid into the chair next to Chris and prepared himself for the worst.

"Mr. Reynolds, I must apologize for asking you to recall the unhappy events that led to this trial." With that as a preamble, Franklyn began the meticulous questioning of John Reynolds about the events surrounding the birth of his grandson.

"Mr. Reynolds, had you looked forward to the birth of your grandson?"

"Naturally. No amount of money changes a man's basic feelings. I wanted sons. And grandsons. Yes, I had looked forward to it. Very much."

"And you followed your daughter's pregnancy quite carefully?" Franklyn asked. Laura knew she should object, but evaluating the consequences she allowed the leading question to stand.

"Most carefully. I would check with Dr. Mitchell every few weeks. He assured me everything was coming along fine," Reynolds replied.

"Tell us, Mr. Reynolds, did Dr. Mitchell warn your daughter . . ."

Now Laura did rise. "Objection. The question clearly calls for hearsay evidence."

Bannon complied with a sound that was partway between a grunt and the word "Sustained."

"Mr. Reynolds," continued Franklyn, "were you ever present at any conversation between your daughter and Dr. Mitchell?"

"I was."

"Did Dr. Mitchell within your hearing ever give your daughter any reason to believe that she would not give birth to a normal baby?" Franklyn asked.

"He did not. He was quite satisfied with her progress and confident about the outcome."

"When did you first learn that the infant was not progressing satisfactorily?" Franklyn asked.

"When Dr. Coleman called," Reynolds said.

"Can you tell us exactly what happened, as you remember it?" Franklyn asked.

"I'm not likely ever to forget it," Reynolds said, the steel coming into his voice for the first time since he had begun to testify. "I had been to the hospital for the second time that day."

"Mr. Reynolds," Franklyn interrupted, "were you apprehensive about your daughter or your grandson?"

"You mean because I went to the hospital twice in one day?" Reynolds asked. "No, it's just that my son-in-law was out of town on business. You see, we never expected that she would deliver when she did. So I took over."

"And what was the initial report from the hospital?" Franklyn asked.

"That my daughter was fine, considering it was a slightly preterm delivery, and the infant was in excellent condition," Reynolds said.

"What was the first sign of trouble, as far as you know?"

"When I went back the next morning. The nurse in charge told me that she had called Dr. Coleman," Reynolds said.

"Did you talk to Dr. Coleman at that time?"

"No, but I did when he called. He was disturbed by one of the lab reports and said that perhaps we had better transfer the child to Metropolitan General," Reynolds said.

"Did you agree to the child being transferred?" Franklyn asked.

"Yes. In fact, I called Mike Sobol, Dr. Michael Sobol."

"Mr. Reynolds, is he the same Dr. Michael Sobol who is a defendant in this lawsuit?"

"He is," Reynolds said, glaring at the defense table.

"And when you called Dr. Sobol?" Franklyn prodded.

"I talked to him first, since we were friends then, good friends. Then I put Coleman on the phone to explain the medical situation."

"Did you hear Dr. Sobol's response?"

"He said, 'We'll send an ambulance over immediately.' He said he was glad to do whatever he could for me or anyone in my family."

"How long did it take for the ambulance to get to Parkside?"

"Forty minutes."

"How do you know that, Mr. Reynolds?" Franklyn asked.

"Because I waited and rode over with my grandson."

"And once you arrived at Metropolitan General?"

"Dr. Sobol met us at the ambulance dock."

"Precisely what did Dr. Sobol do?" Franklyn asked.

"He looked over the transcript that had been sent along with my grandson. Then he examined the baby."

"And when he had done that?" Franklyn prodded.

"He looked over the transcript again. I didn't know at the time . . ."

Laura rose to object. Bannon sustained it and cautioned John Reynolds: "The witness will confine his answers to what he actually saw at that time." Since Bannon did not intend to favor Laura with many rulings, he made an elaborate ceremony of this one. If, at some future time, his rulings were challenged, he would be able to point to at least a few to prove lack of prejudice.

"Then, sir, after Dr. Sobol studied the transcript, what did he do?"

"He had the baby moved into the intensive care nursery and said he had exactly the right man to take over. He called Dr. Grant," Reynolds said, "who I understood . . ."

Franklyn anticipated Laura's objection and cautioned, "Only what you actually saw and heard, sir."

"Well, I heard Dr. Sobol apologize for taking Grant away from his research. So I had to assume . . ."

Franklyn interceded, "Without making any assumptions, sir, did you actually hear Dr. Sobol apologize?"

"I did," Reynolds said.

"At that time did it strike you as strange that a chief of service at a hospital should apologize to a physician working under him because he was asking him to take care of a patient?" Franklyn asked.

"Object!" Laura said, rising.

"On what ground?" asked Bannon.

"On the ground that Mr. Reynolds is a layman. He has no basis on which to judge a given action taking place between two physicians, having to do with their professional relationship. He is not qualified to judge whether it was strange conduct or not."

Bannon resented the fact that she had outmaneuvered both himself and Franklyn by invalidating Reynolds' answer even if he were permitted to give it. "Unless counsel rephrases the question I will have to disallow it," he ruled.

"Mr. Reynolds," said Franklyn, "did you hear Dr. Sobol apologize to Dr. Grant for interrupting his research?"

"I did," Reynolds declared.

"Even though he was calling him to treat a sick infant, less than forty-eight hours old?"

"Yes, sir," Reynolds declared, his indignation plain. "I know it's hard to believe but . . ."

"Regardless of how justified your emotions are, sir, I caution you not to continue," Franklyn said, having achieved his point despite Laura's previous objection. If anything, he had made it more strongly. "Now, sir, will you tell us what Dr. Grant's attitude was when he arrived?"

"He seemed resentful . . ." Reynolds began.

"Object!" Laura called out.

Franklyn did not wait for Bannon's ruling but rephrased his question, "When you met Dr. Grant for the first time what did he say?"

"To me, nothing," Reynolds answered. "He ignored me as if he were angry . . ."

Franklyn raised his voice slightly to ask, "Mr. Reynolds, only what happened. What did Dr. Grant do?"

"He glanced at the transcript. Then Dr. Sobol went into the nursery and Grant started to follow. So did I. But Grant turned and forcibly blocked my way at the door," Reynolds stated.

"He refused you admittance to the nursery?"

"Yes, sir!"

"Even though your sick grandson was in there?"

"Yes, sir!" Reynolds said vindictively.

"Did you say anything?"

"I said, 'That's my grandson. I have a right to know what's being done for him.'" Reynolds said righteously. Several members of the jury unconsciously nodded in agreement.

"And what did Dr. Grant say?" Franklyn asked.

"I don't remember the words. But they were not favorable or polite."

"Object to the word 'polite'!" said Laura.

"It was not a favorable answer."

"So Dr. Grant would not permit you to enter the nursery and see what was being done for your sick grandson?" Franklyn asked.

"He did not! I had to stand outside the big glass window and watch."

Now Harry Franklyn dropped his voice so low that all members of the jury were forced to strain forward to listen.

"Mr. Reynolds, as far as you can remember, did you ever say anything or do anything to Dr. Grant to incur his anger?"

"I had never even seen him before in my life!" Reynolds said.

"On that day did you say or do anything to anger him?"

"I did not," Reynolds said, adopting the same soft attitude as Franklyn.

"Can you in any way account for his hostility?"

"I think he resented being taken away from his research, or else . . ."

Laura came to her feet to object. "The question calls for sheer speculation on the part of the witness!"

Bannon allowed her objection with an intolerant wave of his hand. Franklyn smiled indulgently, then turned back to Reynolds.

"Mr. Reynolds, was anything said at that time that could account for Dr. Grant's attitude?"

"I didn't give it importance at the time. But there was one thing. I was determined to wait all night if need be to see how my grandson was progressing. So I accompanied Dr. Grant down to the staff cafeteria for a late supper. And he made a very interesting remark . . ."

Laura turned to Chris. He could remember nothing of consequence. He shook his head, as intent now as anyone on the jury about Reynolds' recollection.

"When I first asked if I could accompany him to the dining room, Dr. Grant said, 'But you'll have to carry your own tray.' "

"What did you understand that to mean, sir?" Franklyn asked.

"It was an obvious reflection of his resentment against anyone who had accumulated any wealth. He struck me as just another one of these young radical activist doctors to whom medicine is not a science but a political tool!"

Laura was on her feet again, calling out her objection. "That question is irrelevant and immaterial to the issues in this case! I demand that it be struck and that the jury be instructed to disregard the answer!"

As if wearied by constant interruptions, Franklyn turned to the bench, "If Your Honor will permit, please withhold any ruling until my next few questions."

"Continue, Mr. Franklyn."

"Mr. Reynolds, aside from Dr. Grant's obviously prejudiced reflections on your wealth, did anything else happen that day to reveal his attitude?"

"Yes, sir. While my grandson lay terribly sick in that nursery, Dr. Grant left that hospital for two whole hours."

"Did he tell you where he went?"

"He did. He said he was going down to Rixie Square to deliver a lecture. To some expectant mothers."

"Did he say those women were ill or in urgent need of his services?" Franklyn asked.

"They were not ill at all. It was simply another indication of his attitudes and preferences."

Before Laura could object, Franklyn hastened to ask, "Did you try to prevail on him not to go?"

"I certainly did, but he went anyhow. It was obvious

his political leanings were so strong that they overcame his duty to his patient! And his writings prove it!"

"Object!" Laura shouted, rising up out of her chair.

Bannon pondered a moment, then ruled, "If the defendant's own writings constitute an admission against interest, I will allow it."

Reynolds turned slightly toward the defense table. "To confirm my suspicions I had some research done on Dr. Grant's published medical papers. They are replete with attacks against the society. They are political tracts, not medical research papers!"

"Object!" Laura called out, while at her side a red-faced Mike Sobol whispered, "His name should be McCarthy, not Reynolds!"

Franklyn turned to the bench swiftly. "Your Honor, before any ruling is made, we should like to point out one thing. When a doctor is confronted by a choice of therapies, his reasons, conscious or unconscious, for having selected the one he chose are relevant, material and extremely pertinent to the issue. Especially in view of all the highly experienced skilled experts who have since disagreed with him."

While Bannon pondered the question, Franklyn continued, "I would assume that if the witness's statements are incorrect the doctor can prove that to us when he takes the stand."

Now that he had succeeded in challenging Laura to put Chris Grant on the stand, Franklyn was quite prepared to accept any decision from the bench. Even if it went against him.

Bannon finally declared, "The court will reserve its ruling. But it would urge Mr. Franklyn to get on with more factual testimony."

"Of course, Your Honor," Franklyn agreed. "Mr. Reynolds, I believe you were telling us how you were forced to stand outside the intensive care nursery and watch through a big glass window as your grandson was being treated."

"Yes, sir, I was."

"What did you see, sir?"

"Dr. Grant examined my grandson. Then he drew some blood and gave it to a nurse. When she came out, I asked her where she was going and she said to the lab."

"Did you ask her what kind of tests were going to be made?"

"I did. But she seemed in too great a hurry to answer."

"Tell us what else you saw," Franklyn coaxed.

"Staring through the glass, I saw Dr. Grant put on an intravenous attachment, and make some adjustments on some other gauges. Then he did a very strange thing . . ."

"Object!" said Laura.

Bannon leaned forward. "The witness will leave out all qualifying adjectives and opinions."

"Dr. Grant moved an object, I don't know what to call it," Reynolds answered.

"Can you describe it, sir?"

"I certainly can," Reynolds answered. "It was a shiny metal object taller than the Isolette the baby was lying in. He moved it in to place so that the top would serve as a cover for the Isolette."

"Did you see anything about it that seemed unusual?"

"Well, the underside of the lid was composed of fluorescent tubes," Reynolds said.

"How many tubes would you say, sir?"

"I'd guess somewhere between ten and twelve," Reynolds said, using his hands to illustrate, "about this long."

"And then, sir?"

"He threw a switch and turned on the lights."

"He turned the battery of fluorescent lights on your grandson?"

"Yes, sir," Reynolds said.

Franklyn shook his head ever so slightly, glancing at

251

the jury from the corner of his eye. "Tell me, sir, before Dr. Grant turned those lights on your grandson, did he explain the procedure to you?"

"He did not."

"Did he ask your permission?"

"He did not."

"Did he tell you that there were risks involved in that treatment?"

"He did not."

"At any time, before, during or after, did he ask *your* permission to use that treatment?" Franklyn asked.

"*He did not!*" Reynolds said, clipping each word.

Laura sat up stiffly, tense, yet unable to prevent Franklyn and Reynolds from proving one vital cause of action in their complaint, that Chris Grant had not received informed consent from a close relative of the patient. Failure to do so in a case in which a potentially dangerous form of therapy was employed was clearly malpractice.

Franklyn continued. "Mr. Reynolds, have you, since that time, discovered the dangers involved in that form of therapy?"

"Yes, sir, I have."

Laura braced herself for the next question. Chris tried to whisper something to her, but she shrugged him silent with a small but fierce gesture.

"Mr. Reynolds, if you had known then what you now know about phototherapy . . ."

"Object!"

"Mr. Reynolds, if you had known then what you now know about phototherapy . . ."

"Object!" Laura interrupted again, now on her feet.

"On what ground?" Bannon demanded, faced with what he considered a gratuitous interruption in the orderly conduct of the examination.

"There is no evidence whatsoever that Dr. Grant was

under any obligation to inform any relative as to photo-therapy."

The point was well taken, and Bannon had to rule in her favor. Franklyn rephrased his question.

"Mr. Reynolds, if you had been informed as to the dangers . . ."

"Object!" Laura called out again.

With some annoyance Bannon suggested, "Mr. Franklyn, can't you ask your question without including phrases which counsel finds objectionable?"

Franklyn sighed wearily, letting the jury know that he felt hounded by a shrewish, interfering woman who made his work and theirs more difficult.

"Mr. Reynolds, since that day, have you learned more about the subject of phototherapy?"

"I have."

"Precisely how?" Franklyn asked.

"I consulted other doctors. And did quite a good deal of personal research."

"And what was the result of that research?"

"Object!" Laura called out.

But this time Judge Bannon ruled gravely, "The witness may answer."

"The doctors, as well as the medical literature I con-sulted, both agreed on one thing. There is such a vast area of unknown aftereffects that phototherapy is a question-able form of treatment."

"I move to strike that answer in its entirety," said Laura.

Bannon, whose frustration was becoming more evident, turned to her and said, "And on what ground this time, young lady?"

"On the ground, old man, that . . ."

Before Laura could continue there was an outburst of laughter from the spectators. Red-faced, Bannon irately gaveled the courtroom to silence. Glaring down from the bench, he addressed Laura, "Counselor, I deem your remark to verge on contempt of this court. Any similar manner of address will evoke prompt and proper action from this bench!"

Chris noted that, instead of flushing, the blood had drained from Laura's face. He suspected she might break down and start to weep. He had only seen her in that mood once before. And that time, after a severe argument, she did weep. Now, however, she waited till the courtroom was completely silent. Then, her voice sure and strong, she said, "Counsel is quite willing to stipulate that all forms of address based on age or sex be eliminated from this trial."

Challenged, Bannon only replied dryly, "If counsel will state the basis for her objection, this court will rule."

"Since Mr. Reynolds has not been qualified as an expert, any question that calls for an expression of his opinion on medical matters is highly improper," Laura stated.

"Even though Mr. Reynolds is testifying as to what certain doctors told him?" Franklyn interceded.

"Until we know the standing and the expertise of the doctors from whom Mr. Reynolds received his information we object to that question no matter what its form," Laura said. "We will accept expert testimony only from duly qualified experts, only first hand and only if subject to cross-examination."

Bannon glanced down at Franklyn before ruling. "Does counsel wish to rephrase his question or withdraw it?"

Laura said quickly, "If the question calls for a hearsay conclusion, we will object to it!"

Franklyn hesitated for an instant, then turned to Reynolds, who was obviously annoyed that he had not been allowed to answer what he deemed a crucial question.

"Mr. Reynolds, as a grandfather, if phototherapy had been explained to you by Dr. Grant as carefully as it was explained by those other doctors you consulted, would you have given your permission to have it applied to your grandson?"

"I most definitely would not!"

Laura expected that now that Franklyn had succeeded in making his prima facie case on lack of informed consent, she would have her chance at Reynolds. But Franklyn was not done yet.

"Mr. Reynolds, I trust you will forgive me for moving on to still more sensitive subjects."

This alerted Laura even more than Franklyn's intention to keep Reynolds on the stand.

"Mr. Reynolds, can you describe for us the condition of your grandson?"

"Object!" said Laura.

Judge Bannon interceded. "Surely a grandfather does not have to qualify as an expert before he is allowed to testify about his own grandson."

"The condition of the infant, which is the subject of this trial, is medically ascertainable and should be left to duly qualified experts," Laura retorted.

Reynolds turned toward the jury. "It was pitiful to watch the change," he began, "especially after what I had been promised by those two doctors." He glanced at Chris and Mike to make sure the jury made the connection. "They handed him to me and said, 'He's all right now, perfectly okay.' I myself carried him out to the car, and I brought him to his mother. The look on her face when I assured her he had fully recovered . . ."

Reynolds didn't complete that sentence. He let it hang. The look on his face said the rest.

"For weeks we went on that way. You know, most of you, what it's like to be a mother or father. Well, being a grandfather is no different. In fact, because your own time is running out it is more desperately urgent to make sure that the child is healthy, normal. And so we thought."

It seemed Reynolds might break down, but he steadied himself.

Meantime, Laura was furious at the naked ploy that Franklyn had arranged, to change what should be a purely legal issue into an unashamed bid for the jury's sympathy. She knew only too well that to object now would aggravate the situation rather than diminish its effect. She decided to allow Reynolds to continue, trying meanwhile to evolve some strategy to offset the effect of his damaging testimony. It would not be easy.

"We played with him," Reynolds said. "His mother, his dad, my wife, myself. Every day I was in town I saw him at least once. When I had to make business trips, his nursery was the last place I would stop on my way to the airport, the first place I would come on my way back."

Reynolds seemed lost in his own thoughts. Franklyn had to prod.

"And in all respects he seemed to be a normal, healthy child?"

"*Seemed* to be," said Reynolds. "But that's another one of those things I discovered. A baby can seem perfectly normal and then, after three or four months, you begin to notice changes. It's almost imperceptible at first. You notice they don't smile. They don't react. Until suddenly you realize the baby is not advancing, it's retrogressing. You worry, you wonder. You don't dare ask at first."

Reynolds stopped. He shook his head slightly as if to free himself from his own thoughts. Turning back to the jury, he said, "I'm sorry, I keep saying you. I mean *I* noticed all those things. Finally, without telling anyone, I went to the library of the County Medical Association and read up on the subject. I'm not a doctor but I understand enough to know that brain damage, of the kind we are dealing with here, doesn't usually evidence itself until the fourth or fifth month. Precisely the time when I began to detect the first symptoms. The more I read the more frightened I became. Even before we took my grandson to a neurologist I knew the answer."

Reynolds paused, apparently overcome with emotion. The courtroom was so still one could hear distant street noises. Franklyn handed his client a glass of water. Reynolds sipped it, trying to recover.

After a minute, Judge Bannon asked, "Would the witness care for a brief recess?"

Reynolds did not look up, merely shook his head, indicating that he was ready to go on.

"I had no choice but to go see Dr. Mitchell. I told him all my fears. At first he tried to reassure me. But when he had conducted an examination himself, he came to the same conclusion I did. We called in specialists. Not that I doubted Dr. Mitchell, who is a fine doctor, but no one can readily accept such a tragic diagnosis. Four specialists saw my grandson and all agreed that he had suffered irreversible brain damage."

Reynolds was breathing rapidly now. "Despite all of Dr. Grant's promises," he glared at Chris, "that child born perfectly healthy is not well, never will be well. That perfect child."

For a time after Reynolds had finished no one moved. Even Chris felt sorry for the man. Perhaps sorrier than anyone on the jury, for he knew better than they the dreams Reynolds had cherished for his grandson.

Laura saw how cleverly Harry Franklyn had overcome his chief obstacle in this trial. He had done the one thing she would have thought it impossible to do. Despite wealth, position and power, he had made John Stewart Reynolds a pathetic figure, worthy of sympathy. He had also succeeded in virtually cutting off any effective cross-examination. If Laura attempted now to break down any portion of Reynolds' testimony the jury would resent her.

She had no choice but to rise and say, "If Your Honor agrees I would like not to cross-examine the witness at this time; however, retaining my right to recall him later."

Bannon agreed but John Stewart Reynolds sat several more minutes in the witness box, unaware that he had been excused. Finally, he went back to his place at the counsel table.

Harry Franklyn remained on his feet to say, "Your Honor, the plaintiff rests."

Bannon consulted the clock on the back wall and declared, "It being so late in the afternoon, we will reconvene at ten tomorrow morning when the defense will be ready to present its case."

TWENTY-TWO

THEY FINISHED their wine. But left most of their dinner. Chris paid the bill.

"I'll get you home. You need your sleep," he offered.

"I need to get away even more," she replied. "I'd like to go for a drive. I'll drop you."

"No," he said, more intensely than he had intended. She glanced at him and he added, "I don't want you to be alone. Not tonight."

He drove her car out onto the interstate, north of the city to where green fields and stands of trees smelled sweet in the late-night air. The highway was empty. Only an occasional truck roared at them, hauling tomorrow's milk or fresh produce to the city.

"That day . . ." Laura started to say. Another truck roared past them and she didn't complete her thought.

He reached out his right arm, expecting that she would slide close, but instead of pressing against his chest as she usually did, she remained on her side of the seat.

After some moments, he asked softly, "Laurie?"

"Chris," she began tentatively and turned to study his

face. Bathed green in the reflection from the instrument panel, he appeared almost angry.

"Chris, can you remember how you actually *did* feel, the day you treated the baby?"

"What do you mean?" he demanded, half turning to challenge her.

"Keep your eyes on the road. This is difficult enough without you staring at me."

"Well, go ahead."

"First, I should tell you the question of whether to put you on the stand isn't entirely in my hands. True, Franklyn wants to get at you, so it might seem logical to keep you off the stand, but I want you to know that even if I don't call you, he can. As a hostile witness. So we have to be prepared."

"What makes you think I'm not prepared? Or that I'm not willing to take the stand?" he demanded. "Now what were you trying to ask me?"

She said gingerly, "Chris, what *were* your feelings that day?"

"Feelings about what, the infant? The sketchy transcript that came over from Parkside? Old man Reynolds breathing down my neck? How did I feel about *what?*"

"About everything."

"I knew that I wasn't going to trust any lab results from Parkside. I wanted my own and until I got them I decided to use phototherapy as insurance. When I got the results and realized the infant's condition was not too clearly defined, I continued with the phototherapy till we could get a more accurate indication. Once the bilirubin started down I honestly believed that infant was out of the woods," Chris said with an air of finality that seemed not to allow for any further questions or doubts.

"That's what you *did*, but what did you *feel?*"

"What does that mean?"

"Chris, darling," she half begged. "Your irritation just

now when you mentioned Reynolds, did he make you angry then too?"

Chris took his foot off the gas and coasted onto the shoulder of the highway. "What are you trying to say?"

"I didn't say, I was only asking." She paused, then decided to go straight to the point. "Chris, is it possible, just possible, that there is the slightest truth in Reynolds' statement that you had a long, deep, innate grudge against his family because of their wealth?"

"You don't believe that, do you?" he said with muted fury.

"What *I* believe doesn't matter. I have to know exactly how you're going to respond if Franklyn puts that question to you."

"If *you* can ask something like that . . ." He broke off.

"I have to know. Franklyn is one of the shrewdest, craftiest trial lawyers in the business."

"Yes, Franklyn," he echoed. "It's a hell of a profession you practice, my darling. Mere justice is too much to ask. This isn't any longer a trial about what I did or didn't do. It's become a trial to prove how good a lawyer Harry Franklyn is!"

"That is not the point!" Laura insisted.

"Isn't it?" he demanded fiercely. "What you're asking right now is will I be able to stand up to Franklyn and maintain my innocence? Well, go on, ask the real question that's in your mind!"

"Chris." She tried to calm him.

"I'm not afraid to take the stand! I have no doubts about what I did! If you're afraid, then maybe you're . . ."

He didn't complete his accusation. He had no need to. She knew. There was a long, oppressive silence in the car after that.

"Is this what you meant when you warned me how relationships are eroded during a trial?" he asked finally.

"Maybe."

In a while, she said, "It's late. I think we should head back."

He was about to start up the motor when the revolving red light of a police car stopped behind them. The uniformed trooper came to their window, he checked them out and said they were free to go. But he had a word of advice.

"There are motels for this kind of thing. They're safer. Too many lovers have been robbed and worse along this highway in the last couple of years."

They headed back toward the city. Chris, guilty and penitent, tried to lighten the mood. "Lovers. I wonder what he'd have advised if he'd heard what we were saying?"

She didn't answer. They drove the rest of the way in silence. When he brought her to her door he kissed her, but she barely returned the gesture.

"I'll see you in the morning," she said.

She locked her door and in so doing had a forlorn feeling that it was an act as symbolic as it was practical. She had locked him out.

She went about her nightly routine, brushing her teeth, creaming her face, all the time wondering if love could recover from such a charge as he had made tonight.

As angry as Chris had been with her, she was even more furious with herself. The confrontation tonight had been her fault. It should have occurred weeks ago. If Chris had been just another client that was the first thing she would have asked—a complete, honest recital of his feelings and thoughts during the fateful episode. Because she loved him she had trusted him, and then, still worse, revoked her trust.

Mike Sobol should never have called her in on the case. She should never have allowed herself to fall in love with Chris.

She sat up in bed and found her cigarettes. After a while she forced herself to make a cold appraisal of her situation.

One thing was true, if they lost there could be no appeal. They could not afford it. Worse, if Chris had any future left in medicine, it would be far from here, probably in some remote part of the country. So, if they were to have a life together she might have to give up her career or, at best, begin all over again somewhere else. She didn't know whether love could survive such uprooting.

Alone, in the middle of the night, she could admit certain things about herself. Yes, she wanted to marry Chris, and have his children. But that could not be her whole life. Yet, if the jury's verdict went against them, she would undoubtedly have to choose between the two.

She promised herself one thing. From now until the end of the case, she was going to be Chris Grant's lawyer, not his lover. And in making that decision she realized she also had no choice but to put Chris on the stand. No matter how many medical experts rallied to their defense, the crux of the case was Chris's judgment, and only he could justify that.

She fell asleep still working on a defense which must end with Chris Grant on the stand.

"Michael Sobol," announced the clerk.

Mike was sworn in and seated on the witness chair. As Laura rose to question him he thought that if the situation were not so grave he would have been amused. He kept remembering her as a blonde-haired toddler and here she was asking him questions about his schooling, his background, the list of academic appointments he had held.

Slowly, but quite effectively, Laura was qualifying Mike as a distinguished expert. His list of professional accomplishments was so long that Harry Franklyn rose to say, "The plaintiff will stipulate as to the qualifications of this witness."

Judge Bannon was ready to accede, but Laura refused. She wanted the jury to hear Mike's entire impressive career, and only when it had been entered in the court record would she launch into his testimony. Then she elicited from Mike how he first learned of the infant's condition, and promised to send an ambulance to bring it to Metropolitan General.

"Dr. Sobol, when you examined the infant for the first time did it seem to you to be in extreme condition?"

"Not extreme. But any time an infant has a positive Coombs we take it seriously."

"Regardless of the condition of the infant?" Laura persisted.

"Such a situation can become extremely serious in a matter of hours. A doctor must always take a cautious view," Mike replied.

"In the situation you describe, Doctor, what would you as an experienced and expert pediatrician do?" Laura asked.

"Exactly what I did. I turned the infant over to a man in whom I had the highest confidence, Dr. Grant."

"Did you give him any instructions?" Laura asked.

"No instructions were necessary," Mike said.

"Object!" said Franklyn.

"Sustained!" Bannon ruled immediately.

"Doctor," Laura began again, "please answer the question directly. Did you give him any instructions?"

"No," Mike said simply.

"Dr. Sobol, is there any reason why you didn't treat that infant yourself?"

"Well, as you know . . ."

Franklyn raised his forefinger to object. Bannon anticipated him. "The witness's attorney may know these things;

the court and the jury do not. The witness will confine himself to stating facts."

Mike Sobol's face flushed. "There are two reasons why I turned the infant over to Dr. Grant. First, I had a class to teach. Second, and more important, I had as much confidence in Dr. Grant's judgment as in my own."

"Dr. Sobol, presented with the signs, lab reports, and facts stated in the transcript, and based on your examination of the infant in question, in your expert opinion, would any other treatment have been called for?" Laura asked.

"If I had to make the decision again under exactly the same circumstances I would not do anything differently," Sobol declared.

"In your opinion did Dr. Grant's treatment conform with good medical practice?" Laura asked the vital question.

"Without any doubt."

Thereupon Laura began to read back to Mike Sobol parts of the testimony from the plaintiff's medical witnesses, asking him in each instance to agree or disagree. It was a time-consuming procedure, but it was necessary to dislodge from the jurors' minds many of the notions implanted by Franklyn. By the end of his direct testimony Mike Sobol had established some rapport with the jury. One felt that they believed him.

Harry Franklyn rose to the challenge. He advanced slowly toward Sobol, and said softly, "Doctor, did I understand you to testify that you would have followed the same course of treatment if confronted by an infant presenting identical symptoms?"

"I'm afraid that would be impossible," Sobol said.

"You mean there couldn't be another case identical with this one?" Franklyn asked, truly puzzled.

"Not at all. I mean that an infant can't 'present any symptoms,'" Sobol countered softly.

Franklyn reddened. "Do you mean to tell me that you can't detect symptoms in an infant?"

"I mean, sir, that 'symptoms' are what the patient complains of. A two-day-old infant is not likely to present 'symptoms.'"

"There's no need to quibble, Doctor," Franklyn shot back.

Sobol did not raise his voice. "Mr. Franklyn, I'm trying to save you from embarrassment. What the patient complains of are called *symptoms*. What the doctor observes are called *signs*. When dealing with infants we have only signs to go by."

Franklyn suppressed his anger, restated his question. "Dr. Sobol, do you mean to tell us that confronted with the same situation, the same 'signs,' you would have adopted the same modality as Dr. Grant?"

"Precisely," Sobol replied.

"Phototherapy?"

"I didn't say that."

"That is what Dr. Grant used, isn't it, Doctor?" Franklyn asked.

"Only as a *part* of his treatment, sir."

"Did he or did he not use phototherapy on that infant?" Franklyn demanded.

"Mr. Franklyn, do you want an answer to your question or do you want the truth?" Mike asked without raising his voice.

Franklyn had no choice but to say, "We are interested in truth, of course."

"Well, sir," Sobol said, "in medicine, when presented with a problem of uncertain prognosis we have a basic rule. Until you establish a trend, treat the treatable. In this case with an infant presenting certain signs which might or might not be entirely due to an Rh incompatibility, we would treat for all possible causes. That is why Dr. Grant started an intravenous, not only to give the infant nourishment but to administer an antibiotic, in case the basic cause of the infant's jaundice was an infection. At the same

266

time he drew blood for the necessary tests and, as an added precaution, placed the infant in phototherapy. Thus, even before results came back from the lab, treatment was under way."

"Doctor, couldn't all this have been averted by doing what is called an exchange blood transfusion?"

"I don't see how," Sobol said.

"We have heard numerous well-qualified experts testify that under like circumstances they would have done an exchange transfusion at once. Do you disagree with them?" Franklyn asked.

"Did you ask them what they would have done if the cause of the trouble was an *infection?*"

Franklyn appealed to the bench. "Will Your Honor instruct the witness to respond to the question?"

Bannon leaned across his desk. "Dr. Sobol, we do not answer questions with questions. Please try to give Mr. Franklyn a direct answer."

"I'll try," Mike said, mopping his bald head with his pocket kerchief.

"Do you disagree with the opinions of the other experts who testified that they would have done an immediate transfusion?" Franklyn asked.

"Since the severity and prognosis of the condition were not determined, such treatment seemed too radical for the situation," Sobol declared soberly. "The cause might have been . . ."

Franklyn interrupted. "You've answered the question, Doctor!" Then he continued, "Do you consider an Rh incompatibility a serious problem in an infant forty-eight hours old with a bilirubin of sixteen?"

"Any doctor would," Sobol replied.

"I asked whether *you* consider it serious," Franklyn pursued.

"I consider it potentially *very* serious."

"Then do you consider it sufficient to resort to phototherapy instead of a surer method of treatment, namely an exchange transfusion?"

"It depends on the specific circumstances."

"Doctor, I think you're being evasive," Franklyn chided.

"Lawyer, I think you're being misleading," Sobol responded sharply.

Bannon leaned forward. "Dr. Sobol, despite what you may have seen on television, we are not in the habit of trading insults in the courtroom."

Laura rose to intercede. "Your Honor, my witness has been trying to be responsive. But there are medical questions that cannot be answered in precisely the limited form Mr. Franklyn would like. I think a little more latitude in Dr. Sobol's answers might save a good deal of time and bickering."

Much as he disliked being instructed by a woman, Bannon had to agree. "The witness will be permitted to answer in full when necessary."

"Doctor," resumed Franklyn, "between the two methods of treatment . . ."

Sobol interrupted, "I have left some unfinished business, if you don't mind, Mr. Franklyn."

"Such as?" Franklyn asked intolerantly.

"Such as whether I agree with your experts. I do not. For one reason. They were not there. I was. They did not examine the infant. I did. They are judging *after* the fact, and I am not. In my opinion, confronted by an infant with the signs presented, with a bilirubin of sixteen, one might *consider* a transfusion. But when the next lab report comes back showing that the bilirubin has stabilized, I don't think any doctor should urge an exchange transfusion. After all, it is a procedure not without risk and if you will recall the next lab test showed a significant decline. Good medical practice does not indicate rushing into a transfusion."

The explanation was full and complete, more so than

Franklyn would have liked. He decided to sharpen his attack.

"If your opinion is correct, then how do you explain the infant's current tragic condition?"

Laura watched the deep blush rise in Mike's face. "I'm afraid I can't answer that question," he said. "It is not always possible to ascribe brain damage to a specific cause."

"Do you mean that your expertise deserts you when called on to answer the crucial question?" Franklyn asked, the slightest edge of sarcasm in his soft voice.

"I mean that no doctor could definitely state the cause of brain damage in that child," Sobol said sadly.

"Yet we have heard experts here in this courtroom express opinions to the contrary, Doctor. They think it was caused by improper treatment. Treatment that may have actually done more to damage that infant than help it."

"Experts," Sobol scoffed. "I tell you nobody knows the cause. They are only guessing."

When Sobol finished, Franklyn asked, "Doctor, do you accept the fact that the infant, John Reynolds Simpson, is brain-damaged?"

Sobol paused, stared across the well of the courtroom at John Reynolds, then said, "Yes, I accept that."

"Do you know of any other cause besides improper treatment that could have resulted in such damage?"

"Cause? There are many causes. But in this case . . . no, I can't account for it," was his final sad admission.

"Thank you, Doctor," Franklyn said, ending the cross-examination.

Because Franklyn had hurt Sobol's testimony so badly, Laura felt impelled to continue on redirect, but she was limited to those matters that Franklyn had touched upon.

"Dr. Sobol, when you mentioned causes of brain damage, what did you have in mind?"

"A medication the mother might have taken during

pregnancy. Some unobserved viral infection that might affect a fetus in utero. Or some factor we don't yet understand."

"So there might have been several causes for the damage suffered by John Reynolds Simpson?" Laura asked.

"That is true," said Sobol.

Laura did not press him further, but Franklyn rose swiftly to say,

"Dr. Sobol, in the face of all the medical testimony and your own examination of the tragically retarded infant, do you still maintain that phototherapy was the proper form of treatment in this case?"

Mike Sobol, his face damp and red, paused before answering in a voice so low it was only a whisper, "Yes, yes, I do maintain that."

Franklyn did not pursue the matter. There was no need to.

Mike Sobol rose unsteadily, for the first time aware of how strongly his heart was pounding. He was simply not equipped to be a witness. He returned to the counsel table, avoiding Chris's eyes and Laura's. He felt that he had failed them both. Yet he had told the truth. It was the truth which had failed them. A truth that could not be as conclusive as the law would like, but was as much as medical science had to offer.

TWENTY-THREE

AFTER MIKE SOBOL, Laura put several other expert witnesses on the stand. Competent doctors, of excellent reputation, they had volunteered to testify on behalf of the defense. Their testimony was of great value. But Laura knew that the only testimony that could sustain their defense was Chris Grant's. She knew, too, the danger involved in exposing him to Harry Franklyn's cross-examination. Nevertheless, it was a risk she had to take.

After establishing the excellence of Chris's medical training and background and his work at Metropolitan General, Laura questioned him about his experience in phototherapy, the way in which he had developed the program at Metropolitan, the manner in which the treatment worked, its effects, its benefits.

Her strategy was to condition the jury to accept phototherapy as sound medical practice. She also wanted to give Chris as much time as possible to relax on the witness stand before facing the cross-examination.

Harry Franklyn made very few objections. After a while, Laura became uneasily aware that he was going out of his way to give her an easy time. Occasionally he would jot down a note, but that was all and Laura found herself wondering what strategy he might be holding in reserve.

By midafternoon she had led Chris Grant from the generalities of phototherapy to the specifics of the Simpson case. After reviewing the known facts she attempted to explore Chris's own thoughts and motives during the time that was crucial to his decision.

"Doctor, presented with an infant with a bilirubin of sixteen and a laboratory finding of an Rh incompatibility, what thought was uppermost in your mind?"

"To make sure that the bilirubin count did not rise."

"What methods were available to you to ensure that result?"

"The two we've heard discussed in this courtroom," Chris answered. "An exchange transfusion and phototherapy."

"Doctor, wouldn't it have been easier, and safer, to have said, 'Let's start the exchange transfusion and eliminate all other steps'?"

"That could be like using a sledgehammer to nail a thumbtack," said Chris.

"Can you explain that comment to the jury?"

"A doctor selects his therapy based upon his patient's condition," Chris explained.

"And it was your considered opinion that the Simpson infant did not need an exchange transfusion at that time?" Laura asked.

"It was."

"Can you explain the reason for your decision?" Behind her she heard Harry Franklyn stir.

"With a bilirubin of sixteen, you have to study the infant to see if the bilirubin will climb higher or start down. Since in most cases a bilirubin moving in either direction moves fairly slowly, it takes an interval of two hours to discern any change."

"So that it takes several hours to make a determination as to the infant's real condition?"

"Several hours, at least," said Chris.

Usurping one of Franklyn's inevitable questions, Laura asked, "Doctor, wouldn't it have been safer to do an immediate transfusion, rather than wait those few hours?"

"Not necessarily," Chris replied. "A doctor unsure of his own judgment might rush into one, but I always avoid a transfusion if possible. The risks are too great."

"Despite the fact that doctors we heard during this trial have testified that the mortality risk is barely one percent?" Laura pressed.

"When you're dealing with a child's life you don't quote statistics. You can't say to a two-day-old infant if the transfusion fails, 'Sorry, son, you were the one percent.'"

Quite unconsciously, Chris turned to face the jury. "You have to see the newborns in intensive care. They hardly make a handful, tiny red bundles, still bearing the marks of delivery, struggling to breathe, to hold on to life. They lie in pitiful isolation, their little bodies twitching for food when normally they should be pressed against their mothers. Those little ones are engaged in the most dangerous fight of their lives."

Behind her, Laura heard Harry Franklyn stir impatiently. It was an encouraging sign. A restless Franklyn meant that Chris was beginning to score with the jury. She knew there would be an objection at any moment now, but as long as Chris wanted to continue, she would let him.

"It may be that a neonatologist has an unnatural view of early life. We do not deal with healthy infants. We see only the sick, the pathetic. We see them, too, when unfortunately they become laboratory specimens."

At that point Harry Franklyn rose. "Objection! The witness has been granted far too much latitude."

Though Judge Bannon was intrigued with Chris's testimony, he had to recognize the validity of Franklyn's point. "The witness will confine himself to the facts germane to this particular case."

Far from being distressed, Laura welcomed the objection and the ruling. It would make the jury feel that Chris was being prevented from telling his entire story. More confidently she proceeded.

"Doctor, to return to the risks involved in a transfusion. Can you enumerate them?"

"In the main, it can cause infection even when the procedure is carried out with the utmost care."

"Any other risks?" Laura asked.

"It is possible that the very act of transfusing the infant will bring on dangerous cardiac reactions. The procedure extends over a period of more than an hour and during that time the infant may respond badly."

"What does the doctor do then?"

"He stops the transfusion at once."

"And then?"

"After monitoring the heart and blood pressure response, he may decide to continue later, or he may have to abandon the exchange altogether. Not every infant can be transfused and survive," Chris declared.

"Doctor, have you ever had a case in which you have had to stop a transfusion completely?"

"Every pediatrician has had such cases."

"How do you proceed?" Laura asked.

"Well, since there are no choices left, you would put the infant under phototherapy. But at that stage you would not expect a good result."

"Doctor, is it possible that if you had decided to transfuse the Simpson baby it might have reacted unfavorably?"

Before Chris could answer, Harry Franklyn was on his feet.

"Your Honor, since no such attempt was made on the Simpson baby, a fact admitted by both sides in this case, such a question is irrelevant. It calls for speculation."

"Objection sustained!"

Laura desperately wanted to have Chris answer that

question. But she was realist enough to know that no judge would allow it. She proceeded with her examination.

"Doctor, a few moments ago you referred to infants who have become laboratory specimens.What did you mean?"

"Infants who for one reason or another have died during the first week. Where possible, I ask the parents to agree to an autopsy."

"In cases involving an elevated bilirubin, what do you look for?" Laura asked.

"I try to find the degree to which there is brain damage due to kernicterus."

"Have you examined many such specimens?" Laura asked gently.

"Probably a thousand," Chris said gravely.

"Dr. Grant, is a man who has had intensive exposure to such sad cases likely to be casual or lax in his determination of the treatment of any infant with a high bilirubin?"

"Object!" called Franklyn. "The answer would only be self-serving."

"Sustained," Bannon ruled.

Now Laura launched into the most delicate part of her examination—an attempt to disprove Reynolds' allegation that Chris had been motivated by prejudice in his handling of the case.

"Dr. Grant, you heard John Stewart Reynolds testify that hostility toward him might have influenced your decision in treating his grandson. Is that true?"

"It is not. In the first place, I bear no hostility toward Mr. Reynolds. In the second place, he was not the patient. In the third place, no matter how I felt about any other human being I would never revenge myself on an infant," Chris Grant declared aggressively.

Harry Franklyn made another note.

"Doctor, you have just testified that you felt no hostility toward John Stewart Reynolds. Yet Mr. Reynolds testified that your medical papers indicated a prejudice against the society. Particularly against the rich. Can you explain that?"

"Most of the infants I saw in those studies were born to mothers either too poor or too ignorant to know the effect of poor diet during pregnancy. The result is children who start life with improperly developed brains. If they survive they become a drain on society, if they die they become specimens. To doctors like me, it seems inhuman to work in silence rather than attempt to correct the situation. If he has ideas that can prevent sickness and benefit the society at large a doctor should speak out. To do otherwise is criminal negligence!"

Harry Franklyn made another note.

"Was any of the social criticism in your papers directed to any particular person?"

"It was not. It was leveled at the general inequity that prevails in our society."

Franklyn added another note to his growing list.

"So that you did not mean to single out any individual?"

"I did not."

"Or any particular class of individuals?"

"If by class you mean the rich, my answer is no," Chris said firmly. "There are as many rich people trying to correct this situation as there are poor. More perhaps. Much of our research funding comes from the well-to-do. I have no reason to resent them."

"Dr. Grant, was your decision to treat the Simpson infant in any way influenced by anything but your best professional judgment?"

"It was not."

"If you were confronted with the identical set of facts today, would you pursue the same course of treatment?" Laura asked.

"If the facts were the same, yes, I would," Chris said with finality.

Laura stepped back from the witness box and started toward her chair.

"What do you think?" Mike Sobol whispered as she sat down.

"It went pretty well," she said, trying to sound more confident than she really was.

Instead of launching into his cross-examination, Harry Franklyn pointed out the lateness of the hour and asked for a delay until morning, which the judge was quick to grant. Franklyn had no intention of revealing his strategy so the defense could counter it overnight. He wanted to work on Christopher Grant when the advantages were all his, when, with unlimited time, he could proceed to dissect this highly vulnerable young man.

TWENTY-FOUR

THE NEXT morning when Laura, Chris and Mike Sobol entered and took their places at the defense table, no one had yet appeared for the plaintiff. While Laura was laying out her papers, there was a stir at the door.

The court attendants forced back eager spectators while John Stewart Reynolds, his wife, and an unidentified young woman entered. Harry Franklyn led them down the aisle.

Puzzled, Laura whispered, "Who are they?"

Chris identified Mrs. Reynolds, but it was Mike Sobol who recognized the younger woman. "Arlene Simpson, Reynolds' daughter."

"The infant's mother?" Laura reacted with great concern, wondering why Reynolds would have elected to bring her into court at this particular stage of the trial. It must be Harry Franklyn's idea, and the realization gave Laura additional reason to feel uneasy.

Judge Bannon was several minutes late. When he finally entered he was still pulling on his black judicial robe. With a brisk apology he gave the clerk a sign to continue with the case.

Chris resumed the stand. Laura and Mike Sobol sat

alertly upright in their chairs—Laura to make notes for future questioning, Mike to jot down any medical facts that would be of use in Laura's redirect. While Franklyn was gathering his papers, Laura had a chance to glance at Mrs. Simpson. She was a slight girl, resembling her mother, with small, regular features and carefully set, light blonde hair.

Her fragile face made her instantly sympathetic. She appeared younger than she was, less able to cope with the burden of raising a brain-damaged child. Laura could appreciate why Harry Franklyn had chosen to withhold her presence from the jury until now. Much as Laura resented the ploy, she had to concede its effectiveness. Already the jury was staring at the young woman, guessing who she was.

Franklyn waited until he was sure all the jurors had noted Mrs. Simpson's presence and then approached the witness, fingering his notes as if unsure where to begin his attack. It was only a tactic. Harry Franklyn always had his complete strategy in mind. He divided hostile witnesses into two categories—liars and honest men. He had distinctly different techniques for impeaching each.

The liar could be entrapped in his own inconsistencies. Not so the honest man. The way to attack him was to make his very consistency appear a fault, to turn his dedication to what he believed into an Achilles' heel.

Chris Grant had already betrayed a profound dedication to his profession. Both in his examination before trial and in his direct testimony. Several times his emotional outbursts had interrupted the trial. Harry Franklyn had carefully noted all these signs and his cross-examination was structured around them. In Grant's case there was yet another point of vantage: the doctor could be involved so deeply in one phase of his testimony that a sudden switch could leave him temporarily defenseless.

Affably, as if trying to be helpful to both Chris and

the court, Franklyn began, "Dr. Grant, perhaps we should resume with the last point raised by the defense. Would the court stenographer read back both the question and the answer?"

The stenographer found yesterday's stenotyping notes and read aloud, " 'If you were confronted with the identical set of facts today, would you pursue the same course of treatment?' "

"And the doctor's answer?" asked Franklyn.

" 'If the facts were the same, yes, I would,' " the stenographer read back.

"Dr. Grant, can you stand by that statement knowing the tragic outcome of this case?" Franklyn turned to Arlene Simpson. "Would you pursue the same treatment even though you have learned this unfortunate young mother's child is permanently brain-damaged?"

Laura and Mike exchanged glances. Mike whispered, "The bastard!"

"Doctor?" Franklyn prodded.

"Based on the facts as they appeared at the time, I would still have to say yes. I would do the same because it was the correct medical procedure."

Franklyn was delighted. His evaluation of Chris was entirely correct. This was going to be a turkey shoot. For the benefit of the jury Franklyn shook his head in apparent distress. "Do I understand that you feel there was nothing to be learned from that drastic experience?" he asked.

"I mean," Chris said, already beginning to evidence signs of irritation, "that my treatment was the only proper one in the circumstances."

"Despite the result?"

"Despite the result!" Chris said even more strongly.

It was this affirmation that Franklyn had wanted. "Doctor," he proceeded, "is it usual for young men like yourself to be so positive, so dogmatic, if I may use the word?"

"About procedures that have been medically proven we are positive," Chris replied.

"So positive that you continue using such procedures in spite of their consequences?"

"If you're referring to those doctors who came in *after* the fact and testified as to how they would handle the case, I can't accept their statements. At the time I saw the Simpson baby, guided by the known facts and my own professional experience, I would say I chose the right treatment. And so would most doctors forced to make that decision."

"How do you know that?" Franklyn asked with the suddenness of a whiplash.

"Know what?"

"What most other doctors *would* have done?" Franklyn pursued.

"Because it's sound medical practice!"

"Did most of the other doctors testify to that?"

"I told you they were dealing with the case in retrospect, with twenty-twenty hindsight!"

"My question referred to the time you were actually treating the infant," said Franklyn. Chris seemed puzzled. "Doctor," Franklyn continued, "did any other doctor concur in your decision *at the time it was made?*"

"Did they concur . . ." Chris repeated, then recovered to say, "There were no other doctors involved at the time."

"Oh, I see," Franklyn remarked, handling that disclosure as if he had just learned it. "In other words, you did not consult with any other doctor before you placed the infant in phototherapy?"

"No."

"Not even with Dr. Sobol?"

"I talked to him later. I told him what I had done and that I was awaiting the lab results before I decided on any further course of treatment."

"Did you discuss it with Dr. Sobol?" Franklyn asked.

"I reported to him," Chris answered.

"Did you *discuss* it?" Franklyn insisted.

Laura rose to object. "Counsel is trying to force the witness into a semantic discourse. If he reported to Dr. Sobol, I would assume that to be a discussion."

"And I would not!" said Franklyn angrily.

"Allow counsel to continue with his line of questioning," Bannon ruled, disposing of Laura's objection.

"Doctor, do I understand correctly that both before you placed that infant in phototherapy and during the time you were waiting the result of the laboratory tests you did not seek Dr. Sobol's advice?"

"It wasn't necessary to seek his advice," Chris answered.

"Why not?" Franklyn asked.

"Because he would have agreed with my decision, as he later did."

"You don't think it possible that he might have said, 'Young man, I think in such a case we might be well advised to consider a transfusion instead of relying on phototherapy'?"

"Possible," Chris admitted, "but not likely."

"And because *you* thought that it was not likely, because *you* decided that *your* judgment was so far superior to anyone else's you felt you had no *need* to ask for advice or consultation?" Franklyn demanded sharply. When Chris hesitated, Franklyn pressed his advantage, "Is that it, Doctor?"

"I . . . I did not think the case of such questionable nature or so bizarre in its signs that it demanded any additional consultation," Chris said.

"Doctor," Harry Franklyn began, in his lowest voice, "you are aware, aren't you, that it can constitute malpractice *not* to consult with other doctors in questionable situations?"

"This was not such a marginal case as to require consultation, in my opinion."

"In the opinion of a young man, who we have just heard is willing to place his judgment over that of any number of highly qualified men with infinitely more experience," Franklyn said, making it a statement rather than a question.

Laura moved to object. Having achieved his purpose, Franklyn quickly withdrew the remark and apologized. But he had scored. He had shaken Chris by accusing him of not seeking consultation when he should have. More important, he had begun to paint Grant as an arrogant young man, too sure, too dogmatic, to give credence to his elders or to value the experience of the past. It was an eminently effective strategy and with the cooperation of an emotional witness like Chris it was highly likely to succeed.

Franklyn decided on a sudden change of subject, "Doctor, your own counsel asked you yesterday if your treatment of the Simpson infant was in any way influenced by your feelings about John Reynolds."

Laura abruptly interrupted. "That was neither the form nor the substance of my question. I made no mention of Reynolds or any other individual!"

Pretending to have committed an unintentional error, Franklyn turned to Laura, "Perhaps my memory is faulty. Would the stenographer please read the next to last question counsel asked yesterday?"

The stenographer found the place. " 'Dr. Grant, was your decision to treat the Simpson infant in any way influenced by anything but your best professional judgment?' "

"And Dr. Grant's answer?" Laura demanded.

"It was not!" Chris volunteered from the stand before the stenographer could begin.

283

Franklyn then asked, "Doctor, though you are not a specialist in psychiatry, I assume you have some knowledge of the vocabulary. What does the word 'unconscious' mean in medical terms?"

"That question is totally irrelevant!" Laura protested.

"The court considers the question quite relevant and instructs the witness to answer!" Bannon ruled in a loud voice.

"Doctor?" Franklyn pressed.

Chris hesitated, then complied. "As I understand it, it generally means a feeling that motivates the patient even though he is not aware of its existence."

"So that if a psychiatrist were to conclude that someone had an unconscious hostility, that would mean a hostility that the person himself was not aware of. Is that right?"

"Yes," Chris admitted grudgingly.

"In fact, might it not be possible that the hostile person probably would be the *last* to admit his unconscious hostility, which is why he would have needed the help of a psychiatrist in the first place?"

Before Chris could answer, Laura interrupted. "There is no evidence that the defendant is in need of psychiatric help! I ask the court to caution counsel to confine his questions to proper matters for cross-examination."

Franklyn faced the bench with an air of aggrieved innocence. "Your Honor, I didn't introduce the word or the concept of a 'patient' into this testimony. The witness did. In his answer, which went, as I recall, 'As I understand it, it generally means a feeling that motivates the *patient* even though he is not aware of its existence.'" He turned to the stenographer to seek confirmation. When he received it, he said, "Since the word was of the witness's choosing, I think I should be permitted to use it."

Judge Bannon agreed.

Franklyn took advantage of the ruling to say, "We must remember it was defense counsel's own questions that opened up this area of examination. She invited her witness to express his opinion on his motivations during treatment. I think I have every right to explore the subject."

"Continue!" said Bannon.

"Doctor, if someone has an unconscious hostility, might that also mean that he is not qualified to express an opinion as to his motivation in any given circumstance?"

Laura addressed the bench. "Your Honor, Mr. Franklyn's question is based on an assumption, a false assumption, that the witness harbors some secret hostility toward Mr. Reynolds. There is no proof of that. Therefore this entire line of questioning is not only irrelevant but highly specious. It is calculated to mislead the jury and this court!"

Bannon was forced to concede, "Counsel's argument does have point."

"Your Honor," said Franklyn, "we are just about to make the connection between Mr. Reynolds' testimony and Dr. Grant's hostility. If I may be permitted to ask just a few more questions."

Bannon conceded with a wave of the hand.

"Doctor, is it still your contention that you harbored no hostility toward Mr. Reynolds at any time?"

Moving to his table to pick up some papers, Franklyn asked in a soft aside, "Not even now, Dr. Grant?" A faint smile played on his lips, as he added, "You don't have to answer that."

Armed with his documents, the lawyer returned to the witness stand. Chris realized with a sense of shock that the papers were reprints of medical articles.

"Doctor," asked Franklyn, "you have just testified in the strongest terms that you felt no hostility toward John Stewart Reynolds. Is that true?"

"Yes," said Chris, wondering at the needless repetition.

"Dr. Grant, in your medical reading on the subject of brain-damaged infants have you ever come across the term 'Reynolds' babies'?"

Even the spectators in the courtroom seemed aware that this was a pivotal question.

When Chris did not answer at once, Franklyn added, "Doctor, have you ever heard the term 'Reynolds' babies'?"

Chris flushed, then finally admitted, "Yes. Yes, I have."

"Could you explain to the jury who originated that term?"

Chris felt his mouth go dry, but he managed to say, "I . . . I originated that term."

"Oh, did you?" Franklyn remarked before asking, "And could you enlighten the jury as to its application?"

"It was a term I used for the brain-damaged children seen in the course of my recent research," Chris explained.

"Doctor," said Franklyn sharply, "did you create that term before or after you treated the Simpson baby?"

"I don't see what . . ." Chris started to protest.

"*Before* or *after* you treated the Simpson baby, Doctor?"

"Before," said Chris.

"Doctor, can you explain to the jury exactly why you alone among all doctors who have written on the subject use the term 'Reynolds' babies'?"

"It had nothing to do with John Reynolds!" Chris declared.

"Doctor, explain to the jury, please," Franklyn urged, as if inviting a sinner to repent.

"As I explained yesterday, most of the brain-damaged infants I saw came from very poor homes. Their mothers live in tenements or in low-cost housing developments. By sheer coincidence my first few specimens came from developments called Reynolds Houses. So for convenience I simply labeled them 'Reynolds' babies.' "

"And thereafter you 'simply' continued to use that name?" Franklyn remarked acidly.

"It had nothing to do with John Reynolds!" Chris fought back. "Those houses were called Reynolds Houses because they were built by the Reynolds Construction Company!"

"Of course," Franklyn observed. He consulted his notes. "Doctor, have you ever heard the name Wilmot?"

Chris was puzzled and hesitated to answer.

"Let me help you," said Franklyn. "Have you heard any of the following names? Wilmot? Persky? Di Lurie?"

Still puzzled, Chris finally answered, "I don't think so. Are they doctors?"

"They happen to be the names of low-cost housing developments in this city."

"Oh, yes," said Chris.

"Then you *do* recognize them?"

"Now I do, yes."

"Doctor, does Metropolitan General draw patients from any of those developments?"

"Yes," Chris admitted, wondering at the purpose of the question.

"Have you ever received specimens from the damaged brains of infants from those developments?" Franklyn asked.

"Yes, yes, I have," Chris said slowly.

"How many? One? Two? Five? Ten?" Franklyn pursued. "Or would you like to consult your records before you answer?"

"I think we can say that I've seen a number of specimens."

"Did it ever occur to you to use the name Wilmot babies for your paper? Or Persky babies? Or Di Lurie babies?"

"I thought I explained that before."

"Perhaps neither the jury nor I fully understood. Try again, Doctor."

"The first cases I saw came from that development. The choice of the name was simply a convenience. Later I didn't consider it important enough to change it."

Franklyn followed up his advantage. "You didn't think it was a matter of importance that you might be libeling a decent, respectable citizen?"

"I didn't intend to libel anyone. I was dealing with a housing development that reflected a social problem," Chris tried to explain.

"Wouldn't Wilmot or Di Lurie or Persky have reflected that social problem just as well?"

"I don't know," said Chris. "Maybe I used Reynolds because it was better known."

Franklyn seized on the admission. "So there *was* a reason. Your choice of that name *was* deliberate."

"It was deliberate but not hostile. It reflected on a social problem, not an individual. In fact, the building in which I did my research was donated by Mr. Reynolds. Why would I try to libel or defame him?"

"Why indeed?" Franklyn said reproachfully.

Chris realized how important Laura's advice had been about not volunteering information. It only created further opportunities for a shrewd lawyer to exploit to his own advantage. Franklyn was already glancing at the jury, as if to say, To this young man's other faults, add ingratitude.

Before Chris could recover, Franklyn suddenly switched subjects again. "Doctor, when you examined John Reynolds' grandson for the first time, what did you find?"

"Based on the transcript and my examination I found an Rh infant possibly two weeks preterm, but of sufficient weight not to be classified premature. The child was noticeably jaundiced with a bilirubin of fourteen according to the lab at Parkside Polyclinic."

"We heard Mr. Reynolds testify that he saw you draw a blood sample, apply an intravenous and promptly place the infant under phototherapy. Is that right?"

"Yes. Routine procedure under the circumstances," Chris declared.

"Doctor, how much time would you say it took to do all that?"

"Time?" Chris reflected, realizing that he had never before considered the issue. "I wouldn't know."

"Could you make a guess?" Franklyn invited.

"If I had to guess I would say about five to ten minutes."

"So that you examined the infant, took a blood sample, applied an intravenous. And also decided on and put that infant under phototherapy, all within five to ten minutes, Doctor?"

"Working with the information and equipment you have at hand, you do whatever you can quickly while awaiting more definite lab results."

"As we've heard before, 'you treat the treatable,' is that right?" Franklyn seemed anxious to nail down Chris's answer.

"Yes."

"What are the criteria for such swift action, Doctor?" Franklyn asked.

"Whatever may aid the patient without inflicting any harm. We would not take extreme or potentially dangerous steps on the basis of the skimpy evidence that we had at that time."

"Did you consider the use of phototherapy as something that could aid the patient without endangering it?"

"I did."

"Doctor, this phototherapy, it's not without risk, is it?"

Mike Sobol saw Laura's hands clench the edge of the table.

"In the sense that no therapy is absolutely without risk, no. But the risk is so minimal that for all practical purposes it does not exist," Chris said.

"Would you call skin rashes an acceptable aftereffect of any therapy?" Franklyn asked blandly.

"It is an inconvenience but not a hazard," Chris replied. "I explained that in my examination before trial."

"What about stomach upset in an infant, retching, diarrhea?"

"Again, a minor side effect, not a danger, since the infant is fed by IV during the treatment."

"But you *do* admit that these *are* aftereffects of photo-therapy?"

"*Side* effects, not aftereffects," Chris corrected.

"But still results from phototherapy?"

"*Possible* side effects, yes."

Franklyn turned to pick up another clipping. "Doctor, are you familiar with a publication called *The Journal of Medicine?*"

"Of course."

"May I read you a letter that appeared in the issue of September 3, 1970? In fact, would you care to examine it first?" He extended a copy of the clipping to Chris who glanced at it carefully. "Doctor, do you recognize the two names that appear at the end of this letter?"

"I've heard of Dr. Albert. And Dr. Rentler."

"From what you know of them, would you consider them good doctors, men of excellent professional reputation?"

"Yes."

"Doctor, why don't you keep that copy so you can check me as I read."

" 'To the Editor,' " Franklyn began, " 'The many articles you have published in recent years on the subject of photo-therapy continue to omit many risks to the patient, both theoretical and actual. We have compiled a list of the pos-sible hazards of phototherapy that we believe worthy of dis-semination.'

"Correct this far, Doctor?"

"Yes, correct, this far."

"May I continue? 'Animal data.' What does that mean, Doctor?"

"It means results gained from experiments on laboratory animals."

Franklyn continued reading:

" 'Animal data:

" 'Retarded growth in Gunn rats.

" 'Eye damage in piglets at 300 footcandles of light.

" 'Retinal damage in rats at 40 footcandles of light.
" 'Darkness-delayed pineal development in rabbits.
" 'Retarded gonadal growth in rats.
" 'Retinal damage in hamsters, mice and monkeys.
" 'Retinal vascular changes in rats.
" 'Increased liver glycogen values in rats.'

"Lest we overwhelm the jury with medical facts, perhaps we ought to stop here and ask you to define some of the terms used. Doctor, when the article talks of eye damage and retinal damage, to what do the authors refer?"

Aware of the danger of being misunderstood, Chris explained cautiously, "The continued intensity of the lights may inflict damage on the eyes of the patient *if,* and I repeat, *if* the eyes are not properly shielded during the phototherapy." Chris added before Franklyn could interrupt him, "In the case of the Simpson infant, its eyes were securely and properly protected. There was absolutely no retinal damage at all! No one has ever said there was!"

Franklyn waited out Chris's defense. He had expected it. "Doctor, to what does this article refer when it says, let me find it, 'Darkness-delayed pineal development in rabbits'?"

"The effect on certain glandular development in rabbits," Chris stated. "But there have been papers . . ."

"We'll get to that later, Doctor," Franklyn cut him off. "Now, Doctor, tell us, what are the gonads?"

"The male sex glands. The testes."

"Medically what is their function, Doctor?"

"The sperm is manufactured there."

"So that the entire male reproductive process depends on them?" Franklyn asked.

"Of course."

"Then when these two doctors state in their letter, 'retarded gonadal growth in rats' as a result of phototherapy they are actually saying that the application of phototherapy served to retard this vital development in those rats. Is that not so?"

"That's what they're referring to, but that may not be the truth."

"You'll have your turn later, Doctor. Let me continue. Now, under the heading 'Human Data,' these two doctors list the following hazards. That's their word, not mine, Doctor, *hazards*. Let me read them:

" 'Overheating from lights.

" 'Chilling from being exposed.

" 'Retarded growth.

" 'Alteration of circadian rhythms.

" 'Effect on age of sexual maturation.

" 'Rash.

" 'Jaundice masked by light.

" 'Sepsis more difficult to diagnose.

" 'Cyanosis masked by blue light.'

"And finally they list as the last hazard simply the word '*Unknown!*' "

Franklyn turned to face the jury.

"Doctor, do you have any idea what those two doctors refer to when they write of 'retarded growth'?" Franklyn asked.

"There was a paper written some eight or ten years ago which reported that cases had been observed in which phototherapy produced infants with smaller than normal heads," Chris explained. "But that was disproved by later tests and observations. In fact, the doctor who wrote that original paper finally admitted his observations were wrong."

Franklyn did not belabor the point. "Doctor, what does the word 'cyanosis' mean?"

"A patient becomes cyanotic when he fails to receive sufficient oxygen."

"And what is the first and most marked indication?" Franklyn asked.

"The skin turns bluish, starting with the lips and the fingertips," Chris said.

"Then am I right in assuming that what these two doctors mean by, quote, cyanosis masked by blue light, unquote, is that the blue light of the phototherapy may hide the fact that an infant has become cyanotic?"

"That's what they'd mean, *if* they had factual evidence. They're merely raising the question," Chris argued.

"Doctor," said Franklyn, pursuing his own course, "what happens to the human brain when it is deprived of oxygen for even a short span of time?"

Laura realized the trap that Franklyn had set for Chris and was determined not to let him fall into it. Rising, she called out, "Object! The question is immaterial and irrelevant. There is no finding on the part of any doctor in this case that the infant involved suffered anoxia or cyanosis and was damaged as a result!"

"Precisely the point I was making, Counselor," said Franklyn. "I thank you for the assistance." Turning to the bench, he said, "Your Honor, the point that I sought to establish is that phototherapy might *mask* the symptoms of cyanosis. The infant could well have been brain-damaged as a result and no doctor would ever suspect the cause. The bluish signs would have been masked by those blue lights!"

"That's a completely manufactured hypothesis!" Chris exploded. "You've taken bits and pieces, based on theories, not facts, and tried to make a case out of them!"

Franklyn turned on him sharply. "Would you care to *disprove* it, Doctor?"

"It is not always scientifically possible to prove that something *didn't* happen," Chris said, retreating a bit.

To Harry Franklyn that was the turning point of his examination. He felt a surge of elation.

"Doctor, another one of the hazards listed by Drs. Albert and Rentler is, I quote, 'alternation of circadian rhythms.' To what would they be referring?"

Chris glanced at Sobol who leaned over to whisper to

Laura, "What the hell does that have to do with the Simpson baby?" Laura put a restraining hand on Mike's arm. She knew another objection would be futile.

"Doctor?" Franklyn repeated.

"Circadian rhythms are rhythms of life attuned to the hours of the day. It involves many of the biophysiologic activities including sleep patterns, alertness, body temperature, release of stress hormones."

"Doctor, would you say that it is very similar to what is described as jet lag?"

"Jet lag is a form of interruption of circadian rhythms," said Chris.

"Is it possible, then, since an infant in phototherapy is under constant light twenty-four hours a day that it might upset its circadian rhythms?" Franklyn asked.

"That's only a theory."

"I merely asked, is it *possible*, Doctor?"

"Possible, yes," Chris was forced to admit.

"Then that would mean that an infant under those blue lights would have its sleep patterns upset, its alertness and body temperature affected, and its stress hormones affected?"

"I said those were the primary effects of interruption of circadian rhythms. But whether phototherapy would create those effects is pure speculation!"

"Doctor, do you think it is wise to upset the sleep patterns, the body temperature and the vital stress hormones of an infant whom you already know to be sick?"

"I say again, that's pure speculation."

Franklyn nodded his head, not agreeing, only marking Chris's ineffective answer.

"Doctor, how long does it take adults suffering from jet lag to recover?"

"Twenty-four to forty-eight hours," said Chris.

"As much as that?" Franklyn reacted as if he were surprised. "So that the infant, the Simpson baby, who, according to your hospital record, was kept under phototherapy for two days would then need another day or two to recover from the interruption of its circadian rhythms?"

Chris could no longer resist; he turned to Judge Bannon. "Damn it, it's a completely unproven theory! How long is that man going to be allowed to continue this nonsense?"

Laura quickly rose. "Your Honor, we demand a recess."

But Franklyn was not about to give Chris time to relax. "Your Honor, I can understand the witness's discomfort as we draw closer to the heart of his testimony. Frankly, if I were in his place, I would feel equally upset. But the purpose of cross-examination is to elicit the truth. Not to serve the convenience or comfort of the witness, unless, of course, counsel wishes to state that he is ill."

Bannon leaned toward Laura. "Does counsel make such an assertion?"

Laura shook her head.

Bannon said impatiently, "Continue, Counselor!"

"Now, Doctor," said Franklyn, smiling slightly at the jury, "as long as we are all agreed that you're not in any danger, tell me this: Is it at least possible that the Simpson infant could have had its circadian rhythms upset during the two days it was under phototherapy?"

"It's theoretically possible."

"Doctor, among the other possible dangers these two doctors list," Franklyn said, handling the excerpt from *The Journal of Medicine*, "is this last one, 'Unknown!' Would you be good enough to examine your copy and tell me what punctuation mark appears after the word 'Unknown'?"

Chris glanced down and said, "There is an exclamation point after the word 'Unknown.'"

"Is there an exclamation point after any of the other possible dangers?"

"There is not."

"What would that mean to you, as a doctor?" Franklyn asked.

"That Rentler and Albert deemed the last item the most important," Chris replied.

"More important than the dangers already mentioned?"

"I suppose so," said Chris.

Franklyn nodded to underline the answer's significance, but before he could make too much of the moment, Chris said, "If you really want to know, there is another statement in this article that is even more significant!"

Franklyn hesitated only an instant, then, realizing it was better to accede voluntarily, said, "Yes, Doctor, and what is that?"

Holding up the article toward the jury so they would know he was quoting from it, Chris read, " 'We believe that phototherapy used properly is both safe and effective. We point out that no serious clinical toxicity has been documented in over five thousand reported cases treated with light after a period of one to twelve years!' "

The jury seemed startled to receive that knowledge after the effective manner in which Franklyn had belittled the treatment, but Franklyn was not disturbed. With a courteous, "Permit me, Doctor," he retrieved the article. "I would like to read into the record the very last statement in this article, *'Although the known risks of hyperbilirubinemia and of exchange transfusion outweigh the above listed theoretical risks, we affirm that any responsible physician must be aware of the possible hazards of this new therapy, especially to the neonate.'* Doctor, would you follow me as I restate that in laymen's terms and correct me if I make any misstatements?"

Franklyn turned to the jury because this was one of the key moments that he had planned in the cross-examination.

"As I understand it," he said, "these two respected doctors are saying, first, that there are known and proven risks in a high bilirubin and in doing an exchange transfusion."

Chris interrupted, "And that those known risks outweigh the unknown risks of phototherapy!"

"Thank you, Doctor. That was the next point I was about to make. Yes, the known risks of transfusion outweigh the unknown risks of phototherapy *as far as we know*. But these doctors go on to say, in effect, that no responsible doctor should apply phototherapy to an infant, especially a neonate, without being aware of the possible hazards of this form of treatment. Right, Doctor?"

"Which these doctors themselves admit have not been documented in over five thousand patients, some of whom were observed for twelve years!" Chris struck back, hoping to destroy the false impression that Franklyn sought to leave with the jury.

Franklyn remained unperturbed. "Doctor, have you heard of aftereffects of treatment that have been delayed for *more* than twelve years? Haven't you recently read that medication taken when a woman was pregnant produced a cancerous condition in the reproductive organs of her daughter that didn't show up for as much as fifteen years?"

"Such results have been reported," said Chris. "They are being investigated now."

"Then, Doctor, if we may sum up—you decided to use phototherapy, with all its known and unknown dangers, after first examining the Simpson baby?"

"You're giving the wrong impression," said Chris.

"We'll run that risk, Doctor. Just answer the question."

Chris had no choice. "Yes, that is the form of treatment I prescribed."

"And only ten minutes after first laying eyes on that child?"

"Yes," said Chris.

"And you began the treatment without explaining the risks to the infant's grandfather, father or mother?"

"There was no need."

"In your opinion, Doctor," Franklyn qualified.

"In my opinion," Chris asserted.

"Doctor, do you know that in some hospitals it is standard procedure to secure what is known as informed consent before starting phototherapy?"

"There are some, yes," Chris had to admit. "Far from the majority."

"But you didn't think it was necessary?"

"When an infant is sick, it's essential to start treatment as soon as possible. Once the infant was in phototherapy I did explain to Mr. Reynolds."

"Did you? *Did* you warn Mr. Reynolds that his grandson would be exposed to the various hazards we have just covered?"

"Since the serious side effects are only speculations, I didn't think that would serve any purpose. And it would have taken too much time," Chris said, retreating to what he thought was safer ground.

"Too much time," Franklyn said with vicious sarcasm. "Too much time compared to the rest of that poor infant's life?"

"I meant too much time for the situation. At that moment, it was more important to establish the infant's true condition."

Franklyn knew he was on the verge of winning. "Doctor, you have been asked this question before. I ask it again, in the hope that the last few hours of cross-examination might have changed your mind. Would you today, confronted with an infant presenting the same medical signs, apply the same therapy?"

Chris hesitated, then declared, "Yes, I would."

"Despite the risks?"

Chris rose from his chair. "No researcher, no doctor you brought in here, was able to testify that there was any connection between phototherapy and the brain damage suffered by that child."

Franklyn did not argue. He started toward the plaintiff's table as though finished with the witness. Suddenly, half-way there, he turned back to Chris and asked, "Doctor, the pineal gland, where is it located?"

"In the brain," Chris replied.

"And did not Drs. Rentler and Albert warn that photo-therapy could affect the development of the pineal gland, which you tell us is in the brain?"

"That was in laboratory animals, not humans!" Chris responded angrily. "You're drawing a wrong conclusion."

"It's up to the jury to draw conclusions here, Doctor! Did they or did they not warn about damage observed in the laboratory to the pineal gland?"

"Yes, yes, they did," Chris conceded finally.

"And you never thought it important enough to warn Mr. Reynolds before starting treatment?"

Because he felt sure that neither Chris nor his counsel could anticipate his next line of inquiry, Franklyn deemed it safe to ask for a recess at this point. Much as the witness was under strain, Harry Franklyn was more so. He was like an actor who held the stage, except that his lines were never rehearsed. And though he had cultivated an air of perpetual calm his frail body was bathed in sweat.

Yes, he could use a respite. And it would avail the defense little. It might even add to their apprehension.

TWENTY-FIVE

WITH LAURA's admonitions throbbing in his brain, Chris Grant resumed the stand.

Harry Franklyn, a fresh sheaf of notes and exhibits in his hand, advanced toward the witness box.

"Doctor, a little earlier in the day you made use, twice, of some such phrase as 'a social problem of our times.' Is that correct?"

"I used such a phrase," Chris admitted.

"Twice," Franklyn reiterated. "Would you enlighten the jury as to the meaning of the phrase and its relevance to your work?"

Laura stood up. "Your Honor, this is a fishing expedition into waters totally irrelevant to this trial. We are dealing here with matters purely medical."

Franklyn turned to the bench, "Your Honor, when the subject of a lawsuit is a man's subjective decision, it is not a fishing expedition to inquire into his state of mind at the moment he arrived at that decision. Particularly since defense counsel opened the subject. I insist on the right to continue!"

Bannon drummed his fingers impatiently before he ruled,

"The witness's state of mind is relevant. Continue, Counselor."

Laura slipped back into her chair. She had not expected any other outcome and had really objected to warn Chris to be particularly careful and circumspect.

"Well, Doctor, can you shed some light on the phrase 'a social problem'?" Franklyn asked.

Carefully, Chris tried to explain the vital necessity of educating the poor about proper prenatal and postnatal nutrition.

Laura felt Chris retrieved some ground not only by what he said but by the way he had said it. But she knew that Harry Franklyn had not opened the subject to give Chris the chance to redeem himself.

"Doctor," Franklyn resumed, "at what point do you think it a doctor's duty to become a political activist and use his medical practice to achieve sociological goals?"

"I only said we had to make our research findings known for the public good."

"Doctor, would you say that a physician can handle both extensive research and a demanding clinical practice?"

"Yes!" Chris responded sharply.

"Is that why Dr. Sobol found it necessary to apologize to you for taking you away from your research to treat the Simpson baby?"

"You're deliberately trying to misinterpret what happened!"

Franklyn ignored the accusation. He was content that he had again brought Chris to the point where his emotions were taking control.

"Would you care to explain, Doctor?"

Laura hoped that Chris would refuse since it could only entangle him further. But he seized on Franklyn's offer.

"When a doctor accepts an assignment at a teaching hospital such as Metropolitan General he will ask assurance that he will have the facilities and the time to do his research. Otherwise he does not take the appointment."

"Wouldn't you take that to mean that research is more important to such a doctor than treating patients?"

"That's not what I meant!" Chris said.

"Since it's your choice of words, I'm afraid we'll have to hold you to it. At least it explains why Dr. Sobol felt obligated to apologize to you. You really weren't in a mood to treat any patient at the time you took over the Simpson infant, were you?"

"That's not true!"

Franklyn didn't consider it necessary to press the point. He went on: "Doctor, whom did you see first, when you reached the nursery, the patient or Mr. Reynolds?"

"Mr. Reynolds, why?"

"Doctor, in a courtroom the lawyer asks the questions. Now, after Dr. Sobol called you from your research with profuse apologies for disturbing you, the first person you saw was John Reynolds, who, we already know, symbolized a social condition about which you have strong hostile feelings."

"I never said hostile feelings," Chris fought back.

"Can we settle for 'strong negative feelings'?" Franklyn asked.

"A good doctor does not waste his time having negative feelings about any condition. He tries to combat it."

"To the point of being a political activist?" Franklyn asked.

"I am not a political activist," Chris maintained.

"Not even when you urge political action on a group of doctors at a large medical convention?" Franklyn demanded.

"If a doctor observes that a certain set of conditions produces a dangerous and undesirable result, then it is his duty to speak out! And I don't give a damn what you label it!"

Laura and Mike Sobol both reacted with such dismay that Chris shouted at them, "Damn it, I'm a witness sworn to tell the truth. Well, that's the truth!"

Harry Franklyn remained sober, unsmiling, though the moment had worked to even better advantage than he had anticipated. He was ready now for the final thrust of his cross-examination.

"I take it, Dr. Grant, that your answer to the question about being a political activist is *yes?*"

"I'm not going to answer that question!" Chris retorted. "Because to do so would only give you another chance to twist my words out of shape. You're trying to make it sound as if I approached the Simpson infant with a prejudice against it. And that's a lie!"

"Doctor, do you view every patient with the same impartial equanimity?" Franklyn said softly.

"That's an insulting question, in addition to being stupid!" Chris responded sharply.

The witness had completely lost all restraint. Franklyn knew it was the perfect time to move toward his conclusion.

"Doctor," Franklyn asked with a beguiling and disarming gentleness, "isn't it true that you have a reputation in the community surrounding Metropolitan General for being the doctor to the poor? In fact, don't the Hispanic people there call you 'El Medico'?"

"Yes," Chris conceded, wondering why Franklyn had chosen to raise the subject.

"Is there any special reason why they have this marked confidence in you?" Franklyn asked.

"I try to be considerate of their feelings. I try to explain to them. I have saved a number of their very sick infants," Chris said self-consciously.

"Is that all, Doctor?"

Puzzled, Chris hesitated to answer. Franklyn prodded, "Isn't it true, Doctor, that you also deliver lectures in the community?"

"Oh, yes, of course."

303

"Isn't it a fact that you deem those lectures an important part of your political activism?" Franklyn demanded.

"If I can save an infant's life, or its brain, by giving a mother instruction in nutrition, I consider that a part of my work as a doctor. I do not call it political activism," Chris retorted sharply.

Franklyn suddenly switched subjects again. "Doctor, we've heard a procedure called an exchange transfusion described here. Could you tell us how long such an exchange usually takes?"

"If it is done with proper care, and if no complications develop, say an hour. Perhaps a little more."

"An hour." Franklyn dwelled on that for a moment. Then he said, "Doctor, you testified before that bilirubins are tested every two hours. Is that right?"

"You can't discern any noticeable change in a shorter period of time," Chris explained.

"So that between the first bilirubin you took on the Simpson infant and the second one, two hours had to elapse?"

"Yes."

"What exactly did you do during that two-hour interval, Doctor?"

"Well, I talked with Mr. Reynolds. Told him we'd have to wait till the next bilirubin."

"Is that all, Doctor?"

"Yes, that's all . . . No, wait, that was the day I was scheduled to give one of my community talks."

"And did you give that talk?" Franklyn asked.

"Yes, I did."

"Doctor, did Mr. Reynolds raise any objection to your leaving at a time when his grandson was critically ill?"

"His grandson was not critically ill!" said Chris, angered that Franklyn had chosen to characterize the infant's condition in that way.

"But Mr. Reynolds did ask you *not* to leave, didn't he?"

"He did."

"Yet despite that, you did leave?"

"I was scheduled to give a lecture. Besides, there was nothing I could do for the infant until the second bilirubin."

"Nothing you could do, Doctor? Do you really mean that?"

"Of course I mean it!"

"You could have done an exchange transfusion, couldn't you?"

"The situation didn't call for it!"

"The situation didn't call for it? Or you couldn't fit it into your schedule? If you had taken the hour to do that transfusion you would have missed your beloved lecture."

"That wasn't the choice! If the infant had needed a transfusion there were half a dozen men on staff who could have done it!" Chris protested.

Franklyn waited till the courtroom had again subsided into a tense silence. "So, if we can take you at your word, Doctor, you examined the child for five to ten minutes, made some tests, put it under phototherapy, like a housewife puts a slow flame under a pot of stew so that it'll keep, and went off to give a lecture to women whose children were *not at that moment* in need of your services? Is that right, Doctor?"

"No!" Chris protested.

"Is there any part of my statement that you would care to dispute?"

"I did not use phototherapy as a holding action. It was the only thing to do till a trend developed," Chris said weakly.

"Doctor, would you care to amend your previous statement about not giving preference to any patients?"

"It was true before. It's true now."

"Doctor, would you care to amend your previous denial of political activism?"

"No," Chris said simply.

"The talk you delivered that day, where was it given?" Franklyn asked casually.

"I don't recall," said Chris.

"Would it refresh your recollection if I said it was at Public School 146?" Franklyn asked.

"Oh, yes, 146. That's where it was," Chris said, relieved the question was such a trivial one.

"Doctor, what part of the city is P.S. 146 in?"

"What part?" Chris repeated, puzzled. "It's in Rixie Square. Everybody knows that."

"Indeed everybody does," Franklyn repeated. "Doctor, what was the date of your talk?"

"God, I don't know. The same day the Simpson infant was referred."

"And also the same day of the Rixie Square riot?" Franklyn asked, his voice still soft.

"I guess," said Chris, still not sure what point the lawyer was making.

"Dr. Grant, did you know that some of the women who had attended your lecture were in that mob?"

"No, I didn't know that," Chris said, searching for some help from Laura or Mike Sobol.

Franklyn waved a sheaf of newspaper clippings and demanded, "The news reports are here, Doctor, if you care to examine them."

"I would not. They'd have no bearing on this case," Chris said.

"I thought you might decide to withdraw your previous denials of political activism. Or that you might finally concede that it was a mistake to leave the Simpson baby when it needed an exchange transfusion!" Franklyn demanded, raising his voice finally. "That you might finally admit your time would have been better spent at that infant's side, instead of initiating a riot in Rixie Square."

Laura Winters was now painfully aware why Harry

Franklyn had fought so strongly to select a white middle-class jury.

The little lawyer turned away from Chris Grant as from a pariah. If Chris had any response to make, Franklyn did not wish to dignify it by listening. Let that little blonde girl of a lawyer do what she might, she couldn't diminish the impact of his final moments of cross-examination.

Because she could not permit Chris to leave the stand on that note, Laura came forward for the redirect. Since trial practice limited her to new ground uncovered during Franklyn's cross-examination, she could only elicit Chris's denials to Franklyn's specific accusations. When she finished, Laura asked one final question.

"Dr. Grant, at any time in the course of the treatment of John Reynolds Simpson did you give thought to any other consideration than the welfare of that infant?"

"At no time," Chris responded simply, his face drained, his voice barely audible to the jury. "At no time. A doctor . . . a pediatrician . . . is a defender of the weakest and frailest of all patients. I consider myself their advocate, their protector. If I couldn't defend their right to a healthy life to my best ability I would leave the field of medicine altogether. Call it political activism, call it anything you want, I say it is a doctor's sworn duty!"

Laura's eyes filled with tears. As a woman she was very proud, but as a lawyer she knew that Chris had done himself great harm. He had virtually proved Franklyn's thesis that he was indeed a politically motivated partisan. The little lawyer must be extracting great satisfaction from Chris's last statement.

"Thank you, Doctor," she finally said, and sat down. Short of a miracle she did not see any chance left of a favorable verdict.

Five minutes later she stood beside Chris and Mike on the courthouse steps. Reynolds and his family were just getting into their limousine. Suddenly Arlene Simpson turned slightly and as she did her eyes made contact with Chris's. Staring back, Chris was startled. He had expected to see hatred but had instead only found pain. Then the limousine pulled away and he touched Laura's arm to hurry her away. But she was interrupted.

"This time, Counselor, I *can* help."

It was Juan Melez. He seemed so certain that Laura hesitated. After the last few hours she wanted to get Chris home as fast as possible.

"Look," said Melez, "Franklyn's statement about the riot was completely untrue. The only reason the welfare mothers were involved was because a child had been molested."

"Good! Now how do we prove it?" she asked.

"*I* can prove it. Put me on the stand and let me show them the tape of my news report."

"You could actually show that tape in the courtroom?" Laura asked.

"With portable equipment, sure," Melez declared.

"That would help. That would damn well help!" Laura admitted.

Melez nodded. He took her phone number so he could call after he had arranged all the details.

It was past midnight. The eleven o'clock news had been off the air for almost an hour. Juan Melez was in the editing room of Station KTNT, with Irv Kumanoff, the engineer who had agreed to help him. They had found the exact spot in the newscast which concerned the Rixie Square riot. The engineer ran it through twice. Melez listened, watched.

"It's not there! I remember what I said and it's not there! What the hell happened?"

"This is it," Irv insisted. "Exactly what went on the air."

"I remember what I said that night!" Melez insisted.

"Sure you remember. It's most likely in the outtakes."

"Sonofabitch," Melez exploded. "The only way is to do your news live! If you do a tape from location they cut the hell out of it!"

Irv tried to calm him. "They had to. I did that editing job myself."

"What do you mean they had to?" Melez demanded.

"Pressure from City Hall. Soft-pedal all reports on Rixie Square. Otherwise, it could start another riot."

"Irv, where are those outtakes?"

"Juano-baby, getting outtakes out of the vault is a whole *megillah*. Forget it!"

"A doctor's career is riding on it. How can I just forget it? Where the hell are those outtakes?"

"Juano, I have to have permission . . ."

"Screw permission! I give you permission. I want those outtakes!" Juan Melez said in such a fury that Irv finally agreed.

"Only don't tell them it was me," he called over his shoulder as he went toward the vault.

Within twenty minutes Irv had located the outtakes, threaded them up on the machine.

"That's better. It's all there. Now, Irv, I want to borrow some portable equipment and show these in the courtroom tomorrow."

"Not without permission," the engineer protested. "Else I'll get my ass in a sling. My union'll get in a big hassle. No. Not without permission."

"Okay," Melez said, irritatedly, "what's the boss's home number?"

"You going to call him at home? At this hour? Are you crazy?"

"Get that bastard on the phone, Irv! Or I'll cut your heart out. You know a Puerto Rican never goes round without an eight-inch knife." Melez was smiling again. "Irv, please, if it wasn't important I wouldn't insist."

"I'll dial," Irv finally relented. "But you'll have to do the talking."

Five minutes later when Melez hung up, his face was white. The boss wouldn't consider releasing the outtakes without a court order. Not considering all the trouble the station had had with government agencies trying to force its newscasters to reveal their sources, notes and outtakes.

On a point such as this Melez knew further arguments would get him nowhere. It was a good half hour, though, before he had the courage to call Laura.

chapter TWENTY-SIX

THEY WERE at lunch between sessions, Laura and Chris. They ate little. They said less. During the morning Laura had put on the stand two doctors, friends of Mike's, both of whom had testified that Chris's treatment of the Simpson baby had been consistent with good medical practice. But she knew that by the time Franklyn had got through cross-examining them they had had little impact on the jury. Now she was frantically searching her mind for some means, some witness, some piece of evidence that would make those jurors a little less certain that Chris was responsible. At the same time she tried to conceal from Chris the true degree of her desperation.

If there was any chance it would be in Coleman's testimony. Then she remembered with what hope she had photographed the records at Polyclinic. All for nothing, as it turned out. Even Chris and Mike had not found anything there that might shift the responsibility to Coleman. Yet there was something about his testimony that nagged at her.

"A documents expert!" she said suddenly. "If we could find a documents expert, he might prove that there actually were skillful alterations in Coleman's record."

"Even if there were, a documents expert wouldn't necessarily find them," Chris said. "There are ways of changing hospital records without leaving any trace."

"Such as?"

"We had a man at Massachusetts Pediatrics when I was interning. He'd been appropriating drugs from the hospital. And no one could find any visible alteration in the drug supply records. Then someone figured out that he didn't change the records. He simply removed the sheets and replaced them with completely new ones that bore no erasures, no changes, no trace of any alteration."

"If you change the legal effect of a document, no matter how, it's still forgery under the law," said Laura.

After a moment of thought, Chris said, "That second bilirubin. The one that's missing."

"If it came back from the lab after the baby was referred to your care what difference would it make?" she asked.

"Probably none," Chris agreed. "*If* it came back after the infant was referred."

"If it came back before, the nurse would have entered it in the hospital record, wouldn't she?"

"Not necessarily," Chris said. "Some hospitals send the blood sample to the lab. It's processed. The results are noted on the report. The report is sent back to the floor and put into the record. But in many hospitals the doctor must see it and initial it *before* it goes into the chart," Chris explained. "It could work that way at Parkside."

"So that . . ." Laura said, catching his drift.

". . . if a doctor found a disturbing report, instead of initialing it he could simply slip it into his pocket," Chris said. "And it never would show up on the patient's chart."

"You mean Coleman could have found the lab report incriminating and simply destroyed it?"

"Possibly."

"Chris, what could have been on that lab report that would have disturbed Coleman so much?"

"Exactly the same thing that would have made him suddenly decide to refer that infant out of Parkside Polyclinic," Chris stated.

"A bilirubin much higher than fourteen?" Laura asked.

"Yes, a bilirubin much higher than fourteen."

For the first time since the case began they both felt a surge of optimism. Maybe they were not just fighting an inexplicable accident of nature.

"I'm going after that report," Chris said abruptly. "I've got to find it."

"How?"

"If Coleman actually destroyed that report, there's only one place to look—the laboratory log at Parkside Polyclinic. By law, every lab must keep a log of every test they do and every report they issue."

As he strode down the corridor of the Pediatrics Wing at Metropolitan General, Chris Grant was aware that he had now become the object of furtive stares. Before, most of the staff had a smile or quick hello. Now they were afraid of intruding, afraid an attempt at friendliness might be misconstrued as curiosity.

He increased his pace and almost slammed into Alice Kennan. They stopped and smiled, but perhaps because of their past intimacy they now seemed to need to maintain a correct and aseptic distance. Memories brought on by this sudden and unexpected meeting disarmed her. The safest thing was to talk about the trial.

"How's it going?" she asked.

"It's no picnic. But we have a chance." He felt a need to overstate it. "A fair chance."

"Is she a good lawyer?" Alice asked, attempting to appear unemotional.

"Oh, very good. Excellent."

"I'm glad," Alice said, disposing of Laura. "It's been

313

pretty grim around here. No one can talk about anything else."

"I can imagine."

She blurted out, "God, I hope it turns out well!"

In those few words she had given expression to all her fears and expectations of defeat. She had also let him know how much she missed him, how sorry she was she had let their relationship drift on to its inevitable end.

"And you?" he asked, meaning, What had her life been like since they had broken off?

She smiled evasively, trying to appear gayer than she felt. "I took your advice," she said.

"Advice?" He was embarrassed at not remembering.

"A psychiatrist."

"You did? Great!" he said hopefully. "How's it working out?"

"You'd never guess." Then her smile dissipated sadly. "Yes, *you* would."

"What?"

"He's not my psychiatrist anymore. We're having an affair."

"Oh, Allie . . ." It was an instinctive reproach as well as an expression of regret.

Her eyes filled up. "I don't know why it is. After you, I really wanted to find out. Now I guess I'll never know."

He was tempted to embrace her, but they remained apart.

"When the trial ends," he promised, "we'll get together and talk about it. Maybe I can help in some way."

"Thanks, Chris." She tried to smile again. "I think about you. All the time. Look, my class is waiting," she said suddenly. Before she could start to cry, she hurried down the corridor.

Mike Sobol was in his office, poring over some research results that one of the residents had submitted. Mike was impressed by the work, both the method of experimentation and the organization of the results. A good man, Mike said to himself. If ever the need came to advance someone, he would be one to bear in mind. The true import of Mike's thought did not strike forcibly until he looked up and saw Chris standing in his doorway.

Mike extended his hand with unusual feeling because he could see the trial was taking its toll. Without even knowing it, Chris was becoming less aggressive, more withdrawn and self-protective. He had been hurt, badly hurt by this experience.

Mike tried to be encouraging as he asked, "To judge from what I read in the papers this morning, some of our experts did quite well on the stand yesterday."

Because it would serve no purpose to correct Mike's impression of the day's proceedings, Chris just smiled. Then he closed the door and came directly to the point.

"Mike, we must have access to the lab records at Parkside Polyclinic."

"Laura thinks it would help?"

"It would if Coleman deliberately intended to lose that lab report."

"Not necessarily," Mike said, leaning back in his creaky swivel chair. "If the report came down after the infant was transferred it would have no value. There doesn't have to be any malice involved."

"But there just *might* be," Chris insisted. "I need access to that log. I want to know for sure."

Mike Sobol nodded. "So the question is how do we get access?"

"Exactly!"

"Of course," Mike began, "the two most likely people to go investigate, can't. If you or I merely appeared at Parkside alarms would go off all over the place."

"It could be done quietly at night," Chris suggested.

"Like burglars?" Mike asked bitterly. "A nice occupation

for doctors." He stroked his chin, making an inventory of the men he knew who were attached to Parkside Polyclinic. Mitchell and Coleman were out, of course. There was Gunther. Mike had met him at various medical functions, but he didn't know him well enough to ask any favors. Of course, there was always Wellman.

Chris had never heard the name before. Mike explained. "Yes, Wellman. We'll find out if there's such a thing as gratitude left in this world. Fifteen years ago, sixteen, who keeps track of such things, I got a desperate call from Wellman. He had just had a most difficult delivery, a breech position, and had been forced to use forceps to position the child. You know how those cases end up—bruises, lacerations of the scalp, and the chance of damage. He was a young man then, just starting out. You know what that would have done to his career. Well, I took that infant on referral. We spent a very tense thirty-six hours together. Fortunately it turned out fine. He was most grateful and he told me if there was ever anything he could do . . ." Mike reached for his phone. "Well, there is!"

While the operator was trying to reach Wellman, Mike asked, "What date was the Simpson baby referred to us?"

"March sixteenth."

Mike waited till he heard Wellman's voice.

"Mike?" Wellman sounded like a doctor on the run.

"Brad?" Mike asked. "Can you talk?"

"Depends." A sure sign that Wellman couldn't talk freely.

"Then just answer one question for me. Yes or no."

"Sure."

"Last March sixteenth or seventeenth did you process anything through the lab over there?" Sobol asked casually.

"Well, I . . ." Then Wellman stopped.

Sobol understood. "I'll supply the conclusions. You just say yes or no."

"Right," Wellman agreed quickly.

"You can't answer my question without looking up your records. Right?"

"Yes."

Mike could hear the voice of an officious nurse in the background.

"If you want to check your records before you answer the next one, okay. If not, let me know now."

"Yes," Wellman said, but it sounded noncommittal.

"Brad, it is a matter of vital importance to me to have a look at the lab log for March sixteenth."

"Oh?" was all that Wellman said, but Mike could tell that the younger man had jumped to the correct conclusion. There was a long silence.

Finally Wellman said abruptly, "I never like to X ray a patient simply to find out what sex the baby is going to be."

There was an abrupt sound that indicated that Wellman had hung up.

Mike Sobol dropped the phone into its cradle.

"He guessed what it was about," said Chris.

"He guessed," Mike admitted. "I just hope he doesn't say anything to anybody else."

"Is there any other doctor you can contact?"

Mike started to count off the men at Parkside who might be indebted to him. The phone rang. Though it was a distraction he picked it up.

"Mike?"

Sobol sat up alertly. It was Wellman's voice again.

"Mike, sorry I had to cut you off, but I thought it was better to handle this from a public phone on the floor."

Mike laughed to put him at ease.

"Let me understand, Mike. You need something in that record to help you with the case, right?"

"Exactly right," Mike said.

"You want to know what lab work was done on the Simpson baby before it was referred," Wellman guessed.

"Right, again. Brad, I don't want you to get into trouble, but we would appreciate any help we can get," Mike said quite frankly.

"It might take a day or two. But I'll get you the answer," Wellman promised.

"Thanks, Brad."

"No thanks are needed, Mike. You know, the trouble with owing a debt to a man like you? A guy has to wait years for the chance to pay it off. I just hope it turns up the way you want."

"I do, too. And thanks again," Mike said, hanging up.

"He'll do it," Chris said, relieved.

"You see," Mike said reflectively, "how an experience like this can twist your point of view. I first thought he was trying to avoid me. I was ready to call him an ungrateful sonofabitch. Damn it, I wish we'd never got involved in this lawsuit."

He stood up, patted Chris on the shoulder and said, "As soon as I hear anything, I'll let you know."

TWENTY-SEVEN

"TIME IS running out," Laura warned. "We don't have much of our case left to present. And what we do have won't make it," she summed up grimly.

Mike Sobol shook his head. Chris continued his pacing. Neither of them had any suggestions.

Because he could think of nothing else to do, Mike said, "I better phone the hospital."

He reached the night nurse in charge. Had there been any emergencies? Nothing that couldn't be handled. And how was the Williams baby? Took and retained food. The intestinal obstruction seemed to have been overcome by Dr. Baines's surgery.

Was that all? No, there were several messages, all from the same person—a Mr. Bradford. He said to please call him at home. He was sure you would know the number. A Mr. Bradford, Mike wondered. Who was Mr. Bradford? And how would Mike know his number?

Then he realized it was not a Mr. Bradford, it was Brad Wellman. Mike took out his little notebook in which he had listed private numbers of doctors all over the country. It saved time during emergencies. Brad answered on the first ring.

"Well?" Mike asked anxiously.

"I found that second bilirubin report. It's in the lab log."

"Good!" Mike said, gesturing to Chris and Laura to pay attention.

"I had them photocopy the whole page under that date. Told them I needed it for a patient who'd moved to the West Coast whose doctor out there wanted the complete record."

"Yes, yes," Mike said, anxious to get the result. "What did it show?"

Chris and Laura both waited, not daring to breathe.

"I see," said Mike. "Could you drop it by the hospital? And thanks again. Believe me, anything you ever owed me is paid in full."

"That second bilirubin *was* higher, wasn't it?" Chris asked, after Mike hung up.

Before he could take too much comfort in the thought, Mike said, "It was, but only eighteen point five."

"Eighteen point five could have been damned dangerous. Even Franklyn's experts would testify to that, Chris said."

"Not so fast," Laura said. "If you start claiming that damage might have occurred below twenty, then Franklyn can very well ask why you didn't do an exchange when you found out it was sixteen." She reached for another cigarette.

"So, though Coleman's lying, it doesn't help us!" Chris exploded in frustration.

"Still, we know he must have been scared. When he saw that second lab report he knew he was dealing with a very hot baby," Mike declared.

"And that he had mishandled the case," said Chris. "So he destroyed the report, called Mitchell and said, 'Let's refer the baby.' "

"It wouldn't be the first time a doctor copped out by telling the family he was taking 'the best and safest course' by referring a patient," said Mike.

"So," Laura concluded, "he unloaded his mistake onto another unsuspecting doctor. Now, if we could only . . ."

"Prove it!" Mike anticipated her angrily. "Why is it that everything Franklyn wants to prove, can be proved. But everything that would help us can't be!" Immediately, he realized how Laura might interpret his outburst and added, "I'm sorry, my dear, I didn't mean it the way it sounded."

"I know, Mike, I know." But her feelings had obviously been pricked. She forced herself to go over the problem again. "All we have now is a medical assumption."

"Coleman withheld that second bilirubin!" Chris insisted.

"We're only assuming that he did. And even if we could prove it, what does it come down to? The infant's bilirubin went from fourteen to eighteen point five and then started down. The bilirubin you took was sixteen. I ask you both, how much danger could there be in a bilirubin that spikes at eighteen point five if it starts down at once?"

"But who is there to say that when that bilirubin was reported at eighteen point five it was at its peak?" asked Mike.

"Meaning?" Laura prodded.

"Meaning that in the hours between the first and second tests the bilirubin might have gone much higher," Chris explained. "Maybe it was already on its way *down* when the lab caught it at eighteen point five."

"Exactly!" said Mike. "The worse the condition, the swifter the ascent and descent."

"That bilirubin might have exceeded twenty before the infant ever reached Metropolitan," Chris said grimly.

"And if it did . . ." Laura said, not daring to go on.

"The damage would have been done before Chris even saw the child," Mike concluded.

"We still don't have proof," Laura pointed out.

"I could graph the bilirubin during those missing hours," Mike offered. "The rise, the peak and the rate of decline. Even their own doctors would have to admit the damage could have occurred that way."

"*Could* have occurred," Laura repeated, thoughtfully.

"You know the terrible irony of it?" Chris remarked wearily. "Coleman's negligence is exactly what protects him. His failure to follow good procedure by taking a bilirubin every two hours leaves those gaps in the record that shield him. And we have to pay for it."

"Maybe they won't shield him much longer," Laura said with determination.

"Laura?"

"I'm going to recall him to the stand tomorrow!"

TWENTY-EIGHT

As it turned out, recalling Dr. Robert Coleman was not easy. Harry Franklyn made a succession of strong objections. Coleman himself sent messages to the court informing Judge Bannon that his busy schedule would not allow for his return. An obstetrician was not master of his own time. Nature determined when and where he practiced, not courts, and certainly not lawyers for the opposition. Finally, on the ground that new evidence had been discovered, Bannon was forced to demand Coleman's presence.

Laura reopened her cross-examination by trying to refresh the jurors' minds.

"Dr. Coleman, if you will recall, when you were on the stand last you testified that though you felt the Simpson infant was in no immediate danger, you still referred it to Metropolitan General. Can you recall for us, why?"

"As I explained, I was especially busy at the time and I thought the best procedure was to refer the infant to a hospital with a larger staff and larger intensive care facilities," he answered meticulously.

"Doctor, did you follow the progress of the Simpson baby after that?"

"Once the infant was in what I had thought to be dependable hands I felt free to concentrate my efforts on other patients."

"So you did not know of the progress of that infant's bilirubin, its rise, its subsequent treatment and its seeming recovery?" Laura asked.

"Only what has come out during the course of this trial."

"So you do know that the bilirubin went to sixteen at Metropolitan and then began to descend?" Laura asked.

"Yes," Coleman admitted.

"Did those figures supply the reason why the infant suffered brain damage?" Laura asked.

"Some doctors have recently concluded that any count over fifteen can be serious," said Coleman.

"Then sixteen would surely be serious," Laura pursued.

"According to the new theory, yes," Coleman said firmly.

"What about eighteen, Doctor?"

"If sixteen is considered dangerous then surely eighteen would be more so," Coleman hedged, growing a bit uneasy for the first time.

"What about anything *over* eighteen, Doctor?" Laura began to press Coleman without raising her voice, like a sheep dog gently nudging a stray lamb into the fold.

"We can state that according to the new theory any bilirubin over eighteen would be considered highly dangerous," Coleman said, trying to close the subject.

"However, since there's no evidence that this infant's bilirubin ever exceeded sixteen, I agree it's quite academic," Laura said.

Coleman glanced at her suspiciously, wondering why she had chosen to phrase her concession in those particular words.

"Doctor, a number of experts who testified here said that whenever a bilirubin starts to rise the proper course is to repeat the test every two hours. Do you agree with them?"

"I think every doctor would agree."

"And is that what you did with the Simpson infant?" she asked.

"As soon as I learned that the bilirubin had reached fourteen and that there was a positive Coombs, I immediately ordered a second bilirubin," Coleman replied righteously.

"Immediately?" Laura asked.

"Immediately!"

"Doctor, I thought you said the procedure was to wait two hours and then have another blood sample taken," Laura said, pretending to be confused.

"I gave the order to have the bilirubin done immediately because I didn't want to wait two more hours in a case such as this." Coleman could not help but glance toward the counsel table where John Reynolds sat grimly listening.

"Doctor," Laura began again, "let's reduce this to specific hours. As I recollect, you received a call from the nursery while you were in the operating room."

"Yes," Coleman conceded.

"And you learned then that the Simpson baby was exhibiting signs of marked jaundice and had a bilirubin of fourteen . . ."

"I wasn't told that at that time," Coleman interrupted.

"Well, what message did you receive?"

"Such information is not relayed over a squawk box. The doctor is simply asked to call the floor."

"Oh, I see," Laura said, pretending to be suddenly enlightened. "So it wasn't till you left surgery that you discovered what the bilirubin was?"

"Yes," Coleman replied, unshaken.

"Doctor, how long after you received that message on the squawk box did you leave surgery?" Laura asked.

"I wouldn't remember a detail like that," Coleman said.

"Especially on a day when you were covering for Dr. Mitchell and had two hysterectomies to do." Laura seemed to explain on his behalf. Suddenly she asked, "How long

325

does it take to do a hysterectomy, Doctor?" When Coleman didn't reply at once, she offered, "Four hours, five?"

"Of course not!" Coleman replied. "An hour. Two at the most."

"Even with complications?" Laura asked.

"Two to three hours at the most."

"So that if that call came in during your first operation it would have been four or possibly five hours before you could go down to the nursery and see the Simpson baby's lab report."

Coleman hesitated, then replied, "I doubt it would have been that long."

"Backtracking for a moment, Doctor, how long was it between the time the baby exhibited jaundice and tests were ordered and the time you saw the lab report?"

"I don't understand," Coleman evaded.

"Well, blood was sent down to the lab without any instructions from you to rush. How long does that usually take at Parkside?"

"In the normal routine?" Coleman fenced.

"In the normal routine."

"A few hours at the most."

"Can you be more specific, Doctor? Two hours, or is three or four more usual?"

"It could take three hours."

"So that if the jury were to assume the more modest figure of three hours and add to that the four or five hours that elapsed while you were in surgery, that would mean that as much as eight hours could have gone by. . . ."

Coleman interrupted, "No one has said eight hours passed."

"Then how many, Doctor?"

"Nobody knows!" said Coleman, finally allowing his irritation to show.

"Doctor, wasn't the real reason you didn't wait two hours but immediately ordered a second bilirubin that not two hours had gone by, but eight?" Laura demanded.

"Eight hours did not go by!" Coleman persisted. "Besides, since the bilirubin never went beyond sixteen this is all academic."

"Doctor, when an infant is in serious trouble is its bilirubin apt to rise faster or slower?" Laura asked.

"It rises faster, it declines faster."

Laura turned toward the jury. "Doctor, if a bilirubin of fourteen were to rise to say, *eighteen and a half* in a matter of seven or eight hours would you consider that cause for alarm?"

"Cause for concern," Coleman responded cautiously.

"Not cause for *alarm?*"

"Cause for *concern,*" Coleman reiterated.

"What if it had gone higher than eighteen point five?" Laura asked suddenly.

"This is all conjecture. The Simpson baby never had a bilirubin report higher than sixteen. And it started receding after that!"

"Doctor, would it surprise you to learn that the result on the second bilirubin you ordered actually *was* eighteen point five?" Laura asked suddenly.

Stunned, Coleman stared at her. Before he could speak, Laura turned to the bench and said, "I would like to offer into evidence a photocopy of the lab log on the day in question taken from Parkside Polyclinic Hospital."

At the plaintiff's counsel table there was a hasty conference between John Reynolds and Harry Franklyn. Franklyn jumped up. "Your honor, we demand the right to examine that document first!"

Laura held out the copy. "You may keep this, Mr. Franklyn, we have a number of them." As Franklyn took it Laura crossed to her table to take a second copy from Chris's outstretched hand. She glanced at Harry Franklyn, then advanced to the bench to offer her document to Judge Bannon. Bannon inspected it and looked at Franklyn.

"Your Honor, this development is such a total surprise to the plaintiff that we demand a short recess."

Laura turned toward the bench. "Your Honor, I demand to go on with this examination! We believe there has been a deliberate attempt to withhold evidence and I mean to pursue the matter."

"Your Honor, I take an oath as an attorney and officer of this court that I have never seen this document before this moment!" Harry Franklyn protested.

At least Laura had gained a valuable piece of information. The failure to disclose was entirely Coleman's doing. But there was the tactical urgency of time now. She did not want to give Coleman a chance to recover from his obvious surprise.

"Your Honor, whether the plaintiff knew this or not is of no importance now. Unless we are to assume that if he had known, he would never have started this lawsuit. Is Mr. Franklyn offering to withdraw the suit now? If so, we are quite amenable if the proper apologies are made to the defendants."

"The plaintiffs have no intention of withdrawing," Franklyn declared, for once raising his voice to a shout.

"In that event," Laura said, "we offer this report for identification. And when it is accepted we demand the right to proceed with the examination."

Bannon examined the document, glanced toward the plaintiff's table and ruled, "Since it has not been properly introduced and identified, the court cannot accept it."

"I could ask for a recess long enough to subpoena the hematologist at Polyclinic to make a proper identification," Laura offered.

Franklyn didn't respond but it was obvious he was thankful for the respite and the chance to reorient his witness. It was Coleman who interceded.

"Your Honor, if I can have a look at the report I think I might be able to make the identification."

Laura studied him, suspecting some trick. She addressed the bench, "I will accept the doctor's offer provided that if he fails to identify it I will still have recourse to other witnesses."

Bannon granted her request. Laura showed the document to Coleman. He took it gingerly, looked it over quite carefully.

"Doctor, does that seem to be a true and genuine excerpt from the lab log at Parkside Polyclinic?" She waited, puzzled by his cooperation.

Finally Coleman said, "Yes, yes, this seems to be genuine."

Still suspicious, Laura offered it into evidence. Then she asked, "Doctor, would you be good enough to glance down the column to the second entry that appears alongside the name 'Simpson, Baby'?"

"Yes?" said Coleman, glancing at the page.

"Will you read us the entry there, the result of the second bilirubin?"

Without changing expression, Coleman read simply, "Eighteen point five."

"So that when the Simpson infant was referred to Dr. Grant its bilirubin was higher than the fourteen you first told us?"

"It would seem so," Coleman admitted.

" 'Seem so,' Doctor? Is that all you can say, in light of this document?" Laura's words came faster now, as she attempted to corner Coleman.

"The bilirubin was obviously higher when the infant was referred," he said, cool and deliberate again.

"Doctor, did you or did you not see that bilirubin of eighteen point five before?"

"I did not."

"I suggest that you did see it. That it was this report which made you decide to refer the infant to Metropolitan."

"That's not true."

"I further suggest that you turned that infant over not to secure more intensive care, but to get the case out of your hands so you wouldn't be held responsible for any consequences," Laura pursued.

"That's a lie!"

Changing course suddenly, Laura asked, "Doctor, what is the routine procedure in Parkside Polyclinic concerning lab reports?"

"I don't understand."

"Is it the practice there that before it is put on the patient's chart the attending physician must initial it?" Laura asked.

"As a general rule, yes," said Coleman.

"Is there any reason to believe that the 'general rule' was not followed in this case?" Laura demanded.

"Every reason," said Coleman. "Since I did not pay a visit to the nursery at Parkside after I had arranged to transfer the infant that report was never seen by me, never initialed and therefore never entered in the patient's record."

Because she felt the witness was slipping out of the trap she had prepared for him, Laura decided on a desperate move. She retreated to her table. Expecting that the examination was over, Coleman started to rise from the witness chair. She turned to pin him there. "Doctor, we're not done yet."

Holding up a chart in such a way that Coleman could not see it, Laura advanced toward the witness box.

"Doctor, in your opinion, if an infant showed a bilirubin of eighteen point five at one point and then showed a bilirubin of sixteen a few hours later, would that signify to you that the bilirubin was past its peak and on its way down?"

"Of course it would," Coleman said, contemptuous of both question and questioner.

"In your opinion, would that be the only possible medical conclusion?" Laura asked.

"I should think so, yes," Coleman said.

"Isn't there perhaps another possibility since the bilirubin of eighteen point five resulted from a test taken many hours after the previous reading of fourteen?" Laura asked.

"I don't understand."

"Doctor, let me ask the following hypothetical question: Assuming that an infant exhibits a bilirubin of fourteen, and is suffering from an Rh incompatibility, which tends to drive up a bilirubin at a fast rate, isn't it possible that bilirubin might have peaked at twenty or higher? So that when its bilirubin recorded eighteen point five it was on its way *down?*" Laura demanded.

Before Coleman could attempt to answer, Franklyn had risen. "Your Honor, there has been absolutely no testimony in the course of this trial that would support such a hypothesis. The question is baseless, even capricious. I ask the court to rule it out."

"Motion granted," Bannon said gravely. He turned to Laura to invite her to proceed with another question or else end her examination.

Laura was determined to make one more effort. "Doctor, I ask you to look at this chart."

Franklyn was up again, but Laura anticipated his objection. "I have a copy prepared for you, Mr. Franklyn." Chris passed it to the dapper little man who examined it suspiciously.

He looked up at the bench. "Your Honor, before we move in relation to this . . . this . . ." he fumbled intentionally. "It's difficult to know how to characterize it. We wish to know exactly what it purports to be."

Laura turned to the bench. "This is a graph of the possible course of the Simpson baby's bilirubin during those crucial seven to eight hours between the time its bilirubin

331

reached fourteen and the time when its bilirubin was taken at Metropolitan General."

Pretending to be angrier than he was, Franklyn demanded, "Before agreeing to any such invention we have a right to know who supplied these figures, and what their relevance is to this trial!"

"I would be glad to put Dr. Grant on the stand to testify to all aspects of Mr. Franklyn's objection."

"The defendant?" Franklyn scoffed. "Well, that's certainly an unbiased source from which to accept such a hypothesis. Your Honor, we object to this entire line of cross-examination!"

Bannon leaned in Laura's direction. "Counselor, I'm afraid that Mr. Franklyn is right. I shall have to rule against the admission of this purely hypothetical venture."

"Your Honor, in view of the fact that no expert has been able to pinpoint the cause of the damage done this infant, I think any testimony, even speculation, which might answer that question would be helpful and admissible."

Bannon shook his head gravely. But Laura was undeterred. If she could not admit the graph she was at least going to educate the jury on their hypothesis as to what might have happened.

"Your Honor, we fail to see how this method of pursuing the truth differs from that granted to the plaintiffs. They have offered no factual evidence as to the cause of damage. This chart constitutes an opinion as valid as any theory they have proposed. In fact, this chart can prove that the infant might well have been damaged *before* it ever left Parkside Polyclinic!"

Her last words were shouted to override Harry Franklyn's objections. Hoarse, shrill, his voiec did not totally obscure Laura's declaration. Bannon had to resort to his gavel to silence both lawyers.

He glared down at Laura. "Counselor, do I understand correctly that this chart is simply a hypothetical excursion based on the defendant's idea of what might have happened, and that it has no shred of proof as its basis?"

"Your Honor, there is the documentary proof that the infant's bilirubin was higher than the fourteen reported by Dr. Coleman. Having proved that, I think we have a right to explore whether that bilirubin reached eighteen point five on the way up, or on the way down from an even higher, more dangerous figure!" Laura declared strongly.

Bannon glanced at Franklyn.

"Your Honor, since this is sheer speculation intended to mislead the jury, I insist that the court disallow this entire line of questioning," Franklyn argued, his voice having returned to its usual low, soft level.

Bannon considered the matter gravely, then slowly and with an air of great deliberation, he ruled, "Taking into account the arguments of counsel, and being moved by the weight of the evidence actually submitted, as against a mere hypothesis, this court feels forced to rule out this entire line of testimony!"

"Exception!" said Laura, but she knew it was a futile protest.

"The record will show that counsel takes exception to the court's ruling," Bannon said without any show of emotion, though he was well aware that he had virtually wiped out any possible defense Laura might have had by introducing the missing bilirubin report.

To salvage some shred of benefit, Laura turned back to confront Coleman again.

"Doctor, if you had been aware of this second bilirubin of eighteen point five would you have reported it to Dr. Grant?"

"Of course," Coleman replied quickly.

"And what would have been the purpose of reporting that result to Dr. Grant?" Laura asked.

"To help him decide on the best treatment to apply," Coleman said.

"And what form of treatment would that have been?" Laura asked.

Franklyn objected. "Counsel is asking one doctor to guess what would have gone on in the mind of another."

Laura tried again. "Doctor, what would *you* have done if confronted with an infant with a bilirubin of eighteen point five?"

"I would have done an immediate exchange transfusion," Coleman answered, confident now that all risk of culpability had been lifted from him.

"Would you have done an exchange transfusion if confronted by a bilirubin of fourteen?"

"Probably not," Coleman said.

"Then aren't you actually saying that you would have pursued precisely the same treatment as Dr. Grant?" Laura asked.

Again Franklyn rose to object. Turning to Laura, he said, "Counsel knows as well as I do that legally the doctor takes the patient as he finds him. It is no defense to say now that the doctor didn't know this fact or that one. Moreover, there is no evidence indicating that Dr. Coleman saw this lab report before it was shown to him in this courtroom. I demand that counsel apologize for this slur on the doctor's reputation."

"The court deems that a proper request." Bannon glared at Laura.

She did not relent. Finally Bannon shook his head, disapproving of her conduct in such a way that the jury could not overlook it.

Franklyn had accomplished what he had sought to do. He had wiped out the effect of what should have been a startling and effective piece of evidence for the defense. He was content now to close the episode by saying, "Your Honor, I think we have imposed on Dr. Coleman long enough."

If she thought it would have helped, Laura would have

insisted on his remaining, but with things as they stood, she was reluctantly forced to let him go.

As Coleman left the stand, Bannon declared the court in recess till morning, at which time he hoped counsel for both sides would give him some idea of when they would be ready to sum up. It was a strong hint that he was expecting Laura to close her case so it could go to the jury by the weekend.

"Slippery as an eel," Chris exploded.

"It won't do any good to blame him," Laura said. "If you're looking to place blame, put it on me."

"You did the best you could with that sonofabitch!" Chris tried to console her.

Mike Sobol, who had been in deep thought, suddenly said, "You know, I wasn't in court. But listening to the two of you, maybe you're being too hard on Coleman."

"How?" Laura demanded intolerantly.

"Let's reconstruct the pressures he was under that day. He's carrying a double load, Mitchell's practice and his own. He's busy in the OR. He gets a call from the nursery. But the only infant he's supervising there seemed healthy and should not be running into difficulty. Not according to its history. Why should he feel under any pressure of time?"

"He *was* dealing with a first baby," Chris conceded reluctantly. "And a mother who had no positive Coombs during pregnancy, even though she was Rh negative. Statistically that about eliminates the problem. Okay, Mike, I can see where he could have been saying to himself during those operations, 'There's no emergency, it's a first baby.'"

"And it was," Mike insisted.

"How do we know?" Laura asked.

"Because Mitchell or any good ob-gyn man examining a woman could not miss a previous delivery."

335

"Could Mitchell have known and been promised to secrecy?" Laura asked.

"No, my dear," Mike said. "An ethical doctor like Mitchell would still have told Coleman."

"Wait!" Chris interrupted. "Maybe they were both victimized!"

"How?" Laura asked.

Chris glanced at Mike, then said, "There was another way Reynolds' daughter could have become sensitized, so that her antibodies would destroy her infant's blood."

Mike remained silent.

"A previous pregnancy terminated by an abortion," Chris said.

"Then all the time you doctors have been talking about a first baby you really meant a first *pregnancy?*"

"Yes," Mike conceded. "Because a woman will almost invariably confide a previous pregnancy to her obstetrician."

"But if Reynolds' daughter had had an abortion . . ."

"I'd take an oath that she never told Mitchell," Mike said. "Otherwise he'd have taken precautions against an Rh incompatibility."

"She never told *him?*" Laura asked. "Or she never told *anyone?*"

"What does that mean?" Chris asked.

"If she didn't tell her doctor, who *did* she tell? Her mother? Her father?" Laura asked.

"If you had a father like John Reynolds would you tell him?"

"Then a friend? A roommate at college? She married shortly after she graduated. It could have happened while she was still in school. Someone would have had to know."

"Why?" Chris asked.

"Chris, a girl in that condition confides in someone. She wants advice, reassurance, help. If nothing else, she wants someone to share her fears with," Laura said.

Mike nodded. "So Coleman's slow reaction to the fact

that the infant was jaundiced may be the key to our defense." Then he asked, cynically, "But how do we 'prove' anything?"

"If we had time . . ." Laura said exasperatedly. "But we don't." Still her mind kept at it. "The man, she would have told the man involved. I'm sure of that. If we could find him."

"What if you called her to the stand?" Chris asked.

"On what ground?" Laura asked. "For a fishing expedition? Any judge would forbid that, and certainly Bannon."

No one could think of any solution by the time Chris and Mike left at a little past one o'clock.

CHAPTER
TWENTY-NINE

LAURA AND Chris were making their way doggedly up the broad steps to the old courthouse. The lunch recess was over. Mike Sobol had had to go back to teach his afternoon classes. As Laura looked up she discovered Juan Melez waiting on the top step, leaning against one of the soot-gray pillars. He came down to meet them.

"Did you hear my newscast last evening? I tried to make it up to you for not getting those tapes. If you would just give me sixty seconds with the doctor I think we could wipe the riot charge out of the public's mind."

"Can you wipe it out in the jury's mind?" Laura snapped.

"I said I was sorry."

"So am I. Anyway, no interview," Laura declared firmly.

"Well, is there anything I can do? I even considered saying something on the air that might be grounds for a mistrial."

"Juan, forget it. There's nothing you can do, except stand aside and let us into the courthouse," Laura said flatly.

Reluctantly, Melez stepped aside.

Suddenly, Laura stopped and turned back to Melez. "You know, there just might be something."

"What?" Melez asked.

She pledged him to secrecy. Then she revealed the suspicion that had surfaced in the early hours of the morning. Melez listened, his black eyes lighting up with professional anticipation.

"Just remember," Laura said, "this is *not* the usual news story. If you come up with something you're not free to use it till we introduce it first in the courtroom."

Melez hesitated, then agreed. "Off the record until you break it in court."

"We can't give you any real lead," Laura said, "except that common sense says it happened at college. She married so soon after she graduated."

"At least that's a place to begin," Melez agreed. "But you haven't given me much time," he warned.

But Melez did better than anyone expected. As Laura and Chris were leaving court that afternoon one of the attendants handed her a note which read: "Call me soon as I get off the air." It was not signed but there was no need for identification. They went to Laura's apartment and called Melez right after the six o'clock news.

He would not talk to Chris, only to Laura. "Counselor, I didn't have much time, but I lucked out."

"What?" Laura demanded urgently.

"Arlene Reynolds attended Northfield, upstate, for four years, but she did *not* graduate."

"She flunked out after four years?" asked Laura dubiously.

"Not with her grades," Melez said.

"Then what happened?"

"She dropped out two months before graduation," Melez said. "Unless I miss my guess, if what you suspect is true, it must have happened then."

"Is that all you were able to find out?" Laura asked.

"In the time I had," Melez explained. "If I go into this any deeper I'm going to have an obligation to the station to use the story. If you want privacy, take it from here on your own."

"Thanks, Juan," Laura said. She hung up and relayed the information to Chris.

"Somebody would know," he said. "Her roommate. We could find out who her roommate was and speak to her."

"A roommate wouldn't talk, even if she knew. No, one of us is going to have to drive up to the college immediately and make some inquiries."

"You have to be in court all day," Chris said.

"Exactly," said Laura. "You'll have to go yourself."

Chris Grant pulled into the town of Northfield so late at night that he had to wake the clerk at the old inn to find a room. The next morning a stinging cold shower made up for his lack of sleep. A light breakfast and three cups of black coffee also helped, and by nine o'clock he was crossing the broad Northfield campus which was just recapturing its spring green after a long, snowy winter. The girls seemed very young compared to his thirty-six years. There were long-legged girls in jeans and boots. Full-breasted girls in men's shirts of light blue denim. Red-cheeked, long-haired girls with the health of youth and the exuberance.

The bell steered Chris to the Administration Building. There he pretended that he was considering moving to Northfield and wanted a part-time appointment to the college clinic.

He first spoke to Dean Emily Waterston. He was greatly relieved that she accepted him at face value. She even offered to call the doctor in charge of the infirmary to tell her that Chris was on his way over, but he insisted it wasn't

340

necessary. Actually, he preferred to make his own introduction.

There were three students waiting when he entered the clinic. Though the nurse offered to inform Dr. Lumpkin at once, Chris said he would wait. He preferred to see the doctor at a time when waiting patients could not give her a convenient excuse to terminate the interview. He picked up the spring issue of the college publication and leafed through it. In general, college publications hadn't changed much. Some of the slang was different, but the poetry and fiction were still very much the same.

Finally the doctor was free. Dr. Florence Lumpkin was a tall woman, attractive, with coils of rich, gleaming blonde hair wound about her head. Her face was strong, with a reassuring and wholesome look that inspired confidence. She smiled easily. Chris judged she couldn't be more than thirty-nine, forty at the most.

She leaned back in her swivel chair as she listened to his story. Her bright brown eyes gave no hint other than a keen interest in Chris's qualifications and his desire to take up practice in a small town.

"In these times the need for pre- and postnatal care is much more necessary on the college campus than it used to be, Doctor," she observed when he finished.

It was the opening Chris had been seeking and he was relieved that she had handed it to him.

"Have you been here long enough to observe the change?" he asked.

"Eight years."

Good, thought Chris. The time he was concerned with would fall well within that period.

"How did you handle things before the state legalized abortion?"

"In those days, if the girl decided not to have her baby, she had to go out of the country. Or else resort to illegal means. I always advised against that."

"Naturally," he agreed.

"At that point it usually became a matter of economics," Dr. Lumpkin said casually.

Trying to steer the conversation into more revealing channels, Chris asked, "Most girls, when they get into trouble, do they come to you?"

"Most girls," she said, "but not necessarily all."

"Because they're afraid they'll be expelled?"

"No girl has been expelled for that reason in some years," Dr. Lumpkin said quickly.

"How many years has that liberal policy been in effect?"

"Long enough to include the period in which you're interested, Dr. Grant," she said, staring at him defiantly. "Did you think," she added, "that I wouldn't recognize your name?" Then she became almost conciliatory. "You know that I can't help you, no matter how much I might want to. I have my professional obligations to this institution and to the patients I treat here."

"Did it ever occur to you, Doctor," said Chris, "that that was the reason I had to resort to a ruse? At this point we're desperate. Unless we can prove otherwise, I will be unjustly convicted of malpractice."

Dr. Lumpkin did not relent. "Sorry," was all she would say. And she meant it.

"We're not entirely in the dark," he said, hoping to provoke her curiosity. "We know, for instance, that Arlene Reynolds didn't complete her fourth year. She left two months shy of getting her degree. And never came back to finish."

Dr. Lumpkin looked away, a reaction that affirmed the significance of what Chris had said. He continued to probe.

"We have to assume that if she did become pregnant it happened during those last few months. With her money, four years ago she would probably have gone abroad, where she could have an abortion done safely. Then either

342

she chose not to come back here, or her father wouldn't permit it. Is that a fair hypothesis?"

"I can't give you an answer," the blonde doctor said.

"Can you deny it?"

"I refuse to comment," she said.

"Well, I know one thing that I didn't know before," Chris said. "It *did* happen. And she came to see *you.*"

"How can you know that?"

"If you didn't know anything about it then, there'd be no need for confidentiality now. You'd be perfectly free to speculate."

She didn't deny it. For the first time Chris felt that she was actually trying to help him, within the limits of her own professional strictures. It would do no good to push her.

"I'm sorry to have put you in this position, Doctor," Chris said, bringing the interview to a close.

"If I were able to help, believe me, I would," she said.

"Do you have any advice at all?" he asked.

"Keep digging" was all she would say.

"In the time we have left, that may be worse than no advice at all."

Chris stood outside the infirmary. The clock tower announced the end of one class and the beginning of the next. Students were crossing the campus from every direction. A number of them rode by on bikes. One girl passed dangerously close to him on purpose, a tribute to his attractiveness. The saucy, provocative smile on her face told him that.

Chris tried to analyze what little he had gleaned from Dr. Lumpkin. She had said to keep digging, but how could he discover a close friend of Arlene Reynolds' four years after she left. Unless, of course, the doctor was not referring to a student. Some man perhaps connected with the college? Maybe someone on the faculty. By some means he had to secure Arlene Reynolds' scholastic file. That would mean another ruse. More successful, he hoped, than the one that had failed with Dr. Lumpkin.

"I was referred here by Dean Waterston," Chris began, as glibly as he could. "I'm seeking some background information on a student who was in the class of sixty-nine—Arlene Reynolds."

Evidently the dean's name accomplished the purpose. The young girl in charge of the records room repeated efficiently, "Class of sixty-nine. Arlene Reynolds." She disappeared and as time went by Chris wondered uneasily if she had decided to check the dean's office. Eventually, though, she returned with the file.

"Arlene Reynolds," she said as she handed it over. "But you can't take it out of the office." She gestured toward a gray metal table in the corner of the waiting room. Anywhere, Chris said to himself, anywhere, as long as I can get a look at that file! But he restrained himself sufficiently to open the file as nonchalantly as if he were reading his morning newspaper.

He scanned the index of papers. Background. First year. Sophomore year. Junior year. Senior year. Medical record. Activities. He turned to her medical record. There was a list of the usual routine visits to the infirmary. Stomach upsets. Colds. Undiagnosed fever. In her sophomore year an onset of mononucleosis. But not so severe that she was sent home. He now began an intensive study of her senior year. Slight injuries due to a minor automobile accident, in which she was driving her own car. There was also a record of two colds, one complicated by a touch of pneumonia which had yielded to an antibiotic. Then the record ended abruptly. For the last few months of the school year, mid-March through May, no record of any illness. No note of even a routine check up.

It was understandable. The college, particularly Dr.

Lumpkin, was not likely to keep records on an illegitimate pregnancy.

Chris turned to Arlene's senior scholastic record. Six courses. Alongside each was the name of the professor or instructor. His eyes traveled down the list of names swiftly. Of the six, three were women, three men. Henry Wills, Philosophy. Gregory Mayer, Applied Psychology. Arthur Ward, English Literature.

Chris Grant waited outside Barton Hall, where both the departments of philosophy and psychology were housed. He was cautiously formulating his opening remarks, for if any of the three was the man involved, Chris did not wish to jeopardize his academic career.

As it turned out, Dr. Wills had retired two years previously. The secretary to the present chairman of the department offered to give Chris his address, but he saw no reason to visit anyone over sixty-five.

Dr. Gregory Mayer, professor of applied psychology, was also in his sixties. He was a tall man, wrinkled from the shrinking thinness of age. His wattles hung from his lean face like rope.

At Chris's mention of Arlene Reynolds, Mayer looked up thoughtfully.

"Oh, yes. Nice girl. Unspectacular, but willing. I could look up her record, if you wish. What year was it?"

Chris told him. The old man found his looseleaf book for 1969. He flipped through the pages till he reached the R's.

"Yes, here." His eyes focused more sharply as he added, "A better student than I remembered. Three B's. One A-minus." He stopped. "H'mm! Interesting. She failed to finish the course. I should have remembered her."

"Why would a girl do that?"

"Why?" Mayer smiled. "She gets married. She has some

emotional upset. Young ladies in the college years are prone to sudden emotional upsets. But then, you're a doctor, why am I telling you?"

Chris debated asking further questions. One thing was sure, Mayer could not possibly be the man involved, but he was the type of professor in whom girls often confide.

"The kind of doctor I am," Chris ventured, "I know of another reason—a girl becomes pregnant."

"Pregnant!" Mayer scoffed. "These days they don't hide it. They boast about it."

"Yes, but not in Arlene Reynolds' day."

"True," said Mayer, "but I doubt it. She seemed like a timid little girl. Pretty, but not vivacious enough to attract a young man. I ofttimes wondered if it was due to living in the shadow of such an important father. It was quite a burden for her."

There was no further information to be obtained from Mayer, so Chris left as quickly as he gracefully could.

The registry just outside Croft Hall listed *Dr. Ward, Arthur,* English Department, as occupying Room 205. As Chris climbed the stairs he could hear the clatter of several typewriters. The door to 205 was open. When he appeared in the doorway the secretary, middle-aged and plump, looked up, obviously annoyed at being interrupted.

"Did you have an appointment with Dr. Ward?" she asked officiously.

"I was referred by Dean Waterston," Chris lied.

"Dr. Ward has a very busy schedule, but if you have time to wait I'll see if he can accommodate you."

The woman pointed to a worn leather chair. Chris dropped into it and after a few minutes the door to Ward's private office opened. A young woman, obviously a student, was leaving. To judge by the look on her face, her interview had not gone well.

The secretary went in, remained a few minutes, then

346

came out and announced briskly, "Dr. Ward will see you now."

"Dr. Grant?" the tall black man asked, standing behind his cluttered desk.

Dr. Ward was in his thirties, athletically lean, with alert and questioning eyes. His hair was worn in a slight suggestion of an Afro. His clothes were exceedingly conventional, a simple gray tweed jacket, dark flannel slacks, and a blue knit tie. Either Chris concealed his surprise very well or else Ward had become used to such a reaction during his years at the predominantly white college.

"Dr. Ward, I wanted to ask you . . ." Chris began.

Ward interrupted, "Dr. Grant, why did you find it necessary to lie? If you wanted to see me, you had no need to resort to the dean's name." Chris didn't have a ready response. "You've put yourself under a cloud from the very start. A man on an honest mission would have no need to resort to subterfuge."

"Sorry," Chris said. "But I hope that will reflect on the urgency of my mission, not the integrity of it."

Ward gestured for Chris to be seated.

"I'm listening," he demanded.

Chris contemplated Ward for a moment. The man was handsome and strong, his deep voice well modulated and gentle. It was apparent to Chris that this might well be a sensitive man with great romantic appeal.

"Dr. Ward, if straight, simple talk is what you prefer, then I say right off that I am here to find out about Arlene Reynolds."

The involuntary concern in Ward's eyes confirmed what Chris had hoped to learn.

"What would you like to know?" Ward asked.

"It's highly personal. But since my career depends on it, I have to ask."

"Don't apologize, man, say it!" Ward snapped.

347

"This isn't an apology. It's an explanation. I am being sued for malpractice. If I lose this case it'll destroy everything I've worked for, the results of which might be of enormous value to your people in generations to come."

"Are you trying to bribe me with promises of what you're going to do for 'my people'?" Ward asked. He turned away abruptly. "Why do you assume that unless you can do something for black people I will not tell you the truth?"

Ward stared out the window across the campus. He wrung his hands so hard Chris heard his knuckles crack. "What do you want to know?" he asked.

"Was she in love with you?" Chris asked.

"We were in love with each other," Ward corrected him gently. For the first time Chris realized that the man was so defensive because he was still deeply involved in the entire experience.

"I'm sorry," Chris began again, "I know it's painful, but circumstances force me to do this."

"Then do it," Ward said softly.

"We can't go forward with our defense until we know the truth. The entire issue of malpractice may come down to one fact and one fact alone. Had she ever been pregnant before she gave birth to her first child?"

Ward did not respond. The silence became heavy, oppressive.

"Have you considered that it's entirely possible she could have been pregnant and I wouldn't know about it?" Ward finally asked.

"Yes," Chris conceded.

"Look, it would have been bad enough if she had just been wealthy, but to be the daughter of a so-called self-made man was an overwhelming circumstance. I never met him, but I learned enough from her to know precisely the kind of man he is."

"I've met him," Chris observed. "She didn't exaggerate."

Ward continued as if he hadn't heard Chris's comment.

348

"She was really very sweet. Terrified in a way. That was what first called her to my attention. The first time she read a brief piece in class, she trembled so that she couldn't finish. I felt sorry for her. Yet she was a bright girl and quite attractive too. Have you ever seen her?"

"In court, once."

"I don't know what time has done, but she was a pretty girl, slight, with delicate features and such white skin. I know what you are thinking. Well, her whiteness had nothing to do with my feeling for her. It was only a reflection of her sensitivity."

He turned back from the window to find a cigarette. While the match was still flaring he looked at Chris. "I've had a long time to think about it. And I still don't know what the attraction really was." His burned fingers made him stop to flick out the match. "Unless it was a mutual awareness of our vulnerability. Hers in relation to her father. Mine in relation to my race. She helped me very much, because she loved me. And our colors did not matter.

"Then came the day when she felt she was strong enough to face her father. She felt sure she could tell him that, with his permission or without, she was going to marry me. She seemed so strong suddenly. If I suspected anything else I wouldn't have allowed her to confront him. I loved her too much for that."

"She decided suddenly?" Chris asked.

"Quite suddenly," Ward admitted.

"Could that have been because she discovered she was pregnant?" Chris asked.

"I wouldn't know," Ward said quickly. Too quickly, it seemed. For he admitted, "And if I did know I wouldn't tell you."

Ward turned back to the window. "The day she went home to tell him I drove her down to the airport. I even offered to go with her but she said it would be better if she saw him alone. In her own way she was sure. When she kissed me she was so strong and full of conviction that I was certain she would be back. She boarded that plane and I watched it until it was out of sight, and its exhaust had blended in with the dark clouds."

Ward was silent for a while. Then he said simply, "I never saw her again."

Chris could feel the depth of the man's pain. With that simple admission, he had revealed the most intimate and scarring event of his entire life.

"She didn't call, didn't write?" he asked.

Ward shook his head slightly. "The news that she wasn't returning came to me through the college physician, Dr. Lumpkin."

Dr. Lumpkin, Chris marked, wondering if she had alerted Ward to this visit.

"Dr. Ward, did you ever wonder why Dr. Lumpkin was the one to tell you instead of the dean or Arlene's faculty supervisor?"

Ward stared back at Chris, refusing any comment.

"Unless she *was* pregnant?" Chris asked, waiting confirmation. When Ward did not answer, Chris continued, "It would be logical if she were. And being pregnant may have been the reason she felt strong enough to face her father. She had a weapon to use against him, only as it turned out he used it against her. He forced her to fly to Sweden or Switzerland where the thing could be done in utmost secrecy. You were never even told what happened to your child."

Chris paused. If Ward was going to make any admission, this was the time. His ebony face shone with perspiration. He sank down into his chair, reached for a cigarette. Eventually it was clear he would say nothing.

"Dr. Ward, I need your help. I'm not asking you to lie. I'm only asking you to tell the truth!" Chris pleaded.

"I don't know what you're supposed to have done, but if it's something to which the almighty Mr. Reynolds objects, then it doesn't matter what anyone says. You can't win."

"What if you could even the score with him?" Chris asked.

"I am beyond evening scores," Ward replied sadly. Reliving the past had drained him.

"The question is, are you going to let him go on doing that sort of thing to other innocent people?" Chris demanded.

Ward didn't answer. Chris proceeded to tell him the facts involved in the lawsuit, from the moment when he had taken charge of the Simpson baby through the events of the trial.

Ward's only comment was, "It would be like Reynolds to think he could wipe out all memory of his daughter's pregnancy by a black man."

"Do you think he would have gone so far as to forbid her to tell her own obstetrician?" Chris asked.

"Yes. And if he had reduced her again to being the girl I first met, she would have obeyed him."

"Do you understand the consequences of that?" Chris asked.

"Consequences?"

"Withholding that information, she misled her doctors into believing they were dealing with a first pregnancy. They misdiagnosed the entire situation. Vital hours went by, time that was probably responsible for what finally happened," Chris explained.

"The sins of the fathers . . ." Ward mused bitterly. "Or should we say the grandfathers?"

"The question now is, will *you* do something about it?"

"Do something? What?" the black man challenged.

"Come to court. Testify. Let the truth be known finally," Chris explained.

Ward stared at him across the desk.

"I'm sorry," he said at last. "I couldn't do it."

"You'd let Reynolds get away with it?" Chris demanded,

incensed now that the truth was potentially within his grasp.

"It has nothing to do with him," Ward explained, "I . . . I couldn't do that to her."

"It's too late to help her. The child is irrevocably damaged. I've examined it myself."

"That's enough for her to bear," Ward said. "I don't want to destroy what chance she has for making some sort of life. After all, she's married. What will happen if it comes out that before her husband there was a man, a black man? I simply cannot do that to her."

"No matter the consequences to others?"

"I love *her*, not others," Ward said. "And when she does think of me I want it to be with kindness, with love. Is that so hard to understand?"

Unfortunately for Chris, he did understand. He could not bring himself to pursue the man any longer. As they shook hands Chris said, "I'm sorry. But you can understand we're quite desperate."

Ward smiled ruefully. "Do you think it took you to relive those memories? Do you really think a day goes by that something doesn't remind me? I cross campus and a laugh will do it. She used to laugh a great deal in those days. I see the back of some small frail girl and I think that's her again. No, you didn't remind me. You can leave without that on your conscience."

Ward sighed wearily. "Why is it the things we conceal from those closest to us, we reveal so readily to strangers? I'm sure my wife suspects the way I still feel, but I have never told her. In all three years we've been married I've never talked to her about it for as long as I have just talked to you."

Chris started toward the door. "Perhaps you might like to have dinner with us," said Ward, friendly now that the interview was ended.

"Thanks, but I think I'd better start back. There's one

last plane out late this afternoon."

"Oh, yes," Ward smiled. "The guest lecturers' special. That's what we call it. Every visiting lecturer rushes like the devil to make that last flight. Well, sorry, Grant. And sorry, too, that I couldn't do more for you. I can only trust you understand."

"I do," Chris said. But on his way to the plane he kept thinking that all his understanding wasn't going to do his case much good. Laura had wanted proof and he was coming home without it.

Mike and Laura were as disappointed as Chris had expected even though their theory was confirmed.

"A man like John Reynolds, whose pride is as important to him as his power," Mike said sadly. "Of course he would keep it secret. Men with power always think they can change reality, but this time, this time . . . oh, that foolish man."

"What an enormous difference it would have made," Chris replied, "if Mitchell knew beforehand."

Only Laura had not joined in the discussion. Her mind was working on the legal aspects of their predicament. When Chris looked at her she said, "Again it's the damned difference between knowing and proving."

"With everything we have now?" Mike demanded.

"Until someone testifies we have only a theory. Not a fact."

"Who's going to testify?" Chris asked futilely. "I must say I can't hate Ward for refusing."

"Then how *do* we prove it?" asked Mike.

"It has to be a witness who knows the fact firsthand," Laura explained.

"You just excluded the best witness," Mike pointed out. "Who else is there? Mrs. Reynolds? She's completely dominated by her husband."

"Certainly not Simpson," said Chris. "He obviously never knew."

"What about Arlene Simpson herself?" Mike suggested.

Laura shook her head. "She'll never talk with that avenging angel her father glaring at her."

"Even if you mentioned the name Ward to her?" asked Chris.

"Fear and guilt will keep her silent. Guilt about what she did. Fear of her father," said Laura.

"We could leak it to the press. Juan would love that," Chris suggested.

"It wouldn't do us any good with the jury. They have to hear the story from an accredited witness." She was thoughtful for a moment, then said, "There's only one witness who knows the facts, who might be forced to admit them from the stand, and who is not afraid of John Stewart Reynolds."

"Who is that?" Chris demanded.

"John Stewart Reynolds."

"I've known that man for twenty years!" Mike Sobol said. "He'd never admit such a thing."

"Pride can be a weakness as well as a strength," said Laura. "What doesn't bend has to break. It depends on how much pressure we can bring to bear on Reynolds."

"Laura, my dear, don't let us drive you into any foolish moves because of our impatience."

"Mike, your understanding won't help me if we lose," she said soberly. "I'm fighting for more than a court victory. If I lose this case, I lose . . ."

She didn't finish. Tears welled up in her eyes. Mike looked at Chris, who stared back, his eyes admitting the true relationship that existed between them. If Mike had reason to suspect before, they had now told him.

Mike took Laura's hand. He lifted her chin. "Oh, my dear, I do feel sorry. Not that you two found each other. I can't think of two finer young people. But under such a cloud, that's not so good," he ended weakly, not wanting to put into words the gravity of the situation as he saw it.

"There's nothing to be lost by going after Reynolds," Chris said, hoping to restore a shred of hopefulness.

"You're wrong. There's everything to lose," said Laura. "But we've reached the point where we have no options left. It's either put Reynolds on the stand—or sum up and go to the jury with an inadequate defense."

chapter THIRTY

JOHN STEWART Reynolds was waiting for his wife to come down dressed and ready to leave for court. He sat in his library, his fingers idly playing with the electronic market reporter that responded by instantly flashing the prices of stocks, currencies and gold in London, Paris and Zurich. The New York markets had not yet opened.

But this morning he had no interest in the results. Today should bring the end of the trial. The question of guilt, which to his continued annoyance Franklyn kept referring to as "liability," had been clearly established as far as Reynolds was concerned. The question of damages did not concern him. It would be sufficient punishment to be able to plague Christopher Grant for the rest of his career.

He heard his wife's footsteps on the stairs, calling one last order to the housekeeper about dinner. Then she was ready to leave. Reynolds turned off his electronic genie and started out quickly. He did not want to give her time to speak today. They had had several discussions, some tearful, about her refusal to go to court. She had tried to divorce herself from the entire affair even before the trial started. She could not understand that one did such things as a duty, to protect the public from future experiments by young men like Grant.

When she wept at night, and he could hear her in her own bedroom, he wondered if she was crying for poor little John or that damned Dr. Grant. Well, today would be the last sacrifice he would ask of her in relation to the trial. And only because Harry Franklyn had insisted on it.

She called to him. She was ready. Reynolds came striding out of his den on his way to court to listen to the skillful summation Franklyn had prepared. John Stewart Reynolds approached the day with an angry zeal.

Arlene Simpson kissed young John as he lay in his crib. She stared down at him and smiled. The infant, more than a year old now, smiled back only tentatively. Then his face was clouded with the same opaque stare that covered it most of the time.

She turned to Mme. Prochard.

"Try to get him out more today," Arlene suggested. "It's a nice day."

"Of course," the governess assured her. They both knew that Arlene was really hoping the outdoors would serve to stimulate the child in some way. Mme. Prochard knew very well that it wouldn't.

Arlene went downstairs to find her husband waiting at the open door, the car outside, the motor running.

"Come, honey, we can't be late. Today of all days," he urged. "It wouldn't look right walking in after court is in session."

What Simpson meant was that his father-in-law wouldn't like it. The old sonofabitch was a martinet about punctuality. Laddie had seen Reynolds leave a golf course at the eighteenth tee rather than be fifteen minutes late for appointments with men he could buy and sell without straining. The compulsion to be on time exceeded the purpose of being on time. So as long as the old man was alive, Laddie Simpson would have to live by his strict rule. Once the bastard was gone, life and business would be conducted at a more civilized pace.

At times a perverse thought crossed Simpson's mind. That by some damned twist of fate the old bastard would contrive to outlive him. It was just possible. If you knew John Stewart Reynolds you had to believe that he might just live forever. Physically, Reynolds was a match for his son-in-law who was almost forty years his junior. Mentally and emotionally he was as sharp and durable as any amalgam which science had yet invented. Though Simpson feared him, hated him, resented him, secretly planned all kinds of vengeance against him, still he admired him.

The old bastard's hunches were uncanny. Angles other men had to learn, he knew by instinct. If it had to do with business, he was never wrong. If it had to do with men and their motives, he was always right. He could read character. He was right when he anticipated that Grant and Sobol would fight on after the hospital and insurance company had agreed to settle. He was right about bringing in Harry Franklyn to try the case. Franklyn had done an excellent job. Still, it would be good to have it over with.

Though Simpson had not been required to attend every day of the trial, he would be relieved to have the case out of the news. Glad not to have to make the same unspoken declaration each time he met someone—I have a brain-damaged child, a child who is not much better than a moron. If he had had his way there would never have been any trial. What was there to be gained, except some satisfaction for the old bastard? But, as in all things since he had married Arlene, Laddie Simpson had bowed to the old man's demands.

Well, today would be the last day. Thank God for it. After that, he and Arlene could settle down with their own private grief and do what they could for little John.

Other people with similar problems had told them of very fine institutions called "private schools" where such children as John could be placed. They were safe, well cared for, in excellent surroundings, by a staff of specially trained professionals. They were brought along, each at his own rate, to the maximum of their limited abilities. Some were even permitted to come home for brief stays of from a few days to as much as a few weeks, or for as long as their parents could manage them.

That arrangement left the parents free to pursue their own lives, to have other, hopefully normal, children. It placed an enormous financial burden on a man to have to pay out the amount that it cost. Twenty-five thousand and more each year. But for anyone named Reynolds, even an inlaw, that was no great sacrifice.

The great sacrifice came at the time of the original decision. He and Arlene had discussed it. Not at length, not frequently. He was the one who had brought up the subject and there was great guilt involved in merely doing that.

How could any parent justify desertion of a child? Worse, desertion of a child in need. Yes, it was necessary to use such words as abandonment, desertion, for though the children were actually being delivered into the hands of highly skilled professionals, from the point of view of the parents it was desertion.

So, though they had talked about it, they had reached no decision. Laddie promised himself that once the trial was over he would again raise the question with Arlene. He had to do something or she would break down under the strain. She could not take the daily confrontation with little John indefinitely. For some reason she blamed herself, though he had tried to disabuse her of that. None of them should feel guilty, certainly not after the mountain of proof that had been adduced in the course of the trial. Even if the experts whom Reynolds paid so well were wrong, one thing was clear—somehow during the first forty-eight hours of his life, John Reynolds Simpson had been damaged by an elevated bilirubin. Whether the fault was Grant's or not, no one would ever know for sure.

Just then Arlene appeared in her coat on her way toward the front door. He wondered what they would talk about on their way down to the courthouse.

"I think," Arlene said tentatively, "I think this morning his smile was a little different. . . ."

"Was it?" Laddie asked, knowing that she kept searching for such signs. She often called him at the office to report them on the phone. But when he came home everything was exactly the same as it had been. Still, to comfort her, he encouraged her with at least the outward appearance of acceptance.

"Yes," she was saying now. "His smile was broader. Lasted longer, too. I mean, there was something in his eyes. It was like he was trying to get through to me."

"Maybe we'll have a new neurologist come in. I heard about an excellent man up at the Children's Hospital in Boston," he said, knowing that at all costs he had to keep her from weeping on the way to court. Today would be traumatic enough without having her start this early.

It was the old bastard's fault. Even if Franklyn had insisted, the old man had no right to force Arlene and her mother to appear. What purpose could they serve except to fatten Franklyn's case? There were times in court when Simpson actually felt sorry for Chris Grant. Whatever his shortcomings, he wasn't an out-for-a-buck practitioner, looking to profit from the practice of medicine. That he had blundered in this case, that he had earned their hatred, didn't completely erase in Laddie Simpson's mind the fact that Grant had done it in good conscience, believing in the rightness of his treatment.

Hardly a day had gone by since Laddie Simpson married

Arlene Reynolds that he did not make himself resolve that when the time came for him to take control of the Reynolds' enterprises he would not be as tough, vindictive or hostile. He would, in fact, do his best to make up for some of the inequities the old man had committed.

Once, when he and Arlene were on their four-month honeymoon trip, they visited the ancient village of Karnak in Egypt. From their balcony they could look across the Nile. There, in the morning sun, they saw an enormous pink palace set in the sandy white desert, far back from the shore. Later that morning they had visited it and the amazingly broad stone steps were indeed a rosy pink. When he and Arlene had entered the huge structure their guide pointed out the many eleborate frescoes on the ancient sandstone walls. The details of face and figure were still sharp and clear—except that every so often a face was so disfigured as to be unrecognizable.

The guide, an old leathery Egyptian, explained in a decidedly British accent that all the obliterated faces were of the same person, Hatshepsut, the only female Pharaoh in all of ancient Egyptian history. Wily, shrewd, unprincipled, she had fought and schemed her way to the highest position of power. One of her first acts was to build this monument to herself. She was determined to make herself a permanent place in Egyptian history, but so strong was the hatred of her among Egyptians that when she died they disfigured her face wherever it appeared on those magnificent walls.

At the time he first saw the temple, Laddie Simpson had not known John Stewart Reynolds well enough to hate him that much. But now, on his way to court, Simpson promised himself that when he took over the Reynolds' enterprises he would try to obliterate the man's image in all possible ways.

Poor Arlene was still talking. "I ran into Melba Sloane the other day. She said that her sister-in-law had the same problem. Or thought she did and there was a doctor in Mexico City who had helped enormously. Maybe we should inquire. Dad has an office in Mexico, doesn't he?"

He was tempted to answer, "Dad, the old bastard, even has an office in Moscow now." Instead, he said, "Yes. I'll make some inquiries when I get to the office tomorrow."

"It won't take more than a day?" she asked. "The summations, I mean."

"I wouldn't think so."

"Good," she said.

They were silent the rest of the way.

Word has a way of spreading through courthouses. When an interesting case is reaching its climax spectators gather like crowds in the ancient Colosseum, ready to join in the process of observing and judging.

This was one such morning. The seats were filled a good hour before court was called into session. There was a stir of excitement when the Reynolds family filed into the room. John Reynolds led his wife by the arm, as though he were shepherding her down the aisle of a funeral chapel. People stared, impressed by the sight of John Reynolds in person, touched by his wife who dared not look to either side but walked with eyes downcast. Behind them came young Simpson, with Arlene's hand on his arm, and his hand covering hers to give her strength.

In the first row of the press box Juan Melez was making notes. If the other newscasters found little of interest at this point, Melez scribbled with suppressed excitement. He had observed the entry of the Reynolds family. He was awaiting the arrival of the defense.

Laura, Chris and Mike entered the courtroom. They made their way down the aisle, and took their places. Laura made a conspicuous show of setting out several blue-backed memoranda. She wanted Harry Franklyn to believe that she, too, was ready for her summation.

The clerk called for silence. Bannon entered, his black robe trailing like a bishop's cassock. Before he sat down he cleared the court of "all persons who do not have seats." With grumbling protests about twenty spectators deserted their places. The court attendant moved to stand guard at the door.

Since the Rules of Civil Practice provided that the party who opened the case summed up last, Bannon turned to Laura, "Is the defense ready to sum up?"

"No, Your Honor," Laura answered, fully aware of the reaction her announcement would provoke.

"I thought it was agreed that this morning we would commence with summations, in hopes that I might charge the jury before the session is over," Bannon stiffly reprimanded her.

"On reconsideration, the defense has decided to call at least one more witness," Laura said, anticipating Franklyn's objection. She was not disappointed.

"Your Honor, it has been apparent for several days now that the defendant is stalling. At this point I think it is an imposition not only on me but on this court to arbitrarily extend this case any longer. Unless we have some indication of who this new witness is, and what the purpose of the testimony will be, we move to deny counsel permission to continue with any further testimony."

Bannon was quick to rule.

"Plaintiff's request is a fair one in the circumstances. Before permitting any witness to take the stand this court has a right to know who the witness is, and what *new* evidence he might bring to these deliberations."

To provoke Harry Franklyn, Laura mocked his soft voice, "The defense wishes to recall to the stand John Stewart Reynolds."

"What does counsel hope to establish that has not already been established?" demanded the judge.

"In the first place, Your Honor, we specifically reserved our right to cross-examine Mr. Reynolds. The record will show that. Therefore, we can recall Mr. Reynolds without stating any purpose. But if the court insists on it we will."

"Please do!" Bannon ordered.

"Certain matters to which Mr. Reynolds testified have, upon investigation, turned out to be subject to considerable doubt," Laura said, deliberately making her argument as tantalizingly vague as possible.

"Your Honor, we've already been through this performance," said Franklyn. "Her insistence on recalling Dr. Coleman to the stand served only to introduce a missing document which had nothing to do with Dr. Grant's decision. It was a red herring deliberately introduced to obfuscate matters. If this is another of Miss Winters' pointless ruses I strenuously object."

Bannon was nodding his head, agreeing with Franklyn but Laura anticipated him by reaching for one of the blue-backed legal memoranda.

"Your Honor, there is no precedent that deprives an attorney of the right to cross-examine a hostile witness. If you were to so rule now it would surely constitute reversible error."

Her memorandum was of sufficient thickness to give Bannon pause. Reluctantly, Bannon finally acceded to Laura's insistence.

"The witness John Stewart Reynolds will take the stand."

THIRTY-ONE

REYNOLDS RAISED his right hand, his left resting on the Bible, and repeated the oath. He slipped into the witness chair, defiant and contemptuous. The young woman, having lost her case, was obviously hoping for a last chance to avenge herself and he welcomed the challenge.

Laura advanced toward the witness box, her carefully prepared list of questions in hand. If she had learned nothing else from observing Franklyn, she had realized how valuable it was to keep the witness off guard by constantly changing the area of focus. As Franklyn had done to Chris, so she proposed to do to Reynolds.

"Mr. Reynolds, it has been some days since you testified, so may I refresh your recollection as to what you said?"

"I have an excellent memory, but if it makes you feel better, go ahead," Reynolds said impatiently.

"At that time you testified that Dr. Grant failed to explain to you all the hazards involved in phototherapy?"

"That is true."

"You also testified that the first thing he did after drawing blood was to place the infant in phototherapy."

"Yes. True," Reynolds agreed.

"Did you make any protest at that time?" she asked.

"Not at that time. But I did later, when he explained to me that that was the main part of the treatment."

"And when was that?" Laura asked.

"After he dispatched the blood to the lab and gave orders to the nurse. He took me to his office and described what he had done," Reynolds said.

"And you're quite sure that he did not tell you at that time of the possible risks involved?" she said, hoping to absorb him in her diversion.

"Quite sure," Reynolds said firmly.

"Are you also sure that you did not consent to that form of therapy?"

"Absolutely sure!" Reynolds said. "I considered it a ridiculous form of treatment then and I still do."

"Despite the fact that you have sat here day after day and heard many experts say that phototherapy is a perfectly acceptable procedure?" Laura challenged.

"The doctors *I* heard testify said it was damned questionable to use in this case," Reynolds fought back.

"Are you saying you didn't hear the others?" Laura asked.

"I heard them, but it was obvious they were lying to help their friend Dr. Sobol!"

Laura was satisfied that the old man was becoming impatient enough to become reckless.

"Mr. Reynolds, if you were so incensed about your grandson being treated by phototherapy, why didn't you protest it?"

"I made it very clear that I did not approve," Reynolds answered. "I don't know what else I could have done."

"You know Dr. Sobol well. Didn't it occur to you to call him?"

"He'd already said that he had absolute faith in Grant," Reynolds said. "Besides, Grant seemed very sure of what he was doing. He was the cockiest young man I've ever run across!"

"Are you saying that he overpowered you?"

"I'm saying that because he failed to disclose all the dangers to me, he convinced me to await the outcome," said Reynolds.

"Don't you really mean that he failed to disclose the *theoretical* dangers?" Laura corrected.

"Damn you," said Reynolds, "what happened to my grandson is not 'theoretical'!"

"I didn't say that it was. I am asking if at the time Dr. Grant was waiting for the results of the lab tests you really wanted him to discuss all the theoretical dangers?"

"I expect from a doctor what I expect from a business-man—full and honest disclosure!" Reynolds said, his voice beginning to rise.

Laura knew it was time for another diversionary attack.

"Mr. Reynolds, do you ever take aspirin?" He glared at her, wondering if she were trying to make a fool of him. "Do you ever take aspirin?" Laura repeated.

"Not often," he replied, reluctant to agree with anything she asked.

"But on occasion? Say, when you have a headache?"

"I never have headaches!" said Reynolds, rejecting any sign of weakness or fallibility.

"Then when you have a cold?" she persisted.

"When I have a cold, yes."

"Do you take it on your own or on doctor's instructions?" Laura asked.

"I have an averson to medicine of any kind. I only take it when the doctor insists."

"Has any doctor ever told you that, in certain cases, aspirin can cause stomach bleeding, even hemorrhage?"

"No," Reynolds admitted.

"Or that aspirin can affect your heart action?"

"No."

"Has any doctor ever told you that under certain conditions aspirin can cause vomiting?"

"No," he replied.

"That aspirin can serve as a mental depressant?" Laura continued, undeterred by Reynolds' attitude, which had become one of impatient boredom.

"No," Reynolds replied, hardly listening to the question.

"Or that aspirin in certain dosages can cause restlessness, excitement, even visual disturbances?"

Franklyn rose to interject. "Your Honor, I would like to know, as I'm sure the jury would too, what all this nonsense is leading up to."

Unperturbed, Laura looked up at the bench. "I will make the connection very soon, Your Honor."

"I think you'd better . . ." He was about to add "young woman" but Laura's challenging look made him bite back his words. She turned back to the witness.

"Mr. Reynolds, has any doctor ever told you that in certain amounts aspirin can cause rapid pulse?"

"No."

"Or that aspirin can cause low blood pressure, and even convulsions?"

"No," Reynolds answered for what seemed like the hundredth time.

"Do you know that those are not *theoretical* dangers but clinically proved effects from the ingestion of aspirin?" asked Laura.

"I'll take your word for it if it helps you get on with the case."

"Mr. Reynolds, would you expect that a physician would instruct you as to these actual dangers each time he prescribed aspirin?"

"I would not," he conceded.

"And if he did not, would you consider he was guilty of malpractice?"

"There is a vast difference between that and what happened to my grandson!" Reynolds exploded. "When you're dealing with an infant, nothing less than full disclosure is good practice," he insisted fiercely.

"Do you believe in full disclosure in *all* medical situations?" Laura asked.

"In all medical situations!" Reynolds affirmed.

"Full disclosure on *both* sides?"

"I don't know what you mean," said Reynolds.

"Full disclosure by the doctor *and* full disclosure by the patient?" said Laura.

Laddie Simpson felt his wife sag against him. He assumed that the prolonged examination of her father was beginning to tell. He gripped her arm but she pulled away slightly.

"I don't know what you mean," Reynolds repeated, a bit more hesitantly.

Now that she had made Reynolds uneasy, Laura knew it was the moment for another diversion.

"I mean is it possible that your grandson might have been brain-damaged by some undisclosed genetic defect in the Reynolds blood line?"

Franklyn leaped to his feet. "This is the most insulting kind of speculation. It exceeds the bounds of allowable cross-examination. I will not permit my client to be subjected to it."

Laura turned to him and observed, "Well, at least we've been able to establish who is *really* your client in this case, Mr. Franklyn."

Though the slip was not of great importance to the outcome, it did signify to Laura that Franklyn was becoming tense. She hadn't expected it, but after everything the little man had done to humiliate her during the course of the trial, she felt entitled to small satisfactions.

She turned to the bench. "Your Honor, since no real proof has been offered as to the cause of the brain damage to this unfortunate infant, I think we are entitled to dig into all the possible causes, even those that may have been deliberately withheld."

Before Bannon could rule, Reynolds himself shouted, "There isn't a damn thing wrong with the Reynolds blood lines! I'll answer any question anyone wants to ask."

Having provoked Reynolds' challenge to continue, Laura asked, "Mr. Reynolds, have you just told us that there is nothing wrong with the Reynolds blood lines? That there are no genetic defects of which you are aware?"

"True!" He glared down at her.

"How many children did your mother have?" Laura asked.

"Eight!" he replied crisply. "Five boys, three girls, all healthy!"

"Mr. Reynolds, how many children do you have?"

He glared at her, evaluating whether to answer or not. Finally he replied, "One."

"Only one? From a man who has just told us that his father sired eight healthy children? Only one, from the man who some days ago told us how much he desired sons?"

Behind her she heard Franklyn object. Bannon was ready to take up Franklyn's fight. "Young woman, this line of questioning is not only irrelevant. It is a profligate abuse of the right of cross-examination."

"Your Honor," said Laura, "I have been harried by you for the last time! If you want to hold me in contempt, do so! But I am going to ask every question I feel is necessary to discover every possible cause of brain damage that might play a part in this case."

"Young woman, approach this bench!" Bannon ordered, his face crimson with rage. Laura did not move. "Did you hear me?"

"Until I am addressed in accordance with my status at the bar, I do not intend to move."

Chris regarded her with a sudden sense of amusement. This woman, this girl, who could be so soft, so beguiling, had a streak of steel in her. The strength and passion which she had exhibited in her moments of sexual ecstasy could evidently be called upon for other purposes. Finally, Bannon was forced to say, "Counsel will approach the bench."

Franklyn quickly joined the conference. The propriety Bannon had exhibited in his last invitation was no longer present when he whispered fiercely, "Young lady, one more word out of you about my rulings and I will clear this court and hold you in contempt this minute. Now, what the hell do you have in mind with these foolish questions? What are you trying to accomplish, aside from embarrassing the witness?"

"I'm trying to do something that hasn't been done very well during this trial, thanks to you. I am trying to get at the truth!"

Bannon and Franklyn exchanged irate glances. Franklyn said, "Your Honor, unless counsel for the defense has specific information that she is trying to uncover with this line of questioning, I object to it."

Bannon glared at Laura. "Do you have such specific evidence?"

"I do."

"Before the court will allow you to continue, I demand some proof of that."

Laura looked up at Bannon. "I promise the court that before this witness leaves the stand I will make the connection between my line of questioning and the evidence."

"You refuse to inform the court as to the nature of that evidence?"

Laura whispered back at Bannon, *"I damn well do!"*

"Young woman, I warn you now, unless you *do* make that connection I will have you up on charges before the bar association for deliberately lying to this court!"

Laura turned away, presuming she had permission to continue.

"Mr. Reynolds, I believe you were telling us that there is only one child of your marriage. And I had asked if that wasn't surprising for a man who so much wanted sons?"

Reynolds glanced at Franklyn, then at Bannon. When neither came to his defense he finally answered:

"The fact that there was . . . is . . . only one child is not due to the Reynolds genes. There was a son . . ."

Laura had not expected that. She remained breathless as Reynolds groped for words. "The first . . . was a son, still-born, a difficult delivery, very painful despite all they did." His eyes flicked slightly to his wife, as if apologizing for what he was about to reveal.

"The next child, the girl, my daughter, was a caesarian. After that the doctors explained it was too dangerous. I do not remember their reasons anymore. Not that reasons matter. Reasons are only intended to explain failure."

Though his tone had not been accusatory, Mrs. Reynolds lowered her eyes and groped in her purse for her handkerchief.

The courtroom was so still that Laura almost hesitated to ask her next question.

"Mr. Reynolds, was that the greatest disappointment of your life?"

"Yes. Of course," he admitted in a whisper.

"Did you ever feel that it was a reflection on you?" Laura asked.

"It was my wife's fault . . ." He amended that at once. "My wife's condition. The doctors were unanimous about that."

"Did you ever feel that other people might think it was your fault?"

"I don't give a damn about what 'other people' think!" Reynolds protested too quickly.

"It never crossed your mind that friends, associates, to whom you had made no secret of your desire for sons, wondered why you had none? Or did you tell them?"

"I do not discuss private family matters with associates or friends," Reynolds declared imperiously.

"Because you don't care what they think?" Laura asked.

"Because it's none of their damn business!" Reynolds exploded.

"And did your friends always respect your desire for secrecy? I mean, privacy?" Laura asked gently.

"Most of them did. After the first time, *all* of them did!" Reynolds retorted.

" 'After the first time'?" Laura repeated.

"Nobody ever asked that question twice. Not in my presence!"

"Then you made quite clear your desire for privacy?"

"I did!"

"And they all respected it," Laura concluded. "Mr. Reynolds, are you a strong believer in personal privacy?"

"I may be considered old-fashioned by the likes of you, but, yes, I believe that a man's private life is just that, private!"

"How far does one go in an effort to achieve privacy?"

"How far?" Reynolds repeated, puzzled by the meaning of the question, as Laura had intended he be.

"Does one keep things secret only from one's friends?" Laura asked. Before Reynolds could answer, she continued, "Or also from one's lawyer? Possibly even from one's *doctor?*"

Reynolds' steel-blue eyes glared back. For the first time he suspected there was a pattern to this young woman's questions.

"Just how far does this need for secrecy go?" Laura asked again.

"As far as a man wants it to go!" Reynolds asserted, answering yet avoiding the question at the same time. To cover his evasion, he continued, "The trouble in these times is that too much has been made public. The press, the TV are always prying into things that are none of their business!"

Reynolds was breathing hard now, his face had flushed,

his blood pressure having risen under the strain.

All those signs told Laura this was the time to close in. "Mr. Reynolds, I'm sure many citizens feel the way you do. Yet how do you account for the enormous TV coverage of your daughter's marriage?"

"Well," Reynolds conceded, "there are times when you can't keep them out."

"And also times when you invite them in?" Laura commented.

Reynolds bristled. "It was a social event of great importance. The public was very curious."

"So you did invite the press in for that particular event. I wonder, Mr. Reynolds, if you would have been so quick to invite them in if, instead of marrying Mr. Simpson, your daughter had chosen to marry outside your social group?"

While Reynolds was considering the intent of her question, Laura continued, "Say, if your daughter had chosen to marry a Jew?"

Reynolds did not answer. Laura's next question was more pointed.

"Or possibly, if your daughter had chosen to marry a black?"

She hesitated ever so slightly. "Don't you think such a marriage would have made the public even *more* curious?"

Reynolds tried to retain his look of impenetrability. But his tightening jaw muscle betrayed him. He decided finally that her question was an accidental thrust and said, "Since it never happened, I don't see any need to answer."

Laura did not press the point. It was sufficient that she had shaken him severely. She decided it was time to change subjects again.

"Mr. Reynolds, despite your testimony that you resisted Dr. Grant's treatment, that he did not fully inform you about the therapy he gave your grandson, did you or did

374

you not offer him a gift when your grandson left the hospital?"

"I did," Reynolds admitted.

"Will you tell the jury what that gift was?"

"A Continental Mark IV."

"Can you tell us the cost of that car?"

"Somewhere between nine and ten thousand dollars."

"Wasn't that an expensive gift for a man who, you said, refused to tell you what you wanted to know? Who was headstrong and rude?" Laura asked.

"At the time it seemed that he had cured my grandson. The gift was an expression of appreciation."

"Mr. Reynolds, did Dr. Grant accept that gift?"

"He did not."

"What did you do then?" Laura asked.

"I wrote a letter . . . to the board of trustees of Metropolitan General," Reynolds admitted.

"Mr. Reynolds, is this an accurate version of the letter?" She proceeded to read for the record: " 'Board of Trustees, Metropolitan General Hospital, Gentlemen: I wish to compliment you on having on your staff Dr. Christopher Grant. He is not only a first-rate specialist in the field of neonatology but is a fine and sensitive man, as solicitous of the concerns of the patient's family as he is of the needs of the tiny patients he cares for. Your hospital and Dr. Sobol's Pediatrics Department can both be extremely proud of him. Most sincerely, John S. Reynolds.' Is that the letter you wrote, sir?"

"I didn't know the truth then. He told me my grandson was fine. It wasn't till four months later that I knew otherwise."

"But you did write that letter voluntarily?" Laura demanded.

Reynolds was silent and Laura realized it was time to present the real case for the defense.

375

"Mr. Reynolds, you told us in your direct testimony that you went to the medical library to read up on phototherapy and other matters concerning your unfortunate grandson. Since that was some days ago, would you refresh the jury's recollection?"

Suspecting Laura was trying to trap Reynolds in the normal discrepancies that occur when a witness repeats his story, Franklyn rose to demand, "Your Honor, the record is there. I see no need to put the witness through this painful experience again. Why not have the stenographer read it to the court?"

Bannon was about to accede, when Laura intervened. "Is Mr. Franklyn afraid that his witness won't remember the careful coaching he was given?"

Reynolds rose to the bait. "Damn it, you think a man needs to be coached on something like that?"

Since Reynolds insisted, Bannon permitted him to answer the question. When he had finished, Laura allowed some moments to go by while she pretended to search among her notes for her next question. Actually, she had to steel herself for her final attack.

With the precision and the intent of a surgeon, she made the first incision. "Mr. Reynolds, was that the only time you ever went to a medical library to do research?"

"Yes," he admitted, in a hoarse voice.

"Mr. Reynolds, did you know that your daughter is an Rh-negative blood type?"

"Yes. Yes, I did know."

"Yet knowing that, you didn't go to the library and look it up, did you?"

"There was no need. She was in the hands of a very capable doctor."

"Did you discuss the problem with him?" asked Laura.

"Dr. Mitchell is a good doctor. I was confident he would be able to take care of any problem that might arise."

"Even though he was not told all the facts?" Laura

began to drive more sharply now.

Reynolds looked at her with new concern. Laura stared back. If Reynolds had guessed by now that she knew everything, she didn't mind. It was Reynolds whose eyes finally turned away.

Now Laura demanded, "Mr. Reynolds, have you ever done any medical research on the subject of abortion?"

Chris Grant and Mike Sobol glanced at the plaintiff's table where Arlene Simpson sat stiff and breathless. Her delicate face was painfully white.

On the witness stand John Reynolds stared past Laura, past his wife and daughter. Laura called him to account. "Mr. Reynolds, have you or have you not ever done research on the subject of abortion?"

"I have never had need to do any reading on the subject of abortion."

"Then perhaps I should recall to the stand an expert to enlighten you," Laura suggested.

Though he was completely unaware of the course Laura intended to pursue, Harry Franklyn leaped up to object. But Laura wheeled on him and said, "Mr. Franklyn, for the benefit of your own clients, I advise you to withdraw your objection!"

Franklyn was about to strike back in earnest when he felt a hand tug at the sleeve of his London-tailored navy blue jacket. He glanced down into Mrs. Reynolds' face. Her expression warned him not to pursue his objection. Harry Franklyn signified that he was withdrawing it by slipping back into his chair.

Laura addressed the bench. "Your Honor, we would like to interrupt Mr. Reynolds' testimony long enough to recall Dr. Grant to the stand." Bannon signified his approval by a single cautious nod. John Reynolds seemed reluctant to surrender the witness chair. Finally he returned to the table.

Chris Grant came forward. There was no need to qualify

him as an expert. Laura started her examination as swiftly as possible.

"Dr. Grant, will you explain the problems that face an Rh-negative woman in childbirth, especially those that might affect her child?"

Chris faced the jury. He described how the mother's blood could be sensitized and produce antibodies if she had either received a blood transfusion of positive blood or undergone a previous pregnancy. Once those antibodies existed in her bloodstream they could affect the health of any child she might bear. In fact, unless steps were taken, the infant might be severely damaged or even die.

When Laura was convinced that the jury had absorbed the medical facts, she asked, "Dr. Grant, let us assume a woman has been sensitized by a transfusion of positive blood or by an earlier pregnancy. If her doctor knew that, would it modify his treatment?"

"It would make all the difference in the world. The doctor would immediately be alert to an Rh incompatibility in the infant," Chris replied.

"And if he were alert?" Laura asked.

"He would watch for any sign of jaundice. He would be very careful to take a bilirubin every two hours even if the child's color were good."

"Yet Dr. Coleman admitted he didn't do that?" said Laura.

"That was understandable. He *thought* he was dealing with a first baby."

"But, Doctor, the testimony of her doctor was clear— this *was* Mrs. Simpson's first baby, wasn't it?"

"Yes, it was," Chris answered. Then he turned to address John Reynolds. "But a woman does not have to give birth to become sensitized."

"Yes, Doctor?"

"The mother can be sensitized as a result of any previous pregnancy," Chris declared.

John Reynolds turned white. His daughter Arlene pressed back in her chair.

"Doctor, if a woman has had a previous baby would that fact be discernible to her doctor whether she told him or not?"

"Any good doctor would be able to see that for himself."

"Suppose, however, that a woman had had an abortion and deliberately conspired to keep that fact from her doctor. Would he be able to detect it on examination?" Laura asked.

"He would not," Chris answered.

"So that if a woman with Rh-negative blood had an abortion and was forced to conceal that fact from her doctor, he would never know?" Laura asked.

"He would never know," Chris answered, still staring at John Reynolds.

"And if the doctor were kept ignorant of that fact would it affect the manner in which he treated the newborn infant?"

"It would."

"Dr. Coleman testified that he was told by the nurse that the infant was jaundiced. He then ordered a bilirubin and a Coombs test. Did he follow the proper procedure?"

"He did. Except that we know from his own testimony that it was many hours before he saw the results of those tests."

"Despite the fact that in dangerous cases a bilirubin should be done at least every two hours?" Laura asked.

"Coleman was misled into believing he was dealing with an unsensitized mother. So he felt that he had great leeway as far as time was concerned," Chris explained.

"Then Dr. Coleman was working in the dark?"

"By the time Coleman saw the infant seven or eight hours later, the bilirubin undoubtedly had shot up past twenty. The brain damage undoubtedly occurred *before* that infant ever arrived at Metropolitan General."

"Therefore, Doctor, who would you say was responsible for the brain damage suffered by John Reynolds Simpson?"

Chris peered down at John Reynolds. "Whoever it was who made the decision to conceal Arlene Simpson's previous abortion from her doctor."

The blood drained from John Reynolds' face. Arlene turned and whispered an accusation only her father could hear.

His lips twitched but remained soundless. He breathed in shallow, almost imperceptible gasps. Then he muttered, "I . . . I need a doctor. . . ."

Laura turned to the bench. "Your Honor, Mr. Reynolds is obviously under great stress. I urge an immediate recess."

Harry Franklyn called across to Mike Sobol, "Please! Take a look!"

Mike moved to John Reynolds' side, reached for his pulse, loosened his collar to ease his breathing. Reynolds did not respond. "May we have the assistance of the courtroom attendants to see Mr. Reynolds to his car?" said Sobol.

Under Mike's guidance they raised Reynolds up and led him out of court through the judge's robing room, with Mrs. Reynolds at his side.

He moved like a blind man. His face was lifelessly pale, his blue eyes were no longer keen and penetrating. Once he had left the courtroom, Arlene Simpson rose and made her way up the aisle, her husband hurrying after her. Harry Franklyn remained at the counsel table, quite alone.

Laura addressed the bench. "Your Honor, may I suggest a meeting in chambers as early this afternoon as possible?"

With Franklyn's agreement, Bannon set the time for two o'clock, excusing the jury until then.

THIRTY-TWO

At two o'clock Laura, Chris and Mike Sobol presented themselves in Judge Bannon's chambers. Harry Franklyn was fifteen minutes late. He explained that he had been meeting with his clients. With Laura's permission, Franklyn was permitted to make a statement without the presence of the court stenographer.

"On the instructions of my clients I am herewith terminating this action. I have also been authorized to give Dr. Grant and Dr. Sobol any public apology they consider acceptable. Mrs. Simpson is hopeful, however, that it will not entail disclosing events that might cause pain and damage to innocent persons."

Everyone in the room understood.

Franklyn continued, "Mrs. Simpson harbors no hatred toward the man involved. She does not wish to embarrass or injure him personally or professionally. She would not even tell me his name, which I must assume you know and will keep secret."

"Mrs. Simpson has nothing to fear from us," Laura said.

"Thank you," said the little lawyer, adding with bemused self-reproach, "I never thought after all these years that a client could fool me so completely."

Then he said grimly, "If I have any influence left with the Reynolds family I am going to suggest that John Reynolds be kept under continuous observation. I have an uneasy feeling that he might try to destroy himself."

Regretfully, Franklyn started for the door. His hand on the knob, he turned to face Laura. "Young lady . . . and I can call you that, because I have two daughters older than you are . . . young lady, you're one hell of a good lawyer. I'm not so unhappy at the thought of retiring when I see young ones like you coming along."

They were moving down the steps of the courtroom for the last time, Laura Winters, Chris Grant and Mike Sobol. Halfway down, Juan Melez was waiting for them. His cameraman was already getting the three of them in focus in the lens of his hand-held camera.

"Nice day's work, Counselor." Melez beamed at Laura. "Now, can we have that statement?"

Laura glanced at Chris and Mike. She moved forward a single step giving the cameraman a chance to focus on her.

"Miss Winters, would you give our TV viewers the behind-the-scenes story of what really happened in that courtroom? What was it that made Reynolds withdraw his case so suddenly and dramatically?"

Laura smiled into the camera, then answered sweetly, "Sorry, but still no comment."

Juan Melez lost his smile. His face, out of camera range, clearly revealed his disappointment. He signaled his cameraman to stop shooting.

"Look, lady, we had an agreement! Remember?"

"Juan, if we ever release this story to anyone, it's yours. But not at the cost of people's lives."

Melez remained unreconciled.

"Your people are getting their *Medico* back. That should be reward enough," Laura said.

The young man finally nodded and stepped aside, allowing Laura, Chris and Mike to continue down the steps.

They were having their celebration dinner at La Scala. Once he had heard the news of their victory, Guido had called Mike and insisted. He seated them at Mike's favorite corner table. Then Guido summoned the waiter with a snap of the fingers. The boy came at once. No more than sixteen, he was tall, at least a head taller than Guido, and lean, far leaner than the restaurateur, who obviously enjoyed his own excellent cuisine. Still there was an undeniable resemblance. Guido displayed him proudly. He said to Mike, "My grandson. The one you saved. Look at him now. Makes his grandfather look like a midget."

Guido playfully slapped the young man on the back. "I have served squabs bigger than you were on the day you were born. Say thanks to the doctor."

Young Giovanni mumbled his thanks and covered his embarrassment by serving them large pats of butter and a basket of Italian bread. Guido beamed and addressed Mike again, "Tonight I do the ordering!" He smiled. "And the vino, a special bottle for a special night!"

Guido was on his way. Now it was Mike's turn to be embarrassed. He furtively drew a small object out of his pocket. It was a corked hospital flask of deep purple liquid.

"The last of Rose's last bottle of Passover wine," he revealed.

There was enough for three drinks. When he had poured them and admired the color, he raised his glass to Laura. "A toast to our little girl, Chris. A very very smart lawyer. A nice human being. And, as an old hand at being married, I can tell you she'll make a wonderful wife."

All three touched glasses and drank.

"There's a lot of celebrating to do tonight," Mike announced. "For several years now they've been after me to take it easy. To step down, become professor emeritus. No small honor. This afternoon I notified them I would do just that—on the condition that my succeeding chief is Christopher Grant."

"Mike, I owe you too much already," Chris protested.

"Idiot, I'm not doing this for your sake. I'm doing it for the hospital. Now, you say yes, and we'll drink to it. Okay?"

Chris nodded. They raised their glasses again. After they drank, Mike recalled, "Those nights that the interns and residents used to come to Rose's Passover *seders*. When they left, Rose would say sadly, 'Mike, you have so many sons but no grandsons. It isn't fair.'

"Well, I am depending on you two to give me grandsons. And one granddaughter, too, just like her mother."

They started to raise their glasses. But Mike said, "No, please. This time, just Rose and I will drink."

The next morning Christopher Grant, M.D., arrived at Metropolitan General Hospital to resume his work. He entered the Babies' Pavilion, passing the huge bronze plaque that bore the strong profile of John Stewart Reynolds. As he pushed open the door to the hospital floor, he heard the squawk box calling, "Dr. Grant. Dr. Christopher Grant, call the intensive care nursery at once."

He went to the admissions desk and picked up the phone.